❧ PRAISE FOR *THE HARM TREE*:

"A country on the brink of war, and two best friends
turned enemies in a world where nothing is as it seems,
Edwards has created a rich, compelling epic that will leave
even the most hungry fantasy reader sated."
MELINDA SALISBURY

"*The Harm Tree* is absolutely phenomenal. I was gripped from
the very beginning and could not put it down. Rose Edwards
magnificently navigates you through a kingdom on the brink of
war and takes you on a journey filled with fear, grief and power.
You fall in love with characters and experience their journey as
your own. Brilliantly written and absolutely amazing!"
CHARLOTTE ROTHWELL

"It pulls you in quietly but fiercely, like a rip tide . . .
It's sinister, it's beautiful, it's fun, it's exciting, it's terrible,
it's haunting . . . you never find yourself quite where you expect,
and yet you're always somewhere fascinating and right.
The plot feels a bit like riding the outer edge of a whirlpool,
slowly circling at first and then faster and faster
as you converge on the point of no return."
HARI RAI

"Very gripping and unputdownable . . . I hope Rose
writes more because her writing is so good."
RACHAEL

ROSE EDWARDS

The
HARM TREE

uclanpublishing

The Harm Tree is a uclanpublishing book

First published in Great Britain in 2019 by
uclanpublishing
University of Central Lancashire
Preston, PR1 2HE, UK

978-1-9129790-0-4

1 3 5 7 9 10 8 6 4 2

Set in 10/16pt Kingfisher by Becky Chilcott

A CIP catalogue record for this book is available from the British Library.

Printed and bound in Great Britain by Clays Ltd, Elcograf S.p.A.

To my parents
Eddy & Diana
who told me 'just do it'

❧ CAST OF CHARACTERS ❧

THE TELLERS

Torny Vafrisdota: sent away from home, dreams of being a warrior
Ebba Rathnasdota: 'not from round here', dreams of going home

FRITHBERG AND THE PLAINS

Aud: works at the wayhouse, suspiciously good with a rolling pin
Kelda: serving girl at the wayhouse, keeps her hands clean
Jarle: stable hand at the wayhouse, tells dangerous stories
Berger Sorleyson: runs the Frithberg wayhouse, doesn't like trouble
Lord Frithrun: the lord of Frithberg, relies on his reputation
Big Hakon: one of Lord Frithrun's warriors, likes a drink
Spraki Spitnails: Lord Frithrun's skald, doesn't like visitors
Berger Dagomar: a wealthy merchant, looking to expand his market
Sebson: a generous horse breeder, and his sister, Lana Sebsdota

SOUTHERNERS

Berengar of Vellsberg: Erland's protégé, likes lists
Medard: a soldier from the Southern Empire with a sunny disposition
Abelhard: a soldier from the Southern Empire, doesn't speak Northern
The Southern Emperor: ruler of the Southern Empire,
Arngard's neighbour
Theogault of Vellsberg: Lord of Vellsberg on the Vells river,
the border between Arngard and the Southern Empire

HILL COUNTRY

Galen: veteran of the war, a man on a mission

Roaki: Galen's comrade, lost his luck

Fenn: thrall from beyond the Iron Sea, owned by Thorkel

Thorkel: veteran of the war, misses the old days

Laugi: Thorkel's second in command, adapts quickly

ELDINGHOPE, BIRCHHOLD
AND THE EASTERN FARMLANDS

Uncle Ulf Berrson: Ebba's uncle, master of Eldinghope

Cousin Rafe: Ulf's son and heir

Arf Berrson: Ebba's father, Ulf's brother; died when Ebba was young

Rathna: Ebba's mother, outlander; rescued from Raiders by Arf Berrson

Stig Rathnason: Ebba's brother, following in his father's footsteps

Mistress Una: Birchold's village healer

Nanna and Hella: Mistress Una's helpers

Raiders: marauding seafarers, widely feared

GULLCROFT AND THE NORTH

Vigdis: Torny's aunt, Vafri's sister, a Staffbearer

Vafri the Wanderer: Torny's father, died at sea when she was young

Brenna: Torny's mother

Sklep: Torny's stepfather

Thorpe Thorpeson: pigherd

Ranvig: Staffbearer, not to be crossed

Drifa: Staffbearer, a scout

Carr of Hellingap: warrior, wants peace

PALACE OF SUNACRE

King Kolrand 'the Cub': Arn's youngest son and successor, pays tribute to the Southern Emperor

Prester Grimulf: warrior-priest of the White God, raised in the Southern Empire

Erland of Hellingap: captain in charge of the Southern soldiers

The Bearskins: elite regiment under Kolrand's command, known for their discipline

THE WAR OF THE ARNSONS

King Arn 'the Good': Uniter of Arngard, whose murder started the war

Prince Geir Arnson: Arn's eldest son; murdered his father on Bloodnight, killed at the battle of Hellingap

The Slipskins: Prince Geir's warriors, known for their loyalty; hunted after the deaths of Prince Geir and the Sungiven

Sungiven: hero of the Staffbearers, who rallied the Northern forces and rode against Kolrand at the battle of Frithberg

GODS AND SPIRITS

Wise One: Arngard god of death, winter and war

Cornmaiden: Arngard goddess of the sun and the harvest

Staffbearers: magic-workers of the Arngard gods

White God: god of the Southern Empire

Blessed Walpurgis: a saint in the White God's religion, worshipped in place of the Cornmaiden in Arngard

Harrower: ancient spirit of Sleeper's Howe

Luck: spirit that keeps a person from harm, everyone has one

Follower: spirit that appears in dreams to prophecy

Scour: someone who sees visions

Spirit Walkers: shamans from beyond the Iron Sea, who can see and converse with spirits

Spirit Rider: a spirit that has attached itself to a person, invited or otherwise; may try to possess its victim for its own ends

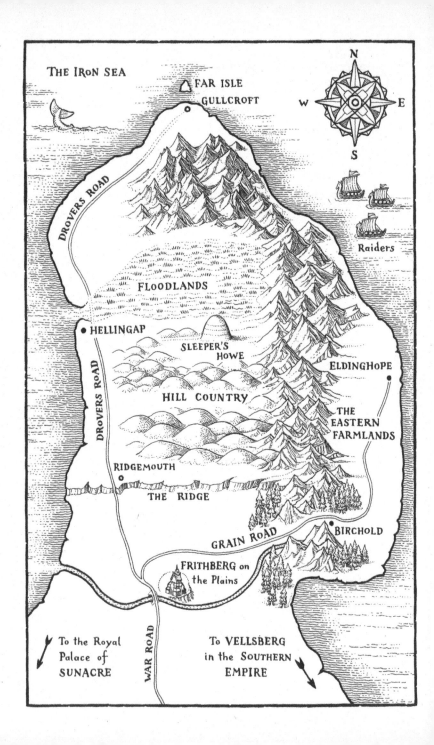

AUTHOR'S NOTE

The names of people and places in Arngard are loosely based on the Norse language. The letter 'j' is pronounced as a 'y', so the name Jarle is pronounced 'Yarle'. People are known by their first names, while their second names are patronymic, meaning 'son/daughter of X'. So Torny Vafrisdota is Torny, daughter of Vafri (her father). In rare cases, maternal names are used: Ebba and her brother Stig are called Rathnasdota and Rathnason, after their mother Rathna.

"Nine years ago, in the year of the eclipse, which was followed by pestilence, Arn, King and Uniter of Arngard, departed this life on the ninth day of the ninth month, which the heathens call Bloodmonth, it being their season for sacrifice. It is said that in the sacred grove at Sunacre on Bloodnight, Arn's own son, Geir, strung his father from the idolatrous tree, slit his throat, and declared himself king. This I cannot vouch for, but it is true that thereafter the King's youngest son, Kolrand, defied his brother's treachery, and the two princes waged war on one another, until there was not a mother in the whole kingdom who had not lost a son. Here in the Southern Empire, it is said that the sun sank the night of Arn's death, and did not rise again until his son Kolrand sat upon the throne and swore fealty to our Emperor and our Lord God, whom they call the White, and promised to fill his war-torn land with the Lord's light. But there are in Arngard those who cling to their idols, and they say the sun rose because a great warrior rode out of the North to rid the land of the usurper, and though she was defeated, yet she will come again."

History of Arngard
Berengar of Vellsberg

"To the Holy Patriarch and Emperor, Ruler of the Southern Empire, by the grace of God, I send greetings and thanks. That Your Holiness should ask further correspondence with me, most lowly of your flock, both honours and shames me. For I must report that, despite King Kolrand's pious rule, and your many gifts to our humble mission, the True Faith remains but a candle flickering in the midst of darkness. Recently I have come to fear that the darkness again gathers, takes shape, begins to move against the will of God. I beg, with the blessing of my King, that you send me men, believers all, to trace this darkness to its source, and cut it out."

Letter to His Imperial Majesty,
Emperor of the Southern Empire,
from Grimulf, Prester of Sunacre

Part One:
FRITHBERG

One

GOLD HORSE

❧

TORNY'S TALE

A gift exchanged between allies, a reminder of oaths

inter is a white wolf with frost on its breath, and a thick coat that darkens the sun. That's what my father's sister Vigdis told me when I was young, and we were waiting for him to come home. Now I'm the one who's missing from the hearth, but no one's waiting for me.

My body is still heavy with sleep, and the first breath of the white wolf has chilled my face. In the dark of the attic, I squint at the bedroll next to me, where Ebba is curled up. I reach out and shake her shoulder. Her straight dark brows draw together over her brown nose.

"Wake up."

Ebba groans and rolls away from me. "Go'way, Torny."

"It's Grainmarket, remember?"

"Uuuuurgh." Ebba drags the blanket over her head, but she'll get up now. I pull my dress on under my covers, crawl past the other bedrolls, and open the trapdoor. The bedroll closest to the trapdoor is empty – even this early, Aud is already up. I slide down the steps and wait in the corridor below, combing my hair with my fingers, trying to plait it. It's springy, almost impossible to tame, white-blonde and short. Before they sent me to Frithberg, my stepfather shaved my head like I was a yearling lamb. I can still feel myself burning with the indignity of it. Now I'm sixteen, I wonder if he'd dare do the same.

Probably.

Still, I've learnt a few tricks since.

Ebba joins me, feet first. She's shorter than me, and with her feet on the planks the top of her head barely reaches my nose. She has brown-black hair that falls in waves, eyes like autumn leaves, and unlike me she actually suits the plain woollen smocks we both wear. Skirts make me itch, I feel like a scarecrow in them, but Ebba's always neat and pretty, even in rough homespun. Used to be I thought I was the only one who noticed her prettiness, but recently I've seen others following her with their eyes. It shouldn't bother me, but it does. Ebba hurts easy, and I don't want her hurt.

I rub my left arm, where a bruise is still tender under my wool shirt. That scuffle with the boothboys down Smithgate left me a few keepsakes to remember it by.

Ebba turns so that I can braid her hair, laughing quietly at my ridiculous plait, wonky as well as short. "Lambtail," she says, tugging it.

"Give over," I say, nudging her. Her hair is soft between my fingers. She's forgotten her hair-tie, so I take my whalebone pin from my breast, twist her braid up, and pin it there. She turns and smiles at me.

"Come on," I say.

It's just before dawn, and the wayhouse is quiet. We tiptoe past Berger Sorleyson's door. He runs the wayhouse, and we work for him. These rooms are for richer guests; when the house is full for the summer fairs we hear their talk coming up through the boards under our bedrolls. This morning the only sound is Sorleyson's snoring. The ordinary folk sleep in the dining hall on the other side of the kitchen. Frithberg's a market town, with plenty of visitors, and the Grainmarket will bring in more than usual.

In the kitchen, Aud is kneeling beside the huge hearth, getting the fire started. Her mousey hair is hidden under her grey kerchief, and a sturdy apron covers her grey dress. Aud's older than us. She runs the kitchen for Sorleyson, and she never talks idly. She looks up as we come in. "Up already, girls?"

"We're goin to market," says Ebba, no trace of her sleepiness left in her dark eyes. "Are you wantin anythin?"

Aud shakes her head. "Just be back in time to help at noon. We're going to be busy."

Ebba bobs down to give Aud a quick hug. Aud tuts, but her usually stern face softens a bit.

"Thank you," I say. "For giving us the morning together."

Aud shoos us out the door into the yard. "Don't be late," is all she says.

Outside the air is cold. Lazy stampings come from the stables across the yard, but there's no sign of Jarle the stable hand. We slip out onto Astgate. Frithberg's main street is bustling. Astgate leads from the town gates to the marketplace, and the wayhouse sits between the two, where travellers can easily find it. Traders have been arriving through the night for Grainmarket, and Astgate smells richly of their beasts' mess. We pick our way between the steaming droppings. Come winter, they'll freeze too fast to stink.

Above us, floating over the morning smoke, the pointed eaves of the kirkhouse glow. The sun isn't high enough to reach the marketplace, but it paints the wooden tower golden. The tower still surprises me sometimes, sitting over the town on its own outcrop of rock, looking down on us.

The market is already full. A hubbub rises from the south side, where sacks of barley are being unloaded from the ox trains and stored in the merchants' warehouses. Grain-traders from the Eastern farmlands, their purses full of merchants' pay, pick their way between the market stalls, looking for goods their farmsteads will need for the winter.

I see Ebba searching their faces, her mouth tight, and I grab her hand.

"Breakfast," I say, tugging her after me between stalls of fruit and cheeses. At the baker's stall I pay for honey twists, and we eat them greedily, our fingers sticky-sweet.

Licking our fingers, Ebba and I slip from stall to stall, ignored by the traders. We're too young and plainly dressed to have money of our own, and the traders are too set on selling goods in bulk to the visitors from the East to bother with local sales today. We make a bee-line for Smithgate, the street where the artisans have their wooden booths. The warm smell of the chandler's booth greets us, bunches of tallow candles hanging from their wicks.

When I was dumped at the wayhouse during the summer

sheep fair last year, Aud took one look at me and dragged me to Smithgate. "What are you," she said, "some kind of barbarian?" I was wearing woollen leggings, the kind only Northerners wear, and one of my stepfather Sklep's old shirts. While Aud haggled over cloth for skirts, a warrior passed us, his forearms and fingers gleaming with silver rings, an axe at his belt. I stared at him while Aud bought me shoes. "If you run after Lord Frithrun's men," she said without looking round, "Sorleyson will thrash you."

She needn't have bothered. I didn't want him. I wanted what he *had*. The way he walked down the street, and others stepped aside. The way people looked at him, and he didn't seem to notice. His name would mean something, and no one could take it from him.

I ran my hand over my sheared head and thought of what had been taken from me. My home, the hovels set among the Northern cliffs, poor, frozen, stinking of fish. There was nothing to mourn. They didn't need me, and I sure as blood didn't need them.

When Ebba arrived with the ox-trains in the autumn, I was sent along to buy shoes for her, and since then we've been friends. Well, almost since then.

At the end of Smithgate, down by the river, are the smithies and the leather workers. The tang of hot metal and ash mixes with the raw smell of new leather. As usual, Ebba and I dawdle outside the smithies, two girls among the small crowd of men. One of the boothboys who bruised me last week is there turning nails for his master, but we ignore each other. This time he keeps his eyes off Ebba.

The crowd grows. One Easterner is haggling over a knife, and another in a blue cloak is running his eyes over the goods laid out on the counter, while the master hammers out an axe head. It's no war-axe, but we look at the swords hung from the rafters and imagine that it is.

"There en't no heroes no more." Ebba sighs, leaning her elbows on the wooden rung between the street and the forge. The old man working the bellows pauses to wipe his sooty face and laughs at her.

"And you should be glad," he says. "You're too young to remember why we needed them." He thumps his leg stuck out stiffly before him. It's made of wood.

"I remember one," I say, and he looks at me. Some of the others do too, and I can feel that strange heaviness that accompanies any mention of the war here, but something about the hammer jumping from the hot metal lulls me, and I say, "She was golden-haired, on a white horse, wearing armour like fish scales."

The hammering stops, and in the sudden quiet the smith thrusts the half-formed axe-head into the fire. Steam rises noisily. The old man bends to the bellows again, his head down, not looking at us.

"The Sungiven?" whispers Ebba, but the smith cuts her off.

"Don't go remembering too much," he says shortly, wiping his face with a rag. His eyes stay on the fire. "She's long gone. Good riddance."

Ebba's still looking at me wide-eyed, but I don't like the way the smith won't meet my eyes. I tug her hand and we walk back towards the market.

"I din't know you'd seen the Sungiven," she whispers.

"I'd forgotten," I whisper back, still feeling that heaviness on me, like eyes. "I was little. I don't know why I remembered it."

"You never said nothin."

I open my mouth, but a weight slams into my back and I sprawl face-first onto the packed earth. Shouting overhead, the thump of a body being brought down, scuffling limbs and kicks aimed from bystanders, and then, right in front of me, the bloodied face of a man staring at me. Something glinting shoots between the legs of the crowd, and I jump up from my grazed knees, stumble, bend, snatch and run. Behind me the man screams.

A hand catches my shoulder. "What's this, girl?"

I look up into the face of the chandler.

"Thief!" I gasp. Behind me the crowd is still yelling and thumping away.

"I think he stole a knife," pants Ebba, catching up to me. "One of the boothboys took him down." The chandler is already looking past us, his suspicion changed to scorn.

"Trying to steal in Smithgate, is he?" He glances down at us. "You seem sensible," he says to Ebba. "Keep an eye on my wares." He hurries towards the fight. Ebba bundles me into the booth behind the display of candles and rushlights.

"What are you *doin*, Torny?" she hisses, as I fumble with my pocket.

I open my hand: a gold pendant, as long as my little finger, in the shape of a horse. It's looking to the east, and across its back is slung a shield, decorated to look like the sun. On other side, where the maker's mark should be, there's a single rune: X.

"Where d'you get that?" Ebba whispers fiercely.

"That Easterner." I'm whispering too.

"He dropped it? That's stealin, Torny!"

"He didn't drop it. He looked me right in the eye and threw it."

"What if he stole it? What if someone sees it? It's *gold*."

She's got a point. Gold is for lords and kings. Even Frithberg's warriors and wealthy men mainly wear silver arm-rings, not gold. I can't keep it. Look what happens to thieves.

There are no more shouts from the crowd down the street, just dull thuds.

"I knew somethin was goin to happen," Ebba growls. "I knew we were goin to get into trouble today."

"Did not," I say, but my mind's busy. Gold doesn't turn up much in Frithberg. Lord Frithrun, the lord of Frithberg, wears some, but that's hardly any help. It just means I'll be dragged before him if I get caught.

Ebba's still scolding me, something about a dream.

"The shrines." I cut her off, looking at her. "Ebba, the shrines in the kirkhouse." The rush of relief makes me grin.

"What about em?"

I'm not the only one struck by Frithberg's kirk. Ebba goes there to pray, and she's told me that merchants from the South visit it when they stop at Frithberg, and leave offerings. Wealthy merchants. I glance up. The chandler's returning.

"Don't you have prayers to say?" I ask Ebba.

When I came to Frithberg, the first thing I saw as the cart bounced down the Drover's Road from the North was the kirkhouse. It rose blackly into the sky, dwarfing the town beneath. I knew then that I was in a different land to the one I'd grown up in, for all it shares the same name. The White God has no houses in the North.

Ebba and I pass Lord Frithrun's hall where it lies at the foot of the rock, in the shadow of the kirk, and start to climb. Aud told me the outcrop is where the sacred grove once stood, with the sunstone in the west, and the Harm Tree in the east. But the grove was cut down by King Kolrand after the war and its wood used to build the kirk, and now Aud never goes up there.

As we climb the path we can see into the yard behind the lord's hall, where Frithrun's warriors spar and wrestle. Any other day we'd stop to watch, but today I don't even glance down, and when I look back at Ebba, she's climbing grimly, her face set. She's angry at me. When we reach the top, we cross the open ground marked with a standing stone, bowing as we pass it. The sunstone is topped by a carving very like the sun on the gold horse's back. Traces of runes curve in ribbons around the stone, but today I don't stop to run my hand over them, or try to make them out. I feel like I did at the forge, as if I'm being watched.

I pass under the carved wooden lintel of the kirk and breathe more freely. It's dim and fragrant, and the thick wooden walls glow warmly in the light of hanging lamps. I look about with interest. I've never been inside.

Six pillars, each made from a single oak trunk, hold up arches and an upper gallery. The pillars are carved with interlocking animals, plants and people. Under the arch at the east end of the kirk is the altar, and the White God hangs above it. I know about the White God of the Southerners, of course, but I've never seen his likeness. In the scented darkness, his pale, naked body glows. All around it, the golden offerings of wealthy believers hang from the walls, shivering in the candlelight. I've heard people say the god himself walks the kirk at night to protect his offerings from thieves.

Ebba bows again before the White God. All I have to do is reach up and hang the horse with the other offerings.

Behind us, the kirkdoor creaks open.

Ebba pushes me through the arch to the right of the altar. In an alcove hung with plaited corn offerings stands a carving of a woman holding a sheaf of corn in the crook of her arm. The Blessed Walpurgis.

Ebba sets the tapering yellow candle she bought from the chandler at the statue's feet, lights it and kneels down to pray. I've seen her doing it back at the wayhouse sometimes, and now I kneel beside her, listening.

Wood creaks as someone walks slowly towards the altar.

Ebba nudges me. "Come on," she whispers.

"Here?" Walpurgis has no gold in her shrine.

Ebba scowls at me. She's right. We can't wait for the coast to be clear.

I feel for the gold horse in my pocket, and set it at Walpurgis' feet, where it peeks out from under her painted hem. Ebba bows hurriedly to the saint, and we leave quietly, avoiding the lone worshipper.

"That's done," I say, feeling my shoulders relax in the morning sun.

I lead the way down the path, glancing back at the kirkhouse once. Does a blue shadow move in the doorway? But then the shouts of warriors sparring reach us, and the clang of their blades from the lord's yard, and a little further down the market is in full swing, traders calling out, animal cries rising over the rooftops.

When we reach the market we're just two girls in scuffed smocks, darting through gaps in the crowd. We avoid Smithgate, winding between cottages down to the gate in the walls. It's wide open to allow the barges lining the wooden dock to be loaded with grain. We cross the bridge over the silvery water to the open ground on the far bank, and walk upstream towards the wooded mountains, leaving the cries of the bargemen behind us.

Ebba sits herself down on the dead winter grass. I can tell she's still angry with me, and that makes me annoyed too. I don't want to fight about it, so I pretend I haven't noticed, and turn some cartwheels instead. I'm upside-down in a handstand when I see Ebba's about to say something. I flip right way up to show I'm listening.

"That could of bin very bad," Ebba says at last, her eyes following some fish wriggling against the current.

I watch her. "You know I'd never steal, don't you?"

She grunts, doesn't look at me.

"Ebba," I say. "I'm not a thief."

"You still picked it up, Torny. Men don't just throw away gold. It must of bin a mistake."

I know it wasn't, but I don't argue. "What did you pray for?" I ask, to change the subject.

Ebba stiffens. "What?"

"In the kirk."

There's a pause.

"A whole day off," says Ebba, "a real day, wi no work."

"Sorleysun wouldn't allow that," I say seriously. "Evil spirits love lazy girls."

Ebba snorts. "They must hate the wayhouse then. Forget lazy, we don't have time to rest."

"We get feastdays off." I hesitate before asking. "Will you go home for . . . for Bloodnight?"

They don't call it that here. They call it Arnsnight, after the old king, and everyone puts on their best clothes and feasts at the lord's hall. But Ebba and I aren't town girls, and in the North and the East it's still Bloodnight, with a Staffbearer chanting the song of the Wise One and making the sacrifices, and when it's just the two of us we can use its real name.

"It's a long way home," Ebba says quietly. "I couldn't make it. Anyway, I don't know if they'd want me. What if they've had another bad year?"

"I'm sure they'll want to see you. Your mother won't recognise you after all those regular meals you've had." That teases a smile from her. Ebba came to Frithberg with the farm's grain last autumn, when her family decided they had too many mouths to feed. It looked like they hadn't fed her properly for a lot longer than a season.

"I miss em so much," she says, like she always does. "When I left, Stig wouldn't come say goodbye to me, an Ma was cryin too much to talk."

"Lucky you." I think about my own family, and the way Brenna – I never call her mother anymore – had looked at me after another argument with my stepfather. *You wouldn't catch her crying about sending me away*, I think.

"Stop it, Torny." Ebba shoots me a look. "It was a bad time. When the crops fail . . ." she shakes her head. "All the grown-ups get scared."

At least they had a reason to send her away. Brenna and Sklep just wanted me gone, what with Brenna expecting Sklep's child. I guess I spoiled the place, hanging around reminding them of my father.

"Tell me about the Sungiven," Ebba says, interrupting my thoughts.

"I don't remember much." I lean over the bank, watching the tiny fish darting through the shallows.

"Try!" Ebba's voice is eager. "We can't talk at Sorleyson's. You heard the smith: people here don't talk about her."

They don't talk about the war at all, here. You'd think they would, seeing how they won.

"It was back home, in Gullcroft," I say. "I remember the boats were coming in . . . I think it was a whale hunt. I remember coming off a boat and climbing the cliff to find Vigdis —"

"Your aunt?" Ebba asks, and glances round to make sure we're alone. "The Staffbearer?" she whispers.

I nod.

"She was up there with this lady with golden hair, and a sword at her belt. I remember her armour was glittering like scales. She looked down at me and she said —"

"What?"

"Something about whales and how they hunt. Maybe she was just asking me how the hunt had gone."

"But you don't remember?" Ebba looks crestfallen. "A real hero, an you don't remember what she said!"

"Not a hero down here."

"Well, she fought on the wrong side, din't she?" Ebba says. "No one here's goin to want to remember a hero who fought *against* King Kolrand."

I squint up at the sun. "We should be getting back."

"Wait."

Ebba and I jump. A man in a blue cloak stands between us and the bridge. His red-gold beard is curled close to his chin, and his eyes are grim.

"You've got something of mine," he says.

"No—" I start, but Ebba glares at me. "What is it?" I finish lamely.

"A trinket. I believe my—" his tongue stumbles "—it was stolen from me. I think you found it."

"You were at the forge!" Ebba says, "You were standin next to us."

The man's eyes dart to her, then back to me.

I feel a weight in my chest. He must have seen me pick it up. "I don't have it."

"I know you do." His voice is not angry, but there is something under the surface, an urgency he's trying to hide.

"Sir," Ebba says, "she's tellin the truth."

The man glances at her. I realise he's jittery despite his firm voice.

"I had it," I say. "I left it in the kirk, as an offering."

The man looks between us, frowning. "Then you'll have to get it back for me, won't you?"

The inside of the kirk is still dim, still pleasant with the scent of beeswax. The man is waiting for us at the foot of the hill, and I'm kneeling before Walpurgis, my mind working horribly slowly.

"What are we goin to do?" Ebba whispers.

"I don't know." I stare at the spot by the saint's foot, where I put the gold horse earlier. All I can think is we're going to be late for the noon meal.

Behind us, both doors are pushed open.

"Prester Grimulf." A man's voice accompanies the creaking. "What a pleasure it is to see you again." By his tone, it's anything but a pleasure.

"Blessings be upon you, Lord Frithrun," says a second voice, deep and measured. Heavy steps come up the aisle behind us. "The doors need greasing."

"I'll send someone up right away," says the lord. "What are you doing here, Grimulf? Has the king sent you?"

Ebba's making shooing gestures, telling me we ought to leave, but we'll never sneak out unseen, and something tells me the lord of Frithberg is not going to be pleased to find two girls eavesdropping. I shake my head and pull her into the shadow of the stalls. Ebba scowls.

"The king is . . . troubled," says the deep voice, the one Lord Frithrun called Grimulf. "We received a petition from the merchants of Frithberg, demanding reassurance." Lord Frithrun snorts, but his visitor continues. "They say there have been attacks on their convoys, and when I arrived today they told me that they had to pay for extra guards to bring the grain from the East here safely."

"You visited the outlander merchants before you came to see me?" Lord Frithrun growls.

"I come at their invitation," says Grimulf, as if snubbing a lord is nothing. "I will stay with Dagomar while I'm here. Tell me, were you aware of these attacks?" Lord Frithrun says nothing. "I hardly need remind you that it is the lord's responsibility to keep his lands clear of bandits."

"The attacks have all been beyond my lands," says Lord Frithrun. "In the mountains, on the road north. Go chide Ridgemouth or Hellingap if you want. Frithberg prospers."

"Yes," says Grimulf, and from his voice he must be standing before the altar. "That is clear. Such splendid offerings, Frithrun. Almost the equal of the kirk at Sunacre."

Sunacre is King Kolrand's palace in the south of the kingdom. From Grimulf's easy contempt of Lord Frithrun, he clearly doesn't care that he's insulting him, and if he comes from Sunacre maybe he's close to the king. But Frithrun called him Prester, not Lord, and I've never heard that word before.

"This one in particular is exquisite," says Grimulf. "Look."

There's silence, then the lord grunts. "A horse," he says. "So what? If you're rich enough to have a horse, you're rich enough to pray for it."

"A horse bearing the sun. Turn it over," says Grimulf, his voice soft. "You see? The gift rune. Don't play games with me, Frithrun. You were at Hellingap, and at Frithberg too, before it was won, and the king gave it to you. You know what this is. They left it by Saint Walpurgis."

Ebba looks at me, wide-eyed.

"Saint Walpurgis is much loved by the people," Lord Frithrun says. "It's probably the offering of a farmer, Grimulf, nothing more."

"Yes," says the prester. "Maybe several, very rich farmers. The Blessed Walpurgis is popular in the East, you know." His voice is low, but we feel it through the wooden prayer stalls at our backs like distant thunder.

Footsteps pace before the altar. I pull Ebba into the shelter of one of the oak pillars.

"Why would they leave it here, to be found?" asks Lord Frithrun. There's an edge of panic in his voice.

"Frithberg is a meeting place," says Grimulf, "a crossroads. This is a message. Either someone in the East is being reminded of their loyalty, or they are affirming it. Her generals wore these tokens during the war."

"But all the generals were killed," says Frithrun. "I should know. I executed most of them myself."

The heavy steps start to pace.

"I've heard what your men say, Frithrun," says Grimulf. "That the White God is a god for women and merchants, not fit for warriors. But believe me, what starts as heresy will soon become treason. You've killed enough traitors to know what happens to them. So think carefully. We both know the source this poison springs from. Help me eradicate this stain from the land. Otherwise the tithes will be paid in the blood of innocents. You know what they're capable of."

We wait, the pacing footsteps drawing near. *Please don't turn the corner. Please don't check the shrine.*

"Very well." Lord Frithrun's voice is chastened. "I've proved my loyalty before, and I'll prove it again. I'll do what's needed."

"Excellent," says Grimulf. "Captain Erland is on his way; he should be here tomorrow. Then we will act." The footsteps head for the door. "Remember, Frithrun. Frithberg is no longer an unknown town in a minor land. It is the edge of God's Kingdom, and the King is eager to see that God's will be done."

The doors creak shut.

Ebba stares at me wide-eyed. "The horse —"

"I know." I wonder if the man in the blue cloak will still be waiting for us, or if he's seen the lord and the prester coming, and fled. "We can't let them see us."

We sit still as long as we dare, then creep to the door. The outcrop is deserted. We run.

Two

FOLLOWER

he people of Arngard, in addition to their idolatrous worship of false gods, and certain rocks and springs, also believe in a multiplicity of spirits. The most common spirit is the Luck. A man's Luck is reckoned to be, not a quality, but a spirit that accompanies him all his life. Of men who die before their time, people say their Luck has left them. Another spirit, rarer than the Luck, is the Follower. They belong to a family, like an heirloom, and appear in dreams to prophesy . . ."

History of Arngard
Berengar of Vellsberg

Most days I forget my dreams till I'm layin back down again at night, but as soon as I saw Torny fall on Smithgate, I remembered this one. My Follower came to me like she sometimes does, dressed in Ma's shape, her skirts an apron, although I knew it weren't Ma at all. "Today'll be busy," says she. I felt like I was back in Eldinghope on Uncle Ulf's farm, with a job needin doin, an Ma there to show me how. The homesickness I carry round wi me every day lightened a bit.

"Take these," says my Follower, pilin weapons into my dream-arms, till I peered at her through a forest of hilts.

"I can't carry these," I say. The grips were all silver, an the axe heads busy wi gold beasts knotted about em. Iron spears shone like new spring shoots. Even one of the swords would of bin too heavy for me awake.

"You'll have to eat em," says my Follower, matter-of-fact, her face shiftin under its stolen shape. She spoke wi the Eastern lilt, an it were soft on my ears like the town-speak of the plains will never be.

So I sit down, an I start to eat the weapons, one by one. The swords were fresh in my mouth, clean an crunchy, like radishes, an the spears thawed to melt water on my tongue. When I finished my meal, my Follower says, "Now you can travel light."

"I don't understand," I say.

My Follower comes up close, an I see a halter in her hand. Next thing I know I feel it over my face. The straps fit across my nose an under my jaw, an at the back of my head, that dip where my spine meets my skull, I feel it tighten. It feels like a tight-plaited braid, pullin at my scalp. An I feel it jerk, like my Follower's tuggin on it.

"Eyes *up*!" she hisses.

Now I'm thinkin on it, I wonder why that was a happy dream. Anyway, I wish she'd of given me a halter for Torny. It's not like I need one, but Torny could do wi some reinin in. I din't have time to tell her about the dream fore she was harin off up the hill to the kirk, an that's the thing wi Torny. She don't listen. Like after, when she tried to wriggle out of tellin the man in blue what she'd done with his gold horse. I nearly kicked her, but I din't have to in the end. I don't think she was brought up to tell the truth like I was. "Tellin the truth is a habit," Ma'd say. I don't think it was a habit in Gullcroft.

Blue Cloak en't waitin for us when we get down from the kirk. We keep runnin, all the way back, an when we duck into the kitchen Sorleyson shouts at us for being late. He's a big man with a big belly, an he scowls like the wind changed an he got stuck.

"If you can't be back in time for work, you shouldn't leave," he growls at us. Luckily his hands are full.

Aud gives us a disappointed look. Any other day I'd feel guilty, but everythin that's happened is still rushin round inside of me. I grab a knife an start slicin onions next to Kelda, the town girl who works with us. Usually I'd try not to get stuck next to her, but Sorleyson's eye is runnin over us. A call takes him back to the busy dinin hall.

"Where've you been?" says Aud, comin up to me.

"There was a fight," I say. I hope Torny don't make somethin up.

Sorleyson sticks his head through the door. "They strung up a thief in the market," he says. "One of the guards who came in with the convoy. You two! Why didn't you tell me?"

Torny jumps. "Strung him up?"

"His carcass is up on the harm — the hanging post," he says, catchin himself.

"We saw em catch him," I say, "but we din't stay to watch."

"Could've told me something useful if you had," Sorleyson grumbles.

After the noon meal we take the greasy bowls an platters out to the trough. Kelda never helps, she's too busy savin her hands from gettin cracked an red in the cold water. She's worried no one'll take her to wife. I don't mind. Ma says white hands mean a bad worker.

Course Torny's happy enough to get her hands dirty, if it means puttin off would-be husbands. She's tall as a boy, an she's got muscles on her too, which Kelda sniffs at. When she tumbles for our fun you can see em.

"Who was your stepdad goin to marry you to?" I ask her. It's a kind of game we play sometimes: Torny the Pigherd's Wife an her mighty deeds.

"What?" She looks at me like she din't hear me.

"Who were you goin to marry?" I nudge her.

"Oh. Thorpe, son of Thorpe, herder of pigs," she says, but her heart's not in it.

We stack the wet platters up an start on the bowls. When the yard gate swings open I look up, then quickly duck my head again before anyone can see me blush.

Jarle the stable hand walks across the yard to the stables, his hair shinin gold in the sun. It's gathered in a sleek tail that flicks across his shoulders. His leather boots fall soft on the cold earth.

"Bet you wouldn't of run away from him," I say, my voice catchin a bit, but Torny just snorts. Jarle ignores us. He don't speak to anyone but Aud less he has to. I check the door. Kelda don't usually miss a chance to see Jarle.

"Are you match-making, Ebba?" Aud sticks her head out the

kitchen door. "At least you got Jarlė," she says to Torny, who scrunches up her nose.

"You can have him," says Torny, takin up a load of clean ware. She carries it into the kitchen.

"Jarle's going to buy a farm and break horses," says Kelda, all curt, comin out on to the step. "He won't want a serving girl for a wife." Her eyes crawl over Aud, but Aud don't seem to notice.

A bit of fire springs up inside of me. Kelda's a town girl, an a beautiful one, but so far as I've seen what she's best at is skivin jobs that might roughen her hands, an sulkin when Aud gives her orders. *You're right,* I want to say, *Jarle'll want a wife who knows how to keep a farm, who can handle the horses well as the labourers. Not some girl who can't get her hands dirty.* But just thinkin about it I know the words'll garble in my mouth, come out silly.

I sneak a look at her. She could be one of the fair folk, with her pale skin an her bright red hair wispin out from under her kerchief. The blue cloth sweeps round her face like bird's wings, balanced all delicate on her slender neck. It hurts me to know it, but she an Jarle would suit each other.

My hair's thick an brown, and no one in the town is dark like me. The moment I open my mouth everyone can tell I'm off the Eastern farms. Sometimes they say they don't understand me, an sometimes they laugh. Sometimes I think even Torny don't really see me, just expects me to be there behind her, like a shadow.

Kelda's turnin to go inside. "When you've done ogling, farm girl," she says, in a voice I hear a lot, "the latrines want cleaning."

I feel my cheeks get hot an my eyes drop.

Aud grabs Kelda's wrist. "You can be rude if you like," she says calmly, "but Ebba works for Berger Sorleyson, not you." It looks like she's just holdin her, but Kelda's wrist is white under Aud's fingers.

"Which do you think he prefers," snaps Kelda, "her face or mine?"

Aud curls her lip. "Hers costs less. Clean the latrines yourself."

She lets go an Kelda flounces off, red-faced.

I keep my head down. I've felt Kelda's pride before, I've got used to it, but now Aud's stepped in it'll be worse.

Aud looks at me. "Don't let her push you, Ebba. You answer to Sorleyson. If you act like she can tell you what to do, she will." Maybe she sees my flamin cheeks cos her voice comes out kinder. "There's Jarle. Finish up and you can get in some practice."

"Come on," says Torny, racin back out of the kitchen. She don't even wait to get the last bowls out of the trough. She lopes across the hard dirt yard with her white-blonde head glowin in the sun. I fish out the bowls, pile em neatly, an trail after her.

Jarle is bringin out the staffs. That's what made Torny run. He don't greet us, just passes a staff to Torny, an they fall to blows an blocks, warmin their muscles before they spar.

Jarle keeps his eyes on Torny's staff. He's got greeny-hazel eyes, an ever since summer I can't help seein how his shoulders are broader, his arms muscled. My heart thuds, an I give up all hope of my cheeks coolin.

"You did well enough against the prentices," he says to Torny, not lookin at her. "But there were only two of them. Did you see the beating on Smithgate?" Torny nods. "In a crowd a fighter has almost no chance. As a girl, your chances are bad to begin with."

That's a long speech, for Jarle. But if he's tryin to rile her, it's workin. Torny swings her staff heavily at his head. He blocks an counter-swings, Torny catchin the blow just in time. Jarle's never really bin friendly, exactly, but he's never complained about our practice. I learnt staff an sling alongside my brother Stig an our cousin Rafe, but things are different back home between the mountains an the sea, wi no lord's warriors to protect us from the Raiders. Here, no town girl would dream of fightin.

A yell brings me back. Torny's standin over Jarle, who's on his backside.

"See that?" she whoops. I take the heavy wooden staff she offers me an settle my hands into the smooth-worn holds. I plant my feet firmly on the ground, Jarle opposite me. I look at his staff to avoid his eyes. If we both do that, maybe he won't see how pink I am.

Our sparrin en't like when he fights Torny. He don't push me the same, which is just as well cos I spend most of the time tryin not to stare at him. I feel like if he looks me in the face, he'll see everythin I feel about him all laid out.

"Look out!" Torny shouts.

I wheel away from a low swing – I seen it too late to block. Jarle pushes forward an I stagger back, tryin to find my footin. I block messily an Jarle's staff cracks over my fingers. I shout an snatch my hand away, cheeks blazin at havin made such a stupid mistake.

"Pay attention!" says Jarle, but he's interrupted by a familiar voice.

"Ebba?"

I freeze, my fingers smartin. My heart sinks. I want to curl into a tiny ball, but I turn to the gate, to my uncle's voice.

My Da's dead, see, same as Torny's. Ma's always tellin us how lucky we were that his brother took us in, stead of turnin us out. An if Uncle Ulf din't always seem pleased to have us, well, that weren't surprisin, because he'd lost his wife an eldest son to the plague the same year Da died. So lookin at us was a reminder of what he'd lost.

But instead of Ulf's thick body an shaved head, the voice comes from a freckled young man with flamin red hair.

For a moment I don't recognise him. He tries to smile an it comes out more like a worried frown, an then I know him.

"Rafe!" I rush into his arms. "You're so tall!"

That's not all he is. My cousin's shoulders are broad under his thick cloak of green wool, an his silver cloak-pins gleam on his chest. There's even some fuzz on his cheeks. The same thing that happened to Jarle has happened to him.

That thought makes me awkward, an I step back. Maybe he feels it too, cos instead of a hug he gives my shoulders a quick squeeze. It's exactly a year since my uncle left me at the wayhouse, an we've both changed. My heart jumps an I remember what my Follower said: *Now you can travel light.*

Is he here to fetch me home?

"What are you come for?" I ask, an it comes out shorter than I mean it.

"I'm come wi the harvest train," he says gruffly, in his voice that en't a boy's no more. The mountains are too steep for laden wagons, so all the grain from the East has to be carried by beasts across the pass. That's how I came last year. I knew Eldinghope must send someone this year, but Rafe's never bin before.

"Ulf said it was time I learned," he says.

"You must be pleased."

I remember how last year Rafe started goin round with Ulf to learn how the farm was run. He should of started earlier, but Ulf treated Rafe like a second son, even though his firstborn had died years ago. Now it seems Ulf's lettin Rafe oversee farm business by himself. No wonder he's dressed like a man now, with his cloak an shiny pins, an a silver buckle at his belt no less.

"En't you got any news for me?" I ask, when he don't reply.

"Oh, aye," he says, colourin up. "Yer ma says she's bin dreamin of you." He pats nervously at the purse on his belt. "She thought you might be needin some more of this." He hands me a small wooden box. I take it, runnin my finger over the simple pattern on the lid. It's the double of one I brought wi me from home. I slide open the lid an smell the sickly-sweet scent of the salve inside. This batch is fresh. It smells stronger'n the one I brought from home. Like always I try to catch a hint of what's in it, but like always I'm stumped. This is Ma's secret cure-all, good for burns, sprains, bruises an wounds. The smell makes my chest tight wi homesickness.

"An Stig?" I ask, my voice muffled.

My cousin is silent so long I look up. His cheeks have lost their colour.

"Stig Arfson is leavin us," he says finally; an just like that I know somethin en't right. Everyone at Eldinghope calls us by Ma's name – Rathna's son an Rathna's daughter. Only Uncle Ulf calls Stig by our Da's name, an Ulf an Stig never were easy together. Hearin Rafe use it makes me shiver.

"Did they fight?"

"No," says Rafe, but he looks away. "He's goin to be useful, same as you. He's fine."

I don't believe him, but his voice says leave it, an he sounds so like Ulf that I heed him. My breath comes shallow like we just had an argument, even though all his words have bin quiet.

"You'll stay with us tonight?" I ask, to change the subject, though it's hardly a question. Where else will he stay?

"I can't"

"Oh." I feel like the air is being squeezed out of me. "Why?"

"The roads en't safe," he says, fiddlin wi the knife at his belt. "The train's leavin soon, an it en't wise to travel alone. We lost one of our guards already. I've got what we need for winter, an I need to see it gets back safe, or —"

He stops but I hear what he don't say. *Or Ulf will want to know why.* Rafe has waited a long time for Ulf to treat him like his heir. He won't take the risk of angerin him now.

My fingers are still sore from Jarle's blow. It's only a couple of minutes since Rafe called me, an now he's leavin. Part of me wishes he hadn't come to see me at all. He goes to ruffle my hair, which he's never done before cos I would of smacked him, but that was when he was only an inch or two taller'n me, an had a boy's voice. Now he's grown I let him pet me, like some kind of stray dog. As he turns away I feel the distance between us grow until it hurts.

"I want to come home for Bloodnight!" The words tumble out of my mouth before I can stop em.

Rafe turns, his face dead white, and grips my shoulders hard. I've said somethin wrong.

"You can't," he says, an his voice trembles. "D'you understand?" He gives me a shake. "You're burden enough without havin you underfoot when the dalesmen come." I try to bite back my tears, but they spill over. "An don't blub! Or . . . or I'll tell Ulf."

I look down, bitin my lip as tears run down my cheeks.

"Hey!" Suddenly I'm lookin down at Torny's back as she

pushes in front of me. "Proud of yourself, are you, coming all this way to make her cry? Well you can tell this Ulf of yours from me to —"

She repeats one of the suggestions we've heard the lord's warriors use in the practice yard. My cheeks burn, as if Ulf might hear her all the way from Eldinghope. I look up over her shoulder. Rafe's cheeks are pink again, an he puts his hand on his knife, but Torny's as tall as he is, an she's picked up the practice staff.

"Just you try it, farmboy," she sneers.

Rafe takes one look at me over her shoulder, an all but runs out the gate.

Torny slings her arm over my shoulders. I'm starin at the ground, tryin to stop cryin. *You're burden enough*, Rafe said. They don't want me back. *Maybe it's another bad harvest*, I think, but a small voice says, *maybe they just don't want you.*

"What was that about?" Torny asks.

"He said I can't go home," I say, an my voice wobbles.

"If he's the best they've got, why would you want to?" says Torny, glarin after him.

I think of Ma an Stig, an fresh tears prick my eyes.

"Oh, Ebba." Torny gives me a proper hug, an it makes me cry more. "They'll have you back soon enough, when they want you for marrying or they need an extra pair of hands. Your cousin's an idiot."

"But what if the farm's failin?" I sob.

"The farm's fine," says Torny. "Did you see all that silver on him? You don't get that with rotted barley."

I don't know what's worse, worryin that they're starvin, or

knowin that they're not an still don't want me. It sticks in my throat like fishbones.

"If that's how they treat you, what's the point of going back?" She's tryin to be kind, but she's impatient wi me too. "You've got your own work here, you don't have to beg them for anything. Being on your own will make you stronger."

She don't understand. I knew she wouldn't.

I pull away from her.

"I'm alright now," I say.

"Let's eat in the barn tonight," she says, still tryin to cheer me. "We'll see if we can't get Jarle to tell us a story."

Aud stands on the kitchen step, callin us in. The sun is low an down Astgate comes the ox-train, headed back East towards the mountains while there's still light. The bells on the ox-bridles tinkle. Even without em the wayhouse will be busy, an for once I'm relieved. Back in the kitchen I barely have time to put Ma's box away. I don't believe what Torny says about bein stronger alone: our family protects us, an it's our duty to add to it, defend it. That's why Uncle Ulf took Ma an Stig an me in when Da died, that's why he sent me here when the crops failed, an maybe that's why Stig's bin sent away.

Thinkin about Stig makes me feel cold; he must of angered Ulf badly this time.

But here I am in the warm kitchen, the heat of the fire on my face, a knife in my hand, vegetables to chop. No time to think, if I want to keep all my fingers.

Next to me, Kelda is choppin turnips like they've offended her.

"Let's all go," Torny is shoutin to Aud across the noise from the hall, where the guests are gatherin. She's turnin the spit, her face rosy an shinin wi sweat. "After the fire's banked. Can we?"

At least I might see Jarle again tonight.

Aud nods an calls Kelda over, loadin her arms wi platters of meat in thick gravy. Kelda disappears into the hall as Sorleyson strides in. He sneers at my vegetables, inspects the spit, an stamps into the store wi buckets to fill. Through the door to the hall I can see the long tables already packed wi men an women. Above em the smoke from the fire itches at the black roof.

There's a yelp, an Kelda reappears, gravy all down her front. "The big one with the beard on the first table," she says to Aud, her eyes narrowed. "He asked for a trick and I said I didn't know any."

Sometimes Sorleyson gets us to do tricks in the hall, on quieter nights when there's space near the fire. Kelda plays the flute, Torny tumbles, an I – I en't got a trick. Not really. Sorleyson had to make one up for me. He even gave me a name an all.

"Go change your apron," orders Aud. "Ebba, pass me that." She points to a rollin pin near my hand. I pass it to her an she sticks it through her apron strings like a sword through a belt. Takin an ale bucket in one hand, she jerks her head at the platters I'm to carry in Kelda's place. She leads the way into the hall, its three long tables packed tight. The guests' mouths gleam wi fat in the firelight.

The jumpin flames make it hard to see. A single eye glitterin in the light, the hook of a nose, teeth ragged against open mouths. The market-traders are callin across neighbours an tables to one another, leanin between the benches, claspin arms an shoutin. I push between em an start laying out platters along the first table. Folk are tellin the fate of the thief on Smithgate for those who en't heard it. Aud stands with her back to the fire, fillin the cups that are passed down the table to her from hand to hand.

The shadow's thick across her.

As I'm layin the last platter, I hear a shout of laughter, an spin round. Aud stands wi the rollin pin raised, an a big man with iron rings in his dirty red hair an a forked beard clutches his hand as if wounded. He's one of Lord Frithrun's warriors; I've seen him in the practice yard as well as the dinin hall. His neighbours are grinnin an pattin him, making 'there, there' noises, all except one. A wiry blond man wi greasy hair sits next to the red-haired giant, his face sour.

"Who dares strike Hakon Kolson, warrior of Frithberg?" bellows the giant, cradlin his hand.

"Aud of the mountains, who's afraid of no plains-boy." Aud turns so her face is lit an folds her arms, still clutchin her rollin pin. "Didn't your mother teach you manners?"

The crowd yells in delight.

Big Hakon stands, his face sombre, an faces Aud. Her chin comes up to the points of his braided beard, an she tips back her head an scowls at him.

"You are too small to be so uncivil, chitling," growls the big man.

"You're too big to be pawing serving girls," says Aud. "You'll crush them without trying!"

"I'll crush you in a moment," says Hakon, to roars of laughter.

"Just you try," says Aud. Big Hakon swipes at her clumsily, an Aud dances back, then swoops forward to tap the rollin pin down on his shoulder. The guests clear space for em. Hakon lumbers like a bear while Aud dances round him, light on her feet, the rollin pin tappin him here an there, makin him spin an growl. It's a good show.

But then somethin changes. Hakon stumbles over his own

feet, an his sour-faced companion steps in to steady him, an says somethin to Aud.

I can't hear what he says, but I see her eyes flash. Her rollin pin whips round, an slams hard into the smaller man's side.

Or it would, but for Hakon movin so fast his sword arm comes between the two, an the pin smashes into his forearm.

The laughter stops. Hakon roars, an swings at Aud, no longer playin. Aud leaps back onto a bench, an people scrabble to get their food out of harm's way.

A hand falls on my shoulder. Sorleyson looks down at me. "Go and get your salve, girl. We'll need it."

I dart through the door where Torny an Kelda are watchin to the store cupboard. Above the lintel are the two boxes of Ma's salve. I take the almost empty one an dash back into the hall between the watchin girls, just as Aud lands a second blow above Big Hakon's wrist that sends his sword-hand numb.

"Harridan!" booms Sorleyson, stridin between the two of em. "Haven't I told you to mind your pots and pans and leave the poor men of this town in peace? Out!" He points to the door, an Aud drops her head an leaves, as if this is all part of the show. Sorleyson moves to the warrior's side, neatly keepin between him an Aud. "Hakon Kolson!" Sorleyson cries. "The only warrior to face the Scold of the Mountains and live!" A cheer goes up, an Kelda nips forward with an overflowin cup of mead, smilin prettily, an presses it into Hakon's good hand.

"And now," continues Sorleyson, "you'll see why our girls need protecting."

He beckons me forward, an I in my turn solemnly approach Hakon, my salve held in front of me.

"This is our Salvebearer, with her magic cure-all from beyond the sea." Sorleyson's voice is deep an strong, carryin through the suddenly quiet hall. "Give her your sword-hand, warrior."

Bemused, Hakon holds out his great fist. I slide the lid off the slim wooden box, dippin the tips of my fingers into the salve, an rub the salve gently into his bruised wrist an arm, murmurin the words for relief. When I'm finished I bow my head an leave, but not before I see Hakon's blond companion starin at me. His sharp eyes are like needles.

I hurry into the kitchen, an behind me I hear another cheer. A song starts up as I replace the salve box on the lintel. Sorleyson nods to me as he passes wi more ale, but he stops Aud with a hand on her arm, an I hear him hiss, "Your Luck was with you this time."

I want to ask Aud what the blond man said to rile her so, but her face don't welcome questions. Instead I tell Torny what I saw.

"Why d'you think she did it?" I ask her. "Was it her Luck leavin her?"

"Everyone's Luck leaves them in the end," says Torny, an shrugs. "That was Spraki Spit-Nails, the lord's skald. He's known for his tongue."

I guess she's right – my Da an hers both lost their Lucks early. But it en't like Aud to lose her temper. Whatever wickedness Spraki put in her ear, it rattled her.

At last the overnight guests wrap themselves in their cloaks an lie down on the hall floor by the fire. Aud banks the kitchen fire an bolts the door to the hall to keep out thieves. The stars are bright above us as we cross the yard. Aud an Kelda carry the small cauldron, full of barley stew wi the dregs of the meat gravy mixed in. Torny an I follow wi hazelnut biscuits an a small bucket of ale.

The stables are lit by a low brazier at the end away from the big double doors, past the stalls. Only two stalls have horses in. Up by the brazier, scraps of leather an tools for mendin tack lie neatly on a chest. Jarle's bed is above us, in the hayloft. Aud puts the cauldron down an starts ladlin stew into bowls. Jarle's bright gold head gleams as he drags hay bales round the brazier for us to sit on. A warm bowl is pressed into my hands an I sit on a bale next to Torny. We don't talk, an by the time my bowl's scraped clean I'm half asleep, my head on Torny's shoulder.

"What story shall we have, Jarle?" Aud asks. Jarle looks up an shrugs. When there are no horses to care for, he hangs round the lord's hall an listens to the skald tellin stories an recitin poems. Then he comes back an recites em to us, if he's in a good mood. Torny says he practices on the horses first.

"Do you know any about the Sungiven?" I ask sleepily. Jarle an Aud's heads snap round to stare at me, an Torny elbows me.

"Why?" asks Jarle, the first thing he's said all evenin.

"No reason," I mumble, an Aud looks like she's going to ask me somethin, when Kelda chokes on a hazelnut. Torny pounds her on the back, an then Kelda has to have some ale to wash it down, an then we all have some, an then – "I have a story," says Jarle, in his storytellin voice, which is the only one most of us ever get to hear.

"An music?" I ask hopefully.

Kelda opens her hands to show she en't brought anythin, but Jarle says, "My pipe's by my bed," an Kelda looks pleased.

"I'll get it," says Torny, an nips up the ladder to the loft before Jarle can argue. We can hear her movin about, then stop.

"Torny!"

"Coming!" Her feet dangle, then she drops, an she sits back down next to me. She hands Jarle's reed pipe to Kelda. Jarle's hunched by the brazier, his face lit from below by the charcoal.

We huddle closer, our backs to the cold empty stalls.

"In the days of honour, when men were free and women true, there was a man called Arn, who people called the Good. He was a lord of the plains, a powerful man who loved the land, and was beloved. First he united the plains, then the western coast, and as his greatness grew, he was crowned king of Arngard. In those days Arngard was bordered by the Vells River in the South, the Ridge in the North, and the mountains in the East.

"Arn dreamed of peace throughout the land, and so he married a daughter of Hellingap, north of the Ridge. His queen was beautiful, with hair like the summer corn, and before long she bore him a son. The boy was as bold as his father and as lovely as his mother. If things had stayed as they were, how happy we would be! But even as the prince grew strong and healthy, his mother's life waned. By his tenth year, the child was motherless.

"The king grieved for his wife, and for many months would not be comforted. But then one day, riding in the borderlands, he came across a young woman in the ruins of a house. In that moment he forgot his dead queen, and carried the woman back to his palace, where shortly after they were married.

"At first the new queen pretended to be kind to the young prince, but it wasn't long before she had a son of her own, and after that things changed. The firstborn prince was brave and fair, but the new queen's son was a sickly child. Of course the new queen was jealous, and did everything she could to make the older boy's life a misery. But even so, he grew from child to man, and he was everything a prince should be."

Kelda's still holdin the pipe, but she's not playin anymore. "I'm not listening to this," she says, breathless. She jumps up, but Aud has her by the wrist an jerks her back to her seat.

I get a sick feelin in my stomach. I know why Kelda's scared. This is the story of King Arn, of the war of the Arnsons, but not the way you usually hear it. I press myself into Torny's side.

Aud en't lookin at Kelda, but she's holdin her tight, an there's a sort of quiet satisfaction on her face.

"It won't kill you," she says. "It's just a story."

Tears glisten in the corners of Kelda's eyes, but she sits still, the pipe in her lap.

Jarle stares into the brazier, his face blank. "He was everything a prince should be," he says, "and although the new queen managed to sour the king's love for his son with fear and jealousy, she could not stop the people loving him. Warriors came from across the land to serve him, and they became famous. It was said the gods favoured them, made them invulnerable in battle, could even change their shape. People called them the Slipskins. They knew the secret ways across the Floodlands in the North, and they won back the barren lands along the Vells River, until the Emperor of the Southern Empire begged for mercy.

"The new queen came from the border lands, so she should have been grateful for the prince's campaign, but instead she determined to destroy him, and place her own son on the throne. She went to the king and in tears told him that she believed his eldest son and heir wished him dead. 'When the Emperor's delegation comes to negotiate the border, you must ask for help,' she said, 'for if you perish, I and your youngest son will not survive.' And the king, so blinded by her wickedness that he believed her, did as she said.

"Now the delegation was led by a man they called Two-Tongue, and like the snake he was named for, he was honourless, a coward. Born in Arngard, he had turned traitor and served the Emperor, with no loyalty for his motherland. King Arn confided in him, and Two-Tongue saw in the king's wild fears an opportunity. So he reassured the king, and told him that he should have imperial troops to protect him, and all the wealth and comfort he could dream of, for the Emperor respected and supported him. In return, all he had to do was denounce the gods of Arngard, the Wise One and the Cornmaiden, and swear loyalty to the White God of the Empire."

I glance at Kelda, an our eyes meet. It's unsettlin. Kelda's always scorned me, but that look makes us brief allies.

Kelda an I both go to the kirk to pray. Not together, an we never talked of it, but we both know. An the others know.

I slip my hand into Torny's, half scared she'll move away from me, but she just squeezes it, still listenin to Jarle.

"In his blindness, Arn turned his back on the gods. He, his queen and his youngest son swore loyalty to the White God, and Two-Tongue smiled, for he knew he had the king under his power.

"When the people discovered what Arn had done, there was outrage. The sun grew black that very day, and a plague passed through the land, killing men and beasts. The crops failed, and all was fear and uncertainty. It was then that the Staffbearers, keepers of the sacred grove, handmaids of the Harm Tree, knew that they could no longer stay silent. They came to Geir, for that was the prince's name, and asked him if he was ready to defend the gods.

"'I am,' he said.

"Then the Staffbearer of Sunacre, still young but wise beyond her years, told him of an ancient law, part of the secret knowledge that the Wise One learned as he hung on the Harm Tree, and his spirit crossed over the border between worlds. The land can be renewed, redeemed. But for that to happen, in the ninth year, on the ninth night of winter, the lord of the land must die.

"Then Prince Geir wept, for he loved his father still. He begged the Staffbearer to find another way, but she told him there was none. The ninth night was fast approaching, and the prince would have to choose.

"Prince Geir was tormented. He honoured the gods, but he revered Arn not only as his own father, but as the father of Arngard itself. But at last his choice was made for him. To prove his loyalty to the White God, Two-Tongue ordered King Arn to cut down the Harm Tree in the palace's sacred grove.

"The prince knew what he must do. When the king came on the ninth night of the ninth year to destroy the tree sacred to the gods, his son, with heavy heart, did what he had to do. The Slipskins surrounded the grove, and no traitor left alive."

Everyone's holdin their breath. This is the story that's told time an again – but not like this. The way it's usually told, it's the prince who's the wicked one, killin his father for power, an the younger son is the victim, driven from his land in fear of his life, brought back in triumph. In the towns an down on the plains they remember Good King Arn on the ninth night of winter, which they call Arnsnight, an that is the story they tell. But east of the mountains an north of the Floodlands, we still call it Bloodnight, an the stories we tell have two sides.

This story don't. I wonder where Jarle got it.

"You know what happened next," says Jarle, scornfully. "Kolrand, the traitor's cub, fled south across the border with Two-Tongue, and returned with imperial troops. He destroyed the sacred groves, murdered the Staffbearers, and Geir Arnson was killed before Hellingap, the town where his mother was born. Now we're ruled by traitors, and people have become cowardly. The gods have turned their backs, and Arngard is in thrall to the Empire."

Jarle sits back, his face in shadow. "This is the story that Spraki Spit-Nails, skald to the Lord of Frithberg, tells, so it must be true."

Kelda sucks in her breath. I know why. For the lord's skald to tell such tales must be treason. In one quick movement, she takes the pipe from her lap, snaps it in two, an throws it into the brazier.

"Tell your stories," she sneers. "I won't tattle. But sooner or later you'll be found out, and then what?"

The charcoal crumbles, showin its red heart. Jarle glances at Aud, an it almost looks like he smiles. Kelda sees too, an turns, dashin more tears out of her eyes with an angry hand, but then the thunder is upon us, wi screams of iron on stone an men shoutin. Kelda shrieks, but Aud is already on her feet.

"Soldiers," she says, an then the doors burst open.

Three

HANGED MAN

❧

TORNY'S TALE

tall man strides out of the shadows, the cold wind at his back.

"Get out, children," he says. "Boy, get your master."

"I'll go," says Aud, brushing off her skirts as she faces him, so the man can see she's no child. "Jarle, help the lord stable his horses. Girls, with me."

She shoos us before her like a mother hen with chicks, but the men – soldiers, Aud called them – are busy leading their horses into the stalls and settling them. They don't even glance at us, but I look at them. All young, all strong-looking, all dressed the same, maroon cloaks and blue tunics. Even their hair is cut alike, ridiculously short on their necks. Jarle is going quickly between beasts, helping where he can, but the soldiers are already brushing them down and cleaning their hooves, using their own brushes and picks. These men are used to caring for their mounts.

As we leave the barn Sorleyson passes us with a flaming torch, his rumpled undershirt shoved into his breeches. The tall man meets him at the stable door, and I hang back to watch. Ebba hovers beside me, her hand in mine.

"Captain Erland," says the leader of the soldiers, looking down at Sorleyson. Sorleyson seems big in the kitchen, but next to the captain he looks stooped and paunchy. "You should have been told we were coming."

Sorleyson mutters something.

"What's a soldier?" whispers Ebba. "Is it like our warriors?"

"No," I whisper back, keeping my eyes on Erland. "You know how warriors have to pay for their own weapons and find a lord who'll take them?" Ebba nods. "Well, soldiers are paid by a lord to fight for him."

"What, all of em?" asks Ebba, surprised. "He'd have to be rich."

"But they wouldn't," I explain. "You could pay poor men to fight for you."

Ebba sounds alarmed. "What're the rich men goin to do if anyone can be a warrior?"

"They'll be captains, like this Erland."

"I can't see it catchin on," says Ebba. "There's no glory in killin a poor man. An who'll work the fields?"

"Farmgirl," I tease.

Ebba smacks my shoulder. "Someone's got to be. Anyway, how d'you know this?"

"Aud told me. It's how they make war in the Southern Empire."

"They're Southerners?" Ebba asks.

"The soldiers are," I say. "But look at the captain. He must be one of ours."

Captain Erland is watching his men stable their horses. His blue eyes are set over wide cheekbones, and his face is toughened from the weather, lined with what looks like soot. His nose has been broken several times, if its hooked and slanted appearance is anything to go on. All his men have horses. Lord Frithrun's warriors go about on their own two feet – only the lord and his wealthiest followers ride.

Ebba tugs my arm, none too gently, and I realise her teeth are chattering. Then I realise mine are too.

Reluctantly, I turn towards the kitchen door, outlined in warm firelight across the yard. Through it, Aud is dark against the fireplace. There's no sign of Kelda.

A hand falls on my shoulder. I look up into the captain's weathered face.

"I need my things taken to my room, girl. Here." He passes me two saddlebags, and I take them, bending a little under the weight but straightening once I have them across my arm. "Go."

Ebba and I go.

Aud is warming stones in the embers. "What are you two doing?" she says. I show her the saddlebags.

"Where's the captain sleeping?"

"First room," she says, "and you can take these too, for the bed." She carefully wraps the stones in blankets and piles them on top of the saddlebags. I have to start moving to keep myself from falling over.

"D'you want help?" I hear Ebba ask behind me, but she seems to be asking Aud. Now I'm out of the cold, I feel sleepiness creeping up my spine, but I fight it. I've never seen a warrior at home before. The door is unbolted, and I push inside. There's a metal brazier lighting the room and the bed is already made. I dump the saddlebags on the floor before tucking the wrapped stones into the bed to warm it.

"I hope you haven't been throwing them around," says the captain's voice from the door. He nods to the bags.

"Soft as down," I say, straightening. "Do you need anything else?"

"Water," he says, "and not from the trough, thank you. Warm."

I raise my brows. "To drink?"

"To wash, you unsanitary child."

To wash? My sleepiness is gone. "He wants water for *washing*," I say to Aud when I'm back in the kitchen. "Not from the trough," I add, as she starts to gesture that way.

"Southerners," growls Aud, grabbing a bucket. "Give this a scrub, fill it up and we'll heat it here." I do as she says.

As I'm standing at the trough in the dark, Sorleyson stamps past me. "That you, Jarle?"

"It's Torny," I call over the splashing, and Sorleyson says, "Odd's blood, where is the boy," and stamps inside.

"Torny," someone whispers in my ear, and I jump.

"Jarle?" I whisper back, seeing the shine of golden hair. "What are you doing? And why are we whis —" I start to say normally, but he clamps a hand over my mouth.

"Where is it, Torny?" he says in my ear. I shake my head. "Where is it?"

I take his hand from my mouth with one of my own, cold and wet from the trough. I do it firmly, my fingers ready to yank his backwards if he resists. I'm not scared of Jarle, but I know he's frightened. "Where's what?" His hand tenses but I have a grip on his last two fingers and I push them back, forcing his hand uncomfortably over his wrist. "What is it, Jarle? And why are you sneaking around in the dark when your master is looking for you?"

He doesn't say anything. What could he say? He pulls his hand away from me and turns on his heel. I put my hands on my hips, and feel my pocket gaping open. So Jarle is light-fingered, and was searching me even while I thought I was in control.

I accept the lesson. It's a good one. Luckily I'm far too sensible to keep secrets in my pockets.

I carry the pail of warm water to the room, slopping some of it on the floor. The encounter with Jarle has sent a fizz of energy through me, but while my mind's busy, my limbs are getting heavy. I push open the door with my foot and stick my head in. "Water, captain."

"Bring it in here, girl." Captain Erland is sitting on the bed with his sword across his knees. In the brazier's light I can see the waves of iron in the blade-edge, and the silver hilt shines under the captain's rough hand. The boss is stamped with a black bear.. "Come on," he says, not unkindly, and I plonk the pail at his feet, my eyes still on the sword.

He rests it on the bed and pulls off his shirt. His cloak and wide leather belt lie across the chair already. He starts scooping the water up in his hands and dashing it into his face and over his body with every sign of enjoyment.

I avert my eyes from this outlandish display, and look about. That sword speaks wealth, but his clothes and saddlebags are plain. His weapon is his only ornament.

"Much better," he says, and laughs at the face I pull. "You

should try it. Not now," he adds hurriedly, so my face must have shown what I thought of that. "Is my face clean?"

"The soot's gone, if that's what you mean," I say stiffly, half-ready to bolt for the door at the first sign of any more washing talk. He's lost the severity he had outside.

"Good." He bends to search for something in his saddlebags, and for the first time I can look at him properly. He's strong, that's clear, and his back is coloured with brown and blue bruises, red grazes, white scars from old wounds – the puckered stars of arrowheads, the grins and frowns of blades.

"Have you been fighting?" I ask, as he pulls a shirt over his head.

"Just riding hard," he answers. "At least the roads will be a little safer for a while, until the bandits grow back." He looks at me. "What's your name?"

"Torny Vafrisdota, captain."

"A strong name," he says, "but you're dog-tired. You can go." He hands me the pail and I leave, almost stumbling.

Up in the loft, Aud and Kelda are both curled silently under their blankets. I pick my way past them, and past the softly-snoring shape of Ebba. I don't bother undressing, just wrap myself in blankets and snuggle into the bedroll. My whalebone pin pricks me; Ebba put it by my pillow for me. I hold it in my fist, the bone still warm to the touch.

My body's so grateful to be lying down. As I fall asleep, Ebba's quiet snores remind me of home, the way we curled up together in the peat-smoke dark, until my father went away, and never came back.

I am awake, my chest tight, my eyes wide, my hands tingling. It is dark and cold as a grave chamber, and something is moaning and thrashing. There is no light. A deep shudder goes through my chilled bones.

"Ma," chokes a voice near my head, and I wriggle out of my blankets and closer to Ebba, who is tossing from side to side. Her eyes are wide open but I know she can't see me. I grab her shoulders and press down. Her breath is short and coming in gasps.

"Ebba," I whisper. "It's Torny. I'm here. You're alright."

She calms slowly, still twitching, and when I touch her face I can feel she's been crying. I wrap my arms around her and hold her. She's so warm, and her thick hair brushes my cheek, tickles my nose. Her breath comes deeper and deeper, until she is still and heavy again. I pull her blankets around her, then lie beside her stroking her hair, like Brenna used to stroke mine before my father died. Ebba never remembers her nightmares in the morning, or at least she never says anything. "What were you dreaming about?" I'll ask, and she'll just say, "Home."

Home.

How can you know a place inside and out – the carved posts at the boundaries, the tracks along the cliffs, the seabirds and their smell, the green turf on the roof and the way the fog rolls in – how can you know it like it's part of you, and then just be pushed out, as if you're nothing?

How can some stranger come in and take over, like it was his all along?

I remember running to Vigdis, in her round hut on the cliff, and saying, "They want me to marry pigherd Thorpe." Just like I'd run to her when Brenna told me she was marrying Sklep, and having his child. Then Vigdis had just said, "Of course," as if I should have known that already. But when I ran to her about Thorpe, she said, "And will you marry him?"

"I'm never going to marry anyone," I told her.

Vigdis looked at me, her pale blue eyes narrow.

"Then what are you going to do?" she asked.

I understood then. Brenna wouldn't have me. Sklep might have been the one to say it, but behind him stood Brenna, her hand on her belly. The home under the green turf roof wasn't mine anymore.

"You've already started teaching me," I said to Vigdis. "Can't I stay with you?"

Vigdis searched my face for a moment, then turned back to her work.

"No," she said. "I'm sorry Torny. I had hoped you might have some ability, but you take after your father. You'll never be a Staffbearer."

I hadn't realised how much I'd relied on that until then. True, I couldn't tell staunchweed from wolfbane, but I could read the runes and I'd watched her bargain for good winds or full nets when I was meant to be sleeping. It didn't seem too much different from any market-day haggle.

I'd thought I didn't have to marry a pigherd. I could learn to be a Staffbearer, like my aunt, and have everyone from the young wives to the headman come round and ask counsel, as they did with Vigdis.

"The drovers will be going south for the sheepfair soon," said Vigdis. "I know a place on the plains you can get work. Frithberg."

That's when I realised she didn't want me. Nobody did, except maybe Thorpe, hard luck to him.

I turned my back on my aunt and went home to pack. Sklep was glad he didn't have to pay bride-price, and Brenna said nothing at all, just watched over her belly to make sure I took everything. "If you leave it, I'll burn it," she said.

"If you're going on the road, you should be disguised," said Sklep, laughing. That was when he held me down and cut my hair off in handfuls. He cut it with a knife, and Brenna smiled.

Vigdis met me at the carved posts. She didn't mention my shorn head and she didn't seem to mind that I was going. A carter with barrels of smoked fish was headed to Hellingap, where I'd join the drovers heading south to Frithberg. Vigdis told me to ask for Sorleyson's wayhouse, and sent me off. The sea wind prickled my neck; my hair was so short I got mistaken for a boy, and liked it.

If I'd been a boy, maybe I wouldn't have had to leave. Maybe I'd have been enough to bring Brenna back, after Vafri died and she went away from us. But if I hadn't left . . .

My arm is still around Ebba. She's breathing softly again, her tears dry.

Beneath me, I hear the creak of a door. The cracks between the wooden boards of the attic glow faintly with light from the room below.

"Prester Grimulf," says Erland, voice muffled. "Welcome."

"It is good to see you, Erland," says the same deep voice I heard yesterday in the kirk. "Did you do as I asked?"

"Two teams from the imperial garrison at Vellsberg, sir, eight men in total. I've brought the Vellsberg boy too, as my armsman. Lord Vellsberg seems to think he needs some experience, and he speaks our tongue."

"He is devout?"

"Very, sir. I believe he hopes to write an ecclesiastical history of Arngard."

"Then he will benefit from seeing the moral rot we work against. Keep him out of trouble, Captain."

"Yes, sir."

"Good. How was the journey?"

"Only one attack, and they soon realised their mistake. Nothing like the fears you describe."

"And yet the merchants are nervous," says the prester. "They have seen more attacks. These are not ordinary bandits. Dagomar found this pinned to the body of one of his agents." There's the crackle of barkpaper. "And when I went to the kirk this morning, I found this. At the foot of Saint Walpurgis."

Even wrapped in my blankets, I feel cold. I imagine the gold horse shining in the brazier-light, gleaming in Erland's rough hand.

"Walpurgis?" says Erland, puzzled.

"Quite. From Dagomar's reports, I thought the trouble was in the North, but Walpurgis is the favourite of the Eastern farms. They worship her in place of the old goddess, the . . . Cornmaiden." The word seems sour in his mouth.

"Gold as well," says Erland heavily. "So they're wealthy, whoever they are. Or maybe this is the wealth of a whole community." He sounds grim. "I had hoped – well. Never mind."

"I understand, captain. It's hard to see one's people so resolute in their evil." Erland doesn't answer. "But God is with us. A man was caught stealing today, one of the guards who came in with the grain. He had a companion, a one-handed man. If we can find him, we'll know more. The tide turns."

"Has Frithrun given you his support, then?"

The prester snorts. "He prevaricates, hoping that the king will overlook his laxity. He does not believe, Erland. If it was left to him, the Staffbearers would forment heresy and sedition on the plains just as they do over the mountains and beyond the Floodlands." *Staffbearers*. He spits the word. The hair on my neck stands up.

"You're sure it's them?" asks Erland. "The Staffbearers?"

"It was them when Arn swung from the Harm Tree at Sunacre," says the prester, "and when the dying lay at the gates of Hellingap. It's always been them, Erland. They are the worm beneath the bark. They were at its heart nine years ago, and believe me, that is where we will find them again."

"But why now?"

"I don't know yet," says the prester, and his steady voice frightens me. "But there's a dead thief strung up in the market place, and before they killed him he said something about the Staffbearer of Gullcroft."

This is true wakefulness, not driven by curiosity or fear. I lie waiting, waiting, after the creak of the door, after the light goes out below as Erland covers the brazier. I remember Ebba saying the Sungiven's name, the man at the forge bolting, knife in hand, and the way he looked at me as he threw me the gold horse. The way the prester recognised it. He'd seen one like it before. *Her generals wore these tokens during the war*, he'd said. *They use Frithberg as a meeting place.* And in the stables, the way Jarle's head snapped round at the Sungiven's name. And then —

I can feel the weight of it on my chest. I pull the cord over my shirt, run my thumb over the shape of the bronze pendant that I stole tonight from the hayloft in the stables, when Jarle asked me to get his flute. A horse. Not gold, this time, bronze, but the same horse, the sun on its side, the X scored into the plain side. Polished, as if someone has held it and turned it over and over in their hands for years.

Why did I take it? Truth is, I didn't think. I just wanted more time to look it over. But the soldiers came, and Jarle looked for it before I could put it back.

Somewhere in the back of my head, Vigdis asks me, *What are you going to do?*

Gullcroft didn't want me. Vafri who left me, Brenna who replaced me, Vigdis with her secret knowledge she wouldn't teach me. But now this man who talks about blood and evil has named my aunt, and no matter what bitterness I feel, I can't ignore this, and I can't tell anyone. I have to warn them myself.

As a girl, your chances are bad to begin with.

I grit my teeth. If I'm to do this, I'll need all the Luck I can get.

Floor-shaking snores are coming up through the boards. Moving as quietly as I can, I get up and creep past the others to the trapdoor. I lower myself into the corridor below, easing the trapdoor back into place, but just as I turn it lifts suddenly, and I nearly swallow my tongue. Ebba stares down at me, her dark eyes huge.

She's silent as we pass the rooms where Sorleyson and Erland sleep. In the kitchen I sit to tie on my leather shoes. Ebba hasn't brought hers. I roll my eyes at her and give her mine. I find Aud's sharp little paring knife on the counter and thrust it into the cord at my waist, and walk out into the yard. There's a thin frost on the ground, and I wince. The cold has come quickly, in earnest. My soles are thick from running barefoot all summer, but they still ache.

We walk up Astgate towards the deserted market place. It's before dawn, still dark, but the clear sky above is littered with stars.

Ebba doesn't ask questions. She doesn't say "Where are we going?" or "Why have you got Aud's knife?" which I know must be bothering her. Like yesterday with the man in the blue cloak. She doesn't like lying. Ebba is so honest some people think she's stupid.

I steal a glance sideways at her and catch the outline of her eyes, her lips. She's wearing that stubborn expression, the one she wears when she's asleep. Maybe that's her true expression. I wonder what I look like when I sleep.

The marketplace opens around us, wide and empty, the well at its centre. Close to it stands the pole, and the corpse hangs from it, its feet lashed high up. We stop at the end of Astgate, staring across the space.

"Stay here," I tell Ebba.

Now she does catch my sleeve and hisses, "What're you goin to do?"

"Look," I say, hooking the cord from under the neckline of my shirt. I pull it over my head and show it to her. She has to peer closely in the dark, but I feel her stiffen and I know she's recognised it.

"Where d'you get that?" I can hear the edge of panic in her voice.

"Shhh," I say. "It was in the stables. Up in the loft."

Ebba drops the bronze horse pendant as if it's on fire, and it twirls on the end of its thong, shining. "Jarle," she says. "He jumped when I asked for a story about the Sungiven."

Ebba is the least stupid person I've ever met.

"Jarle," I agree. "He found me when I was out on my own

❦ 54 ❦

last night. He tried to pick my pocket." Ebba looks shocked. Impulsively I kiss her cheek. "Go back now," I tell her. "You don't want to be here."

"Don't be an idiot," she says, "I'm stayin. What are you doin?"

"Making an offering," I say, but we both know that's not the whole of it. I start towards the corpse. I have very little time.

Wells and rivers are holy places, everyone knows that. Any kind of treasure can be offered. In Frithberg the warriors make offerings of weapons in the river, to keep enemies from crossing, and the townspeople throw coins in the well for riches. It makes sense that a thief would be strung up here, another kind of offering.

He's been stripped of almost everything. Rings and cloak pins, I expected that, but his clothes are gone as well, and I can see how he died – battered, bones broken and collapsed. His face is almost shapeless, and as I approach I try to see any remainder of the living man whose eyes I met yesterday morning. It's cowardly, but I'm grateful to find nothing. His eyes are already gone, plucked out.

I don't even know if what I'm trying to do can be done. Has anyone ever taken a dead man's Luck before? How do I start?

Everything is a bargain, Vigdis taught me. *Offer payment.*

I place the few coins I have along the lip of the well, then the bronze horse. I face the corpse.

"Dead man," I say. "I can help you."

The mottled skin of the corpse seems to shiver.

Closer.

It's not a voice, more like a thought of my own. I take one step towards the corpse, then another. My eyes are level with its ruined face. I can see how the nose broke, how blood must have poured over his mouth and beard. There are questions I don't want answered. Was he dead when they hung him up, when the crows came? What killed him – the blood in his lungs, or these blows that dented his skull, here and here?

What did he think would happen today?

You want to be a warrior? the thought comes. *This is what warriors make. This is what you will make, over and over, and this is what you will become. The wolf's glut, the wife's bane, a feast for crows. This will be your glory.*

I look into the bloody sockets. "You had a heavy duty," I tell him, "but you died a thief. You will never enter the Great Hall with your task left undone." I reach out and push one of the coins over the lip of the well. "I'll finish it for you, but I need help. I can give you burial." Another coin. "Weapons, armour. I promise you the spoils of my first kill."

Wolf's glut, wife's bane. So be it. I've chosen.

"In return, I want your Luck." A warrior with two Lucks: two chances, two near misses. A warrior who'll rise up from the battlefield and walk away.

A cold gust of wind blows at my back, lifts my skirts, whistles past my ears. The corpse sways back against the pole. I stare into the empty sockets, clear now in the grey light, itching to turn around. I stand my ground as the gust slithers under my hair and down my spine. There, at the very small of my back, I feel something like a gimlet hole, a tiny opening through which a skein of cold air creeps like a worm.

I shudder the length of my body, and then it's done. My body is whole, frozen.

It's dawn.

I need something of the corpse to bury, when the time comes

to keep my oath. I gather the corpse's wild, bloodied hair in my hands, and start to saw at the roots with the blade. Just as I'm cutting through the last strands, a movement catches my eye. An arm reaches out and takes the bronze horse from the lip of the well.

I leap backwards, stifling a scream.

The corpse's arms hang useless, dislocated from their joints. They can't have moved.

The man in the blue cloak steps out from behind the corpse of his companion. The bronze horse dangles from his hand, and the eastern sky blushes red.

"What have you done?" he asks, and his voice cracks. He's very different from the man who spoke to us by the river. His breath smells of stale drink, and he looks half-dead himself, except for the anger in his eyes. A knife is thrust through his belt, unsheathed, put there in a hurry. It's not a paring knife: the blade is a hand-span long.

I fight the urge to take a step back. Something tells me that would be as bad as running. Instead I thrust out my hands, the knife in one, the hank of hair in the other. I think of Vigdis, her pale eyes and hard face. "It's no business of yours," I say.

In one movement he draws the knife from his belt, the pendant still clutched in his fist. "How dare you shear him," he says raggedly, but I can hear doubt.

"How dare I?" I ask, stepping towards him. Part of me is terrified of stepping into range of that knife, so I take another step to show it who's in charge. "How dare I do what? Offer him blood to wash away his murder? Or to complete the task he was given? Which is it that disgusts you?"

The blade wavers, then drops. His red-rimmed eyes are wide. They dart from my hair to my eyes to my knife. He looks exhausted, and I wonder if he's been crying.

Lucky, I think. I know now whoever the dead man is, he didn't steal the gold horse off the man in the blue cloak. They were friends.

"Is this what you want?" I ask. "For him?"

"Who are you?" he says. The anger seeps out of his eyes, replaced with doubt. He puts the knife back through his belt, but fumbles it, and his left hand comes forward to catch it, except he doesn't have a left hand. The falling knife knocks away his glove, which falls to the ground. His left arm ends in a knob of scarred skin. My mind jumps back to Erland and the prester.

"You're hunted," I tell him. I hear footsteps running up behind me, light and fast. Ebba must have seen someone coming. "You have to leave. The prester is here, and he's looking for you."

Fear twists his face. Whoever the prester is, he scares this man.

"We were meant to carry a message," he says, glancing at the dead man. "The horse. Without it . . ."

Ebba's reached my side.

"There en't time," she says. "They're stirrin down Astgate."

"Hide," I say to the man, thinking quickly. "When the soldiers leave the wayhouse, go there. Speak only to Jarle, the golden-haired boy in the stables. Show him that." I nod to the pendant. "Tell him you need help. He'll understand." *He'd better,* I think, *or I've just planned your death.* I hand him his glove and knife. "Remember: Golden Jarle at the stables. Now go."

The man staggers back from me, pulling on his glove. He stuffs the pendant inside his clothing, turns and runs.

"Come on," says Ebba, taking off in the opposite direction. I follow her on aching feet, shoving the corpse's knotted hank of hair into my pocket. She leads me between two buildings, and we weave our way through yards and round the back until we're behind the wayhouse. There's movement in the yard, and noise from the kitchen and stables. "Latrines," Ebba says, and we both slip inside the wooden stall.

The cold cuts out some of the smell, which is a mercy. Coming here when you need it is all very well, but the stench is hard to bear. We crouch over the pit.

"They're all up," says Ebba. "We'll of bin missed."

A wave of dizziness washes through me, and I nearly lose my balance. Ebba steadies me, alarmed. It passes, but I feel weak, and the smell isn't helping. "I need to lea —" I start to say, but nausea grabs my guts and twists. Ebba jumps up and I lean on her. She steers me towards the door, even though the yard is ringing with voices. Before I can protest, we're outside, and Aud is only a few paces away.

"Where have you —" she begins, but at that moment I catch sight of the tree behind her. The leaves are flaming yellow and red, and hanging from its feet is the corpse, twisting in the breeze.

I fall to my knees and throw up, all over Aud's wooden shoes.

Four

FEAST

EBBA'S TALE

he most revered among the gods of Arngard is no mighty warrior, nor yet a bringer of justice, but the lord of death and deceit. They call him the Wise One, but he himself is nothing more than a usurper."

History of Arngard
Berengar of Vellsberg

"Where were you?" asks Aud. Ahead of us, the captain carries Torny easy as a child.

"Torny felt sick," I says.

Aud gives me a warnin look I only ever seen her give Kelda before. It sets my insides twistin, but I can't tell her the truth. What'd I say? *Torny wanted to talk to the dead man.* Oh yes, that'll clear things up. I bite my lip, hopin she'll leave it be.

Erland carries Torny into his room, an lays her in his own bed.

Aud protests but Erland quiets her. "She can't use the ladder," he says, "and you'll need to watch her. She's white as a maggot."

"You're very kind, captain," says Aud. "Ebba, get some water."

Lookin sideways I see Aud runnin her fingers under the collar of Torny's undershirt. I bet I know what she's lookin for. I think of Jarle's bronze horse in the one-handed man's fist.

When I come back wi the basin, Aud's face is thundery. Seein how she usually keeps it smooth even when she's riled, I'm worried.

"Wash her feet," she snaps. "I don't want latrine filth on the sheets." I wet a rag an start wipin Torny's feet. They're cold an smeared wi dirt. "Why did Torny have my knife?" says Aud, sharply.

I can't help it, I can feel myself blushin. "I dunno," I say, wishin Torny was awake to tell her own lies. "She weren't makin sense." I have an idea: "You know her aunt's a sta —"

"I know," says Aud sharply, glancin at the door.

"I thought maybe it were to do wi that."

"What do you mean?"

"You know," I try to sound dim. "Gatherin things, like they do."

Aud gives me another of her looks an leaves. I let out a breath I din't know I was holdin, an Torny wriggles her toes in my face.

"Good work," she says quietly. I almost dump my pail of water over her.

"You were *awake*?" I hiss. "You *rat*. Why din't you help me?"

"You were doing so well," she teases, but her voice is weak.

I tuck her feet under the blanket an sit next to her. She looks about her. "The captain's room?"

"He carried you here."

Torny groans. "Now he'll think I'm a weakling."

I stare at her – since when did Torny care what anyone thinks? But then I remember how she frowns when she faces off wi Jarle, all serious, an how closely she watches the warriors when they spar, like she's hungry.

"You want to be like him," I say. Sparrin, stories – for me they're work an play, two different things. But for Torny, they're haft an head, all part of the same. They show her what she could be.

Torny's watchin me. "What?"

"I din't know. You want to be a warrior, don't you?"

"Lords don't take girls to be their warriors."

"But you think Erland might?"

"Maybe he would have," says Torny, but her thoughts are elsewhere. "Ebba, I – I made a deal. With the dead man."

What can you say to that? "What kind of deal?"

"That I'd give him the spoils . . . from my first . . . kill."

Torny, you idiot. "Well," I say, no-nonsense, "you'll just have to make it your job to clear out some bandits or somethin. No help for it now, so you might as well make yourself useful doin it." *I sound like Ma.* "You don't have to do it today. Get some rest." I hesitate. "What d'you ask for?"

Her voice is so low I have to bend forward to hear.

"His Luck."

My mouth falls open. "Can you do that?"

Torny nods, curlin up on her side. I en't never seen her like this before.

"I felt it," she whispers. "It's inside me."

I feel her forehead. She's dead cold, not fevered. "You need sleep." I get up, but stop wi my hand on the door. "Does anyone . . . visit you? In your dreams, I mean."

"What?" She yawns.

"To give you advice."

"Last night I dreamt I saw my aunt."

"Was it —" this is tricky "— was it *really* your aunt?" I ask. She's droppin wi sleep, but she still gives me a strange look. "Never mind. Sleep well."

I rush out the room, pullin the door shut a bit too hard. I en't never talked about my Follower to anyone. The first time I asked Ma, she just said, "She was your Da's." An that was that, because on Uncle Ulf's farm no one spoke of Arf Berrson, not ever.

In the kitchen the air smells of toastin barley. Kelda is crouched by the hearthstone, poundin warm brown grains with a pestle. She scowls at me out of habit.

Through the open door I catch glimpses of the men in the yard – *soldiers*, that's what Aud an Torny called em. I see things I missed last night. Long faces wi narrow cheekbones. Dark heads, brown an black, hair cut short above their shoulders. They all wear the same kind of tunic down to their knees. I stifle a giggle an Kelda pulls a face. I guess she finds men in long tunics pretty funny too.

We're cookin the barley into gruel over the fire when Erland comes to the door. His shoulders fill the openin, an he has to duck his head under the lintel.

"Where's your mistress?" he says. "My men need feeding."

"We'll do it," says Kelda, an there's none of the eyelash-battin men usually get from her, nor any reaction to him callin Aud her mistress. "Will you sit in the hall?"

"We'll take it in the yard," Erland says.

Kelda sends me out wi the soldiers' gruel, an that surprises me even more. I try to keep my eyes modestly down an look at em through the steam at the same time. They talk quietly, but their tongue is harsher than ours. There are ten of em, countin Erland. He must be nearly forty, but the others are younger. Their faces are softer, not broken in like his. Under their daft long tunics their bodies are strong, an there's not one with a limp or a stump. *In their first strength*. The words come to me as I look at em, an I realise I en't keepin my eyes down at all.

An they look back at me, curious. When I smile, they smile. One of em thanks me, a young man wi curled black hair like crows wings. His accent is strong but he uses the right words. They reach out for the bowls, an their hands an arms en't scarred, except for the small scars of work, the nicks an burns we all have. *The war*, I think. *It weren't just our fathers we lost. Where are our young men?*

Jarle stands by the kitchen door, wolfin his breakfast, an though his hair is still as gold as it were yesterday, now he looks like a boy, not a man. I look back at the soldiers. All around me as I've grown I've known boys an old men. Like I din't notice there was somethin missin.

The crow-haired one is watchin me over his bowl. While I've bin lookin his fellows over like horseflesh, he's bin seein me do it. I colour an look down.

"Well, Captain." Aud's on the kitchen step, wipin her hands on her apron. "How long will you be staying?"

"Until Lord Frithrun releases us from his hospitality," Erland says. "We feast with him today."

"That'll be around midnight, then," says Aud, an her smile is polite, but tight. "Your men will have to sleep in the stables again. What must they think of us?"

"King Kolrand's hay no sweeter than yours, mistress," says a fair-haired soldier, an there's some back-thumpin from his grinnin companions.

Aud is all in grey like always, her hair hidden, but her blue eyes are sharp. "And why did Kolrand send his guests to Frithberg? This must seem a small, mean holdings to a Southerner."

Erland opens his mouth, but the serious-lookin crow-haired soldier speaks first.

"Frithberg is an important town," he says. "The Frithberg treaty was signed here, nine years since. It has witnessed three great wonders: the end of war, the first church built in Arngard and the beginning of the White God's rule. Frithberg is the city of peace, praise God."

I can feel the hush on my skin, in my dry mouth. Aud's gone very still, an all these strong young men seem to sense it. The air gets thick.

So that's how Southerners see it, I think. He's right, in a way. Kolrand Arnson was only a child when his half-brother Geir killed their father Arn and Kolrand fled across the southern border. The Emperor helped him, sent troops with him to take back the palace at Sunacre, to face Geir in the battle of Hellingap. But the war tore the land apart. Troops under Kolrand's command killed Staffbearers an destroyed the sacred groves, while Geir's men took their revenge on anyone they thought should of fought harder, resisted more. When the final battle of Frithberg was fought, the land was already steeped in blood. So the Southern Emperor helped Kolrand, but in return . . .

In return the kirktower was raised over Frithberg.

I can understand why Aud won't go near it.

Erland clears his throat. "Thank you, Berengar. The king is keen to see how the White God's believers fare in Arngard," he says to Aud.

For a terrible moment, I think Aud is goin to spit. I don't know what might happen if she does.

Instead, she turns her eyes on me. "Ask Ebba. She goes to the kirkhouse."

Erland, some of the soliders, even Jarle, all turn to look at me. I feel my cheeks get hot. I hold the tray against my chest like a shield.

"*Credens*?" asks the crow-haired soldier, the one Erland called Berengar. Their attention sharpens.

"What are they sayin?" I ask, nervous.

"You're the first believer they've met north of Kolrand's palace." Erland looks me over, then smiles. "Would you like to be introduced to the prester?"

"Me?" I look from him to the open, interested faces of the Southerners, then to Aud. Her face is demure again. Does she know about the horse? Does she know who this stranger is, this prester, who thinks it's a sign, an called these men here to – what did he say? – to *act*?

"I think that's a very good idea," says Aud, her eyes not leavin mine.

The soldiers seem interested in everything. The houses, the kirkrock, the way I speak. When they see the dead man by the well, they're interested in that too.

"Mistress," says the fair one, "what he do?"

"Thief," I says, keepin my eyes on the kirk. "What's your name?" I ask, fore he can ask more.

"Medard," he says, smilin. "You wife?"

I shoot him a look. Erland's just ahead of us, pretendin like he can't hear. "No, thank you," I say, glarin. Erland's shoulders bob like he's tryin not to laugh.

The crow-haired soldier, Berengar, scowls at the fair one, who shrugs an smiles.

It's not like the kirk is hard to find. I feel stupid, walkin along wi these men, the tower risin over us like a beacon. I've no place here. I can feel the pink still in my cheeks an I think, *What would Ma say, me trailin round like this when there's work to be done?* Torny would love it. She'd be talkin to the soldiers, even if they din't understand, an askin them about battles an swords. She'd be in the lead. And what am I? Just some kind of pet, some . . . *credens*, whatever that means. Some ugly Southern word.

We pass the painted doorposts of the lord's hall without a glance to spare. Erland must know what it is, but he don't even pause.

"Don't you want to see the lord?" I ask.

"That's where we're going," he says. I follow him, puzzled. When we reach open ground I halt to bow to the stone, but Erland walks right past it. I make myself follow him without bowin, an sneak a look over my shoulder. None of the soldiers bow either. Their eyes are on the kirk.

The prester – it must be him – stands in the doorway. He's wearin white under a red cloak. Instead of claspin arms, Erland drops to one knee, an all the soldiers follow him. I dip down too, half a second behind em.

The prester's eyes fall on me as his gaze sweeps over us. He raises his right hand an draws a cross in the air. "Blessings be upon you," he says. "In the name of God, welcome."

Erland rises an waves me forward. "This girl brought us here, Prester Grimulf. She is the first believer we have met so far north."

I can't meet the prester's eyes. I don't really know what Erland means by believer, but it sounds like somethin important. I'm not sure visitin the kirk on my days off to ask Walpurgis to watch over the farm is the same thing.

The prester puts his hand under my chin an raises it. He's not as tall as Erland an he's thick-set, but his bare forearms are muscle, not fat. His head is square on a neck like a bull's, an covered wi short white curls. His heavy jaw is shaven, the bristles white an grey. He looks at me wi pale blue eyes, not kindly, but steadily, like he's searchin for somethin.

"Where are you from, girl?" he asks at last.

"Eldinghope," I say. That's not what he means. He means, *You aren't from here. Outlander.*

"The Eastern farmlands," he says. His hand is still under my chin, so I can't nod. "So you must be a farmer's daughter, I think. And who do you pray for? Saint Walpurgis?"

My heart squeezes in fear. I wish I could make my face smooth the way Aud does. The hand under my chin seems gentle, but I feel like my head's in a yoke.

"What's your name, child?"

"Ebba Rathnasdota, prester."

"Rathnasdota? Don't you have a father?"

"He died. I grew up in my uncle's home."

The prester's eyes change, get . . . heavier. I can't tell you how, but I feel their weight on me.

"The war made many orphans," he says at last. "We'll speak next time you come to pray, Ebba Rathnasdota. But remember, the blessed Walpurgis is but a vessel. You should come for that which fills it."

I dunno what he means, but he lets go my chin an draws a cross over me. I feel like I got away wi somethin. Erland an the soldiers follow him into the warm dark of the kirk, filin around me.

When I'm sure I'm alone, I bow to the stone an run back down the path.

Torny sleeps through noon, an Aud keeps me too busy to go to her. A small boy comes from the lord's hall askin for a barrel of mead an is sent back doubled over, rollin it in front of him. "They'll be drunk as pigs," says Aud, but Kelda says, "I wish I could serve first cup to the warriors," an I say how I used to serve first cup on my uncle's farm, when the dalesmen came an feasted on holy days. I can tell Kelda's envious because she sneers an says it must be a great honour, servin pigherds.

I take care not to mention which holy days, or whose.

Aud goes out later, when the place is quiet. I wash the bowls by myself, then sneak in to see Torny.

She's asleep. I sit on the edge of the bed, wonderin if I should wake her. I want to tell her about the prester, an ask if she thinks he knows I'm mixed up wi the gold horse. I want to tell her about Berengar an the others, an what I felt when they were crowding round me in the yard, like I was bein seen for the first time.

I look at Torny. Sweat shines on her forehead. I sigh an go to the kitchen. Kelda's standin on the step sunnin herself.

"Have we got any yarrow?" I ask, "or —"

"Salvebearer!"

Kelda an I stare at each other, then stick our heads out the door. A warrior is leanin on the yard gate, drawin breath for another yell.

"He wants you," says Kelda, but I shake my head nervously. "We can't just ignore him," she says, "Lord Frithrun sent him."

I back away, but Kelda drags me out onto the step. The warrior squints at us, then pushes off the gate post an weaves towards us, the silver on his arms winkin in the sun. He stops a few paces away an leers at Kelda. I'm surprised he can even focus. The smell of mead is strong, an the sun catches droplets in his red beard, makin em twinkle. It's Hakon. I shrink back. He's very big an very drunk.

"Salvebearer!" He shouts again, as if we weren't only a few steps away. "Where's tha bantam?"

"What?" Kelda's already impatient.

"The fighting bantam," he says, swayin. "Rolly pin."

"She'll be back . . . soon," Kelda says. "What do you want? Isn't there a feast?"

"Feast," says Hakon seriously. "Feast, Southerners . . ."

"Don't take all day," Kelda mutters.

"I've bin tole to bring the Salvebearer," says Hakon.

I find my voice at last. "Has someone been hurt?"

"Yes." Hakon nods slowly, grinnin like a dope. "Someone's *very badly hurt.*"

"She's coming," says Kelda, pushin me back inside. "He's mucking you about," she says, "No one's hurt. They're all drunk and they want you to entertain them."

"I can't go," I say, panicked.

"He's the lord's warrior," says Kelda, "you have to. Get your salve."

My head's spinnin as I climb up to take the salve from the lintel. Back in the kitchen I say, "Boil up some staunchweed for

Torny, she's fevered," an I hear the shake in my voice. Kelda grunts an says, "I'll tell Aud," but I don't have time to ask if she means about Torny or me fore I'm out an walkin beside Hakon, who en't very good at straight lines. *He'll have a head on him like a sheep's bum come the mornin*, Ma would of said, but she'd've said it after Uncle Ulf had drunk himself to sleep, not before. Before, no one said anythin.

You can hear the shoutin an the singin halfway across the market place, but Hakon puts his finger to his lips an winks. Least, that's what I think he's tryin to do. His finger slides up his nose an he screws his eyes closed. It would be funny, if he weren't four times bigger an heavier than me, with a sword at his belt.

I think of the gods an the glorious dead in the Great Hall, gettin drunk an fightin. An I think of Uncle Ulf an Stig. I follow Hakon round the side of the hall an into the kitchen, my hands clenched. The lord's cook is lollin at the table, a big woman who sometimes comes to argue with Aud an borrow things. Her head is in her folded arms, an she raises it stupidly as I pass. Her too. Somehow, that makes things worse. The noise from the hall comes in roars, an I begin to feel sick.

Hakon puts a hand on the nape of my neck, an steers me into the dark hall, filled wi smoke an noise. The benches are ranged in a square round the great hearth in the middle, an I can see Lord Frithrun's warriors massed on two sides, their hair long an braided, their arms an necks thick wi metal rings an torques. The soldiers, wi their short hair an long tunics, are seated opposite the high table, between the fire an the door. That's the lowest bench, where women or labourers usually sit. To place guests there is an insult. I wonder if they know it? On the bench between the fire an the high table sit the merchants. At the high table sit Lord Frithrun, Captain Erland an the prester. Standin beside the lord is the wiry blond man who was with Hakon last night: Spraki Spit-Nails, the lord's skald.

I feel sick. If I could run I would, but Hakon's huge hand is still on the back of my neck, pushin me into the space by the fire. Through the flames, over the heads of the merchants, I see Spraki watchin me, the same fixed look he gave me last night. Not drunk, I think. He's bin savin himself. Then I look along the table an see the prester watchin me too. Steady. Searchin.

Hakon holds me close to the fire till I can feel its harsh heat on my face. "The Salvebearer!" he bellows, though it takes a few goes before the roar dies an everyone is watchin us. "Last night, my hand was broken," Hakon shouts in my ear. "Now look!" There's the clink an slither of a sword being drawn, right at my back. I see it flash past me, lit by firelight, as Hakon thrusts it overhead.

His wrist was bruised, I think to myself. *The salve just brings down swellin and dulls the pain. No one can mend a broken bone overnight.*

What have I got myself into?

Lord Frithrun is also drunk. He might not be staggerin, or stickin his finger up his own nostril, but he sits back lazily, his mouth in a slack smile. He was made lord of Frithberg by King Kolrand cos it was his arrow killed Prince Geir at Hellingap, but now he's old an runnin to fat. Because Frithberg is a town wi walls, he don't go abroad, just sits inside his circle of sticks. That's what Aud says, anyway.

"Well, Hakon. Well, Spraki. What did you want to show me with this, this . . . Salvebearer?" He waves a hand at me.

Spraki walks down to the fire, wavin Hakon away. A skald's

a warrior, but also a poet, someone who tells the stories of the warriors who've gone before. His nose is long, his mouth too wide over a sharp chin. He comes right up to me an circles me, so close that when he smiles, I can see the way the diseased gums have pulled back from his yellow teeth. His mouth must hurt him.

"A remarkable thing, Lord," he says, an he has a voice that makes up for his face. It's sweet, an when he speaks, all talk stops. "We have had a treasure in our midst, and we have not known it."

Out of the corner of my eye I see someone stand up among the group of soldiers. I don't dare turn to look.

"Last night I saw with my own two eyes a thing I had heard whispered, but not believed. My shield-brother Hakon was struck in a brawl, and this girl, with only the touch of her magic salve, did mend him."

Damn Sorleyson an his mystery-peddlin.

"And today our honoured guests from the South, here by invitation of the *king*," Spraki continues, "tell me that they have found the only true believer north of the king's palace. They tell me that such powerful healing must be from the White God himself."

There's some mutterin from the merchants. They are the ones who leave expensive offerins at the altar, whose trade an taxes support Lord Frithrun an the king. They probably en't happy that a girl they don't recognise is being called the White God's best believer. My eyes flick up to Erland. His face is pale, but he's sittin back in his carved chair, tryin to look at ease. Next to him, the prester's watchin Spraki with a venom that shakes me. These men hate each other.

"And since our honoured guests are here to report on the White God's success in Arngard, and the god is known for his displays,

I have brought the girl here to show us what the White God's believers can do." Spraki turns to the prester. "What are such displays called, Grimulf of Vellsberg?"

The prester scowls. "That's Prester to you, skald."

Spraki mock-bows, his hand over his heart. On his thumb is a blurred tattoo, a snake's head with its mouth open. "Forgive me if my tongue slips. What's the word, Prester?"

"Miracles," growls the prester. "But I warn you, skald, the White God does not perform tricks, like a dog."

"No," says Spraki, "but I believe he listens to the prayers of his true believers."

Hakon lurches through the door from the kitchen, draggin somethin. In one hand he has a club, an over the sounds of benches scrapin an people gettin out the way, I hear a growl that sets my hair on end.

"Got your salve, Salvebearer?" asks Hakon cheerily. "Reckon you might need it."

Dragged by the leather leash round its neck, its long teeth buried in the wood of the club, one of Lord Frithrun's wolfhounds limps into the firelight.

It stands as high as my shoulder, so I can stare into its eyes an see the thin black lips linin its wet, snarlin mouth. If it stood on its hind legs it could lace its paws over Hakon's shoulders. I take in all the small things: the soft grey fur under the long black guard hairs, the two yellow fangs lodged in the club, each as long as my little finger.

There's a furious yell from the soldiers an Hakon shouts wi laughter as a fight breaks out. I hope he don't forget what he's doin an let go that leash.

I drag my eyes away from the hound's teeth. One of the front paws is a mess – a claw hangs from it, the joint is swollen, an I can see fresh blood weepin over dried crust. There are scratches in the dog's side, not deep, but open.

Beside me, Spraki says, "Where's your magic salve, believer?"

I think, *You want to see me torn open, all so's you can thumb yer nose at these Southerners an their god.*

It angers me, but I can't meet his eyes.

"Get me a muzzle," I say, nearly chokin. "I've got a use for it."

My Uncle Ulf is a big man, but folk say his brother Arf was small an bent. Least, Uncle Ulf says so, when he's drunk. Sometimes, when he'd bin drinkin so's his fumey breath could make you choke, he'd grab my brother by the shoulder an pull him from the bench where the boys an workers sat. "Why should you sit wi my son," he'd ask, "when your father was a hunch-backed coward, an your mother's an outlander bitch?" An he would thrust Stig down among us women on the low bench, while we all kept our eyes down.

Ulf used to say our Da died of the plague that killed Ulf's wife an firstborn, but "He's lying," Stig told me once, when we were alone wi the sheep. "I remember Arf, an he weren't hunched, an he din't die that summer. He died in the autumn. That bastard Ulf knows our Da died a warrior's death, but he'll die on his back in his bed, like an old woman." An he spat, to seal the truth into his words.

Stig's the same age as our cousin Rafe. When their turn came to move from the boys' bench to the men's, my heart was squeezed all day in my chest. It was early in the year, an the earth was soft enough to cut open an sow. We spent the day scarin crows away from the seed wi slingshots. I was ten, old enough to be with em, but nothin compared to their twelve years. Stig an cousin Rafe were shoutin insults at the crows, like they was enemy warriors.

"Your ma will be mournin you tonight," yelled Rafe, loosin a shot at a crow braver then the rest.

"Your brothers won't never drink wi you again," Stig shouted, though his voice were still high. The crow skipped sideways an jumped into the air.

I was sittin behind em, tryin to cover my part of the field. I saw the raven land a way off, a big glossy un, head turnin from side to side, like it were lookin at em both. Stig raised his arm but I cried stop. "That's the Wise One's bird," I said.

Stig looked unsure, but Rafe turned on me. "You know this en't the Wise One's land," he said scornfully. "You know it's given to the Blessed Walpurgis."

"Oh yeah?" I said, angered he was treatin me like a baby. "So I suppose you'll kill it, will you?"

Rafe turned red.

"D'you believe her too?" he said, turnin to Stig. "And you meant to be joinin the man's bench tonight."

Now Stig went red. "No," he said, but he wouldn't meet my eyes.

"Kill it then," said Rafe, as if he didn't care.

"He won't kill it, so why should you?" I said, grabbin Stig's arm.

Stig din't say nothin; nor did Rafe. He din't need to. Stig pushed me hard, so's I fell back into the mud, an picked out a pellet.

The raven hadn't moved. It watched us, not twenty paces distant. It looked carefully, like it was rememberin each of our faces. The rough loose feathers of the throat shone like black water. As Stig swung the sling the raven fixed its eyes on him.

The shot whistled, hit hard an sure, an the bird fell in a spray of blood.

I threw mud at my brother's back, so angry I couldn't speak. Stig ignored me, just looked at Rafe, but Rafe was lookin away as if he hadn't seen anythin. After they'd gone, I ran to where the body lay in the soft dark soil, but the stone had crushed the skull. The raven stared one-eyed at the low grey sky.

That night the boys had the mud washed off their faces, an Ma put em in red shirts. My uncle's foreman, his righthand man, came an put braids in their hair. When the men sat down to feast, Uncle Ulf was already at his bench with a cup in his hand. My heart was twice as tight. Ma an I stood waitin to bring in the meat, an I could see Ma's knuckles clenched white against her apron as Stig came in behind Rafe. As the boys came up to the bench where they usually sat, the labourers banged the table wi their bowls an chanted "No room, no room!" Then they walked to the bench where the freemen sat, an the freemen banged the bowls an howled, "Only men, only men." Finally they stood in front of Uncle Ulf, an he bellowed, "Who stands here?" so that all the bangin an the yellin stopped. The foreman stepped up, all serious with his duty, an said, "Two new men for your service, master."

"Are they brave an strong?" asked Ulf.

"Brave as a bear!" yelled the labourers.

"Strong as a stallion!" yelled back the freemen.

"Are they tall an straight?"

"Tall as a tree!"

"Straight as a spear!"

"Will they bring honour on this farm?"

"The honour of honourable men," all the men yelled together, already raising their cups to toast the boys onto the men's bench.

"Honourable men," said Ulf, suddenly quiet, "don't kill the Wise One's bird."

The hall fell silent a second time, but this time it was a horrible silence. What I said in the field was true. Ravens belonged to the Wise One: they ate at his table, which was the battlefield, an they knew his secrets. It din't matter that we carried the carvin of the Blessed Walpurgis through the fields on the first day of spring, or that we laid a sheaf of corn in her arms every harvest, an asked her blessin for weddins an births. Her realm was the field an the farm, the seed an the fruit. If on Bloodnight we left the fields, went up into the forest to the sacred grove, an offered up another kind of sacrifice – well, what happens at death's door is a different question, one no one can claim to answer. Not even Walpurgis.

Ulf stood, towerin over Stig. Rafe stepped back.

"You'll never be a man," said Ulf, an Stig seemed to sink into himself. "You don't belong here, an the land knows it. Half-breeds have no honour."

Next to me I could feel Ma shakin.

"Rafe told him to!"

That was my voice, high an childish. Everyone froze, like they could make me unsay it by pretendin I weren't there.

"Rafe told him to kill it! Rafe said it din't matter! If you beat Stig, you'd better beat Rafe."

An finally they looked. Not the men, cause men don't listen to little girls. Not Ma or the women, because their eyes were down like always. But Uncle Ulf, his face growin red, an Rafe, fear in his eyes . . . an Stig. Stig, glarin daggers at me, like it were all my fault.

Then Ulf turned to Stig with a small smile an said, "Is this true?"

An Stig said, "She's lyin."

So my uncle gave Stig the job of beatin me, there in front of everyone, an then, as his reward, Stig went an sat on the men's bench next to my cousin. *The honour of honourable men.*

Everyone was very merry, even Ma, an there was singin. After Uncle Ulf went to bed, Ma kissed Stig, who was pink-cheeked with happiness, an said, "He'll have a head on him like a sheep's bum come the morning," an they laughed. That night I slept on my front, so's not to open the cuts on my back, an after that I kept my mouth shut an my eyes down.

Get me a muzzle and a knife.

"No muzzle," Spraki says. "Your god will muzzle it for you."

He wants to stop em givin me the knife too, but Hakon is already handin over his, an I grip the wire-bound hilt an glare back at Spraki.

"Three things," I say quickly, though my voice is uneven. "I'm allowed three. My salve, the knife an a cloak. Get me a cloak."

Spraki's annoyed, but three is a good number. In the stories, three questions reveal a person's true nature, three tasks test their strength. Even through my fear, I know he can't refuse me. The cloak is laid down beside me, thick lambskin. Hakon leans back on the leash, cranin to get a good look at the fight behind us. The hound's eyes are rollin, rimmed wi white.

My hands shake as I take the salve's slim case from my pocket. The hound still growls, still tries to yank its teeth free of the club.

The fire is hot on my face, an over the dancin flames I see the prester, his broad head lit up like a mask. He en't taken his eyes off Spraki.

I kneel, an wrap the cloak clumsily round my left arm. The scuffle's died down, cause I hear men pushin back benches to watch. I kneel at the hound's feet, usin my cloak-wrapped arm as a shield. I grasp the bad paw above the joint wi my left hand. The knife is in my right hand. I look up at the animal, as it strains against the wooden gag, an from down here I see how its chest is heavin, how its neck is arched painfully high. From down here I can see how scared it is.

"Shhh," I say. "This'll only hurt a bit."

I hold the paw as firmly an carefully as I can. The hound makes a horrible noise in its throat. The ripped-out claw dangles from the tendon, an I have to hold it down to cut it. The hound bucks wi fear an pain, its choked howl fillin my ears. But Hakon keeps his knife sharp, an the claw comes away from the bleeding pad. I drop the knife, reach down for the salve an fumble it open. The hound's desperate whine drills through my head. I take too much salve in my hurry, feel its cool stickiness coating my fingers. The hound jerks wildly as I rub its paw with the balm.

Maybe Hakon's arm is tired, or maybe he just lost interest. The hound wrenches its fangs free at last an lunges at me. I whip my arm up to save my face, an the long teeth close on my salve-covered hand.

Like in a nightmare, my scream makes no sound.

I feel pain, but it is remembered pain. I feel my back blazin wi bruises an cuts. I hear my Follower whisper in my ear: *Eyes up.*

I stare into the hound's wide dark eyes an feel the heavy jaws lock. Then I feel the warm wet tongue on my palm, hot dribble down my wrist, an the salty red where one fang has opened the smallest of cuts.

The tongue rolls over my palm, between my fingers, soft, searchin.

I stand, my hand in the hound's mouth. The hall is silent.

Then the hound opens its mouth an lies down at my feet.

I rub balm into the scratches on its side and then I tuck the curly white fleece of the lambskin around the hound's limp body. It raises its head once, to lick my hand. I check the hound's paw again. The bleeding has stopped and now the hound is asleep.

All around me a voice rings out: "*My soul is among wolves, I am forced to dwell among ravenous beasts; among men whose teeth are spears, whose tongues are sharp swords.*"

Over the cracklin fire I see the prester standin, prayin, his tongue the only tongue in a room full of empty mouths.

Five

FLIGHT

TORNY'S TALE

I was cold to my bones. All around me the mist rose in a pale haze, and water slapped against wood. I swayed with the swell and drop of the small boat, but all I could see was the hooded shape of the oarsman in the stern, labouring over the long-handled oar. Splinters from the rough seat needled my thighs. About my neck a thick rope scratched the soft skin of my throat, and the weight of its tail trailed down my spine. I wore a shift of undyed wool against the cold, and nothing else.

The swell lessened, and the mist grew opaque. The oarsman sculled us gently into quiet waters, until I felt the bump of the bows on rock. A murmur rose behind me, through the slap and suck of the waves, over the creaking of the boat. Cold strong hands, many of them, caught me under my arms and hauled me up. Under my bare feet was black rock, set in pillars like steps. Around me cloaked figures held out their hands for me to grasp for balance as

I climbed. I couldn't tell if this was a guard of honour, or whether I was a captive. Maybe both.

At the top of the rocks, a figure taller than the others held out its hands to me, almost as if it would embrace me, though the face remained hidden. I walked towards it, the mist so thick it hid everything else, though the murmur still ran through the unseen crowd at my back. It sounded almost like hissing.

I slipped on the wet, uneven stones beneath my feet, but the figure stretched out both arms to me – women's arms, tattooed and strong, the hands scarred. I grasped the sinewy wrists, found my balance, and the figure led me, walking backwards into the white mist.

We walked between lines of small white stones. The figure did not let go of my hands but drew me onwards, and around her hooded head bloomed red tongues of colour, like frozen flames. When I realised what it was I cried out and pulled back, but the figure wouldn't let go; her fingers tightened on my wrists. Above her rose the tree, its bark and branches black as stone, its leaves red, orange and yellow. Over her shoulder I saw first the legs, then the body, then the whole of the dead man. His head was shorn, and his arms dangled uselessly. His ragged eye sockets looked right at me.

Tell me your name.

I yanked my arms away from the figure, but she held me like iron. *Your name.*

The branches of the tree were outlined against a growing light, slowly staining the mist red. I felt someone grasp the heavy rope that trailed down my back and jerk it, yanking the rope at my throat tight.

They'll hang you up next to me. Tell me your name, and I will save you.

I gritted my teeth and tried grimly to pull myself out of the figure's grip. The more violently I pulled, the tighter her grasp was. Black spots whirled before my eyes as the rope shut off my breath.

Once you've invited one thing in, it's hard to keep the others out, said the voice, and as I collapsed, the hole in my back, where the Luck-worm crawled in, opened like a rotting fruit.

"Can you walk?" a low voice says in my ear.

"Aud?" My voice is muddled with sleep. I'm slowly returning to myself, to my limbs warm and dry, to a throat unconstricted by rope.

"I don't know what you're playing at," she growls, "but get up."

She pulls me up and walks me out into the yard. Dizziness makes me stumble, but she drags me into the stables, and kicks the doors closed behind us. The Southerners' horses shift in their stalls. At the far end, Jarle is sitting at his workbench, fidgeting. Aud pushes me down onto a hay bale.

"You took something of Jarle's last night," she says, "and now there's a man outside telling us you said we'd give him a horse. Torny, what have you done?"

"Why don't you tell me what the pendant means?" I say. Jarle's cheeks flush.

"Why did you take it?" Aud asks.

If they're not going to answer me, I'm not going to answer them.

"It looked familiar," I say.

Aud and Jarle exchange glances.

"Did you show it to anyone else?" Aud asks.

"Just him," I say. "Ask Ebba. She'll tell you."

"You showed Ebba?" says Aud.

"She'd already seen the other one," I say, defensively.

"The other one? What other one?"

So I tell them about the stranger who threw me the gold pendant of the horse just before he was killed, and how we took it to the kirk, and how the prester found it.

Jarle covers his eyes with his hands. I look from him to Aud.

"Who is the prester?" I ask. "What is he?"

Aud looks grim. "He's the Cub's holy man," she says, using the insulting nickname for King Kolrand. "But from what I've heard, he's more than that. He's been around since the Cub was crowned, and he was here at the battle of Frithberg."

My eyes widen. "So he's a warrior? I thought he was an outlander!"

"He's dangerous," says Aud. "Whatever you do, keep away from him, you understand?"

"He was here," I tell them. "Last night. He visited Erland."

Jarle groans, his head still in his hands. Even Aud looks shaken.

"What's the matter?" I ask.

"I sent Ebba with the soldiers this morning when they went to greet him," says Aud. "I was angry. It was stupid. Just before your friend showed up, Kelda told me Ebba was taken to Frithrun's hall by one of his warriors. I was in such a hurry to get Kelda out of the way I didn't think anything of it, but . . ."

"I don't understand," I say. "What's so bad about it?"

"Ebba's a good girl," says Aud, "but do you really think she can keep her mouth shut?" I open my mouth to argue but she cuts me off. "She knows about the horses, your one-handed friend —"

"He's not my friend," I snap, and then I realise something else. "The prester knows about him too. He wants him hunted down.

And he knows he's connected to the Staffbearer of Gullcroft. The dead man said so before he died." I feel a tug in my chest, the faintest pull. "I have to go, Aud. She's my —"

"We know," says Aud shortly. "I know Vigdis. That's why she sent you here. This is worse than I thought."

She reaches across and takes Jarle's hand. I've wondered about them sometimes, wondered whether for all Kelda's mooning and Ebba's matchmaking these two are already lovers. But the way Aud looks at Jarle is more like a mother.

"You have to let it go," she says softly. "It's not safe anymore."

And to my amazement, I see Jarle's crying.

"You're right," Aud says, turning to me. "You have to warn Vigdis. Can you find your way home?"

"I think so, but —"

"Jarle, they'll need horses."

"They?"

"You said the prester is hunting this man?"

"But if they know about Gullcroft, he won't be safe there."

"You can't go alone," Aud says. "It's too dangerous. He'll protect you while he believes you're important. And if the prester's men catch you, you can say he forced you to go with him."

"Aud!" Jarle and I are both shocked.

Aud takes me by the shoulders, and looks hard into my face. "They will kill Vigdis, Torny. And because of who she is, it will not be quick, or secret."

My mouth tastes foul. "But Gullcroft is tiny! There's nothing there. Why would they care?"

"Believe me, her death will be the least of it," Aud says. "You're not old enough to remember what people will do for power. Let the man protect you while he can, and when he can't anymore, do what you have to do to protect yourself."

"But what is all this? The horse, the Staffbearers – what does it mean?"

Aud turns, her hand on the stable door. "They're bringing back the Sungiven." She and Jarle share a long look. Jarle looks away. "I'll make up a pack for you, Torny. Go get your things."

I've been using my few things from Gullcroft as a pillow, so they're already bundled up. I stop briefly at Ebba's bedroll. I'm not stupid. Aud won't be telling her where I've gone. I lay my hand in the hollow where her body lay last night, straining against her dreams. "I'll be back soon," I promise the empty room.

"Skirts won't do," says Aud, when I rejoin her in the barn.

"How about these?" I pull my leggings from the bundle. They're woollen, striped and zigzagged in blue. I haven't worn them since I came south to Frithberg. Aud makes a face.

"Why don't you just leave a message at every farm you pass through? 'The idiots went this way'," she says in disgust. She has a point. A girl in zigzag leggings will draw comment. "Here, try these." She hands me some worn but sturdy trousers in a thick brown weave, and woolen socks.

I strip off my smock and pull on my leggings. They don't even reach my ankles anymore, and there's a gap left when I put on the socks. I must have grown more than I thought. I put the trousers on, and I can feel an extra layer of cloth in the seat.

"Who did you steal these from?" I ask, lacing my shoes.

"They're mine," says Aud, handing me a woollen shirt. It's too big, but I pull it over the one I'm already wearing, tucking it into my belt. Wordlessly she hands me a leather vest, sleeveless and well worn to a shape that isn't mine. I've never seen one like it. I slip my arms through the holes and she laces the front tightly. Her face is grim. I'm wondering why Aud, a servant who runs a kitchen, owns trousers made for riding and a —

"What is this?" I ask, tugging at the leather.

"A corselet. It'll keep you from bouncing," says Aud, "though there's little enough to bounce." I stick my tongue out at her, but her face is set, and she just turns away from me. I wish Ebba were here, to laugh at my flat up-and-down frame with me.

My bundle is barely that without my leggings in it. There's a scruffy blue scarf that held it all together. Aud takes it and ties it over my lamb-bright hair, then hands me a plain knife in its own scabbard. I slip it onto my belt.

"If you need to stick it into someone, do it point-first," she says. "Anything else?"

"There's something I need to protect," I say, thinking of the hank of filthy hair in my pocket. After a brief search we find some waxed linen, and I wrap it in the material and tie it tightly. I put it inside my clothes, next to my skin. I don't like it, but there's nothing else to be done. I can't lose it.

Wordlessly, she gives me her sheepskin cloak.

"Aud," I say, "you'll freeze."

"You'll freeze quicker," she says. "I'll be sleeping inside tonight. You won't."

I hadn't thought of that.

"There's something else," I say, my mind still on the dead man. "I don't want him to know my name."

"Makes sense," says Aud, handing me my pack and leading me out of the barn. "What's that name Ebba gave you?"

"Lambtail," I say, my heart sinking. "What will you tell Ebba?"

"She can't know," Aud says. "No one can."

The sun is low in a clear blue sky, and I realise that there are hours and hours of night ahead once it sets. I've never slept out except in the summer. Aud leads me round behind the stables and between the buildings.

"Where are we going?"

Aud nods towards the jagged line rising ahead of us. It's the earthen slope that marks the edge of Frithberg. It's topped with wooden staves, and falls away steeply on the outside, so that anyone trying to get in is faced with an earthen barrier higher than their heads, and then the sharpened points above that. I guess two horsemen leaving by the town gates would be remembered.

Luckily, sneaking out is easier than sneaking in.

There's a hole where the wooden posts pointing upwards make way for the staves sticking out at angles. A full-grown man couldn't get through, but a girl can. I wriggle out onto the strut of the pole. Aud doesn't follow me. She hands me the pack and says, "There's food, water and a bedroll in there. Your friend's waiting for you in the forest behind the kirkrock. You'll have to take the path up behind Sebson's farm, then loop back. You can't be seen heading north, understand?" I nod. "If you have to leave him behind, do it. Don't trust anyone."

I look back at her through the hole. I'd meant to ask her to let Ebba know I'm alright, but now that I'm here, excitement bubbles up like a spring in my chest. "Thanks for the clothes," I say. "I'll try not to freeze to death."

Aud narrows her eyes, studying my face. Then she grins suddenly, worlds apart from the serene young woman I know.

"Good luck, Lambtail," she says. "I wish I was going with you."

Then she's gone. I drop from the pole and roll as I land. I follow the ditch at the foot of the palisade round the town, until I'm behind the kirkrock. As I pass behind Lord Frithrun's hall I hear the voices of men raised in song. The rocky crag where the kirk sits forms a cliff on the outer edge, and the palisade ends here. I halt at the foot of the cliff, my back to the stone.

At the edge of the forest waits a mounted figure wrapped in a blue cloak, accompanied by a riderless horse. Between us lie the hummocks of the burying ground. I feel my stomach knot, but I set my feet apart and my right hand strays to the knife at my belt.

The man in the blue cloak turns his face towards me. His horse is steady, its head still, but the riderless horse turns too, its pale gold coat crisp against the black trunks of the trees.

That's what makes me walk forward. I'm wary of the man, but that long gold face with its spray of white and brown mane over black-tipped ears, both trained on me as I approach, and the black and white muzzle soft as I put out my hand to be sniffed and then nosed – for that I cross into the shadow of the woods, where the ground is still frosted, and look into the face of the man in the blue cloak.

Part Two:
THE WILDS

Six

SCOUR

GALEN'S TALE

Frithberg and the Hill Country

I wake up warm, a thing I try to take comfort in, seeing as there's not much to be had otherwise in a great man like me lying frit inside a hutch. Straw pokes my neck. If I dreamed I can't remember it, and that's a relief, for poor dead Roaki did not leave me alone the whole of last night. I wriggle out backwards and beat out the feathers and mess of hens from my blue cloak. *Galen*, I tell myself, *you're cock of the roost, but there's only so much you can joke about lying with fowl.*

The gold-haired boy appears with a steaming bowl, and I eat crouched on my haunches, an eye to the ale skins he's got at his shoulder. He doesn't offer.

At least it's not the hard-eyed skivvy. She knew how to prick a man's throat, for all that she was dressed like a mouse. No, she and the boy were not pleased when I appeared with their bronze horse in my hand, and told them who'd sent me.

I look up at the boy. "Can you get me a horse?" More than anything I want rid of this town, with its tall black tower, its blood-thirsty craftsmen.

"Yes," says the boy, but before I can get too cozy with this answer, he adds, "The girl's going with you."

I know he doesn't mean the skivvy with the knife, but the girl who sent me to them this morning, the girl who sheared poor Roaki.

"Why?" Imagine after the knife and the coop, I am not so very pleased with this.

"She's not a Staffbearer," says the boy slowly, "but I suppose you might call her a fledgling of the same nest." And with that he straightens and motions me to bring my pack, and he leads me bold as you like down the main street to the western gate, where there are none but some lads playing at guarding, all the real guards being gone to the feast he says. He takes them honey cakes and tells them a skivvy named Kelda has sent em, and the lads all coo and flutter before remembering to be gruff. We're out.

The Ridge rises up dead north, sheltering the plains from the cold north wind, and the Drovers Road cuts up and over it. But the boy turns away from the road and heads across pastureland towards a farm. Behind it stretches black forest, leaves dead and rustling. The farm's pasture runs up the slopes of the Ridge, and sturdy horses graze the sunny grass. Even thirsty, it's good to see them.

"Do you see the line of trees above the farm?" the boy asks suddenly. "Behind them is a path that leads over the Ridge, and joins the Drovers Road on the other side. Cross that tonight."

"Where are we going?" I ask, bolder now that we're out of the town, and with horses in sight.

"Gullcroft," says the boy. "I heard that's where you an your friend were bound. Do you know the way?"

"Aye," I say hoarsely, not wanting him to see that I know the place. Part of me wants to grab him and demand, "Don't you know who I am?" but of course he doesn't. No one does or has these nine years.

"The girl's from there," says the boy. "Make sure she gets there safe, and soon. You'll have company on your heels."

I don't say the message entrusted to me and Roaki has already gone awry, fallen into the worst hands it could. They must know that, to be helping me.

"D'you want yours back?" I ask, reaching inside my shirt, but he shakes his head and won't meet my eyes.

At the farm a bandy-legged man called Sebson welcomes the boy, and uncomplainingly shows me two horses. I find them healthy and strong, so I know this Sebson is in as deep as any of us, to give us two such valuable beasts. "Does the girl ride?" I ask the boy, but "She's capable," is all he says.

We ride the horses down the length of the forest's side, to the shadow of the cliffs under the tower. Low mounds on the open ground say this was once a burying place. The girl will meet me here, the boy says, giving me the second mount's reins. Then he hands me the two fat skins with a look, but being grateful I swallow down two mouthfuls without caring, by then he's gone. There's singing in the distance, so I toast them with another swallow.

Everything grows clearer with the first gulp, as it always does. The soft mounds of the buried are white-edged with frost, the air stings my good hand's knuckles, and a needle of cold tickles my left wrist, like there still was a hand to feel it. My bad hand, I call it, although it's no hand at all.

The dun mare I ride smells like hay, and her sides warm my legs. I hold the reins long, and she scuffs the frosted leaves with her muzzle, looking for grass. The other mare is younger, light gold, standing calm like she knows what is expected. I try the second skin, but it's just water, so I tie it with the bedroll behind the saddle. I raise the ale skin again, but there'll be no more after this, maybe for days, and I think to save what I have. Regretfully I tighten the plug and tuck it into my belt.

The forest crackles above me like a fall of arrows, and a scrawny figure pulls itself out of the earth at the foot of the cliff. It stands, pale smudge of face turned towards me. The forest shivers. The last leaves drop.

Tall and sure between the mounds, I know it's her though her hair is hidden, though her bare feet are now in leather boots. If she was grim this morning, with her pale hair and grey eyes, now there's a sort of spirit about her, burning through her pallor. Something . . . familiar. If she said she were risen from this burying ground I would be all believing.

She comes up to the gold mare first, and I'm glad to look on her before she looks on me, to see her have her hands nuzzled and the happiness in her face. I wasn't looking to find anything like that in her.

"And who are you?" I ask, and she turns up a white face with dark shadows. I hear a touch of fever when she talks.

"The Staffbearer's messenger," she says, "so don't worry, everything is as it should be." She smiles, the mare's breath filling her hands with mist.

I snort, passing her the reins. "Nothing has been as it should be since the war. What's your name?"

"Lambtail," she says, a hand tugging at the cloth covering her hair.

I laugh. "Lamb for a wolf to take," I say, "and me what the wolf left." I raise my left wrist and grin. She hesitates. Companions should take each other's arms, to show their trust, but there's no trust between us, so she fixes her pack behind the mare's saddle and pulls herself up easily.

"Let's go," she says.

I lead her through the forest and up the path behind the farm, the trees shielding us in the dusk. Above us the sky loses colour like dye. We follow a stream, white skeins of scum uncoiling on the black surface. The steady stump of hooves is our company; we don't talk. As we pass behind the farm the horses turn their noses to home, but I drive the dun mare past, and the gold mare follows. The ground rises, the trees thin, and the sun slides under the earth without a whisper, almost without blood. The town lies girded by its walls, and I'm glad of the dark rising to hide us from the bleak stare of the kirk. I glance back to see if the girl is taking a last look, but her eyes are straight ahead, fixed and wide.

I follow her gaze ahead, where a final tree stands almost on the hump of the Ridge. Its bare black limbs twist upwards from the darkening earth, but the sky behind it is still blue, though deepening. All in a horror the girl sits, and her mare stops, knowing it.

Normally I'd tell you a tree is a tree and no use glaring a curse on it like the girl's doing, but it comes to me what she was like at dawn, shearing poor Roaki without a tremble, and I think there's no scare in her that isn't there for sense. Maybe she's scouring, seeing beyond what's there. I get down and take the reins from her fingers. I start walking, leading the two horses, and though the gold mare is worried by her rider's fear, she follows quietly. The girl's hands are clenched, and I wonder if the fever I sensed in her is serious. "What do you see?' I ask, my voice soft.

"He – he's following me," she whispers, and I jerk my head to look behind us, too used to being followed. But her eyes stay forward, and the slopes are clear.

"Who is he?"

"I don't know." A breeze skimming over the Ridge's back finds our faces, sifting her words. "I thought he was just a man, but – I think I called something else. Something that speaks through him."

I can't help it, I shudder. We're exposed on the bare ground, the tree looming over us now and the stars springing out of the night like fleas.

"Is it speaking to you now?"

She shakes her head, bent all the way back now to look up into the bare branches, and then like a body cut down from a hanging, her head drops to her chest, and she slumps over. The gold mare jumps a little, but settles again, and I'm at her side. Her forehead is clammy, her cheeks burning, but with a normal sickness, not that strange spirit I saw on her when we met. I take the blanket off the dun mare, wrap the girl in it, and prop her upright. "Can you ride?" I ask, and she nods and mumbles.

We're on the north side of the ridge now, with no shelter from the wind. I turn my face into it and lead the horses down into the night. After a long black time, the ground evens out, and then, luck with us, the moon rises, so I don't stumble so much. The girl is quiet, but she doesn't fall, and the path heads north. At such times, not much is all you can ask for.

Still, I'm near dropping when the moon shows me a tumbled hump of stones ahead. It's a shepherd's hive, barely as high as the girl herself, with a round low entrance like a hole for the world's biggest rabbit. I lift the girl from her horse and she crawls inside. I peg the horses' reins so they can graze, and crawl through the hole myself, pushing the packs ahead of me. Inside it's wide and very dry, and there's no wind anymore. I wrap up in the gold mare's blanket, my nose full of horse-sweat, and curled round the sleeping bundle of the girl I set myself to dreaming.

There's no sign of Roaki in my dreaming, which I think on as I wake, chewing on an end of straw. The first night after his death he tormented me, but now I have laid down twice ready to see him, and twice he has not come. This to my mind is unusual, since my thoughts have been turning over his death and our travels together, whether I like them to or not, and that is sure feed for dreams.

Also the girl is not here, and the light outside the hole is morning-light, so I take out the blanket to beat it, and find her sitting atop the hive in the sun. By day I can see what kept us so warm: the earth creeps up the hive's walls, coating it in grass like a winter coat. Only the top of its dome is bare stone. This is where the girl is sitting on the horse blanket, watching the two mares.

"You missed the turning," she says. "At the foot of the ridge. We should have joined the Drovers Road there."

I am beating the blanket, so I let her think about it some more. I check for burrs or thorns, but there's just straw. Her face is still pale, but the shadows under her eyes are gone, and she isn't shivering. We were lucky to find the hive.

"Maybe it's best," I say. "If they're hunting us, they're like to stick to the road. I'm not sure we can outrun them, so not being where they're going is a good thought." She's biting her lip. "Spit it out."

"We're meant to reach Gullcroft before them."

"We won't reach Gullcroft at all if they catch us first." Her teeth are still worrying her bottom lip, but whatever it is she doesn't speak it. "The road follows the coast," I say, trying to convince her. "That's miles out of our way. We can go quicker and safer if we follow the paths." The hill country ahead is better hiding than the coast, where the world stretches flat around you for days. It's not just that of course. This is my country. We'll have no trouble until —

"What about the Floodlands?"

"What about them?"

"How will we cross them? That's why the road follows the coast, so it can cross at the mouth."

"I've crossed the Floodlands before."

"When?" I can see she doesn't believe me.

"During the war."

Oh yes. She glares at me but she doesn't argue. The Floodlands protected the North. Only one road across their mouth at Hellingap, and that cut off most of the winter. First these hills, then the North was our sanctuary. For a little time.

I feel good here. Safe. Maybe if I show her, she'll feel it too.

"We'll need to hunt," I say. "Can you use a sling?"

She gives me a pitying look. Now she looks more like the girl I first saw by the river with her friend, nothing eerie about her. Good. Maybe she'll stay that way.

"Here." I pass her Roaki's sling and his pellets. "You'll load quicker'n me."

She tucks the sling into her belt and the pellets into the pouch at her waist. Then she slides down from her seat on the hive and checks her blanket for thorns like I checked mine. I saddle first my mare then hers, checking their bridles and girths, glad to see they're rested.

"Do they have names?" She's standing ready with the packs, her sheepskin cloak on her shoulders. Little white-blond curls of hair have escaped her scarf, more clumsily tied today than yesterday.

"None that I was told."

I can see the gladness in her face, and wonder if she's already picked a name for her mare, like any child would.

"What about you?" she says, "do you have a name? I know what you said yesterday, but 'wolf leavings' sounds like wolf droppings."

I scowl at her. "Who brought you to this nice warm bed, instead of leaving you out in the cold when you fainted?"

"I didn't faint!" she snaps.

"And I didn't want a sick girl to coddle," I snap back. Red blazes in her white cheeks, and she squares up to me, but I laugh and push her away gently, my hand on her shoulder. "Don't try it. You wouldn't even land a punch. Now have you breakfast or not?"

Her pack has cheese and bread, and we eat in silence, leading the horses. There are still red smudges in her cheeks when we're done, but she says stiffly, "I'm sorry I was rude about your name."

"It's not my name," I say. "I'm Galen. Now will you tell me yours?"

But she shakes her head. "Lambtail is what my friends call me. It's best you use that."

Seven

SHEEP

EBBA'S TALE

Frithberg and the Grain Road to the East

 rn was not the first to dream of unifying the land of his forefathers, but before him none succeeded. The land is like a jagged spur, ringed by cold grey waters. It is divided from within, and the winter snows or the spring thaw make unimportant distances impassible to men. There are only three roads, and without them there would be no unity. Arn built the War Road when first he united the plains, and it stretches from the palace at Sunacre in the South to Frithberg beneath the Ridge. At Frithberg the three roads meet: the Grain Road crosses the mountains into the farmlands of the East, and the oldest road, the Drovers Road, follows the coast to the inhospitable North."

History of Arngard
Berengar of Vellsberg

"You can't hide in here forever," Erland tells me.

"I en't hidin," I say, "I'm workin." I'm in the kitchen, cuttin fat from a piece of mutton. I keep my eyes down. Blood leaks into the knife-scores on the wooden tabletop.

"Same thing," says Erland, lettin Kelda by. He's a big man an he's in the way, but he don't seem to care.

There's some mutterin from the door. Two soldiers have poked their heads through an are watchin us. Watchin me. They've bin doin it all mornin.

"Captain, tell your men to leave my girls alone," snaps Aud on her way past. Between Torny vanishin an all the sudden interest in me, she's tetchy.

Erland says somethin sharp to the men in Southern, an they retreat.

I nearly din't come back here last night. While the prester's voice was still ringin out, Erland spirited me from between Hakon's club an the skald's teeth. We were almost across the marketplace when Aud strode out of the dusk. She an Erland haggled over me like a market goose, an somehow this big man ended up handin me over half-asleep. It was only in the mornin I noticed the cold on my back an realised that Torny was gone.

"I know it must have been hard for you," Erland's sayin. "Spraki has an evil tongue on him when he's riled."

"It weren't his tongue I was feared of," I say.

"I know," Erland says. "You were very brave. You could have cried, or run away. No one would have blamed you. But you didn't."

That's a lie, I think, an my knife slips. Uncle Ulf taught me long ago that cryin an runnin don't save you from anythin. The anger's burnin like a slow fire deep inside of me. I fight to keep my hands steady.

"If we thought you were going to be hurt —"

I stop listenin. *It would just of bin a stranger-girl bein hurt*, I think, *that's all. The only reason anyone's interested in me now is cos they saw somethin more'n they thought to.*

"Are you keeping her from her work, Captain?" Aud's back, an her voice is sour.

"Not so as you'd notice," Erland says, showin the first seed of impatience. "The prester wants to see her."

"And I'm one girl down, so the prester will have to wait till after noon." Aud's a servant an of course she can't throw a warrior out, even one so mannerly as the captain. Still, somehow he ends up outside on the step, bein shooed into the yard.

"When are they leaving?" Kelda asks soon as the door's shut.

Aud shakes her head, her mouth a line. "Let's hope it's soon," she says. "I've had about enough of this." She gives me a look, but it's not as hard as it could be. "What did you go catching their notice for, Ebba?"

"It's not her fault," says Kelda, an me an Aud are both so shocked by this that we turn to stare at her. She rolls her eyes. "Well, it's not. It's Sorleyson's tricks that got her noticed."

Aud sighs. "It's my fault too," she says. "I shouldn't have told them you go to the kirk. That's what's got this lot going."

I shrug. Nice as it is havin Kelda be civil for once, I don't need to be told this en't my fault. I might not say it to Erland, but I *know* I en't the one who's done anythin wrong.

While my hands trim the meat, I wonder where Torny is. Sorleyson's story – "Sent with supplies for the Sebsons" – is horse dung. Sebson's farm is barely an hour away. So she's gone somewhere, an neither Sorleyson nor Aud are tellin where. I guess Blue Cloak did come callin for Jarle after all, an for some reason Torny's gone with him.

This mornin I found somethin I'd missed last night, layin under my pillow. It's her pin, long as my palm, with its head carved like a whale. I can't think why she'd leave it, save if she were tellin me she went herself, by choice. The thought of her out there alone with that man makes me uneasy, but there's nothin I can do. I have to trust I'm right.

The food is nearly ready when there's a polite tap on the door. Aud pulls it wide, scowlin.

"Mistress Salvebearer?" someone asks, an as Aud hesitates the speaker sticks a curly black-haired head round the door an looks straight at me.

"What d'you want, soldier-boy?" Kelda asks.

"My name is Berengar," he corrects her, steppin inside. Aud gives him a disgusted look but lets him be.

"An I'm Ebba," I say. "Mistress Salvebearer en't a name."

"Ebba," he says, an his tongue makes it light an curt. He bows. "Berger Dagomar invites you to his table."

I goggle at him. Berger Dagomar is one of Frithberg's richest merchants. A handful of the gold offerins hangin in the kirk are his.

"She's working —" Aud begins, but Berengar hands her a leather purse an bows again. It clinks.

"Prester Grimulf understands, Mistress. He pays for her time. Please send her well dressed."

Aud's face is smooth as she opens the purse. She counts the

money then turns to Berengar, even droppin him a curtsey. "Ebba will clean herself and join you," she says sweetly. "Please wait outside. Ebba," she says briskly as the door shuts, "clean yourself up."

I din't think Aud was one to turn so easily for money. "But —"

"No buts. Kelda, give her one of your good smocks. No, don't *fuss*, Kelda, do it."

So I'm trussed up in Kelda's soft blue smock — "If you get grease on it I'll kill you," she hisses helpfully, pullin it hard over my head – an sent out to Berengar – "Don't tread on the hem, little Miss Important!"

The hem's pretty, sewn wi fine white vines. I'd kill me for dirtyin it too, if it were mine.

Berengar smiles when he sees me. I must look like a child dressed up in my ma's clothes, wi my skirts too long an hitched up in both hands.

"What do they want wi me?" I ask him as he leads me down Astgate.

"You do not need to talk," he says, "just be seen."

I shut my mouth. I feel like I'm walkin a thin line an I have to look like I know what I'm doin, even if I don't.

The merchant lives across the market from Lord Frithrun's hall. His house is in the Southern style, new stone walls, the upper floor made of wood, same as the wayhouse. That means built after the war. No carved doorposts like most folk have, an no signs for protection or prosperity.

The door is opened by a servant. Her hair is covered like the townswomen wear it, an she don't meet our eyes.

My skin prickles.

There are bruises on her inner arm. I doubt Berengar notices. He walks straight past her. I duck my head an follow him inside, feelin her eyes on me. I know what she's thinkin. What's a scut like me doin in this rich man's home?

The main room is lit by horn windows. I en't never seen such things before. The light falls cold like milk, makin the prester's white curls glow. He sits at the head of the table, Berger Dagomar at his right hand like he's the guest, for all this is his home. The merchant sits hunched in the prester's shadow, his hair a dirty mix of black an grey, the skin on his sharp red nose peelin off in flakes. The rings on his fingers have pressed red weals into the white skin.

Erland sits on the prester's left, across from the merchant. His naked sword lies on the table in front of him, to show he'll not have need of it among friends. Berengar seats me next to Erland, where Dagomar can see me when he raises his eyes. The prester don't name me, an I can see there's no need. The merchant knows who I am. The way his close-set eyes travel over me makes my skin crawl.

The prester's voice flows like wind through corn. His eyes are half-hooded, an his fleshy lips are pink against the white bristle on his thick-set jaw.

"You know too well," he's sayin, "that even here in Frithberg, the people have shut their ears to the word of the Lord. You see it in the empty kirkhouse, which your own wealth helped build. We had hoped for a flock, you and I, yet believers come to the shepherd's call like lost sheep, lonely and few. And when the sheep are scattered, the shepherd has need of dogs."

Next to me, Erland places his hand over his blade, and Dagomar's eyes slide to him.

"But such things can be ugly," the prester continues, "if the dogs are not well trained, they may nip harder than desired, and no shepherd can abide to see his flock's fleece bloodied without need."

His rollin voice makes me heady, his words callin up memories of my uncle's broad-faced stock in the fields, the way they turn together as the dogs run em.

"To the shepherd, even one lamb returned to him is a great joy. That one lamb gives him hope that the rest of the flock may follow." His eyes flick to me, and Dagomar's eyes follow. "You are a merchant, and your sheep are ships sailing the oceans, but I wonder . . . what would you advise an old friend, a shepherd of men if you will, who wishes to see the lamb become a flock?"

This time Dagomar looks me over like I'm livestock. He takes his time before answerin.

"As you say, Grimulf, my sheep are ships, haha." He makes the noise of a laugh without the warmth. "So I know nothing of the shepherd's tricks. But my ships sail further west and south than even the Empire reaches, and everywhere I find man most desires those things that come from far away, which suits me very well. And one thing he desires the whole world through is other men, to do his bidding." His eyes linger on my hair an face. "Now, to the East are other ships, sailing a sea I cannot breach for fear of being plundered. Those ships carry not just their brigand crew, but also rare, far away goods; black sheep, for instance. Biddable ones."

He turns to Grimulf an I realise I've bin holdin my breath. I don't understand his words, but my skin feels greasy from his look.

"I have heard the Eastern flocks are yearly assaulted by these same brigands. If a wise shepherd were to protect them from such assaults, might not the flocks come gladly to him? A lamb of their kin would afford him a hearing."

I cannot make it out, this talk of sheep an lambs an shepherds. It's like a secret way of speakin hidden inside the common tongue, an it comes to me that the prester spoke like this yesterday, when he tole me the Blessed Walpurgis was a vessel, an again after I faced the hound, when he talked of wolves. I look over at Erland, who's bin sittin there this whole time with a face as empty as a deaf man's. Has he understood it?

The servant brings a cup to the table an the prester an Dagomar each drink from it. Then the woman puts down meat an fresh bread before em. That seems to mean it's decided, whatever it is.

Erland rises an beckons me from where I sit foolish an forgotten. He takes me from that place, but not unkindly, an he hands me some bread as we walk back to the wayhouse. It's not warm or new-baked, but yesterday's crust.

"I don't understand," I say between chewin an tryin to keep Kelda's nice hem out of the mud.

Erland gives me a look almost like pity, but he don't say nothin.

The wayhouse yard is empty. Aud opens the kitchen door to us, an Erland puts his hand on my shoulder. His face is serious.

"Yes?" she says, her sharp eyes dartin between us.

"The girl's coming with us," says Erland.

I'm up before true dawn, hands pullin me from my place between the merchant's daughters. Dagomar's wife took one look at me an put me wi them. I'm grateful. Between what Sorleyson tole me an my distrust of the merchant, I'm heavy wi the sleep I din't have. The servant who rouses me is the same woman who opened the door yesterday. She dresses me like I'm a block of wood, till I would of preferred Kelda's pinches to her stony glare. I know why she's angry. I'm not in my proper place. Why should I be protected, when she's left to collect bruises an whatever else her master chooses to give her?

They've another use for me. That's all.

Outside Dagomar's house stands a covered wagon, an a great horse wi strange long ears, tacked out for ridin. The prester holds the reins, gold shinin on his fingers as he speaks wi Dagomar. He's wrapped in a fine red cloak, his white hair bright in the torchlight. The servant pushes me to the wagon. It's slung low behind two stocky horses that en't nothin like the prester's long-legged creature. Hunched against the cold on the seat is one of the soldiers. He raises his head an I recognise Berengar. He jerks his head to show I should get in behind.

As I climb in, I glimpse Erland in the half-dark, talkin wi two warriors in red an furs.

It's black in the wagon, but there are packs an blankets. I could jus wrap myself up an give in to sleep, but I want to see the wayhouse one last time.

I hear Erland's voice outside as he an the warriors draw closer, leadin their mounts.

"Ride hard," he says, "an you may catch him on the Drover's Road. One hand, remember. If not, keep north."

His words don't really reach me, my head's so full. The sour feelin thoughts have when they circle your head at night en't worn off yet, an it's like they've worn ruts in my skull.

Erland almost din't let me into the wayhouse when he brought me back from Dagomar's last night, but I begged him to let me get my things myself. He had his hand on my shoulder like a leash.

"All right," he said at last, "but be quick. You'll need your salve, an keep that dress. You stay here, Mistress," he said to Aud when she moved to come wi me. "I have things to discuss with you."

What he had to say I don't know, but that he was keepin her from me was clear. I climbed to the loft, changed into my own smock, an packed away what other small bits were mine along wi Torny's pin. When I climbed down, carryin Kelda's blue smock, Berger Sorleyson was standin at the door of his room.

Sorleyson always left our care to Aud, not wantin to be bothered wi chits, he said. He might speak to us as we worked, but otherwise almost never.

"When your uncle sent you to me," he said now, "you know that was for money?"

I started to nod, but somethin in the way he said it made me stop.

"You're indentured," he said, talkin like he would to a child. "That means I gave your uncle money, and in return you came to work for me."

I stared at him. "No one tole me." I'd thought I was makin wages all this time, like Torny an Kelda.

Sorleyson shrugged. "The prester has paid me for your loss," he said, "and he's paid what remained of your uncle's debt."

"His debt?"

Judgin by his face, Sorleyson must've thought I was an idiot.

"Yes, girl. One payment after the first harvest, one after the second. If the debt weren't paid, you were the surety." My mouth drops open. "You didn't think one girl's work could pay off a whole family's food and supplies for a winter, did you?"

That's when I remembered Cousin Rafe's visit. I knew he was here on business, but suddenly I saw the nature of that business. He was payin the first half of the debt.

My cheeks were flamin red, I could feel em. I felt stupid, but also angry. The feelin that started when I listened to Erland's lies was back, like hot embers under my ribs.

"So what am I now?" I asked.

"You work for the prester," said Sorleyson, like it's obvious.

"I've bin sold?"

"We agreed the terms remain," said Sorleyson huffily. "Same terms as your uncle and I had. You work off part of it, your uncle pays the rest. The prester's paid off what your uncle owed me. If the prester chooses to collect it from your uncle, that's his right. This is better for you, girl, you must see that."

I had no words for him. To find out Sorleyson had sold me on, that made me feel I was on marshland, but only later. When I was first told, all I could think was I'd bin sent away not to keep me safe an fed, but so's Ulf could have money.

Standin there it slowly came to me what Sorleyson had said, that this was better for me.

"What d'you mean, I was the surety? What would of happened if my uncle hadn't paid?" I asked, but Sorleyson wouldn't look at me, just jerked his head to show I should leave, an that was how I knew the answer.

I'd of bin sold for real, I realised. *That's how Sorleyson would of got his money back.*

So maybe you can see why I went quietly, though Aud's eyes were blazin as Erland kept himself between her an me as I collected my salve, an though Kelda spat curses, though that weren't for me, but for her blue smock that she'd bin made to give up.

I have that smock wi me now, wrapped tight in a bigger pack. There are other things the prester required I have – a new undershirt, leather shoes, woollen stockings, a cloak an a comb – riches by any servant's measure. They were brought to me at Dagomar's where I was kept in his daughters' room. There's also a plain white dress, like I en't seen before. It's not to be touched yet, I've bin told.

I'm bumped awake. The wagon jerks as the horses pull, an I bang my head on the planks as I try to find an openin to peer through. We're crossin the market place. It's just light. The soldiers have joined us, hooves clatterin fit to wake the dead. We head down Astgate, an at the wayhouse I see her, Aud, standin straight an smooth-faced in her grey kerchief an dress. She watches us pass, an I wish more'n anythin that she knew I were watchin her too, so's she could tell me where Torny's gone, or what's to become of me. But her glare is fixed ahead of me, where the prester rides, an soon we're past an out of the gates. All I can do is curl up among the tumbled packs, Torny's whalebone pin in my fist, an cry.

Whatever else I am, I'm still a servant. When we stop an make a fire it falls to me to make up the gruel from a pack of toasted grains. Berengar shows me how much to use an how to mark the level on the pack. The soldiers crowd round me again, hands holdin out their bowls, but somethin's changed. Their smiles are quick an bashful, an they duck their heads away from me when I meet their eyes. They mutter words of thanks; some I understand an some I guess.

"What's wrong with em?" I ask Berengar when we're alone by

the fire again. I'm tired an the cold mornin has dampened the bit of fire I had in me yesterday.

He's playin with a length of beads, flickin em this way an that. "Mistress is a believer now, not a servant."

"Then how come Mistress is makin your breakfast?" I snap, before my ears hear what I'm sayin an I bite my lip. Somethin I en't felt for nearly a year washes over me like ice water.

I cower.

Everythin about this feelin is familiar – the fear that moves me quicker'n thought, the way I'm already hunched for the blow. The way my eyes drop.

But there is somethin new. I'm ashamed. *What would Torny think if she saw me like this?* I wonder, an the shame freezes me as bad as the fear.

Nothin happens. After a moment I look up.

Berengar is watchin me, his face surprised, not angry. "You are… unhappy?" he says.

"No," I say quickly, an I straighten up. "I just . . ." I just remembered Sorleyson's words, that I'm bought by the prester, an I remembered too that masters can beat their servants. But I don't say that. "I just want to know where I stand."

Berengar looks down, frowns, an opens his mouth.

"I mean," I say, "I want to know what I am. Am I a mistress or a servant? Seems to me I'm a servant."

Berengar thinks, fiddlin with his beads. I see now they're seeds on threads, each painted a different colour.

"All men are servants of the Lord," he says at last. "Like your lord in his hall at Frithberg. But God is lord of the world, and his hall is heaven. So all of us are servants."

Pretty words, I think, *but I don't see Erland or the prester down here in the ashes.*

Maybe he guesses what I'm thinkin, cos he shrugs, his lips twitching up in a lopsided smile. Maybe he means some of us must serve more lords than one. He turns back to his coloured seeds an I start packin away.

Erland comes up to us. "You settling in?" he asks me. I eye him, uncertain. Is he the captain who's polite even with servants, or the man who took me from my home?

"Berengar's showin me what food to use," I say.

"He's got a knack for that," says Erland, an I can hear approval in his voice. Berengar's face lights up.

"Cookin?" I ask.

"Supplies," says Erland, noddin to the bright coloured beads in Berengar's hand. "Those counting-beads keep track of our foodstuff, coin and feed." He must see I'm confused cos he adds, "Berengar makes sure we have what we need, and he looks after my weapons and horse."

"He's your servant?" I ask. Berengar's cheeks flush.

"Berengar is cousin to the lord of Vellsburg, a knight of the Holy Emperor," Erland corrects me. It's my turn to go pink. "He rides with me to learn how to command. It's his job to learn while he serves me, and it's my job to see that he goes home to his lord knowing everything he needs to. Speaking of which," he says, "Berengar, please see to Prester Grimulf. Make sure he's ready for the day's ride, and check his mule's feet."

Berengar hurries off and Erland turns back to me. "Now," he says briskly, "what was all that cringing about?"

I en't able to speak.

"Whatever they did to you in Frithberg," he says, "that's finished. No one here will beat you."

"Why am I here?" I ask, my voice thin.

"You're a remarkable girl, Ebba. Prester Grimulf saw that. He wanted to save you."

"Save me? From what?"

Erland puts a hand on my shoulder and looks into my eyes. "From whatever you were afraid of just now."

I can't tell him. The fear I felt has drained away, but I en't forgotten the shame, an to tell him it weren't the people I was sold to who did the beatin, but the family who sold me . . . I can't. I just drop my eyes an nod.

"Finish up then. We're leaving."

I pack away the supplies in the cart. I dither, wonderin if I'm meant to ride in the back like before, but Berengar calls me round to the front an gives me a hand up next to him. He don't say nothin, but I guess I'm forgiven for thinkin him like me.

We travel east. The sky is blue, an soft clouds stand out against it, pink an gold. The forest rises up about us, black-barked beeches standin in their fallen copper leaves. The cartwheels crunch ruts through loam an twigs. Sittin next to Berengar, my fingers itch from doin nothin. I twist my skirt in my lap, an watch the soldiers. Some walk their mounts along the Grain Road with us, while others ride ahead in pairs. Erland an the prester ride up front.

"This country is familiar to you?" Berengar asks.

I shake my head. "I bin through it once, a year ago. I come from the Eastern farmlands."

"Are Eastern lands like the plains of Frithberg?"

"Not so flat," I say, rememberin the farm, an the way the folds in the land hide one field from the next. "When me an Stig an Rafe watched the sheep we'd stand on the ridges an we could see all the way down past the farmstead to the sea."

"Stiganrafe?" asks Berengar curiously, an I laugh to hear how he runs it together. They were like that, always taggin after each other, even when they'd fallen out.

"Stig's my brother," I say, an I feel a twinge of worry, wonderin how he is. "Rafe's my cousin."

"The sheep?"

"My uncle's sheep."

"I watched sheep too, when I was a child," says Berengar, an he sounds wistful. "Are Easterners all like you?" I raise my eyebrows, an he gestures to my face an hair.

"No," I say, turnin away. "More like Frithbergers. Me an Stig an Ma are different. Ma was taken when she were young from her land." Berengar glances at me, an I say, "They never put the collar on her. She weren't a thrall. They was goin to, the Raiders I mean, but Da rescued her from them an they fell in love an he married her. Anyway," I say, calming down a bit, "that's why I got black hair an brown skin."

Berengar's eyes light up. "Raiders!" he says, like I've given him a treat. "There are very few raiders in imperial waters."

"Lucky you," I say.

"You have seen them?"

"Course I bloody seen em." I'm annoyed now, that this bead-countin lord's pet seems to think Raiders are somethin to see, like a hen layin gold eggs. "Every summer we set night watches for em. They kill an mutilate our people, they take slaves, an they burn. Once they burnt all our fields from the sea to the foothills. When they come down on us everyone takes up arms. We fight em off, we try'n save what's left. It en't no summer fair for lordlins to gape at."

"What do they wear?" Berengar asks, like he en't heard me.

"What do they *wear*?" I repeat, near speechless. "What d'you mean?"

"Their style of dress," says Berengar seriously.

I stare at him. "I dunno," I say finally. "I'm usually too busy tryin to stop everythin from burnin an help Ma bandage up them as got cut to notice."

Berengar looks disappointed. "I am writing a history," he says.

"What's that then? A list of clothes?"

Berengar looks offended. "A story of what happened," he says, all reproachful. "Here. In Arngard."

"Like King Arn an his sons?"

"Yes!" says Berengar, tuggin the reins in his excitement so that the horses pull up an stamp. "The war and King Kolrand, his treaty with the Holy Emperor, and how God came to Arngard."

"Oh." I watch him coaxin the horses into movin again. I'm not sure I can tell him anythin about those things.

"I know how King Kolrand faced heathens at Frithberg and under the Lord's protection crushed them. Then the treaty agreed churches to be built at Sunacre and Frithberg," he says. "I do not know how the Lord God came to the East. Tell me."

This is goin to be the Raiders' britches all over again, I think. *How am I meant to know this?*

"Well, we don't have a kirk," I say. "My uncle's farmstead is maybe the biggest in the East. It's called Eldinghope. Like I tole you, it stretches from the sea to the mountains, an the sacred grove is on his land, so everyone around comes for Walpurgis Day an Bloodnight."

Berengar's frownin. "What?"

"The first day of spring an the first day of winter," I say. "On Walpurgis Day we welcome the Blessed Walpurgis and take her round the fields an pray to her —"

"The other," says Berengar. "Bloodnight. What is it?"

"Nothin," I say, realisin my mistake. "Forget it."

But Berengar has caught me by the arm, so hard it hurts. His fingers bite into the flesh above my elbow.

"I know what it is," he hisses.

"Then why d'you ask —"

"I asked about God!" he says. "These things you say. They are not holy days. They are heathen."

"Heathen?"

"They have nothing to do with the Lord!" Berengar's face is white under his crow-black hair.

I'm frightened but I try not to shrink from him like I did by the fire. I try to be like Torny.

"What's wrong?" I ask, keepin my voice low like his.

"Wrong?" He laughs, like he don't know where to begin. "Prester Grimulf brings you with us as a believer. But you are not."

For a warrior to show fright, even if he is a grain-countin, clothes-listin outlander, it must be bad.

I close my eyes as fear leaps in my chest like a hare. If only I could up an run like that, run far an fast so's they'd never catch me. But I can't run from men on horses, an if I'm goin to make it through, I need to know more'n how to look down.

I meet his gaze.

"Help me," I say.

Eight
CHOKE

❧

ero." I whisper it, because I don't want Galen hearing me. "Come on, Hero."

My mare flicks her ears back to me, as if she understands that's her name now. I smile as my hips roll with her gait. The sun is bright but the air is cold, and I'm glad of Hero's warm sides, and Aud's sheepskin cloak. The brightness burns away the night before, the darkness, the tree, the dead man . . .

Yes. Under the morning sun I can think about it without flinching. The dead man.

Whatever Galen says, I didn't faint.

Hero snorts, and tosses her head. I can feel her dancing underneath me, longing to break out of her trot into long, open strides. I lean back and push my seat forward, keeping the reins long. I feel her gather herself and leap forward, like a powerful wave running up a long beach.

"You'll frighten the rabbits," Galen says sourly, catching up to us a mile or so later. He holds the reins easily in his one hand, while his left wrist rests on his thigh.

"There'll be more." I look around. "Where are the sheep, anyway?"

"They'll be taking em down off the hills for winter," says Galen, glancing round. "We'd better hope the snows don't start while we're out here."

"The snows! They won't start till after Bloodnight."

He gives me a patronising look. "We're not on the plains now, girl."

"Don't call me girl. Anyway, I'm not from the plains, I'm from Gullcroft."

Galen gives me a hard look for a moment. Then he grins and rallies. "An egg-hunter, eh? No wonder you're such a skinny thing. I would be too if I had to walk over a cliff every time I wanted a snack."

I open my mouth to tell him that a long walk off a short cliff is just what he needs, but suddenly I remember what the spring sea looks like under the scudding clouds, and the feel of the wind all around me, like a powerful animal, and the tough rope tied round my waist. The thrill of stepping backwards over the edge, resting on the wind's back, while the gulls scream murder.

Then I'm back to the warmth of Hero's back, and the green hills. I'm filled with a longing so strong it takes me a moment to recognise it.

"What?" Galen's watching my face.

"I . . . I miss home."

"You're in luck, girl, that's where we're going." Galen urges his mare forward, leaving me at a loss. I don't even tell him not to call me girl.

He mustn't think there's anything strange about it. I don't try to tell him that in all the time since I left, my anger's been too strong to miss Gullcroft. All I could think about was Brenna's smile while Sklep sheared me, or Vigdis telling me I wasn't good enough. I've never felt the need to go home, like a hook in my heart.

This must be how Ebba feels about her family. I never could understand the way she'd cry for home, but if it felt like this . . .

Ahead of me, Galen starts singing. He's in a good mood. Whatever the rabbits felt about Hero's galloping, they can't be any happier with the tuneless bellow that passes for his singing voice. Hero and I keep an arrow's flight behind, and I pull my scarf down over my ears. But I'm sort of glad of his caterwauling, because it saves me from having to think too much, about the sudden ache in my chest or . . . well. Other things.

Come noon Galen lays off the songs and finds us a stream. We eat bread and cheese again. I fill our water skins and then run my fingers through the pebbles in the stream-bed, idly looking for shot for the sling. Galen's humming through his beard. There are crumbs caught in the red-gold hairs.

"You weren't like this yesterday," I say. "You were all jittery."

He doesn't seem to hear me, but he stops humming.

"Well?" I say.

After a pause he says, "Nasty place, Frithberg. Bloodthirsty."

I watch the stream trickle between my cold fingers, the sun glinting off it. "Who was he?" I ask. "Your companion?"

As I say it my neck prickles. I look behind us. There's nobody, of course, only the grass rippling over the hills like the tide.

"His name —" Galen starts, but Hero rears, her eyes rolling white, and I rush to her and hang onto her reins, pulling her down with all my weight. I talk to her the way I would talk to Ebba when she woke with night-frights. "It's alright Hero, I'm here, it's nothing, there's nothing here . . ."

Galen's blue eyes are narrowed. "She didn't spook once last night," he says at last. "And how did you haul her down? You must weigh next to nothing." He strides over to me, puts his hand around my upper arm and swears. He makes to grab me again and I sidestep behind Hero, so she's between us.

"Don't touch me," I tell him.

He holds his hand up. "I didn't mean anything."

"Keep your hands to yourself." A trickle of the fear that ran through me when I faced him at dawn yesterday comes back to me. My feet settle into a fighting stance. The knife Aud gave me is on the bank by the cheese. I can just imagine what she'd say to that. *You can't use the pointy bit if you don't keep it to hand, you idiot.* I glare at him, putting my anger at myself into it.

He takes a few steps back, his hand still up, scowling. "It's only the one hand. And you're all over muscle," he says.

I relax a bit. "I can do tricks," I say. "Walking on my hands, stuff like that."

He relaxes too. "Oh, tricks," he says, dismissively. "Did I hear you call that horse Hero?"

"And?" Now I'm scowling.

"Does she look like a hero to you?"

I glare at him but this time it doesn't have any effect. "Out of the three of us, I'd say she's the best bet."

"Hear that, Sweetpea?" Galen says to his mare. "She's not even counting you. What an ill-mannered girl."

"Don't call me girl."

The afternoon's quieter than the morning. The singing has stopped, and Galen seems to be looking for something. We're deep in the hills now, long out of sight of any kind of road or path other than sheep tracks.

Galen's humming grows less and less tuneful, and each time we crest one of the hills he scans the horizon. My eyes turn to the west, where the Drovers Road lies hidden, as if some magic might let me see whether we're being followed. An unpleasant thought comes to me – what if we fall behind? What if we reach Gullcroft too late?

"Galen," I call, riding up to him, "are you sure you know —"

"There!" He throws out his arm, finger stabbing north east.

I look where he points. I can't see anything. "What?"

"I knew it," he mutters under his breath, and he takes off on Sweetpea. I have no choice but to follow. We cut east until we reach the foot of a domed hillock, quite different to the rolling slopes around it. Galen leaps off Sweetpea, pushing her reins into my hands, and runs up the dome. I slide down from Hero's back and tether the two horses, then hike up after him.

Galen's bent over, pulling at something. As I get closer I see it's a cairn of stones.

"Grab that," Galen grunts, and I lift away some of the bigger stones.

Underneath the pile is a bundle in waxed cloth. Awkwardly, Galen pulls it loose and slings it under his right arm.

I follow him back down to the horses. He's in a fine mood, whistling between his teeth as he spreads the packet's contents out on the ground. Flexible willow switches, wooden pegs and a large, tough sheet made from sailcloth.

"What is it?" I ask.

"A shelter."

I sit back on my heels. "How did you know it'd be here?"

Galen's face is strangely animated. "We used to use them."

"We?"

"During the war," he says. I look from him to the tent's materials. "When we were stuck out here," he adds.

"I thought the war was mostly fought on the plains?"

"These hills are where we hid. This is where my prince came with his men when we heard Kolrand had returned to usurp his kingdom." Galen runs his hands over the switches almost lovingly. "We hid these packs so we could survive out here if we had to."

He sits back, gazing at something only he can see. He has a dreamy look in his eyes.

"During the war," I say. "Nearly ten years ago. And you just knew they'd still be here?"

Galen's smile fades. "I wasn't sure, of course —"

"These look new."

"The stones keep the animals off," he says, but he's frowning, and he leads us well away from the hillock before we make camp.

My thoughts are all tangled up like fish in a net, but a few small ones get through. The first is that Galen fought for Geir Arnson during the war. That means he was on the side that killed the old king. Lots of people must have been, of course, but when people talk about the war, they don't talk about who they fought for. They talk about the war like they'd talk about a pestilence, a curse that visited death on everyone. But it wasn't a pestilence, it was people. The stories all say it – kin killing kin – but how did the survivors heal themselves when it was over?

And Galen smiles when he speaks of the war. I've never known anyone do that. I wonder what it means.

The second thought is simpler. I don't care how strong the sailcloth is, how well buried. The willow switches are still green.

That shelter pack has not been sitting on a hilltop for nine years.

Galen chooses our camp before sunset; neither of us wants to be caught in the dark without shelter. He sends me to collect wood from the hunched thorn trees huddled on the slopes above us. The hollows between the hills are in shadow, but as I climb I come back into the sun, and I turn my face into it and close my eyes, bathing in it.

While the light lasts, I break off dry branches and twigs from the thorn bushes. The clump I've chosen doesn't yield much, but there's another above me, and as I climb I watch Galen, doll-sized, sliding the flexible willow struts through the sailcloth. He works methodically, slower with his one hand, but his movements are practised.

I reach the higher clump of thorns and start piling up wood. After a while I glance down and see that the shadows in the valley have risen almost to my feet.

My heart kicks in my ribs. Panic trickles down my spine.

I prick my hands all over in my hurry to be done before the shade reaches me, but it rises like a flood. It laps at my ankles and then slides up my body, swallowing me whole. I freeze as it covers me, and the cold steals in at my mouth and reaches down, spreading through my lungs.

I don't want to see him again. Even though there are no trees here, nothing for him to hang from. Somehow I don't think that will matter.

I force myself to climb down into that gloom. My heart's thumping, and I feel eyes on my back all the way down. When I set down my bundle next to him, Galen gives me a strange look.

"You alright?"

I nod my head. My mouth feels like it's been sewn shut – my lips prickle just like my scratched hands. I drop to my knees and start building the fire while Galen crouches over a nest of dry grass. With his foot he holds a curved iron hook in place over the nest, and strikes down on the iron with a piece of stone. I watch the tiny red sparks to keep my eyes busy, I lay the wood to keep my hands busy, but all the while unseen eyes are boring into my back, and behind me the dusk rustles with a murmur I can't quite hear.

The sparks catch the tinder, and Galen curls low over the nest, breathing red life into it. He tucks it into the pile I've built, and the red light blooms, making the gloom into darkness. Woodsmoke blows into my eyes, and they stream with tears. I squeeze my lids closed to clear them, and I wish ferociously that I could stay like this, head bowed and eyes shut tight.

Galen prods my shoulder. "Do you want food or don't you?"

Reluctantly, I look up.

Across the flames from me, his feet lashed high among the stars, hangs the dead man. He grins.

When I wake, it's dawn. I drag my thoughts out of cloying grey mists. I spent the whole night in the thick fog, the hooded figure gripping my arms, the freezing stone under my bare feet. And that voice in my head, over the waves, over the murmuring: *Tell me your name.*

My jaws ache from keeping my teeth clenched shut.

Light filters through the sailcloth, and my face is numb with cold. I tuck it into the sheepskin hood and breath into the wool, trying to warm it, but the rest of my body joins in the complaint. My feet are chilled, my bladder is full, and my fingers ache too, as if they've been curled into fists all night. Sure enough, when I look at my palms there are four half-moon dents on each where my nails have dug into the skin.

I slither awkwardly out of my bedroll, eyes still gummy, legs stiff, and stagger away from camp to relieve myself.

When I get back, Galen is hunched over the low remains of the fire. He looks haggard, more like the wild-eyed sleepless man who confronted me over the body of his companion than the whistling adventurer of yesterday. I see he's cradling a half-full skin. I reach out for it, hoping to wash my mouth out, but he passes me a bowl instead.

I sniff the steaming water, but it smells harmless.

"Found the herbs in your pack," Galen says, wearily.

Aud must have included a packet of Ebba's herbal tea. I sip it until the warmth has spread from my mouth to my belly, and my hands around the hot cup have loosened and stopped aching.

"What happened?" I ask.

"That's what I want to know." Galen sips from his skin. "After I lit the fire you fainted dead away. I couldn't wake you. You got so cold I wondered if you'd left us." He sips again. "Towards dawn you got a little warmer, so I wrapped you up and went to sleep."

"You stayed up all night with me?"

"By the fire," he says. "I thought you were dying, girl."

No wonder he looks awful. He must be exhausted.

"The night we climbed the ridge, you said you were being followed. You said something was speaking to you."

"I don't remember."

"But you know what it is, don't you?" Galen looks at me, hard.

My throat closes up, but I nod. Just like last night, I can feel eyes on the back of my neck, but now I know I'm not imagining it.

"Tell me," says Galen.

It feels like someone has their hand around my throat. I shake my head, my lips pursed.

Galen looks like he might hit me. "This is no time for games," he growls, and I can see the fear plain in him.

I try to swallow against the grip on my throat. It hurts, and my blood begins to throb in my head. My breath is being forced out. Galen's eyes are wide with fear, and as I raise a hand to scratch at my throat I see his hand come up too.

The grip on my throat loosens as Galen's slap lands on my cheek. I sway back with the blow, then launch myself at him, red spots and grey mist behind my eyes. Whatever force closed up my throat now pushes me forward, and I hit him full in the chest, smacking him to the ground, winding him. My hand's on the knife Aud gave me before I can think, and there are voices roaring in my ears.

I blink, look down at him, and release him quickly, walking away while he sits up and catches his breath. We don't take our eyes off each other.

I hunker down by the fire, out of reach. I have to find a way to make this right, now, before we end up killing each other. There's a warning pinch at my throat, as if to remind me what will happen if I try to explain. I pick up a part-burned twig and fiddle with it, my eyes on Galen as he wheezes and glares at me.

"Galen," I say, poking at the ashes with the twig. "Listen to me, this is very important." I speak loudly and slowly, and I hope Galen's too shaken to interrupt me. "Thank you for looking after me. I don't want to fight. It's going to happen again, and I'll need you while I'm – asleep. I think —" my concentration wavers, and I breathe deeply, trying to hold the words in my mind, to find the ones that won't cause my throat to close up. "I think if you try to hurt me, I'll be forced to hurt you. There's something . . . here . . . with me." The grip tightens again, hard and fast, and then releases me, and I fall back, choking and panting.

Galen stares at me, then looks down. I force myself not to look down at the ashes until I'm sure the grip on my throat is gone, and I can't feel the unseen eyes boring into me anymore.

Then I glance down. In the ashes, my twig has sketched a man, hanging upside down from a tree. It's rough, but Galen looks at me grimly and nods.

He offers me his hand to help me up, and we silently set about packing up the shelter and the bedrolls. We set out under the low grey sky, leading the mares up the slope. All we leave behind is the black scorch mark of the dead fire, and the ashes blown smooth in the morning breeze.

The solid clouds above us show no hint of the sun all day. The north-facing slopes of the hills grow steeper and steeper, and the narrow track we follow winds back and forth as it descends. It means we can stay on the horses, but it takes us longer to ride than it would to walk. True, my feet aren't hurting, but my thighs and back are aching, and my seat is sore; I've never spent this long on horseback. The worst thing is imagining those soldiers on their big glossy mounts galloping along the flat road north, passing us and leaving us far behind. I catch myself grinding my teeth with frustration more than once. Under me, Hero seems as nervy as I am.

Galen doesn't seem worried. Despite a sleepless night, and this morning's excitement, he's almost cheerful. The dark circles are still etched deep under his eyes, and he sips from his skin often. I offer to fill it when we stop at a stream, and when he refuses I realise it doesn't hold water. He scans the hills when we crest, same as he did yesterday when he was searching for the cairn where the shelter was stashed. I wonder if he's looking for other signs, invisible to me.

We eat in the saddle, stopping only for water at the streams. I've got a good number of pellets for my sling by now, so I practise on rabbits. I start off rusty, not helped by being on Hero's back, but after a few hours I've brought down two. I start thinking about the coming night.

"Galen, can we keep going in the dark, like we did the first night?"

He shakes his head. "The hills are too steep. Even with moonrise the slopes will be in shadow, and the path isn't straight."

"Can't we make a torch? There's no one to see us, is there?"

Galen opens his mouth and closes it again.

"They'd only see us if they were very close to us, or standing lookout on the top of one of these hills," I go on. "And who'd be watching the hills?"

"We don't know," says Galen. "Anyone could be."

"Who?" I ask. "We haven't seen a single sheep or shepherd."

"I told you, they don't want to risk the snows."

"Are you sure? Because the first frost was only a few days ago, and I haven't even seen any droppings. I don't think there are any shepherds up here."

"I'm taking you through the deepest part, aren't I?" demands Galen. "To keep us out of sight."

"So why can't we use a torch?"

"Because," Galen growls through his teeth, "others might be here keeping out of sight, like us."

We don't speak for a while.

"The shelter is new, isn't it?"

Galen sighs. "Yes. The willow is green."

"And you think it might be some of your friends, is that it?" My voice comes out hard, even to my ears. "The same men you fought with in the war, hiding out in the hills and raiding and killing until your prince was killed?"

Galen reins in. "You don't know *anything* about the war, girl," he says angrily.

"I know Geir Arnson killed his own father!"

"Oh yes, kind King Arn," Galen says with contempt, and spits. "The man was no more kind than winter. It's thanks to him I have this." He raises his stump. "The kindness was that he let me keep my sword hand, and in remembrance I took up my sword against him as soon as I could."

"He had your hand cut off?" I ask, staring at him. "I thought you lost it in the war. What did you do?"

"I told him I was his son's man, not his. He said that since

I would only serve one master, I would need only one hand."

I don't argue. It sounds like the kind of thing a king might say ... just not the king everyone calls the Good.

"You liked it, didn't you?" I ask after a while. "Living out here with the warbands. That's why you've been so happy."

"Happy?" demands Galen. "Happy? With a sick child and being hunted, and poor Ro —"

Sweetpea rears, like Hero did yesterday, dumping Galen heavily on his back. I keep Hero's reins short as she sidles in panic, but Sweetpea quiets, and Galen's still breathing. I jump down to help. This time I can guess what caused the upset.

"Don't say his name," I tell Galen. "He'll just stop you."

Galen looks shaken, but he takes Sweetpea's reins and leads her downhill. I follow, leading Hero in case the dead man feels like trying the trick again. I'm tired, and the muscles in my neck are tight. I've been tensing them in case the dead man's grip returns. He can scare horses, and he can close my throat, but he doesn't seem to be able to touch Galen directly. And he can hear us talking, but he doesn't seem to hear my thoughts, otherwise he would have stopped me drawing in the ashes. And the dreams ... he's trying to get me to say my name out loud.

More than ever I'm glad I haven't shared it with Galen. But when I get home ... well. I'll worry about that later.

Again, I get that pull, that tugging under my ribs. The homesickness is back, with a strength that twists my insides. Like I'm being dragged back to Gullcroft, heart-first.

Under the dull grey sky it's hard to keep track of time, but Galen calls a halt before I sense sunset. When I try to argue he glares at me. "You're the one who drops like an anchor when the sun goes down," he says. "This time I want to be ready. And you need to eat, or you'll weaken."

We build the fire, set up the shelter and cook the rabbits. While they're browning, Galen beckons to me. "Let's see these tricks then," he says, and I limber up, grateful for anything to take my mind off the coming dark.

I turn a few cartwheels, then kick up into a handstand. I walk about on my hands a bit, then balance on one hand, the other held straight out from my body. I settle back onto both hands, and let my legs fall slowly into the splits. Galen claps his hand against his thigh. I bring my legs up and curl them over my head, so that I look out from between my hanging feet. Galen's smiling. My muscles complain a bit, and I can feel some stiffness in my back and neck, but it's not so bad, considering I haven't practiced these last few days.

When I stand again I'm sweating a bit, but I feel better than I have all day.

"When I found you," Galen says softly, not looking at me, "you were shearing him. Why?"

"Something to bury," I say, braced for my throat to close. Nothing happens.

"Is that what he wants, our . . . companion?" asks Galen.

I nod. "That's what I promised. And things," I add.

"Burial and grave goods," says Galen. He looks thoughtful, but all he says is, "Do you know how to use that knife?"

We practice with the knives, and I don't shame myself. Then we eat as the dark comes on, and not a moment too soon, because right after I feel the prickling in my lips again. Too late, I wish I'd asked Galen to tell me something about the dead man, something about what he was like when he was alive, before he was this grinning, bloated corpse. But I don't think the dead man would have let me ask anyway. Here he comes, hanging from the dark, starless sky, and I stare into his sockets and fall, and keep falling.

Nine

WOLF

EBBA'S TALE

The Grain Road to Birchold

'm up to my elbows in the trough when he comes
to me.

"Come wi me," he says like a friend, though I
en't seen him before.

"I can't," I say, "I've got to get these clean." I look down again,
but the trough is full of mead. Little golden fish flash between my
fingers.

"Come wi me," he says again. His eyes are dark like mine.

So I wipe my hands on my apron an I follow him out onto
Astgate. There are others with us, but I can't see em. I just know
they're there.

He comes to the market place, an the people are waitin for
him. The old man who works the bellows at the smithy is there,
an the dark-eyed man touches his hand to the old man's forehead.

The old man gets up an walks about on two legs, leavin his wooden leg lyin on the ground.

We come to the well by the hangin pole. The dead man is still strung up. The dark-eyed man touches the dead man's forehead like he did the old man's, an the dead man lifts himself an unties the rope bindin his feet. He drops to the ground an gets up an I see he's got eyes again, an his body is whole.

We climb the outcrop to the kirk, but the kirk ain't there, only a great oak tree growin on its edge, the carved stone before it. The man climbs up on this tree an people tie him to it. Spraki the skald hammers long nails through the man's hands an feet, laughin. The man don't cry out once. He bleeds an dies.

When he's dead, they bring him down off the tree.

"Look," he says to me, in his dead voice. An he shows me the wounds in his hands an feet.

I take out my salve, an I rub it into his wounds. His red blood turns golden. An he stands up, an he says —

"I am the blood an the mead, the bread an the meat. *Wake up, Ebba!*"

I squint blearily into the light. Someone's shakin me.

"Get dressed," says Berengar, his voice low. "The prester wants you."

I sit up, tangled in blankets in the back of the cart. Outside I can hear the soldiers an their horses. Everyone's up.

My head's still blurry wi the stories Berengar told me yesterday. I slept in my dress so there's no helpin that, but I pull my new comb through my thick hair. I don't have anyone to braid it, so I just pin it up wi Torny's whalebone. I wrap myself in my new thick cloak an climb out of the cart.

Erland an Berengar are by the fire. They both see me, but Erland lets Berengar come to me alone.

"What does he want?" I ask him. I'm uncomfortable. My stomach growls, and I'm in need of the latrine.

"He did not say," says Berengar. His face is white, an his hand clasps my shoulder too tightly. He steers me away from the fire an hope of breakfast.

Berengar leads me to a stream a little way from the camp. The prester sits by the stream, wrapped in rough-woven grey wool. His white curls shine in the cold mornin air. One of the slim kirk candles stands before him on a small wooden altar. His hands are in his lap, an between the thick, short fingers I see a flash of gold as somethin is turned over an over between em.

"Ebba Rathnasdota, my lord," says Berengar. I en't heard him speak to the prester before. There's respect an wariness all mixed up in him.

The prester's head nods, but he stays starin at the pale flame.

Berengar gives me a worried look an leaves.

I stand there, listenin to his footsteps crunch away, the stream runnin swift, the crows in the trees. The prester don't move, save the bulk of his shoulders risin with his breath. The sweet smell of beeswax wraps around me as I shift from foot to foot.

At last he beckons me to join him. I kneel beside him, hands on my thighs. Since he's still gazin at the flame, I do to.

"I believe the Lord has led me to you for a reason, Ebba Rathnasdota," the prester says. "I believe he desires your gift to be used in his name, to his purpose."

"My gift?" I say.

"Your salve," he says. "He has bestowed the power to heal men's bodies, but also, I believe, to heal their souls, by leading them to him. For if they know not God, their bodies may be hale, but their souls are lost."

I cling to what I know. "You want me to heal people?"

"Child," he says, "you must understand. *You* do not heal people. God uses you as a vessel. It is he who heals them, working through you."

I think of the way Ma's salve calmed the hound, when I know it should do no more than calm a swollen joint. Maybe that was the White God workin through me. Berengar explained how the Blessed Walpurgis en't a goddess, but a woman who believed so deeply in God that she became wise an just. Maybe I'm meant to be like her.

"Before you do the work of God," says the prester, "the body must be made ready for God to enter into it. Are you ready for God to enter into your body, Ebba?"

What kind of a question is that? *Not right now, if you please*, I think, but weakly. I wish I could go, but he wraps his thick fingers around my wrist and brings my hand to the flame.

I want to pull away an curl myself up on the pine needles, or run all the way home to the wayhouse. Panic so pure I can't hear anythin but a clangin in my ears like the bells of the kirk overhead.

Eyes up.

I force myself to hold still, to meet his eyes. He knows. Just like Erland knew, only the prester en't wastin time tellin me not to be afraid. He wants me afraid. He wants to see what I'll do with it.

The pale flame dances against the dark trunks of the pines, an I let him guide my fingertips through the flame. Away an back again.

My fingers are cold an the flame barely warms em, but my whole arm tingles an flinches away. Or tries to. His fist holds me too firmly for that.

He makes me do it again, an the flame brushes the underside of my knuckles. His pale blue eyes bore into mine.

The third time, he pauses, an as the flame leaps up to kiss my palm, I remember Spraki's malice. This en't that bad. I bite my lip an hold still.

But he lets me go, an I snatch my hand back before the kiss can blister. I lean forward an plunge my hand into the small stream. The cold water bites into my palm.

When I sit back, he's still watchin me.

"What if it don't work?" I ask. "What if I can't do it?"

"If you prepare yourself for God to work through you, if you trust in him utterly," he says, "you will accomplish all that he directs you to do."

"But how'll I know what he wants?" I ask. "I en't meant to talk to gods!"

The word falls between us.

Do not, Berengar tole me, *talk of these things as equal. The Blessed Walpurgis is not a god, she was a holy woman. The Wise One is a false god. And most of all do not speak of these sacrifices, this Bloodnight, as something that you have done and seen. There is one God. The rest is devilry.*

The prester's eyes are fixed on me like millstones, an I feel the weight of em pinnin me down.

"You poor child," he says at last, softly, though it's the softness of a growl. "You have been raised in ignorance and darkness, and yet the purity of your faith shines like a candle. We must build it into a torch, to light the way for others."

I keep my mouth firmly shut. I seem to have got away with somethin, an I don't want to mess it up.

"We will prepare you, Ebba. The Vellsberg boy can teach you the proper words. You must learn them before we reach Birchold. Can you do that?"

I nod.

"Then go and tell him. You must be ready."

That seems to be the end. I stumble to my feet, stiff an eager to be gone.

"Thank you, Prester," I say, bowing to his back.

"Call me Father, child," he says.

A sick feelin twists in my stomach. I don't want to call this man father. But I don't see how I can refuse without bein rude, an I can't be rude. I belong to him.

"Father," I say, stiffly. I bow again an walk quickly back to the camp.

I spend the mornin copyin the words Berengar recites for me. He's tense, an snaps when I get it wrong.

"*Unigenitum!*" he hisses, so the others won't hear. "I have said it a dozen times. *Uni-geni-tum.*"

"Well you try learnin nonsense!" I hiss back, sick to my teeth of sayin sorry over these stupid words.

"This is not nonsense, you stupid girl. This is what will save you!" Now he sounds like a lordlin.

"I en't stupid! The prester said he wants me to light the way for others." Berengar snorts. "How'm I goin to do that if they don't understand what I'm sayin?"

"*You* do not understand what you are saying," he says. "The whole thing is mummery."

"Berengar. Ebba."

Erland's leadin a horse beside us. I feel myself goin red an then see Berengar's blushin too.

"Berengar, take Steady for a ride," says Erland. "You must be tired of sitting."

Berengar halts the cart, hands over the reins wi bad grace, an rides off. Erland swings himself up beside me.

"Nice to see you're over the cringing," he says. I look at him sideways. "Oh, don't start it again with me," he says. "These words Grimulf's having you learn. Do you know what they mean?"

"Berengar won't tell me," I mutter.

"Berengar's been brought up to this faith, and his father, and his father before that," Erland says. "He doesn't know what it's like to come to it new, and he thinks it's a sin not to have known it already. But people like us, Ebba, we come to it."

"You chose it?" I guess I thought he had no choice, bein the king's man.

Erland hears my surprise an smiles. "I first heard of the White God when I served King Arn," he says, "and I was with Prince Kolrand when he signed the treaty with the Southern Emperor saying he would take the White God as his master. I took the oath with him when he was crowned."

"So it's an oath I'm learnin?"

"Yes," says Erland. "A heavy one. So you should know what you're sayin. There's a reason our laws say children can't take oaths, and it's because a broken oath can be cause enough for death."

"I en't a child," I say.

For a moment his face is sad, but it passes so quick I think I must of bin mistaken.

"Then I'll teach you," he says.

Berengar don't come back all that day, though Erland says he's just huntin. He says to concentrate on the words. I learn em easy enough in our shared tongue, an though I don't understand all of it, there's a story wrapped inside of it. The White God's tongue is harder. The sounds are different, an without knowin what the words mean I get muddled. There's a rhythm to em, I can hear that, an when I say so Erland tells me they're chanted by believers in kirks. There are great stone kirks that hold hundreds, ten times higher than any hall, an the stone ringin wi voices as they chant. I think guiltily of Bloodnight, of the grove an the blood, the way it feels to be part of somethin bigger'n you.

The dusk comes quickly, the sun racin low over the horizon. In the forest it skulks between trees, makes the sky flush red between black branches. The ground's bin risin, an now the trees are pines, bare trunks wi dark, feathered tops. I remember crossin the pass on my way to Frithberg, so I know we're comin to it.

"Will we cross tonight?" I ask Erland, but he shakes his head. The soldiers are ridin up in ones an twos.

"They've found a camp for us," he says.

When we reach it, I see the camp has bin used recently. There's a fire pit, a neat store of wood, a long tetherin post. It could be the same spot where me an Ulf stopped on our way to Frithberg last year, an maybe Rafe laid his head here just a few days ago. Once the fire's goin I take out the bags of food an cook. One of the soldiers,

Adelhard, sits beside me preparin what's bin caught. He don't speak anythin but Southern, but I bin watchin, an I can see the soldiers are divided into two teams of four. Adelhard, short an broad-shouldered, is in charge of one, an the laughin fair-haired soldier, Medard, is in charge of the other. He smiles at me when he passes, an once or twice when I should of bin concentratin I was really tryin not to think about how he's like Jarle might be in a few years.

When the meal's ready, the men pass round their bowls, an I ladle food from the cauldron, the fire playin over our faces. Their smiles are a bit easier than yesterday, when they treated me so different, an in turn I unknot some, smile back. The last person I serve is Berengar. He don't meet my eyes, just pushes forward two bowls – one for him an one for the prester. I fill em like I don't mind his unfriendliness, but I find I do.

As we sit eatin there comes a howl, not too close, an we all stop to listen. Adelhard laughs an says somethin, an the others look at me an laugh too.

"What're they sayin?" I ask Erland, for I don't want to ask Berengar, who still won't look at me.

"They say you've been brought to live among hungry beasts," he says. "It's a joke. Them and the wolves, see?"

"That's what the prester said!" I say, an some of the soldiers, the ones wi bits an pieces of my tongue, turn to look. "At the feast."

"Mistress," says fair-haired Medard. "Country-wolves more safe than town-wolves." He looks pleased with himself, an says somethin in Southern tongue for the others, who laugh agreement.

Town-wolves, I think. *He means Aud an Sorleyson an Jarle.* I open my mouth but Erland's got hold of the back of my smock an is tuggin me back, his hand hidden from the others.

"Don't," he says, pleasantly.

I close my mouth. *I guess they mean Spraki an Lord Frithrun too,* I realise. *I wonder what they thought when they saw me brought me in like that to face the hound?* An for the first time I believe Erland a bit, that maybe if it had gone wrong, some of these men might of helped me.

"Mistress scare of wolves?" asks Medard.

I shrug. "They won't bother us this early," I say. "It en't even snowed yet."

Erland translates, an to my surprise the soldiers cheer.

"What did you tell em?" I ask.

"They liked your answer," he says.

"Brave Mistress," says Medard, smilin at me.

"All right Medard, that's enough —" Erland says, but he's interrupted by Berengar, who says somethin in Southern an spits into the fire.

There's a tense moment. I look between him an the others, not sure what's happened. Berengar sees me lookin.

"I said you are indentured," he says. "Of course wolves do not scare slaves."

"I'm not a slave!" I shout, jumpin up quicker'n Erland can stop me.

Erland drags me down, but the rest of the soldiers have jumped up now, all lookin at Berengar. My mouth drops open. This is new.

Medard says somethin sneerin to Berengar, whose cheeks flush red. *He blushes as easy as I do,* I think.

"What's this?"

The prester's voice rings out over the fire as he strides towards us, out of the dark woods.

As one, the soldiers hang their heads, lookin like guilty children. "Captain?"

Erland sighs. "A bit of over-excitement, Prester." He says somethin in Southern, an the soldiers stand to attention.

The prester's eyes fall on me, half hidden by Erland's side.

"The girl shouldn't be here, Captain. A soldiers' campfire is no place for her."

So I'm sent to my bed in the cart. Outside I can hear the prester speakin to the men in their tongue, while I wrap myself in a nest of straw an blankets, an then it's quiet, an I'm still too cold. I curl into myself, tryin to warm my fingers an toes. I think I hear howls again, but I might just be dreamin.

After a long cold time, I hear scrabblin at the cart's openin. I'm about to shout out, thinkin maybe the wolves are hungry after all, when a voice stops me.

"Ebba?"

"Who's that?" But I know it's Berengar. "What d'you want?"

"I am sorry."

"Go away."

"I brought you this."

He fumbles wi the openin an pushes somethin through. I take it. It's a rock, warm from the fire pit, wrapped in rags. I tuck it against my stomach, at the heart of my nest.

"Go away," I say again, but softer this time.

He goes.

I lie in the dark, tryin to recite the words of the oath, until I fall asleep. I can't tell you what I dream. I know the prester's there, an the hound, an maybe, somewhere at the back of everythin, Torny's there too. I just can't remember.

I wake early, at first light, an climb out to find the latrine. By the fire pit, the big cauldron lies on its side. When I go to look at it, I see it's bin licked clean. The pine needles are scuffled, an in a patch of mud I find a paw print. I cover the print with my own, an by the time the others wake, I've washed the cauldron, built up the fire, an started breakfast.

I look back once, when we're on the bare saddle of the pass. We're all on foot to spare the horses, the men takin turns to help push the cart up the last steep climb. The trees stopped a while back, an now we can see over their crowns to the plains.

Smoke rises in lines in the distance, a few late fields bein burnt of their stubble. Frithberg's kirk tower sticks up on its outcrop, black above the town's smoke, an the river loops around the kirkrock's foot, spoolin across the land to the dull grey sea. To the south the plains stretch hazily away, an to the north the Ridge rises like a dark wave, split by the Drovers Road. The hills beyond are a grey-green blur. Is that where Torny went with Blue Cloak? Back where she came from? Is that what her whalebone pin was meant to tell me? I raise my hand to my hair to touch the carved head.

This is the first time I've seen the west spread out like this. When Ulf brought me to Frithberg I stared as long as I could east, back towards Eldinghope, an when we crossed over I couldn't bear to look at the place I was goin.

Now I find it's just as hard to look towards home as it once was to look away.

It's all right, I tell myself. *You'll just be on the same side of the mountains. A bit closer to Ma. That's good, en't it? I thought you wanted to go home?*

So I look, even though I flinch from it, like the sight'll scorch me same as the prester's candle. The wind hits my face, bitterly cold. *Go back*, it seems to say, pushin against my body. *Go back.*

"This is your country, Ebba," says Erland, comin up beside me.

Is it? I wonder. *I wanted so badly to come back. An now . . . now it feels like a mistake.* I remember Rafe tellin me I must stay in Frithberg, an for a moment relief fills me. *That's why I feel bad!* I think. *He tole me not to come, an I here I am. But that was when Ulf wanted me to stay wi Sorleyson, to pay his debt, an now all that's changed. So I'm not really disobeyin him.*

But the relief I felt dies again, an the uneasiness is back. It stays even as we dip down into the trees, an the wind softens to a chill breath.

We stay on foot the rest of the day. I don't mind. It's easier than the joltin planks of the cart, an my new leather boots are snug. Erland calls me to him to practise the words of the oath, an hands me strips of the dried meat the soldiers eat. In the afternoon I'm made to practise the words in the White God's tongue wi Berengar, an he's more patient than yesterday, though he still clicks his tongue when I get it wrong. He's not friendly, but the memory of the warm rock keeps me from hurtin, an I don't mind so much that he won't look at me. Now I'm takin heed I can see it's worry that's eatin him, not anger.

The prester walks at the back of the train, slow an steady, but I feel his eyes on me. None of the other soldiers talk to me, though they sometimes smile quickly, out of the corner of their eyes, an I wonder if they can feel the prester watchin em too. Once Medard looks like he's goin to speak to me, but Berengar glares an Erland calls him away.

Dusk falls, but we keep movin. Torches are brought out of the cart, an we lead the horses in a train. Once one of the soldiers calls that he sees wolf-eyes, glitterin in the dark, but the others laugh at him.

It's true dark when we see a pale gleam in the black ahead. A soldier shouts, an Erland pushes to the front, then waves us on. The gleam en't a ghost, but the first of the silver birches that give Birchold its name. The trunks rise white an waverin in the dark, just a few at first, then growin thicker an thicker until the black pine trunks are forced out.

The people of Birchold know we're comin, it seems, though I don't know how. We come to a small village with a hall at the centre. I'm hustled into the arms of two women, their hair covered town-style in kerchiefs. They en't like Dagomar's maid, with her blank face an hard hands.

"Poor lamb," one of em coos, an even in my drowsiness I think, *No one ever called me that before.*

I'm put to bed. A real bed, not straw in a cart, not a bedroll on the floor, but a sweet stuffed mattress an clean blankets, an a sheepskin that smells of home. It's all I can do to sit upright while one of the women combs out my hair an hands me Torny's pin. Then I slip into a dark sleep girdled by pale white birches an glitterin eyes that howl lullabies.

I'm shaken roughly awake, an for a moment I think I'm back in Eldinghope, an this is Ulf come to punish me.

"No!"

"Be quiet."

I squirm away from the thick body blockin me in, but the heavy hand on my arm yanks me back.

I'm in the dark in a strange room, the prester sittin so close it's almost like bein crushed.

"Please," I say, tears chokin me. "Please don't."

"You have not been truthful with me, Ebba Rathnasdota," he says, an he squeezes my arm painfully. "You have lied to me."

Hot tears are coursin down my wet cheeks. I must of bin cryin in my sleep again. I feel the shame of it hot in me, unbearable, an more'n anythin I wish Torny were here wi me, her arm around me, her head up. *It's all right Ebba, I'm here.*

But she en't. I'm alone.

"You're no believer," the prester says. "You're as sinful as the rest of them. I've been watching you, girl, and I've seen the way you smile at the men – even Captain Erland, who is only trying to save you. No decent woman would act the way you do. What do you have to say for yourself?"

That en't true!

That's what Torny would say. But my mouth's bin sealed up, an my body's gone limp. My muscles en't got no strength in em. The prester pushes me back onto the bed in disgust.

My hand falls on somethin sharp.

Torny's pin.

I wrap my fist around it, runnin my thumb over the carved head.

"Don't hurt me," I say, my voice shakin, my fist clenched.

"I've done many things in the service of God," says the prester, standin, "but violation is not one of them. Commend yourself to God, girl, and get up."

My legs are weak, but I stand before him.

"Put this on," he says, holdin out somethin white in the gloom. I take it, feel it rough against my skin.

He don't turn, an I don't ask him to. This is part of it, I understand. It's dark, an my long hair covers my chest, but still my cheeks burn wi shame, an still it is a violation, whatever he says, to make me strip like this before him.

I pull the plain shift over my head, the pin still clutched in my fist. When I'm covered he steps towards me. He don't touch me, but he don't have to.

"You are filth," he says, soft an steady. "You are nothing, and you belong to me. Do you understand?"

I nod at once. I don't even need to think about it.

All my life, I've bin learnin this lesson.

"You will obey me," says the prester. "You will do everything I tell you. If I tell you to pray, you pray. If I tell you to die, you die. Do you understand?"

I nod, but in the dark I press the point of the pin into my thigh an I think, *No*.

An that surprises me. Maybe Torny's planted some of her courage like a weed in my obedient heart.

I'm goin to live, I tell myself.

The prester leads me out into the empty village. Somewhere there's a drum an a pipe, muffled by the forest. At the edge of the village a narrow path descends between the white-skinned trees, an the ground is cold under my bare feet.

The music is sweet an heady, an the path twists an opens. Red sparks fly upwards, an underneath em I see people swayin, their hands raised. I could be back in the Eldinghope grove on Bloodnight.

The music stops, an the people turn an part before us.

The prester leads me. Now I can see he's wrapped in his

red cloak, rich in the glow of embers. His white curls gleam. He raises his arms, an that voice rolls over us, like thunder over wheatfields.

"Good people of Birchold, I have brought you a sign from God! A child, sent to show you his great mercy in these troubled times."

What do they see when I step forward? An outlander, a half-breed? A girl? Or am I somethin else now, changed by the white shift, by the prester's hand on my shoulder, by his words?

The Blessed Walpurgis was a woman, Berengar said, who loved the White God so much she died for him. Maybe that is what the prester would make me.

But how can you love somethin you've never known?

Walpurgis makes the seeds grow, watches over the fields. She brings in the harvest, an we thank her. The Wise One stands at the gates of death, an every Bloodnight since I was old enough, save one, the blood of the sacrifices has marked my face as we welcome him. I know them, they protect us.

The White God I have never known, an when I say this oath that Erland has bin teachin me, it will be dead in my mouth. An yet I will be bound.

The prester is right. I'm a liar.

I let him press me forward again, to the heart of the crowd, an now I see where the sparks come from.

A long walk of red fire lies between the watchin men an women. The heat strokes my cheeks as the prester leads me to its edge. The sparks fly up an up, an at the far end a waterfall plunges into a pool.

"The true believer must be forged, like the sword on the

anvil," says the prester in my ear, "and all that is impure must be burnt out."

I look into the fire, an I see Uncle Ulf pullin back his arm for the blow, an Ma huggin Stig an laughin. I see Spraki grinnin with his bloody gums, an I feel the hot wet tongue of the hound on my palm, on the tender spot where the prester held my hand steady for the candle's kiss.

This is a lesson I've bin learnin all my life.

I'm ready.

Eyes up!

I look into the unfamiliar faces, an they stare back at me, wide-eyed, like they en't never seen the like of me before.

You en't, I think, clutchin the pin in my hand. *You think you can buy me, can hammer me, but I've got spears an swords inside of me. I din't break before, an I en't goin to now.*

Under the sky where night an dawn do battle, I step onto the burnin path.

My flesh shivers like it wants to crawl off me. I take a step, an my bare soles feel the warmth, but inside my blood has turned to steam. Another step, an my eyes are blinded by red mist. The heat lifts my hair, spreads it out, makes a dark cloud in the sparks.

Heat ripples over me like its own spirit, an I think death might be like this, a body meltin away like a cloud in summer.

Is this it?

With each step I'm waitin. If a god's goin to crawl inside of me, it'll be now.

But all I feel is the ash stingin my eyes, the smoke catchin in my lungs . . . an a strange peace, like a ghostly embrace. It's so strong I almost stop. Just for a moment I feel like if I stop, I might feel those arms, cradlin my whole body against everythin that's ever hurt me.

But my palm throbs, my head comes up, an I step on, quicker now, out of the peace of the shimmerin air an onto the hard cold ground of the grey dawn. My feet an calves are black with ash.

I turn an look back across the fire.

The silent villagers are frozen, their faces laid open for me. Now that I'm lookin properly I see the soldiers too. Erland's face is as bloodless as it was in Lord Frithrun's hall. Berengar's lookin at me strangely, half-fearful. I wonder if even the prester has fallen into this wonder – but no. The look he gives me is like a master whose dog has learnt a new trick.

For a moment, wi the fire between us, I think, *I could say anythin. He couldn't stop me, not right away.*

But what could I say? There's only one endin they'll believe.

So I open my mouth, an although my voice is choked from the ash, it grows stronger, an the White God's oath rolls from my mouth, his tongue on my tongue, flowerin like flames.

They listen.

Part of me thinks, *They don't even know what I'm sayin!*

An I see it don't matter. The wonder is stronger *because* they don't know. The oath en't dead. It's livin, burnin. I made it so.

I finish, an there's a moment of silence, stillness.

Then the spell breaks, an the prester comes forwards to claim me, his arms raised.

I can't help myself, I shrink from him.

A howl deeper than any wolf shakes the clearin. I feel it in my chest the same way I feel the prester's voice.

A long grey shape streaks over my head. It lands before

me, shakin off drops like starlight. It puts down its head, an growls.

The prester steps back. It's only one step, an he hides it well, but I see it.

The wolfhound crouches before me. Its long black lips are drawn back over its yellow fangs, but it's snarlin at the watchers, not me. It's protectin me. No one moves.

A sign from God, in these troubled times.

"Shhh," I say, wi what little breath I have. "It's me."

I kneel down an hold out my hands to be sniffed. When it's satisfied, the hound licks my hands an sits back on its haunches.

It's over.

The prester blesses us both, me an the hound, but he does so from a safe distance. Erland takes off his own cloak an wraps me in it, an the hound growls a little, to show he's allowin Erland to do it, an not to get too familiar.

One by one the villagers come forward an kneel before me, an I place my hands on their head an say the words Erland tells me. The prester stays across the fire, as if he knows not to come too close, an he tells the story of how I healed the faithful hound, in a house of men who wished to kill me. It's more or less the way I remember.

He says, "She wrapped it in sheepskin. She tamed the beast. She made the wolf a lamb."

Ten

BURIAL

TORNY'S TALE

Hill Country, near Sleeper's Howe

ambtail! Wake up!"

My nose crinkles, full of fumes. I look blearily into Galen's grinning face and yawn, turning my face into Hero's rough white mane. I drag myself upright and see the sun's past noon.

Great. Now I've started falling asleep during the day too. I pat Hero, thanks for not dumping me while I dozed, and she wickers.

Galen's been drinking again. The ale skin flops at his belt, almost empty.

I wonder what will happen when he runs out.

"What are you so pleased about?"

"Din't you wonder why you hadn't fallen off yet?" He grins wider, and spreads his arms.

That's when I see we're on a path, and not just a sheep trail.

It's wide enough for two riders side by side, and it runs along the top of a bank between two deep ditches. It's grassy, not packed earth and mud, so I guess no one comes here much. In this hilly land it runs straight and level between the slopes.

Galen's almost bouncing in the saddle. This morning I could tell he was looking for something again, that he had some kind of plan, but I was still groggy from my third night in the grey mists.

"What is it?" I ask.

"We used to call it the Corpse Road," he says.

"That's a nice name for a road," I say, biting down the giggles that are welling up inside me.

"Are you fevered?" Galen asks suspiciously.

I shake my head.

"Just tired," I say.

I wish Ebba were here to laugh with me.

"You'll see why when we get there." Galen sees my mouth opening and guesses my question. "We're nearly out of the hills," he says. "We'll cross the Floodlands tomorrow."

Good. It's not just thoughts of soldiers that needle me now. Under my ribs, the hook of my homesickness tugs me North.

I wonder if this is what the gulls feel, flying back to their nests in the spring. I've decided it can't be what Ebba feels. If she felt this, she would have left the wayhouse, would have walked all the way home by herself, no matter what anyone ordered. No matter who waited for her.

I miss Ebba. If she were here I bet she'd know what herbs would help me in the mornings, when the mists leave me beached and weak. I could tell her about my dream, the way it feels to be battered night after night with the same question, the same struggle. Maybe she would hold me, the way I used to hold her, and I could bury my face in her thick hair, take comfort in her warmth.

When she came to the wayhouse last autumn, her dreams woke me every night. At first I didn't understand. It took a while to find out what was happening. During the day, the way she talked about them, you would have thought her family was just like any other. It was only at night, after the dreams woke her and we were lying together in the dark, that she'd say anything about that uncle of hers.

It made me angry. Sklep tried to marry me to Thorpe, and he sheared me for fun, but really he just wanted me out from under his roof. But Ebba's uncle wanted to keep them there, all of them, and beat them and marry them off, and no doubt keep beating them if he could. It drove me wild that Ebba never saw how wrong it was. She'd talk about how she'd go home when the harvest was better, and marry whoever they'd chosen, and when I told her to make her own way and pay back her uncle with whatever she earned, she laughed and said I was a typical Northerner, full of sea-wind.

"Farmers know you don't just pay off a debt like that," she said. "I owe him every mouthful I've had since my Da died."

Every mouthful. And Ebba came to Frithberg with not much flesh on her, believe me.

But being out here, no chores, no family . . . I feel free.

I wish we could be free together.

Galen stops, bringing me back. I look up, and shiver.

Ahead of us the hills open out around a wide valley. The raised road drives straight down the middle. The ditches are gone, and standing stones line the path, each as high as my waist. To either side rise long, low barrows, like the kind in the old burying ground at Frithberg, but bigger, and much older.

The road ends at the foot of a hill.

The hill is unnaturally regular, rising straight up from the flat valley floor. The afternoon sun shines down on it, and its grass seems lusher, greener. Up near the summit I can see a slash of earth-red, as if the turf's been lifted away.

"Corpse Road," I say, understanding. This valley is an ancient burying ground.

"That's Sleeper's Howe," says Galen, nodding at the hill.

"It looks like someone's tried to open it," I say.

Galen frowns. "No one's idiot enough to do that," he says.

I glance at the barrows on either side of us. Some of their doorways are blocked with a door-stone, but others stand open, their dark passages gaping.

I look questioningly at Galen.

"We buried some of our own here," he says gruffly.

"You opened them?" I ask, shocked.

"Of course not," Galen says. "We found them empty. Prince Geir ordered that those of us who fell in battle should be laid to rest here, among comrades, ready for the Great Hall. Using an empty tomb, that's different. You'd have to be a fool to open one yourself."

"Why?"

"Sleeping's better than walking, when it comes to the dead."

But he takes a deep draught of the spirits in his nearly-empty skin, and the way he looks at the barrows makes me wonder what he's thinking. A buzzing fills my ears, and a clatter like weapons against shields. I shake my head to clear it and it's gone.

"Was that you?" I ask, touching the packet of hair under my shirt.

"What?"

"Nothing," I say, because I wasn't talking to Galen. But I get no answer from the dead man either, no prickles or pinches.

As we reach a barrow near the foot of Sleeper's Howe, Galen dismounts and stands before it. He takes the ale skin from his belt and upends it, pouring the last of the golden liquid into the grass before the barrow's stone doorway. He says something, but too softly for me to hear him. I guess he's greeting those he knew, the ones he helped bury here. By the time I've tethered the mares, he's gone to the back of the barrow and reappears with two spades and some wedges. Supplies like the shelter, maybe, for times of need.

"We can bury him here," he says, passing me a spade. "He can join his comrades in the Great Hall."

"He was one of you?"

"We served the same master," he says, and unconsciously he raises his left wrist to his breastbone.

"Do you think this will work?" I ask.

Galen turns to me, but I don't think he sees me. It's as if he's looking through me, and although the sun catches in the red-gold of his beard, his lips are pale and bloodless.

"Everything I ever loved is here," he says. "If there was some way I could die here and now, with honour, I would take it."

The way he says it turns me cold.

As he stoops to set a wedge between the door-stone and the lintel, I feel the dead man grip my throat. It's sudden and silent, cutting off all air. I flail out, hitting Galen's shoulder. He turns and grabs me as my knees buckle, but the blood is thumping in my temples, and I can't draw breath.

I turn to crawl away from the barrow, and the grip releases me as suddenly as it came. I choke on the air rushing into my lungs, and Galen drags me up to sitting. I turn to the horses but the grip comes again, hard and merciless, and lights dance before my eyes. Under the thumping of my blood there's the thrum of the bullroarer, the clash of metal —

Galen pulls me back round to face him. The grip loosens again.

"What do you *want*?" I cry, my eyes watering and my throat raw. The chill air hurts as I breath in. "I don't understand —"

I look over Galen's shoulder. The howe rises behind him.

"Oh *no*," I say.

It's easy enough to check. Each time I try to walk away from Sleeper's Howe, my throat closes violently, dropping me to my knees.

Galen gets more and more jittery. For a moment he looks like he doesn't believe me, and I wonder if he's going to drag me away, but he seems to remember what happened when he tried to force me to talk yesterday.

"If I had a choice, I'd take it," I tell him.

"You do have a choice," he says grimly.

"Dying of choking is not a death I want," I snap.

"You might be glad of it, rather than wake whatever's in there."

We both look at the hill. Of course I know the stories. Corpses bloated blue-black with rot, rising to defend their hoards. Sharp-toothed ghouls feasting on thieves' flesh. Galen said all the barrows had been opened, but this one sits undisturbed. Even grave robbers knew it wasn't worth the risk.

"Come on," I say. "Maybe it's already been opened."

We don't speak as we climb the steep green sides. There's

a fresh-trod path zig-zagging up the side. Glancing over my shoulder, I see the straight line of the Corpse Road stretching between the rolling hills. The sun hangs almost directly over the western end of the road.

Just below the crest the path ends in a narrow ledge before a door. Like the barrow doorways, it's made of two posts and a lintel, with a fourth stone laid across them, but unlike the barrows, these stones are still red with traces of the earth that covered them. The jagged lines of the green turf stand out against the fresh red soil, but it's the door-stone itself that catches my eye.

Against the red-smudged surface, a newer carving stands out. The cut rock is pale, and the carving is not particularly skilful, but it's clear enough. A snake eating its own tail.

Galen steps back so quickly I have to grab him to keep him from tumbling off the narrow ledge. His face is grey under his beard, and his eyes are rimmed with white. He shakes me off.

"We have to go," he says.

"I can't," I say, grabbing him again as my throat clenches in warning.

He turns unseeing eyes on me, then looks again at the snake. "They're here," he says, and his voice breaks. I can't tell if he's scared or excited. "All these years —"

"Galen! I need you. You don't have to go in, but please, wait for me."

But his eyes are wandering past me, out over the valley to the north.

"I'll not wait here," he says. "Down there, look. I'll wait for you there." He points to the north, where a path leads from the valley between two hills.

"I thought you said you wished you could die here?" I ask, as icily as I can manage.

That seems to cut through to him.

"With *honour*," he says. "Whatever you do, don't take anything, or you'll wish you'd choked."

And that's it. He turns and hurries down the path.

I watch him go, my fists clenched. I want to yell after him that he's a coward. That it's not my fault this dead man he knew in life has become such a bastard in death. I want to beg him not to leave me, with the sun already in the west. But there's no point.

I look down at the spade in my hand. It has runes carved on the handle, but they're the normal inscription: *Thorkel made me.* Nothing magical. I sigh. A magical spade probably wouldn't have helped anyway.

I knock the large wooden wedges into place between the door-stone and the post-stones. Using the spade, I hammer them in, flinching at the metal ringing against stone. I think I hear the bullroarer again, and voices howling. I'm soaked in sweat, and not just from the work. The sinking sun on my back is the only comfort I have.

The flat stone judders open, and I lever it wide enough to creep through. Grasping Thorkel's spade, I walk out of the sun's reach and into the earth.

The tunnel is close and dry, running straight and then sloping down and to the right. I thought I was going to have to feel my way along, but instead of pitch black, the walls and floor are shades of very dark grey. If I look directly at them, everything seems dark, but if I look ahead, they swim into sight at the edges.

"Are you doing that?" I ask the dead man quietly, but I get no answer.

The passage curves onwards and downwards. I notice that the tug under my ribs is shifting as I follow the passage. If the tug is pulling me North, then this passage must be a spiral, like the whorl in a seashell, digging down into the heart of the hill. My eyes have got used to gazing ahead, and now I glimpse earth walls shored up with wood and stones to each side of me.

The first block I come to isn't much – I almost walk into it in the gloom. Sharpened staves have been planted in the ground across the passage, tilted slightly away from me, downhill. They remind me of the palisade at Frithberg, only smaller. I climb over them awkwardly, avoiding the sharpened points. A thought nags at me, but then I see something glimmer out of the corner of my eye. It's gone before I catch it, but as I follow the curve of the passage, something rises through the soles of my feet.

Whuuuuuuum ... Whuuuuuuum ... Whuuuuuuum ...

It's the bullroarer, and this time it enters my bones first, bypassing my ears, and I feel my whole body buzzing. It washes over me, then fades.

I want it to come again. While it filled me, I felt no tug to the North, no pain in my throat, no ache in my muscles. I didn't miss home and I didn't miss Ebba. Now it's gone, I feel all those things sharply.

Ebba, I think, but then the glimmer comes again. This time it seems to have a ripple to it, a texture. I follow it, and come to the second barrier.

This time the passage is completely blocked. By touch, I guess it's a hurdle, like the kind we use for fencing, woven from split branches and daubed in mud. I put my shoulder to it and push. It gives a little, and I shove harder. The dry mud crumbles, and dust fills my mouth.

It's salty. I roll the dust on my tongue, and I can feel the rough crystals of salt mixed into the fine mud before I spit it out. I unwrap the scarf from my hair and tie it over my mouth and nose, then get to work. It takes a while, but the spade is solid, and the hurdle is very old and dry. The dust settles all over me, mixing with my sweat and dripping into my eyes, stinging. The salt in my mouth burns my tongue, makes me thirsty.

I step through. The air behind this barrier is different, stale and thick, dragging through my lungs like smoke. I can't seem to breathe deep enough. I start to turn back, to stick my head through the remains of the barrier into the upper passage where I can breathe freely. A warning clench of my throat stops me, so instead I take off the scarf and beat out as much dust as I can before tying it on again.

The passage ends in a doorway of stones like the one at the top of the hill, except the two stones to either side of the opening have niches carved into them. In each niche sits the long, white skull of a horse, resting at head-height. They look out at me like sentinels. Beyond them I can dimly make out an open chamber. At the centre are slabs of stone, set against each other, propping up the ceiling. I take three steps towards them before my throat closes.

The dead man's grip has become familiar, but it still makes lights pop and dance before my eyes, still fills my veins with the blood-roar.

Through streaming eyes, I look around for the problem.

At my feet, a line of fist-sized white pebbles blocks my way.

I cast around, trying to unfocus my gaze as I survey the chamber from the corner of my eyes. The whole floor is lined with pebbles, in long curved lines.

It's a labyrinth. The standing stones form a sort of chamber in the centre of it, and all around them the pale lines ripple and shift under my ghost-given sight.

All right, I think. *I know how these work. I follow the path, and the path leads me to the middle.*

My mouth dry from the salt, my throat raw from the grip, and my lungs fighting the heavy air, I start to trace out the path.

Following the uneven white lines calms me. I'm thrumming, not with the bullroarer's overpowering buzz this time, but with a deep, steady hum. It starts so low that I only notice it when I realise how painless my body has become. There are no twitches, no pulls, just steady movement, almost like I'm floating. The labyrinth's path leads me round, circling, doubling back on myself, and where at first I saw only an open room, now I see the pebble-lines are as solid as walls, leading me on a journey whose route is invisible, and whose destination is known, but never directly approached. I almost forget the stones at the centre, waiting for me.

I lose all sense of time. I think sunset must have come and gone in the world above, but down here there's no light, no change in the air, no sounds except the hum that seems to fill me from the inside, and the hum doesn't waver, doesn't pause for breath. It warms me in this silent place, it seems to be the same stuff as the wavering white lines, as the waiting stones that I creep towards. Now and then I catch a flickering glow on the dark, distant walls, like the rippling light that led me down the passage.

When I finally come to the stones, the space between them glows. I hesitate, thinking of those bloated corpses from the stories, but the floating feeling pulls me forward, pulls me into the stone chamber, and into the light.

The body is lit up as if lying in sunshine, although there's no source of light. It wears an open helm and gold-washed armour, both dulled by time. On its chest lies a round, polished mirror, the skeletal hands crossed over it. The feeling of floating is gone, and I stand looking down on the withered thing. No horror, just sprawled bones.

The body is lying on a chariot of some kind, taken apart and piled up to form a bier. The wheels lie at the body's head, and around them are pots and metal cups, all broken or dented.

Nothing's been left whole. The armour, the helm are both damaged, and a broken sword lies at the body's side.

I turn to the foot of the bed, noting crushed gold rings and scattered beads, and that's when I see the other body.

This one is smaller, curled up. No weapons or armour, but mixed in among the bones are golden bangles and beads on rotting leather tack.

What was done to the sword, and the chariot, and the rest of the goods, was done to this body too. The bones are small, and curled the way a dog lies at its master's feet.

But it's not a dog.

It's a child.

Anger floods through me, blotting out the warm hum. I reach out to touch the child's skull, and a jolt travels through me, blinding me for a moment.

I see a young boy; his face is blurred but I make out dark hair and lively eyes. I feel the hot, sweaty sides of the horses he cares for, and their sweet-grass breath on his skin, and the pure joy of riding them. I feel the weight of the gold bangles at his wrists and ankles. I feel his love for the one who holds him and pets him, who tells him he is her joy, her guide. And then I feel the hands that hold him, and a bitter drink, and the sharp kiss of the the knife in his throat and his blood gushing into the bowl where the drink was before, and finally, just as the last beat of his heart joins mine, I feel the land all around me, the dozens of men in their barrows, the earth piled over my head, the cold, grey presence of the dead man at my shoulder, and something dark stirring behind me, on the ancient wooden bier.

I whip round to face the body, but of course it hasn't moved. I bite down the fear and look hard at it, this gilded mound of bones.

"You had so much," I say. "And everything you had was put here for you." I remember the sentinel skulls at the entrance. "Even your horses joined you. You could have left him alive. You'd still have had all of this —"

And I look up. And on the stone ceiling, reflecting a light that can't be real, is a flickering glow, flung upwards by the mirror.

The one thing in the chamber that isn't broken.

Maybe it's spite. Maybe it's greed.

Ebba would say it was stealing.

I reach out, and take it.

My fingers barely brush the warrior's chest, but my body jolts again with another rush of images, and the rotted wood collapses, tumbling bones, armour, sword and goods into a dusty heap on the ground. The bullroarer starts, growing louder and louder, and I try to block my ears. I push my way out of the stone chamber, the mirror clasped tightly to my chest, and stare hopelessly across the coils of labyrinth. The door is right in front of me, but I'm stuck, trapped by the snaking white lines and the disembodied grip on my throat. Behind me I feel that stirring again, and the thought that nagged at me as I crossed the first barrier comes back, fully formed.

The labyrinth – a barrier of salt – the line of stakes pointing downwards – they were trying to keep something *in*.

Fear stronger than anything I've ever known fills me, freezing me solid.

Galen was right, I think. *I should have let the dead man choke me.*

Something moves in the doorway. This time I do scream, because someone is moving towards me, leaping over the white lines. They land beside me, and I look down into lively eyes under dark hair.

"I'll lead you," says the boy from my vision. "Follow me. *Quick.*"

Eleven

FAITH

THE PRESTER'S TALE

Birchold

There are times when the Lord calls, and we must answer.

The young imagine this call to be a glorious thing; a light breaking through clouds, a sweet horn inviting them to the battle they have longed for all their short lives. I see it in the faces of the initiates, as they pray in the darkest hours of the night, and in the scribe bent at his desk, his brush loaded with gold, bringing light to the page as the Lord brought light to the world. They yearn for it, and it does not come.

That is why we must have faith.

The Lord leads us on strange, untrodden paths, and we must follow. At new moon I lay in my own apartments in the palace at Sunacre, close by the king's chambers, and my head was busy with matters of state: which lord's daughter might suit his highness as a queen; how to keep the army from boredom; whether new trade might bring us the wealth required for new churches, new followers. I was comfortable, I had influence – and then came the merchants' letter, and with it the scrawled parchment, marked in blood.

Now I lie in a hut so ill-made the moonlight shines between the hinges, and my bed is a heap of straw mattresses (two, because they honour me) and a rough wood frame. I share this palace with an ignorant child and her cur. The beast is always between us, and I know why.

My Lord has many enemies.

I close my eyes and see Dagomar's letter, the parchment he sent with it: the uneven circle, the gaping mouth. The snake that devours itself. That alone was enough to bring me to Frithberg, to the edge of civilisation.

And then . . .

Heavy in my palm lies the golden horse, weighing on my thoughts.

I believed myself free of these things, but if I have learnt anything since coming to Arngard, it is that here the dead walk. One cannot call any matter closed while still there are those who will talk of it.

The straw itches, the wind blows through the hinges, but I am here, and I will not turn from this.

Do not long for toil other than that which is set before you. So I learned at my foster father's table, long before I was anything but a snot-nosed brat, and an outland brat to boot.

Well might I wish that I had been the first-born son, not the second, so that my brother might take my place in the Southern lord's home, that I might not face extinction if the peace treaty between my people and theirs was not honoured. Well might I wish to be a boy in Arn's land, learning nothing but hunting and war, speaking unthinking in my own tongue, instead of a child in imperial Vellsberg, where not one but three tongues are needed, and to grow them requires daily beating.

But it was my lot, and no other's, to be sent as a hostage into the home of my enemy, and mine to bear the beatings until the tongues of Empire and Church lay obedient in my mouth. And the peace held, so I lived, and old Lord Vellsberg, my enemy, became a better father to me than my own. He could not bequeath me any worldly wealth, so he gave me those things that cannot be taken: learning, ambition and humility.

It took me longer to acquire humility than the others. I despised my people for giving me up as surety, but most of all I resented my foster brother. He seemed to me unlordly: cautious, meticulous, uninterested in war. I thought that I should be a better lord than he, and his father saw it and laughed at me.

"You would ruin Vellsberg," he told me one day, when I was nearing manhood, "or she would ruin you. She is the mistress of merchants and trade, and she requires peace to prosper, while you desire conquest."

He had called me into his study, and I stood while his page poured hot spiced wine into two goblets. My lord sat half-turned from his desk under the south west windows, and I remember how the light fell in scales through the thick glass, speckling the pages of account books and the side of his face.

"The only war you could wage here would be against your own people," he said, taking a goblet the young boy offered him, "and no man can do that without paying a heavy price. But this stretch of the border has been quiet these ten years and, God willing, so it will remain."

I knew it had not been quiet elsewhere. I knew there were boys and young men, second sons like me, sent to other lords whose lands bordered Arn's, who had been deemed expendable by their families. I comforted myself that at least my family had cared well enough not to provoke my murder at the hands of the man who had raised me.

Sometimes I wondered how he would kill me, if they ever stopped caring. Would he do it himself? Would my head be sent to my family as proof? Would they know me?

"Vellsberg needs a bookkeeper, not a warrior," my lord said. "Do not begrudge my son his birthright, for he is suited to it."

"I have no birthright, suited or otherwise," I said. It came out more bitterly than I meant it to.

"That is your freedom," said my foster father, "and you would be a fool to wish it away. Vellsberg would do you no good, you are too bold, and accounts bore you. I suppose I could have kept you unlettered and savage, and returned you as you came to me, but I hate waste. You are a man of the Empire now, not some backwater chieftain, and your father's lands, were you to have them, would be a millstone around your neck. You like power, Grimulf. Neither of the inheritances you covet would provide it. I suggest the Church."

And Lord forgive me, I laughed. I will not say what I told him then, for though pride is a sin, yet must a man be allowed a little. We are all ignorant when we are young.

My lord laughed too.

"Tell me," he said, "at whose feet do I kneel every day?"

From then on, I watched. I saw my lord and all his family kneel before the bishop, and heard him praised and chastised during the sermons. The bishop sat at his right hand when he held council and when he passed judgement, and when letters came from the Emperor's court to Vellsberg, the bishop received his own, sealed and heavy, and secret from everyone, my lord included.

In my eighteenth year, when my birth family did not send for me, I was among the initiates on my knees before the bishop, my head shorn, my lordling clothes replaced with sombre habits. To renounce the lands I had never known was no great loss, but to renounce the sword, the horse, the hawk on my fist . . . these things were dear to me, they told me who I was and what I might do. Without them I felt naked. To bend my head in submission not to my lord, whose authority was plain, but to a God who had never shown the least interest in me – how little I knew then! – was hardest of all.

I see now how well my foster-father equipped me. I did not know it, but I had already been taught submission beneath the blows of my masters. I learned quickly and well. Already I could speak and write the church-tongue, while many of my fellows laboured at it, and I soon learned to recite the holy texts. At first they were little more to me than the blocks with which to build my future, but you cannot carve words in your mind without their meaning shaping you.

I learned that though I had renounced battle, the God I served loved warriors just as well as the devil of deceit they worshipped in the North. My God's words became a sword, ready in my mouth and in my hand. The faith that sprang in my breast as His words filled me became a shield, and His promise was a helm. It covered my head, and showed me the path that would lead me to its fulfilment. I learned that there is another battle, a constant battle, beneath our daily lives, and I too longed to be called.

And one day, the call does come. It comes not as we kneel in the dark, not as we ache at our toil, but when we are quite comfortable. When, perhaps, our faith has led us to a hilltop where we can see our works, and the good of them, and we know there is more good work to be done. Then comes the call, and then it is the hardest to obey.

Birchold is the first village of the East, the gateway of the mountains. After the Treaty of Frithberg was signed and the kirk built, merchants like Dagomar needed reassurance that the route to the East was secure. Birchold converted, and now its wealth comes from housing the merchants' agents and the yearly convoys of grain. From here the faith has spread east. I have not been here since the conversion. It has changed. When I first came, Birchold was a wretched place. They traded charcoal and barkpaper, and its people were half-starved. Now they have a long barn to house the caravans, and a shrine to Saint Walpurgis, and their headman has even built himself a hall.

On the first day, I order the girl to be cleaned and put to bed. The hound will not leave her, nor be leashed, so they put them both in the hut we are to share, and I call the headman to me in the hall.

"We are blessed," I say, before he can begin to babble his thankfulness. "The Lord is capable of many wonders, but to witness one is a rare honour."

"Indeed," he says, hands clasped. "I believe my people have

already sent word to our neighbours of the great good fortune we've been visited with."

I smile. "And so the work of the Lord is made plain," I say. He bobs his head. "Tell me, has the barn been cleaned?"

"Not yet, my lord," says the headman, frowning.

"It must be done today."

"My lord?"

I beckon him closer. I can see the nits moving in his unwashed hair.

"This child is a beacon of hope," I say, "and many will flock to her. They will come to be healed." He nods, face blank. "They will need somewhere to stay," I say, and at last understanding dawns.

It is like speaking to children.

"I'll have the barn cleaned right away, my lord," he says. Rubbing his hands, his hair twitching with vermin, he winks at me.

I smile. I have learned to smile, to hide my distaste.

"Very prescient of you," I say.

This is the first way she will serve me. I have no qualms about that. When I first met her, I recognised the signs of obedience thoroughly taught. She was prepared for me, the perfect tool. Demure, uneducated, pretty enough to inspire, but not to incite. Soft-hearted Erland tells me she was beaten by her master in Frithberg, but Erland plays big brother to everyone, and even after all these years, his compassion blinds him.

It is the work of a family, not strangers, that instills such dependable submission.

And that is the second service she will render.

I summon Erland and his two lieutenants. The Vellsberg boy

spreads out the maps, and Erland dismisses him. I see a spark of defiance in the boy's eyes, but it burns out immediately. He may be of noble blood but he has been born and bred to weakness. Just like the rest of his family.

Beneath my hands spread the Eastern farmlands. How different from the first map of Arngard I ever saw, with its blank stretches of unfilled parchment, its unknown reaches. The merchants have prepared this one, and their work is thorough.

There between the northerly spur of the mountains and the sea lies Eldinghope. Above it shelter the dales, inhospitable and sparsely populated, but Eldinghope itself covers more land than many lords lay claim to. Rich land, too. Dagomar reckoned that the grain from Eldinghope's fields accounts for a third or more of all the grain from the East.

The only difference between a wealthy farmer and a warlord is the tools his people wield.

Adelhard and Medard receive their orders without comment, but I see the fire in them, clear as day. What they witnessed at dawn has entered them, and now they do the Lord's work.

"Are you sure it's Eldinghope?" Erland asks me as his men leave.

"I am certain."

"There are other farms in these lands . . ."

"But none so wealthy."

"The war did not cross the mountains."

"But men did, and they fought and died for the East, though they did it on the plains. There is even some suggestion that *she* came from the East, did you know that?"

Of course he did. Poor, soft-hearted Erland.

"We have been brothers a long time, you and I," I say softly.

"The Lord brought us together to protect and uphold the innocent. I would no more seek to bring suffering to these people than I would have given up our young prince to his doom ten years ago."

"I know," says Erland. "Forgive me, Grimulf. But this could start it all again. I am loath to relive those times."

I clasp his forearm hard. "I long for peace, brother. But this is a cancer. It breeds beneath the skin, and to save the whole it must be cut out. Even now our orders will have been received, your men will have embarked. We cannot halt this."

Erland sighs. "I'm worried for the girl. If anyone is innocent, she is, and yet if what you say is true . . ."

"I know." I rest my hand on his shoulder, still gripping his forearm. "To confront evil in strangers requires only righteousness. To confront it in one's own kin leaves a wound that never truly heals."

I've been with him so long, I can follow his thoughts as if they were my own: the terrified boy Kolrand, brought to Erland by his mother in the dead of night, and her refusal to flee. Her murder at the hands of Geir's Slipskins, and Erland powerless to prevent it, bound by his oath to protect the child. The snake daubed in blood on the door of her chamber, still eating its tail when we returned months later, an army at our heels.

"Come," I say, clapping him on the shoulder. "Have faith. We have been shown wonders, these last few days. Let us pray for one more – a bloodless peace."

Erland nods, and I watch him walk ahead of me towards the shrine, his head bowed.

There is no such thing as peace without blood. You would have thought Erland, of all people, knew that.

I did not go to the court of King Arn because I was called. I went because I was the missing piece, with my mouthful of tongues, my sword and my book. King Arn was no longer young. He had spent his life uniting lands under his name, marrying a Northern lord's daughter, cajoling and crushing, marrying again when his first wife died, and now he had a kingdom that bore his name, and he was learning, as his hair turned grey, that a king can never rest, can never call his lands secure.

Arn had decided to accept the Emperor's patronage, and I was charged with negotiating the terms. By then I was in my prime. I had entered the Church twenty years before, and I had even served at the Emperor's summer court at Ban Granis. I had fought for the Empire against the uprising among the Qesar, and I had some experience of command, but my lack of lands or income told: I watched younger, better connected men surpass me, enter bishoprics, become patrons in their turn.

My foster-father secured me the role of negotiator. *No one has bothered to barb their tongue by learning the babble of the Northerners,* he wrote to me, *and the Northerners themselves are too insular to imagine another tongue than their own might be necessary. All understanding rests in you.*

I knew what he was telling me. Any hope of advancement lay there, in the cold North, in the lands and people that had disowned me. Without their submission to the Empire, I would forever be orphaned.

That evening, when the girl awakens, she is brought to me in the shrine, and I explain what she is going to do.

"The Lord is with you," I tell her. "He held you as you passed through the flames. You have a calling."

The hound growls, but she places a hand on its neck – the brute's head comes to her shoulder – and it quiets. She has a sweet solemnity, her dark hair loose, her brown eyes cast demurely down. If I did not know what I do – if I had not seen the fire-walking trick done before, many times, in the festivals in the South, or if I had not seen her smile and blush at Medard's advances – even I might see something saintly in her.

"All you need to do is repeat the oath to me when I ask you for it," I tell her. "I will bless you, and then you will stand here, and the people will come to you for healing."

"What if I can't heal em?" she asks, her voice burred with the Eastern drawl. I will have to teach her to speak properly before I take her back to Sunacre, should it come to that.

"No one expects miracles of you, child," I say. "Place some of your salve on the place where the hurt is, or on their forehead, and bless them in the Lord's name."

"But the salve —"

"The salve is the agent of faith," I cut her off. "As are you. It is their faith in God that will heal them. Not you, not your salve. You may be the Salvebearer, but in truth you bring them salvation. Do you understand?"

She presses her lips together and nods. A lie, I'm certain, but all she needs to do is follow instructions.

"Good." I beckon in the village woman who has appeared by the door. "This is Mistress Una. She will house the sick who come to us. When you leave the shrine, you are to accompany her to visit them, and offer comfort and prayers. Mistress, is the barn ready?"

"It will be, my lord," says the woman, dropping a curtsey. She is like the servants at Sunacre, respectful and sensible.

"Prepare food for the Salvebearer," I tell her. "She will eat in her room, not in the hall."

"Of course." The woman curtseys again and leaves.

"I will present you twice a day," I tell the girl, "three times if necessary. Of course your hound must be with you. He is part of your story. When your duties are done, you will stay in the cottage. The Vellsberg boy will be your guard." From what I've observed, he has little regard for her. I need not fear any closeness between them. "He can instruct you in the lives of the saints." Maybe the little heathen will learn something from them. "You remember what I told you before you went to the fire?"

She blushes, and the hound growls again, but she silences it, and nods.

"Yes," she says.

"Yes what?"

"Yes, Father," she says, dropping her eyes. Her fist clenches in the hound's mane, and I can't help smiling.

"Very good, my child. Now go. You must eat and sleep, for you will have work enough come tomorrow."

The hound growls again as she leaves, but I don't let it worry me. A hound is only a hound, and I can be rid of it when I need to be. For now let her have her companion, her protector. When it is gone she will be all the more alone.

In charge of a circus of scribes and soldiers, I spent my last night on imperial soil in Vellsberg, the home of my childhood. I had seen bigger towns by then, all more ancient and more beautiful than the small border town I grew up in, but as we entered the valley, the early autumn sun turned the Vell river golden, and the city walls glowed warmly, and my heart grew light.

My foster-brother Theogault received me in his father's study, his hands ink-stained like a clerk's.

"My father's ill," he said, without further greeting, and I knew it must be bad if the old lord could not even descend one flight of stairs to his study. "I'll take you to him in a minute."

He held out his hand for the sealed letters I carried, but I didn't hand them over.

"Is he too ill to read?" I asked.

Theogault barked with laughter.

"Father's been blind these last two years," he said. "Not that you'd know. I read everything to him." He looked me up and down. "You look more like a barbarian than ever."

I held my tongue. If my foster-father was close to death, the time when I could rely on his influence would soon be past, and my foster-brother would be my only link to the Vellsberg name. As it was he knew all that I had thought private in those letters between my foster-father and me.

Theogault raised an eyebrow. "Don't tell me you learnt manners while you were away?" he said. "Wonders never cease. Wine."

A small boy got down from a stool at the narrow scribe's desk next to Theogault's. His hands were no better than his lord's, and the white cuffs of his undershirt were also ink-spattered. Theogault caught me looking at them as the boy poured wine.

"He has a good hand," he said, and the child blushed with pleasure. "Maybe he can be a monk, like you."

I bit back my irritation while Theogault broke the seals, and the child returned to sharpening quills. Theogault ignored me as he read, and when he set the letters aside, it was only to say, "Your escort arrived today. I put them in the stables where the smell can't upset anyone."

"I would like to pay my respects to Lord Vellsberg," I said.

Theogault's mouth twisted upwards. He gestured me to follow him up the stairs set into the study's wall.

I had never been into my foster-father's chamber before. There, in a heavy oak bed, lay what was left of the Lord of Vellsberg.

His strong frame had withered, and the skull stood out under the skin. His eyes were watery and unfocused, the whites yellowed, but by then I had seen his mouth, and I was glad he was blind.

The right side of his face sagged, dribble spilling from the corner of his mouth. His right arm lay useless on the covers, and I knew that he had been visited by the half-death, that curse that only the saints can lift.

"My lord," I said, seating myself on the bed beside him.

The left side of his mouth turned up, and he gurgled.

The shock of that was worst of all, and I couldn't hide it, even though I knew Theogault would take pleasure in it.

"Does he know me?" I asked, and Theogault shrugged.

But the Lord of Vellsberg raised his left hand and felt for me, and I took it, and he gurgled again, and would not let me go, so that Theogault turned sullen and left me there with the all-but corpse of the only father I ever knew.

My foster-father's grip was strong, and he gave little grating cries when I tried to leave, so that after a while I stopped, and faced him as a man, my pity and my grief heavy in me. Instead of running I began to speak, and I thanked him for all he had done for me, and I told him I would honour Theogault as I had honoured him. Then, as he still held me, I told him about the court and the towns where I had served, the things I had seen and done. I even told him how my heart had lifted seeing Vellsberg again, and he squeezed my hand tightly.

I left when he fell asleep. The study below was empty, but the page had laid out food and wine on a folding table, and I ate there.

When Theogault returned, we didn't speak of the father we unwillingly shared. We spoke like two men conducting business, arranging the details of the next stage of my journey to Arn's court at Sunacre. The map laid out between us was unfinished, blank where imperial knowledge fell short.

"The river is the border," Theogault said, "but beyond that you have a good day's ride before you reach any holdings." He looked at me out of the corner of his eye. "Of course," he said, "this *used* to be your family's land."

He pointed to the borderlands north of Vellsberg. I did not intend to show my foster-brother that I had been wondering whether any of my birth-family still remained, but he must have known. What orphan can help but wonder?

"Bloodfeud?" I asked, deliberately looking ahead to the sketch of a longhouse that marked Sunacre. "Or has Arn learned that redistributing land is a good way to break up resistance?"

"Oh no," said Theogault in mock-surprise. "Why, they've been empty for twenty-five years. Ever since they broke the treaty."

I couldn't help it. I stared at him.

"What?" I said at last.

"The treaty," he said. "They broke it. You must have been fifteen or so."

My mouth hung open, but I couldn't close it.

"It was just a raid," he said, "just some sheep. But that's how these border people do it. They steal a few sheep, to see what they can get away with. It breaks the treaty, but they know that if the lord kills the hostage for a few sheep not worth a man's bloodprice, it looks bad. So they keep pushing. Father knew it wouldn't stop. He had to choose whether to execute you and be accused of unlawful killing, or whether to let you live and appear weak. So he disguised his troops as bandits, sent them over the river, and ordered them to kill every last one of your family."

He paused, flicking dirt from under his ink-stained fingernails.

"I suppose you could say," he said, "that it showed how much he loved you."

And so they come, as I knew they would, seeking health, seeking hope. Several dozen on the first day, scores more on the second. Birchold is overrun. When I bless her, the crowd spills out of the shrine onto open ground, they climb trees to see her over the heads of other worshippers, they cry out to her. Soon the long barn is almost full.

I see how much she hates it. I see how it weighs on her, their eyes, the cries of "Salvebearer!" as she passes. She won't leave the cottage where we sleep unless she has to. When the sick pluck at her hem from where they lie on their pallets before the shrine, or in the barn, I see her flinch as if they mean her harm.

There are too many of them, they want too much of her. That strength I saw in her when Frithrun's drunken men led the hound before the fire back in Frithberg is soon stamped out.

Anything so easily killed does not deserve life.

On the third night, I overhear the Vellsberg boy berating her. She has taken to hiding in the cottage, and he sits outside, his portable writing desk across his knees. He's writing on a new sheet of barkpaper. Notes for the history Erland mentioned, no doubt. The ink blotches his hands.

"You do not understand," he says, in his clipped, Southern accent. "I have spent my life praying to the Lord, waiting for His call. And you! You have been called, and you flee from it. Do you know what honour you have been shown? For such an honour many lives have been spent in fruitless hope!"

I remember a boy, ten years ago, his hands spattered with ink, his cheeks pink with pride at a single backhanded insult from his lordly cousin. He will learn.

The rewards of faith are never yours, and if you would have faith until the very end, you must be willing to set them aside, and come when you are called.

My foster-father died that night. I left Vellsberg the next morning. I could have stayed for his burial, but I could already tell the negotiations would be difficult, and I didn't wish to delay.

My escort was headed by a warrior, respectful and more intelligent than I expected, but too young to be anyone of great importance. Still, he was what passed for noble in Arngard – he was the nephew of Arn's first wife, cousin to Prince Geir, and his father was the lord of Hellingap. If Arn was sending me this boy to be my escort, that told me he did not wish to appear too eager for Southern support.

Soon I had guessed from his unguarded talk that he was hopelessly in love with Arn's queen, and devoted to her son

Kolrand, the younger of the Arnson princes. I remember thinking that must put him at odds with his own family, linked as he was by blood to the elder prince.

To spare his youthful indiscretion, I asked him if he knew whose lands we were riding through, but he only shrugged. It was then that I realised I couldn't remember my birth-father's name.

"My lord," said my escort, "forgive me, but you aren't a Southerner, are you?"

"My name is Grimulf," I told him.

"So you're from Arngard?"

"I was born before King Arn united these lands," I said. "But yes, I was born north of the Vell."

"That's good," said Erland. "We need someone who values this land. An outlander wouldn't understand, but when you're born in a place you have it in your blood. It's like family. You can't turn against it without angering the gods."

I did not tell him that my God had no interest in land or blood.

When we reached Sunacre, I knew at once that Prince Geir would cause difficulties. I didn't want to sign one treaty, only to be recalled when Arn died, and face Geir and his army. Besides, if I didn't make these lands mine, I would remain an orphan of the Empire for the rest of my life. I refused to die in some monastery, stripped of all importance.

I may have said something to someone regarding some ancient custom of the land that I had learned in passing. It was ten years since, and my memory is not the memory of a young man.

Besides, Kolrand was a good child, most obedient, and I have always had a sympathy for second sons.

Twelve
PROTECTOR

EBBA'S TALE

Birchold and the East

 e reach an arrangement, the prester an me. It en't agreed through talk, but through looks an warnin glances.

I use my salve on the people who come to me. At first it's just the villagers, but on the second day people come from the foothills below Birchold, an on the third they come from the farmlands. They come to be cured, an the prester knows I can't cure em, not all of em. But I kneel before him durin the ceremonies he holds in the shrine, an I use my salve on all who come, even those I know it can't help, an I keep my mouth shut when he calls me the Salvebearer, bringer of salvation.

Because I am what he said. I'm a liar.

In return, Fetch never leaves my side. That's the name I give the wolfhound, because he followed me an found me. He won't let himself be leashed, an no one dares rile him. Fetch knows when my heart hurts. Havin him beside me is all that gets me out of this cottage an into the hall. He an the prester have bin civil since the first dawn, but the prester keeps out of Fetch's way, an that pleases me.

Right now I'm in the cottage, my back against the door. I hate goin outside. Birchold is filled wi people come to see me. When I leave the cottage they call to me, beg me to heal em.

I can't bear it.

"Are you there?" I say.

"I am here," says Berengar.

For three days now he's sat himself outside the door. Never mind that the ground has bin frozen solid since the day we arrived.

"It would be nice to write the history of the Salvebearer," he says through the door. "For example: '*And on the third day she wore a fine blue dress with embroideries, made in Frithberg, very reasonable prices offered.*'"

"Don't," I say, my heart achin. Fetch comes up to me an I put my arms around him, buryin my face in his rough coat. He whuffs, an its like the ground shakin. "Are you sure he en't listenin?"

"The prester is in the hall talking with the captain," says Berengar, an I hear the scritch-scratch of his pen on barkpaper. "I have a lecture prepared if he comes out. This one is called, 'You are a Very Ungrateful Child and should be More Thankful to your Generous Benefactor.'"

"It sounds like a long one," I say, my mouth twitchin despite myself.

"He will like it," says Berengar, gravely.

We sit there, back to back, the splintered door between us.

"Berengar?"

"Yes?"

"You believe me, don't you?"

There's a silence.

"Yes," he says. "I do not like to, but I do. All the things you told me are things I believe he would say."

We're both quiet for a bit.

"He tole me a decent woman shouldn't talk to men," I say, "so why'd he make you guard me?"

"He believes I dislike you," says Berengar. "Also, he does not see me as a man. None of them do."

"They treat you differently," I say. "The other soldiers. Why?"

He sighs. "I am the cousin of Lord Theogault of Vellsberg. I am noble, and they are not."

"You don't seem too noble to me," I say.

He makes a strange noise, an I realise he's laughin. "I am aware of that," he says. "No one has ever spoken to me the way you do, Ebba."

"What d'you mean, 'the way I do'?"

"Yes, like that."

Smilin, I scratch Fetch behind the ears, an he beats his long tail against the packed earth floor. I en't smiled properly for so long.

"How much salve do you have left, Ebba?"

The smile drops from my face.

"Enough," I say.

"Enough for what?"

"Just enough, all right?" I snap.

"I know you have finished one box," he says. "How much of the other have you got left?"

That's the problem wi not leavin the cottage. When he does this I can't get away.

"Half." I say. "I've got half a box left."

"You need to make more," he says.

But that's the thing, en't it?

"You only have enough for a few more days," he says.

"Maybe there'll be less people."

"There'll be more."

"They can't keep comin forever!"

"Ebba, this is just the beginning," he says. "Tell me, what do you need?"

But Mistress Una interrupts him.

"Is the Salvebearer in?"

"She is," Berengar replies. "Salvebearer, your attendance is begged for," he calls to me.

Though I know he's just doin it to protect me, I hate it when he puts on that voice. I hate that name, too.

"Shall I help dress her?" asks Mistress Una.

"No," I say. "I'm comin." I get to my feet an hitch up the hem of Kelda's pretty blue smock in one hand. I take up my half-empty box of salve in the other an walk out to face my fears, Fetch at my side.

It's dusk when Berengar finds me again, bearin my food on a tray.

While I eat, feedin Fetch from my plate, he tells me another saint's tale, sittin outside where he can be seen an heard. Wouldn't do to have him alone in a room wi the Salvebearer, of course. Even though the prester sleeps alone in here wi me every night, an no one seems to mind that.

I shudder, then notice Berengar's fallen silent.

"Do you know," he says after a while, "people are taking ashes from the fire in the grove. They are taking water from the pool. They are saying that God made the pool spring up to bathe your feet after you walked through the fire."

I stop eatin.

"That's crazy," I say. "Anyone can tell em the pool was already there."

"They are calling it Ebba's Spring," he says.

"They know my *name*?"

"Of course they know your name."

"What if someone tells my uncle?" As I say it I hear how childish I sound. Fetch noses my hand for comfort.

"*That* is what worries you?" asks Berengar. "Your uncle, if he has any sense, will not interfere. This place is now a holy place. You are a holy person."

"No," I say, "I en't."

"I know," Berengar says. "I have read the lives of the saints, and you are not one of them. Not yet."

"What d'you mean?"

He don't answer straight away. I hear him shiftin on the cold ground. Then he says, "Open the door."

I do as he says, an look into his face for the first time in days. We've bin so busy pretendin to hate each other I en't done more'n glance at him. He looks different. When I met him in Frithberg he seemed young an eager, but now I see how his hazel eyes are grown serious.

"There are certain saints," says Berengar, an now he looks away, "who are like you. Young heathen girls who took God's faith and took his oath, although their own people did not believe."

"Well? Did any of em heal people?" Maybe I can learn from them, maybe what they did can show me what I should do. "What were they like? What did they do?"

Berengar's face is still turned away.

"They died," he says. "They had to choose between their faith and their lives, and they chose to die."

"That's no use," I say, frustrated. "I en't goin to do that."

"It is not a choice!" snaps Berengar. Fetch growls under his breath. "It is a story! A story that works very well. A beautiful dead girl. Do you understand? That's what he was telling you. If you are not good, if you do not obey him, you will be dead. And then he will control your story completely. He may even make me write it."

Somewhere in the woods, an owl hoots. My hand strays to Torny's pin, holdin my braid in place.

"That is why you must make more salve," he says quietly.

"I can't," I say. "I don't know how. It's Ma's recipe."

"Then make it up," he says, his voice harsh. "It won't matter."

He rises an leaves me in the dark cottage, with only Fetch to guard me.

That night I barely sleep. My breath catches when the prester comes in, and I lie wi Fetch between us like a shield, his heart racin against mine. I wish the prester snored so I could tell when he was sleepin, but his breath is deep an even. I feel like if I looked across at him I'd see his eyes shinin through the dark, fixed on me even as he sleeps.

When the first light comes in through the cracks, I get up as quietly as I can, put on my cloak an shoes, an walk out into the frost-laden dawn.

The cold has deepened since we crossed the pass, an for the first time I can smell snow in the air. Fetch trots from tree to tree, sniffin like any hound, as we follow the path to the grove.

I want to see this for myself.

The ashes from the burnin path are scattered an trodden into the hard ground. The edges of the pool have bin churned up by many feet an then frozen, white ice caught in the ruts. In some places it looks like it's bin scooped up.

The sun's comin up now, an the trees are turnin ghostly. The edge of the clearin is lined by young birches, an their white bark glows softly. The trickle of the stream fallin into the pool, the sharp air, all of it feels alive. The beauty of it fills me.

I want to see the sunrise. I need some way to get above the trees, but the mountain's too steep to climb. The birches en't much use, but I peer between em, an this time I notice a dark, twisted trunk, too heavy to belong to a birch.

I have to find a path through the brambles, but once I do it leads straight where I need.

It's an old oak, huge an heavy, its branches spread in welcome. A bundle of bright green mistletoe sprouts in a cleft above me. I throw off my cloak an hitch my skirts through my belt so my legs are free, heedless of the cold. I grab hold of a low branch an kick my legs round it.

It takes a couple of tries, but I swing myself upright. The trunk is huge, gnarled an split, an it don't take me long to get higher. I look east, through the thin bare branches of the birch wood.

It's so clear I can see the edge of the world, the gold fire reflected in the strip of the sea, the white mist liftin from the valleys in the foothills. The land is still asleep.

The dawn's fire kindles somethin right at the centre of my body, a spark buried under the dread that's bin suffocatin me since I came to Birchold. The spark soars inside me, yearnin upwards.

I feel numb an alive all at once.

The sun clears the horizon, an the cold bites through my dress. I slide down a couple of branches, an then my fingers find a scar in the bark, the kind you get when you tie rope round a tree an leave it too long.

Suddenly I want to get down as quick as possible.

I slither off the scarred branch onto the next, but I'm stiff an tired, an I misjudge it. I land heavily an overbalance backwards, the bark scrapin the backs of my knees painfully as I swing upside down.

Fetch bounds towards me, barkin. Not angry barks, 'follow me' barks. Then he reaches me an jumps up, lickin my face. Between the tongue an the slobber I see he's not alone.

"Ber —" I start, before Fetch gets in the way an I have to close my mouth against his dog-kisses.

I finally hook a hand round the branch an drop down into the leaves. Fetch licks me some more. It's like bein one of em babes brought up by wolves.

"Stop it," I say, pushin him away. He trots off, tail high an proud. I can feel my cheeks go pink, an when I look over, Berengar's are too. He's sort of half turned, tryin not to look.

I unhook my skirts an check I en't lost Torny's pin.

"It's all right," I say, "I'm decent." He glances at me like he needs to make sure himself. "It en't that bad," I say. "You must of guessed I had legs."

He gives me a baleful look, an opens his mouth to give me a tellin off, but somethin catches his eye.

"What?"

He points down at the oak's roots. At first I can't see anythin, but when I do it gives me a sick feelin.

"Oh," I say.

Tucked into the knarled roots of the old oak are dozens of rough mud shapes. Some of em are fallin apart already, but others are fresh-made.

They're body parts. Feet, hands, legs, faces, even breasts an genitals.

It all comes together – the new saplins growin round this tree, like they only bin allowed to seed in the last few years, the way the oak stands in the east. The rope-scarred branch.

This is a sacred grove. It was holy long before I came along an walked through fire. An this is the Harm Tree, where the sacrifices were hung.

But these offerins . . . I en't seen that before. I think of the mud by the pool, the places where it's bin scooped out.

"This is wrong," Berengar says. He looks green. "We must tell the prester."

"We can't do that!" I hiss. "Who knows what he'll do?"

"The White God is the one true god!"

I don't know what to say. Berengar's face is screwed up, like a little boy tryin not to cry.

"The White God's new here," I say, tryin to calm him. "The people don't know Him. Can you blame em for keepin in wi the others until He's proved himself?"

Berengar thumps his fist on the oak's trunk. "You should be the proof," he says. "You! It is your job to prove His power."

"It's *His* job," I say coldly, pullin back.

Berengar don't answer, just sinks to his knees before the oak an sits there, huddled over. I think he might be cryin.

I'm wonderin what to do when I hear footsteps behind us.

It's Erland. I en't seen him save wi the prester for days, but here he is. He looks at us, then the oak.

"Haven't you got sick people to see to, Ebba?" he says.

The guilty feelin starts up again. I open my mouth to argue, but his look says not to bother.

I feel naked, walkin alone through the village. Well, not alone. Fetch is wi me. You can't really be alone with a hound who stands as tall as your shoulder. An people give me my space, even if they do stare.

It takes me a while to find Mistress Una, an when I do she looks at me in surprise.

"How can I serve you, Salvebearer?"

"You can call me Ebba," I say. I suddenly feel ashamed I never asked her to before. I can feel the blush reachin my cheeks. "Can I help you in the barn?"

She looks me over, an somethin in the way she does it reminds me of Aud, the first day I came to the wayhouse.

"I'm takin em breakfast," she says. "You can help me wi that."

It's better than I thought. When I come after the ceremony the worshippers follow me about, wantin to watch me, but this time it's just me, Mistress Una, an those who need care. It's still difficult, but I feel better for facin them. This is a duty, after all, like any chore Ma or Aud might of set me, save the people I serve an talk to en't payin guests or farmhands, but people lookin for hope.

Fetch is better at it than me. He lies down besides those who can't sit, an lets em pet him. I see Mistress Una eyein me sideways, an I try to think what Ma would do. I can't give em what they need, but I can at least talk to em. I ask people about their hurts, an they tell me.

It surprises me that I know a little of what to do. Helpin Ma means I know that this one should be given yarrow against fever, or that one should have a hot compress to ease joint pain. I start askin Mistress Una what herbs they have. Halfway through I think how useful it'd be to have Berengar here, keepin a list of what they have an what they need.

They all want the salve, of course. They've all had some before, durin my visits after the ceremony. Surely if it was as powerful as they believe it is, it would of cured them by now, but that don't stop em askin. I say today I bin tole to go among em an treat em as myself.

The way they look at me shows they think it's the god who's bin tellin me.

But it gets me thinkin. Somethin did happen wi Fetch that first night in Lord Frithrun's hall, somethin no one can make sense of save to say it was the White God protectin me. I was there, an still it seems unreal. Because of that the prester brought me here, but whatever happened wi Fetch en't happenin to these people. The salve is bein wasted, used on wounds it can't possibly heal, sometimes just dotted on a sick person's forehead if their pain is all inside. I *know* it don't work like that.

I remember my dream, where the White God touched the lame man, an he walked.

Nothin like that has happened, so why do they trust me?

Another thought nags me. I try to grasp it but it breaks off like a splinter, an before I can get hold of it there's someone else to talk to, another question for Mistress Una. Then Erland comes to get me for the mornin ceremony, an I lose it, though I can still feel it lodged in me, prickin me, as I kneel an pray.

It's only when the prester puts the piece of bread on my tongue an offers me the cup of mead that it comes to me.

I din't treat Fetch; I put the salve in his mouth.

I don't do anythin about it straight away. What if I'm wrong? I finish visitin the sick an I run to find Berengar, Fetch at my heels.

I find Erland instead.

"I sent him hunting," he says. He's whittlin somethin out of a round of birch wood.

"En't you upset?" I ask.

White feathers of wood fall around Erland's boots as he works. He don't look upset.

"Berengar has grown up knowing the White God is the one true god," he says. "He's grown up learnin to write an read from God's book, by copyin out the lives of the saints an their miracles. He's grown up surrounded by faith, so he's never had to have faith. An now he's in a foreign land where the White God is just one among many, where he an his companions are the strange ones. Why do you think they were so pleased when we met you?"

I shrug.

"They're homesick, Ebba. You being a believer made you a bit like their sister."

I can't meet his eye, so I run my hand through Fetch's coat instead. I feel like I've bin lyin to all of em, Berengar an Erland's men, Mistress Una an the sick people who come from miles around.

"I shouldn't of done it," I say. "I should of told the prester I weren't a believer."

"I don't think you had a choice," Erland says, "not after you healed the dog." There's a strange edge to his voice. I wonder if Berengar told him about what the prester said to me.

"You're his friend, en't you?" I say. "Can't you ask him to let me stop?"

Erland don't answer right away, an when he does it en't an answer.

"Do you know who Grimulf is?" he asks.

I shake my head.

"He was sent by the Emperor to Sunacre ten years ago. It was his job to negotiate the treaty between Arn and the Empire. It was my job to look after him, and spy on him." The wood is startin to gain shape under his knife. Soon he's goin to need a smaller blade. "I was meant to find out if he meant to betray us. Instead, I discovered too late that it was Prince Geir who was planning to betray us."

Between his calloused fingers, I can see a rough mouth forming, gaping open, a tail caught in its teeth.

"Grimulf saved Prince Kolrand," Erland says, his voice catchin. "Without Grimulf, the king I serve would have been murdered along with his mother and father, and I doubt I would have survived that bloody night either. Without Grimulf, Arngard would not be as it is. I know," he says, before I can say anythin, "there are still people who believe it should have been Geir. But who would you have chosen, Ebba? The prince who would kill his father, or the outlander whose god directed him to save an innocent boy?"

His knife slips, an blood wells between the feathery wood flakes. I reach out an catch his hand.

"I en't a believer," I say. "Not in any god, if I'm truthful. I'd of chosen him too."

Erland looks at me, his face troubled. "Grimulf believes the White God has sent him a tool," he says. "You. Not to make use of you would be against his master's will."

"So you can't stop him."

"No." He shakes his head. "I don't think I can. And I don't understand. He's a good man, so why —?"

I've got no answers for him. All I know is even though he says the prester's a good man, he's bin hidin my friendliness wi Berengar from him.

"Then I'll do what he wants," I say. "But tell me. Would you protect me, if it came to it?"

Or is it only princes who can hope to be saved?

So I go back to playin the part the prester's given me. I rope Berengar in easy. "Think about all the questions you can ask em about what people were wearin," I say. He huffs a bit, but whatever Erland said to him seems to of calmed him, an it turns out Mistress Una can tell him all about the buildin of the Birchold shrine, so he's satisfied.

In return he writes lists of herbs they have an don't have, an what supplies Birchold needs. The only problem is we need him to read em back to us.

"You'll have to teach me," I say.

He goes off in a sulk. Erland sends him back, an he starts wi just the letters. There are more'n twenty. This might take longer than I thought.

The next mornin I'm strugglin over em, Fetch across my feet, when I hear horses. I walk over to the hall an see Adelhard an his men dismountin.

Erland beckons me over to the hall. "Prester Grimulf is waiting for you," he says.

I tell Fetch to stay by the door an walk over to where the prester talks wi the headman. Berengar's standin stiffly to attention beside them.

The prester looks me over before speakin.

"By the grace of God, Adelhard has brought news of your family." I din't expect that, an he must see it on my face. "When did you last see them, child?"

"A year ago, Father." The word is still distasteful on my tongue, but I'm gettin better at sayin it.

"You must miss them very much."

If he'd asked me back in Frithberg I would of said yes. I might of cried. I can't count how many times I dreamed I was home again. But that was before I knew my uncle was willin to sell me to secure a loan. I nod, but only because he's expectin it.

"Well, I have good news indeed. We leave for Eldinghope immediately. You will be home by the full moon."

He don't mention Bloodnight, so I don't either. Ulf hosts the Bloodnight feast for all our neighbours, so the farm will be busy. My uncle won't have time to bother wi me, an maybe I can get the recipe for the salve from Ma. Maybe she'll have some spare supplies I can bring back for Mistress Una. Din't I tell Torny back in Frithberg that I wanted to go home for Bloodnight?

"Your kindness shows your greatness, Father," I say.

The prester looks past me to Berengar.

"Vellsberg. Help the Salvebearer prepare for the journey."

"It is my honour," says Berengar, hand on his heart. I look at the ground an try not to giggle.

"Very well. We leave as soon as you are ready, child."

Berengar waits till we're safely out of earshot before he rolls his eyes at me. "'Your kindess shows your greatness'?"

"What about you? Honoured to look after a farm girl, are you?"

He shoots me a quick smile an my stomach turns over. I en't seen him smile freely in so long, an I find I missed it.

Thirteen
BUTCHER

TORNY'S TALE

Hill country, near Sleeper's Howe

A bird calls, and the mists roll back. I'm wrapped in a stinking blanket. Something warm lies against my back, chewing.

Chewing?

I roll over. A chorus of baas starts up, and I scoot away from the sheep I was lying against, only to bump into another. I try to stand, but my head bumps against branches, and thorns prick my scalp.

I crouch awkwardly, surrounded by irritated sheep, trying to untangle my hair from the thorns. Where am I?

I remember the boy pulling me over the lines of the labyrinth, as if he couldn't feel the way they tried to hold us back. I remember staggering up the tunnel, tripping over the line of stakes, the sharp pain in my shins. I remember bolting between the stones towards the thick red light, and small hands catching my clothes to hold me back from plunging headfirst off the narrow ledge.

And now I'm here, in a sort of cave under some thorn-trees that the sheep use for shelter, if the fleece-lined walls are anything to go by. But how I got here is another question.

The bird calls again, two notes, falling and rising, like a question asked over and over to the grey morning sky between the twisted thorns.

Morning.

Galen. I have to find Galen. What if he gives me up for lost, leaves without me?

Panic bubbles up my sore throat. I tear the last strands of my hair free of the thorns.

The bird's call changes, from sharp, clear notes into an ugly chattering scream. Something drips onto my cheek. I brush it away, hoping it's not rain, and look at my hand.

It's blood.

I stare up into the knotted twigs, and another drip falls on me, just missing my eye, and then I see a tiny, struggling body. As I watch, it twitches and stills.

The sheep baa, the thorns shiver, and a small dark head appears between the roots. It tilts up and looks at me with narrow, smiling eyes like upturned moons.

"Awake? Good, good." The boy wriggles the rest of his boney body into the small space. The sheep get to their feet, still baaing, and he shoos them out of the strange thorny cave, leaving us alone.

He looks me over, taking in the blood spots on my face, and clicks his tongue.

Can this be the boy I saw in my vision? But the feelings that raced through me then came from inside the dead boy, and the flash of his face I did see was blurred, imperfect. And anyway, the boy I saw died long ago, longer than I can count. This boy before me is too solid, too practical.

"Who are you?" I ask.

"Fenni," says the boy, and makes a face. "Fenn. I like better." He straightens up and I see the plain iron thrall collar round his neck.

"Who's your master?" I ask, and the boy suddenly looks sly.

"I help you," he says, "yes? I save you from the Sleeper, yes?"

"Yes," I say, sensing there's a bargain coming.

"So you help me, yes?"

"What kind of help?"

"Easy," he says, smiling disarmingly. "Easy help. Help your one-hand friend also."

"Galen? The man with one hand?"

Fenn nods. "My master Thorkel," he says, "take your one-hand Galen. I told stay wait for you. But you," he smiles again, widely. "You have butcher with you."

"What do you mean?" I ask.

He nods upwards. I look. A bird is hunched in the branches above me, tearing at the tiny body I saw before. More blood spatters down, dark spots on the filthy blanket, and I flinch away.

"That butcher on this side," he says, nodding at the bird. "Your butcher on the *other* side." He looks at me and grins nastily. "He hungry. You not feed him."

I look up through the branches, and now I know what I'm looking for, I can see them – impaled shrews and field mice. I've been sleeping under a shrike's larder.

"My butcher?" I ask, but already I'm remembering that grey

presence I felt for a moment in the depths of Sleeper's Howe. My hand strays to my chest; the packet is still there, against my skin.

Fenn smiles, a half-smile this time, and reaches out a slim hand to touch my throat where it feels bruised from the dead man's grip.

"You have collar too," he says. "You also thrall."

I throw the blanket away from me in disgust.

"I'm no thrall," I tell him, and my voice snaps more than I mean it to. "Where's Galen? Why has your master taken him?"

Fenn shrugs, and I notice how pointed his shoulders are under his ragged clothes. There are tattoos under the dirt of his forearms, even though he's still a child, strange spindly lines and dots.

"Old friends," says Fenn. If this Thorkel is the same one who owned the spade from the barrow, he must be one of Galen's old warband. "But . . ."

"But what?"

"Master Thorkel have many friends, all dead. Keep them in long halls near Sleeper's hill." He means the barrows.

I look into his cheerful, hungry face. "He's going to kill him?" He nods. "We have to do something."

Fenn smiles winningly. "Come," he says. He snatches up the dirty blanket, pushes his head through a hole in the middle, and wearing it as a cloak, turns and ducks back onto his stomach.

I follow him out from under the thorns, pulling myself along. Crawling out onto the spiky winter grass, I can see we're in a dug-out hollow. There's a pot over a small fire, and a worn patch next to the firepit. It looks like a shepherd's summer camp.

Fenn uncovers the pot and spoons some heavy lentil soup into a chipped bowl. He hands it to me and watches me eat. When I'm done he fills it again and eats from it himself. I huddle by the fire, missing Aud's cloak. The dull tug to the North is back again, lodged under my ribs. I'm growing used to it, but it's not a pleasant feeling.

Still there? I ask the dead man, but I get no reply.

I can't see Sleeper's Howe from here and I'm glad; I don't want to think too much about what I saw, or thought I saw. But I remember something, and start to my feet.

"Where is it?" I ask.

Fenn watches me. He's smiling, but it's the kind of smile that keeps your face busy, while his legs tense, ready to leap up.

"What, Butcher-girl?" he asks.

"The thing I took . . ." I hesitate, remembering Galen's warning. But I also remember the rippling patch of light that led me to the Sleeper. If I had to guess, I'd say the mirror wanted to be taken.

Still cautious, Fenn reaches inside his clothes. Wordlessly, he holds the mirror out to me.

I almost refuse it. I almost tell him to bury it between the thorn roots and have done with it, but . . .

I take it.

It's a little bigger than my palm, and the back is decorated with loops and circles, light and dark, intersecting and binding. I try to follow the curves, but my eyes slide over them, unable to pin them down. Around the rim are three loops like you find on horse tack. It's heavier than it looks.

I turn it over and stare at the dull face. An opaque greenish bloom covers the surface.

"But —" I say. "It was —"

Fenn shrugs elaborately, as if to say that what it may have been and what it is now is none of his business.

I flip it over again, tracing the flowing lines with my thumb. "Was it real?"

Fenn shrugs again. "And this?" he asks, reaching out to touch my neck again. "This real?"

I jerk back. "How do you know about that?"

"I see him," he says, nodding over my shoulder.

Then he says that I see the dead man too, in my mind, the way he was when I went to him at dawn: inverted, the empty sockets watching me.

"Who is he?" asks Fenn.

"I don't know his name," I say. "He died five days ago. Now he's following me."

"You ask him?"

I nod, and Fenn clicks his tongue disapprovingly. He sits back, his chin in his hands, as if he's trying to work out a riddle.

"Is that who you meant by my butcher?" I ask.

Fenn nods. "Your butcher on other side," he says again. "Take you to Sleeper. Sleeper's hill on this side, but Sleeper on other side too."

All these sides are giving me a headache. "You mean I . . . crossed over?"

Vigdis never spoke about it, of course. You don't get told the secrets of a trade until you enter it. But everyone *knows*. Maybe not how, or why, or what the price is. But that's what being a Staffbearer is about. Sometimes, when it's necessary, you cross over, and walk among the shadows.

That would explain why I could see in the dark. And the way I couldn't cross the stones in the labyrinth, and the visions, the feelings of being inside another person's skin. But then . . . I touch my neck, right over the place where it feels bruised. If the dead man can reach through, can hurt me, here, in the daylit world . . .

Fenn's still watching me, his dark eyes large in his hungry face.

"How do you know these things?" I ask. Staffbearers are always women. I've never heard of them training a boy.

"Back home," he says, "the Spirit Walker chose me." He holds up his arms and shows me the strange dot-and-line tattoos. "They marked me. I see both sides."

I look him over properly. He's older than I first thought; although he's underfed and dressed in rags, he's about the age when boys move to the men's table. If I had to guess, I'd say he comes from the far North, beyond the Iron Sea. The thrall collar has rubbed raw calluses around his throat. He reminds me of the Sleeper's body – not one thing on him is whole, except the collar.

"What do you want?" I ask.

Fenn smiles, but there's a hardness to it.

"Two winters I am thrall," he says. "Three winters is too much."

"Help me free Galen," I say, "and you can come with us."

Fenn shakes his head. "Master Thorkel follow. Master Thorkel keep his friends close. They leave, he hunt them."

"Is that why you haven't run away?"

He raises his eyebrows at my stupidity. "Boy wearing collar, always someone's thrall."

He's right. If he's found on his own, he'll just be returned to his master, or enslaved again.

"You need protection," I say.

"You need guide," Fenn counters. I can tell he's enjoying himself. I suppose bargaining isn't something he gets to do much.

"Galen's guiding me," I tell him.

"Where?" he asks.

And there he has me. So far, Galen has led me a merry chase right into the arms of his old warband.

"What makes you better?"

"Two years here," Fenn says promptly. "Floodlands dangerous. I know crossing."

"All right. How do we stop your master from coming after us?"

"You fight him," says Fenn, still smiling.

I argue.

"I don't have a sword," I say.

"If you challenge, they give you."

"I can't fight all of them."

"No need. Just Master Thorkel."

"Since when did bandits follow rules of honour?"

"Not bandits," Fenn says. "Warriors."

Warriors without a war, just like Galen is a bondsman without his prince.

The next thing I say shames me because it scares me, but it's true.

"I'm not ready."

Fenn cups his sharp chin in his hands, and studies me.

"You have help," he says, nodding over my shoulder to where the dead man seems to be. "We help you. With that."

I look at the dull mirror lying heavy in my lap. The dead man led me to it, after all, and the dead man knew Galen, who knew this Thorkel. Between them they brought me here, the dead man and the living man who wants to die. And I asked for it, didn't I? I wanted help.

I stop arguing, but now I'm scared and impatient all at once.

Fenn is unhurried. He says Thorkel and his men won't do

anything until sunset, and settles into concocting something over the small, steady fire.

"What if I fall unconscious at sunset?" I ask, but he just smiles. We both know I won't.

This is what the dead man wants too.

So I burrow back under the thorns and try to sleep. I doze fitfully, and I dream Ebba is with me, curled up against my back. I can feel the warmth of her, the comfort. I want to turn and bury my face in her thick hair that smells so sweetly of woodsmoke, want to feel her hand slip into mine. My heart squeezes in me.

En't this what you always wanted? she asks. *Glory? The chance to prove yourself?*

What if I die? I ask her. I never thought I'd be a coward, but I'm scared.

We all die.

After that I don't ask questions. I just want to feel her near me a little longer.

Finally Fenn rouses me and I join him, so nervous I can't speak. He hands me the bowl, full of a thick, bitter liquid.

"Drink," he says. When I look at him questioningly he says, "To calm you."

The first mouthful turns my stomach, and Fenn carefully takes the drink from me while I vomit. When I'm done he hands it back to me, and I finish it. My stomach cramps, but after a little while it passes. The sun dips down to the hilltops.

Fenn leads me from the hollow. We follow a sheep trail through a long, narrow gully, then climb a steep slope to where more of the low, knotted thorns provide cover. We creep to the top on our bellies and look over.

The Floodlands glisten between shadowy clumps of rushes. The surface looks almost greasy, rippling with black and silver, and a thin mist covers everything, obscuring the far shore. I'd imagined something with edges, not this confusion, this muddling of water and earth. There's no clear shoreline, no telling when a path becomes a channel. Even the horizon has been devoured: a dark line to the north could be high moors or low-lying clouds.

At the foot of the slope is an open space of tramped down dirt, with a ramshackle smithy at one end, and a firepit at the other. The fire is burning, though no one's in sight. Smoke also rises from the slope below us, and I realise I'm looking down on turf roofs. There are shacks built into the hillside itself. Now I know what I'm looking for I can see wooden posts, stone foundations.

A large man appears from the smithy. A hiss from Fenn tells me this is Thorkel. He's wearing a smith's heavy leather apron, and his hair falls down his back in long beaded braids. His face is grained with soot, and one eye shines in its socket. He takes something from his belt and with a flick of his wrist he starts the thing whirling round his head.

The bullroarer whirs like a captive hornet, filling the air and the hills. The thorns over our heads seem to shiver. I put my hands over my ears and screw up my eyes, and with horror I sense something stirring, something twitching —

The slap brings me round. Fenn glares at me. "Hold," he commands, pushing the mirror into my hands, dull side up. "Watch."

From the hillside shacks, men are emerging. There are no women. Like Thorkel, they're filthy, but dressed as warriors. They make a ring around Thorkel, and as he whirls the bullroarer over his head, they shout together, and bring their swords up. One of them draws a measure of something from a barrel an the cup travels the circle. Another joins Thorkel, and sets up a steady beat on a hand drum. Then the men begin to dance.

On fine days, Ebba and I used to sit on the path up to the kirk, watching Lord Frithrun's warriors spar. Sometimes one would perform a sword dance for the others. Then those hulking men had a grace I found entrancing, though not in the way Aud meant when she warned me off them. Their weapons became part of their bodies, and their bodies became weapons. The power of those dances lay in the way flesh became . . . something else. And the watching men would whistle and cheer, while we sat above it all, unseen, closed out.

But this is different. This is dozens of men stamping and roaring together, their moves perfectly in time. They drop, spring, lunge and slash. The earth shudders like a cliff battered by the sea.

And all the time that buzz, sawing into me, opening me up.

My eyes sting. In my hands, the mirror is shining.

I yelp, pulling back from the edge, trying to hide the light.

"What do you see?" Fenn slithers down beside me.

But I can't see anything. I've got my eyes shut tight against the harsh light, and my head feels as if it's cracking open.

Fenn tugs my arm. It's all I can do to follow him back down the slope and round, until we're huddled behind the smithy. Fenn digs through a bundle. I find can't loosen my grip on the mirror and my teeth are gritted against the nausea.

"You know sword dance?" he asks. I shake my head and the world loops crazily. But my feet are twitching in time to the drum, and my arms know the weight of the sword, remember the feints and lunges.

"Your butcher knows," says Fenn. "His time now. Let him in."

"No!"

Part of me is surprised by how vehemently I fight it, the slipping control over my own limbs. The world is spinning in time with the *whuuum* of the bullroarer, yet I cling to it. The mirror burns white, and I can feel the cold grip of the dead man seeping through my hands, filling my muscles. The Luck-worm ripples up my spine to meet him, sending ripples of nausea through me.

Fenn takes out a knife, and knicks his own wrist. Blood wells up, and he smears it across my cheeks. He doesn't look like a boy anymore. Black splotches are bursting across my vision, blinding me.

As the dancers thunder to their conclusion, metal clashing upon metal, Fenn reaches out and grips my neck, leaving a hot, bloody hand-mark over the ring of bruises.

Cold fills me. The drum stops and I feel like I'm travelling upwards, through the dark. My blood pumps to the thrum of the bullroarer. My limbs are slack, their twitching stilled. The mirror drops from my nerveless fingers.

"He comes," says Fenn softly.

The bullroarer falls silent, and it's as if my heart has forgotten how to beat. It's unbearable, this yearning.

A harsh voice calls, "Bring him out!"

Somewhere near us, men are cursing, stumbling. Then I hear Galen's voice.

"Thorkel! Is this how you treat a comrade?"

Enough of me remains to cringe at his desperate whine.

"You're no comrade of ours, Galen." This contemptuous voice must be Thorkel; all by themselves, my hands bunch into fists.

"We fought together often enough, Thorkel. We were both his followers."

"You snuck away in the night, like the coward you are. Did you slither away to serve the cub Kolrand? Or have you spent the last nine years snivelling over the man you betrayed?" Thorkel shouts with laughter. "Galen the Golden, the prince's right hand man! Your kind always do turn."

The other men howl.

Galen the Golden.

Dimly, through the cold invading my head, I remember that I used that same name when I told Galen to seek out Jarle. Some people are like that, so beautiful they glow, but the Galen I know is dulled and drawn. The only time I saw anything like that in him was by the barrows. *Everything I ever loved is here*, he said. His face was lit then, but by a sick gold, a cursed gold.

"I thought you hated women's magic, Thorkel," says Galen, as the howling dies. "But here I see you've lost an eye, and broken the turf on the Howe. Have you gone crazy out here in the wild, or are you so afraid you mutilate your own body in offerings to a bogle?"

The men fall silent.

"You're a coward and an idiot," says Thorkel. "We've found something better than magic."

"Who's the coward?" says Galen. "He who lives in the world, or he who hides from it?"

"We have been preparing," says Thorkel, "and we will be bloody midwives of a new world. We have discovered a power beyond the dreams of men, and soon it will wash us all clean."

"If you had fought at Frithberg, instead of hiding here, you'd know we tried it," spits Galen. "The Sungiven failed, the war ended —"

There's the crunch and smack of a blow.

"The war never ended," says Thorkel. "Look about you. These are the last true men in a kingdom of degradation. We are the Slipskins, and we will bring bloody reckoning to the traitors who laid down their weapons before their lives!"

"You're a bunch of drunken madmen," Galen says thickly. "Gods rot you in your muddy shithole."

Another smack, then a rising clatter of swords on shields.

Fenn shoves something into my hands.

"They kill him now," he says, "unless you fight."

My heart hammers in my chest. As Fenn runs out into the open space, I look down at the spade in my hands, and the cold burns its way into my skull.

"Master!" Fenn cries, "She's here! *She dug her way out!*"

Fourteen

HOMECOMING

✤

EBBA'S TALE

The East and Eldinghope

he wave starts at the shore an gallops inland. White horses become gold, the hot, liquid kind, an their manes fly up red. A black tide follows. The east is already dark, the sun's gone down behind the mountains, an below us the soft fields are bein overrun. It must be late summer, cos the crops are ripe, an the black tide laps up around the foothills an starts to climb to where we're tryin to pen the frightened sheep.

I have my arm over my mouth an nose, but the wind pushes the hot ash before it, stingin my eyes. The sheep are panicked, breakin like water from an overfull cup, an the dogs are hard pressed to pen em. Rafe an Stig are there. Stig's holdin my hand. Ulf's first born son, just a year short of manhood, is watchin the fire an cryin. Least there are tears on his face. They might just be from the ash.

Someone takes my other hand. I screw up my eyes an see my Follower. She's wearin the face of a field thrall. I can see her wrinkled skin an the collar at her throat, but I know it's my Follower from the way her face don't quite fit.

"It's the Raiders," I tell her. "They set fire to the dune grass. Everythin from the shore to the mountains burned."

"An why d'you remember that?" she asks.

"Cos it was the year my Da died."

As I say it, I see him.

The glow from the burnin fields lights up his face, streaked black an pocked wi scars. Sweat scours fresh tracks in the ash, an he comes towards me an picks me up. I sit balanced on his hip, an I feel him holdin me, strong an certain. His tawny hair has a reddish tint, like mine, an his eyes . . . to tell the truth, I can't see his eyes. He's blurred, just like my memories of him, an the scars, the sweat-trails, the glint on his hair, are only fragments. What I have instead is my feelin of him.

I en't scared of the fires no more. In his grasp I stop frettin, even as the red horses throw themselves at the slopes. I lean my head against his shoulder, out of harm's reach, an watch our home go up in smoke.

I smell the snow on Fetch's coat when he sticks his head through the cart's coverin an licks me. I pull on my overshoes an wrap myself tighter in my cloak. It's the second day out of Birchold, but the pleasure of sleepin in the cart again en't worn off. The prester sleeps in his tent, Fetch keeps me warm, an I am happier than I've bin in days.

Everythin has turned white. I jump down into a hand's depth

of snow. Fetch's neat paw prints ring the camp, crossin bird an rabbit trails, but the rest of the world is still asleep. The two tents where the men sleep sag wi the snow's weight. Behind the tents, the foothills fold their slopes softly into one another, an higher up on the mountains, the black woods are lined wi white.

I tramp round the cart an up a short slope, Fetch beside me. The land opens out, the sun hangin low in the east. The gold drop turns the snow blue an the clouds red. I feel awake, but somewhere inside me the fire in my dreams keeps on burnin.

I start lookin for landmarks, but the snow leeches the shapes from the land, an anyway, I en't familiar wi the road beyond Ulf's markers. All I can make out is two ruts cuttin lines of shadow through the white. There'll be milestones along the road, but I can't see one nearby.

Footsteps crunch behind me. I spin an see Berengar makin his way towards me. I breathe out, my breath a cloud. Fetch goes to sniff Berengar's hands. He's the only other person Fetch will greet.

"Your home is close," Berengar says, feedin Fetch a strip of dried meat. "Your family will be proud."

"I doubt it," I say. Somethin about the empty land makes me say what I'm thinkin for once. "Ma'll be happy to see me, I think. I dunno about the rest of em. What does the prester want with em anyway?"

"You were there."

"When?"

"When I brought you to Dagomar's table." Berengar stands beside me on the raised road, lookin out towards the sea.

I try to recall the prester's strange speech, all about shepherds an flocks.

"I din't understand what they meant."

"They want a route," he says. "From the East coast to Frithberg and the South."

"What for? The grain already crosses the mountains."

Berengar blows on his hands to warm em. His nose is red wi cold. He's not meetin my eyes.

"Where did your mother come from, Ebba?"

"I don't know, do I —" I begin but then I stop. "The Raiders. She was rescued from the Raiders. They'd of sold her." I watch him to see if I'm right, an I am. I wind my hand in Fetch's ruff for comfort, but my voice still comes out small. "A slave route? Is that what Dagomar wants?"

Berengar's eyes flick to my face, but he don't say nothin. We stand there in silence.

"What about you?" I ask, pettin Fetch. I can't think about this. I need talk in my ears, to keep it out. "En't you missin your family?"

Berengar shrugs. "I miss my mother, and our orchard. But they are glad Captain Erland took me," he says. "No other knight-master would have me. Writing is the work of a monk or clerk, not a soldier."

"Why'd Erland take you then?"

"He knows Prester Grimulf," says Berengar, "and the prester is known in Vellsberg. He is half-monk and half-soldier. It was the best my family could hope for."

"D'you want to be a monk?" I ask.

Berengar looks into the dawn, an I look at his face, really look at it. When your mind wants to be busy it can see things you never glanced twice at before. I see the paleness of his skin, white like the snow, an the black of his hair. His dark brows are drawn together, an under his straight lashes the sun catches his eyes like it's travellin through water. I en't noticed before how his eyes are the same hazel as the forest in summer, nor how deep they are, nor the soft pink that spreads across his high pale cheeks in the cold.

"I would rather marry," he says shortly, turnin his back on me an the sun. An that's all I get, cos when we get back to camp Erland an Adelhard are hunkered down by the fire.

As I cook breakfast I keep an eye on Berengar. I see how the soldiers' tent gets taken down by Adelhard's three men, who shake off the snow an fold it down as they work an talk, an how Berengar is left to take down the other tent on his own. He's still at it when the gruel's bein ladled out. Erland sends a soldier to help him an they finish the task without speakin.

We travel slower today. Fetch trots close to the wagon, sniffin the air. There must be smells to tempt him, but he stays close. Berengar's quiet, an my mind slides dangerously back to this mornin. When I hear the thump of hoofbeats behind us, I twist round in relief. Four riders are comin up the road. The one in front trots past us an I recognise Medard's floppy fair hair. He winks at me as he passes an throws a salute for Erland, who frowns an beckons him up front where the prester's ridin his mule. I turn back to see Berengar glowerin after em.

"Are you jealous?" I ask.

"Jealous? Of that illiterate idiot?"

"He's all right," I say. "He's just a flirt."

Berengar sniffs. "Is Arngard so barbaric that her daughters are uncompromised by the lax attentions of swine?"

"I dunno," I say. "You tell me."

He gives me a sideways look. "Medard should be careful," he

says. "Captain Erland protected him from the prester once already."

I open my mouth, but Medard's back.

"Prester Grimulf want speak with you," he says, smilin. I can't help it, I smile back.

Medard leads his horse alongside an gestures that I should get on. I hesitate, but the prester's a fair way ahead on his mule. Surely it's all right if he asked Medard to bring me?

"Horse more safe than wolf, Mistress," says Medard, his eyes glitterin wi laughter. Berengar snorts, an that annoys me. I grab the back of Medard's saddle an swing my leg awkwardly over his mount's haunches. Fetch gives a warnin growl, but nothin more. I hang on as Medard kicks his horse into what I think is a canter. It's hard to tell wi my face buried in his cloak.

"No ride?" calls Medard over his shoulder. It must be pretty clear from my grip that I en't feelin at home.

We reach the prester an I stiffen, expectin a rebuke, but he just looks me over briefly.

"Is this your first time on horseback?"

I shake my head, but truthfully it's only the second or third time.

"These horses en't like ours," I say. "I'd rather be closer to the ground. The fall's shorter."

Medard laughs, an I feel it through his back. The prester's gaze moves to him an waits till he stops, then switches back to me.

"The men found almost no one at the farmsteads they called at," he says to me. "Is this usual?"

"Most'll be at my uncle's," I say, "for the feast."

"What feast is this?"

I'm stuck. The prester must know it's Bloodnight, but I can't tell him Eldinghope still keeps a heathen feast.

"Arnsnight," I say, hopin we'll be gone before he can find out any different.

"Of course," he says. "Tell me, does your uncle often gather his tenants together like this?"

I look at Erland, who's come up on the prester's other side. His face is blank.

"They're always invited on feast days," I say. There can't be anythin wrong wi that, surely? Anyone wi the means for it provides a feast, just like Lord Frithrun did for the prester an Erland. It shows you have wealth enough.

Rememberin Lord Frithrun makes me feel better, but the prester's gaze is still on me. He runs a hand over the white-grey stubble of his cheeks.

With a flick of his hand he dismisses me. Erland takes up his reins to turn with us, but the prester holds him back, an Medard returns me alone to the cart. He hands me back to Berengar with a bow. Berengar's cheeks are pink, an Medard sees an laughs.

Berengar's short wi me. I don't bother tryin to coddle him out of it. Instead I think about how it felt when Medard laughed, his back against my chest, an I turn my face into the wind an pretend that's what turns my cheeks pink. I remember how I used to spend my time in the wayhouse moonin over Jarle to make my chores more excitin, an it seems years ago.

At noon we eat without stoppin, an soon after we get down to ford a stream. Medard circles round but Erland's already swung me onto his horse. I hide my disappointment as well as I can. I like Medard's flirtin, even if it is dangerous wi the prester watchin. It stops me thinkin of other things. Soon as the cart's up the other bank Erland sets me back on it. Berengar's still sulkin.

225

A strip of woodland breaks up the white fields as the cart climbs a long gentle slope. At the top I forget Berengar's prissiness. The woods end, an the road runs due north to two uneven standin stones.

I'd recognise em anywhere. The one on the right is a milestone, but the stone on the left is taller than a mounted man. A rough grey triangle, scoured by the wind an carved wi the form of a man an three spirals in each corner. The carvins have bin newly painted in red an blue. On the side facin away from us are the names of Eldinghope's masters in runes, right down to Grandpa Berr an Uncle Ulf. I can't read em, of course, but Rafe used to recite em for me. His name will be carved under Ulf's when he takes over the land.

About a hundred feet back from the stones is a young man with a strung bow. The cart moves slowly, but the soldiers trot towards him. The bow comes up, though he en't got a chance against so many riders.

Erland must be sayin somethin to him, cos the man answers, but I'm already down off the cart quicker'n Berengar can stop me. I run across the uneven snow towards the loose circle of horses, Fetch lopin beside me.

"What's yer business?" the young man's sayin.

"Rafe!" I call. "Rafe, it's me!"

My cousin looks up, his red hair burnin in the weak sun.

He just has time to unsling the arrow before I fling my arms around him.

"Gods, Ebba," he says, steadyin us both. "Yer for it."

Uncle Ulf can't whip me, but I can tell he'd like to.

"My name is Grimulf, prester of Sunacre." The prester is leanin back in the high chair while Ulf stands before him like he's the guest. I can see Ulf's hands clenchin. "This is Captain Erland of the king's guard. We are here on the king's business. You will provide lodgings for our men and beasts."

Ulf's eyes flick over me, but I keep my attention on the cauldron over the hearth. We're in Ulf's hall, an Rafe an Ulf's foreman are standin a few paces behind my uncle. The soldiers are lined along the walls by the door. A terrified servin girl is hidin in the kitchen.

Ulf weren't home when Rafe led us in, so the prester made himself comfortable. In Ulf's chair.

If I weren't under the prester's protection, I'd be breathless wi fear. As it is, it's all I can do to stir the cider without droppin the ladle. I wish I'd kept Fetch wi me, but I ordered him to guard the wagon an horses. I din't trust em not to come to mischief.

"An say I do," Ulf all but snarls, "will ye tell me what my brother's daughter is doin in yer company?"

"The girl's contract has been purchased from Berger Sorleyson of Frithberg," says Grimulf. "As has your debt."

Ulf grunts, but I see a vein poppin on his thick neck. Ulf's used to people fearin his temper. Maybe the shock of bein treated like a nobody will finish him off.

It en't goin to be that easy, but a girl can dream.

"Your debt is now owed to me, Farmer Ulfson," the prester says. "Payment is not due for a year, as the contract states, but since we were passing, courtesy demanded that I inform you in person."

There's an uneasy pause. The prester sits back, Erland a little behind him to his right. Erland's face is blank again, an now I know his history wi Grimulf, I wonder how many times he's stood like this, keepin himself unreadable, ready to enforce Grimulf's authority.

Ulf's gaze travels between the two, an his hands loosen.

"Lot of trouble fer one servin girl," he says, an there's a new note in his voice. "My son came back from Frithberg less'n ten days ago, an she were still Sorleyson's then. What would a fine lord like yerself want such a costly one for?" He leers.

I feel sick. I know what he's meanin. Grimulf gives my uncle the long, dead look he has that searches every part of you, but Ulf don't care. He's got his way in now, an he's gleeful.

"No," he says, all false an scrapin. "I can see yer not like that, bein the King's man an a holy man too. So it en't for beddin ye have her. Less she learnt to stop burnin meat it en't her cookin neither. She must have some other talent I don't recall."

I can feel his eyes on me, all over me, like pig slurry. Without meanin to I put my hand to my belt, where my salve box is strung in my pocket, but I catch myself an I make like I'm straightenin my skirts instead. I glance up into eyes like poison. If wishes were fishes, I'd be a dead one.

"Tell you what," Ulf says, lookin back to the prester. "My debt en't due a year, I know, but what wi the harvest in an the tithe I take from those on my land, I'm richer than I thought. Yer lordship's shown great charity towards a low girl like our Ebba, an that makes me anxious to show our gratitude. Let me pay you now, an you can release her back to me."

His words hit me like I bin kicked in the chest. My heart stops, my guts feel like they're spillin out of me.

If Ulf gets me back, he'll kill me.

I know it the same way I know the sun rises an fire burns. I know it from watchin him beat my brother, my mother an me ever since I can remember. Ever since the farm went up in fire an my da died.

Grimulf studies the thick gold ring on his left hand. "The girl has a year of service left," he says, soundin bored. Ulf opens his mouth, doubtless to say he'll pay, but the prester smiles down on him. "The contract does not specify early release upon payment of debt," he says. "I will take your payment, and you may have the girl in a year."

My heart slams back into action, an I choke a little as I remember to breathe.

I've never seen my uncle so furious. He gestures to Rafe, who almost runs from the room, his face a sick greenish white.

It weren't just us, I realise. *Me an Stig just got the everyday anger.*

An hard on that thought's heels: *I wonder who's bin catchin it since I left?*

I din't think to see Stig or Ma in the hall of course, but now their absence worries me. Where's he got em? Are they hidden away, or is it worse'n that?

I want to ask but I can't. The prester wants me silent, an he's all that's sittin between me an Ulf's anger.

Rafe comes back, followed by two farmhands carryin a great chest.

Ulf's hands shake wi rage as he unlocks it, an sets out a double handful of silver before the prester. Then he takes out a set of scales, but the prester holds up a hand. Ulf stops, fuming.

"We will use our scales too," says the prester, smilin at Ulf. "That way neither party can claim they were not fairly dealt with."

At his order, Berengar an another soldier leave their place at the door. The hall is tense, waitin for em to come back so's we can finish. The two farmhands standin by the chest look to Ulf, but wi eight armed men linin the walls, he can't do nothin.

A loud hiss makes me jump. The cauldron I'm tendin has boiled over, an I swiftly lift it out of the fire an set it down. I ladle the sweet hot cider into the cups, an stand to lay em out on the table between Ulf an the prester.

As I lay the last cup Berengar comes back wi the scales. As we cross paths I look up into his face.

I en't prepared for the pity I see there.

I see myself as he must see me – a girl from a family led by a brute, where fear an coarseness are the only things deservin of respect. That's all Ulf is to Berengar: too stupid to know he en't important, too used to usin his fists to know when he's bin beaten.

The shame hits me harder than I ever felt it before. I'm worse than a thrall. There were no chains, no collar holdin me here. Only my own lies. *Blood is thicker'n water. Your duty is to the family. Every mouthful of food you ever ate, you owe to him.*

But they en't my lies, are they? I din't get born knowin em, I learned em.

Too late I turn an look into Ulf's eyes. Too late I know he's seen everythin, from Berengar's pity to my shame, an everythin between us that made us feel em. All he needs is a way in. Now he's got one.

Side by side, Ulf an Berengar measure out the silver while the prester watches. Rafe fidgets next to the chest. His freckles stand out like ticks, an his eyes are firmly down. I stand back, hands twined so tight behind me I can't feel my fingers. Ulf might not have me yet, but my heart's racin, an I can barely see for dread.

He's still got Stig an Ma.

The payment is made, an Ulf an the prester sign the contract, followed by Rafe an Berengar for witnesses. The prester lifts his cup of hot cider an toasts Ulf.

"We thank you for you hospitality," he says. "Show the men their quarters, and have the girl's mother sent in."

My heart flips over. What if Ulf decides the next best thing to hurtin me is to hurt her?

Ulf pushes away his own cup.

"There can be no hospitality," he says.

Rafe an the foreman look horrified. To refuse hospitality is unheard of save between the direst enemies, where no trust is possible.

The prester knows it too.

"And why is that?" he asks, wi the softness of a whetstone.

"Because I've guests, an there's no room for more," says Ulf.

The prester narrows his eyes, an Erland's hand twitches on his belt, movin to his hilt. I hear the slither of eight swords being half-pulled from their sheaths as the soldiers respond to their captain's movement.

"If you refuse me, you refuse the king," he says.

"The king en't here," says Ulf, "an he won't be, not him nor his foreign dogs, till next spring." He stares at Erland an spits. "The snow's started. The passes will be closed before the half-moon. Yer on yer own, holy man, an round here, you don't mean shit. You have ten men, and a slut who's already beddin at least one of em."

For a moment my whole body goes numb. Berengar an the few soldiers who understand some of our tongue draw their blades. Ulf grins, not takin his eyes off the prester.

"Four of em, then," he corrects himself. Berengar's cheeks flame, but Erland puts a hand on his shoulder. I daren't look at the prester.

"Now," continues Ulf. "I have more'n a hundred men who work for me or who pay me tithes for the right to work my land. An tonight they come here to worship an feast, an not for no dead god who couldn't even save himself." Ulf spits again, an his spittle flecks the prester's boots. "So go. Tell yer king the men of the East don't want yer weaklin god. We prefer our own."

The prester rises, with a hand signal to Erland. "You're making a mistake," he says. "The Lord is a man of war, and he teaches my hand to war."

Ulf sneers, an moves aside to watch the prester pass. Rafe moves aside too, steppin deliberately into my path. Our eyes meet an I open my mouth, but Ulf beats me to it.

"Don't bother askin," he says, shovin Rafe away. "Rathna's dead. Serves the bitch right for whelpin you."

I'm stuck to the spot, my head swimmin. I try to speak but nothin comes out. Berengar grips my arm an pulls me out into the shadowed yard. Fetch runs to me immediately, growling low in his throat, an I put my arms around his neck. All around me the soldiers mount up swiftly, swingin shields over their backs. Berengar coaxes me up onto the cart, jumps up himself, an cracks the reins. The horses start forward, an I nearly spill off the cart as it jumps.

Somethin soft an wet finds my ear. Fetch balances behind me, licking my ear. Even he can't bring me back. I'm full up of hurt, loss worse'n anythin I ever felt. I can't move.

Ulf's farm falls behind us, an it may as well be the world. I feel like a spirit travellin a long white road to nothingness.

"Ebba." Someone shakes me, hard. I slowly come back to my body. It's cold an stiff.

Erland is leanin over me from his mount. The east is growin dark, though the sun's still above the mountains to our right. I take the skin Erland offers me an drink, then sputter as the mead hits my throat. It burns my nose, but I swallow it down an take another mouthful. I offer it to Berengar who shakes his head, his eyes on the road.

"We're nearly at the stones," Erland says. "We'll ride through the night. We need you awake, Ebba."

I nod dully. Erland rides ahead. I see the soldiers in formation, Adelhard's team ahead, Medard's behind.

"Your cousin gave me this," says Berengar softly. It's the first thing he's said since we left. He passes me a small wrap of cloth. Heavy. I stare at it blankly.

There's nothin in me. I bin gutted like prey, all my insides scooped out an fed to the dogs.

Fetch is in the back of the cart, whinin.

Fetch's hot tongue, lappin at my hand.

My hand in Fetch's wet mouth.

Like in a dream, I put my hand in my pocket an slide out the salve box. I open it. There en't much left. This is all I have left of Ma, I realise, an a pain so deep I think I'm dyin goes through me.

I dip my fingers into the slick white cream, an put em in my mouth.

It tastes waxy an foul, like ditch water, or the mushrooms you ate when you was little, an your ma thumped you to knock some sense into you.

I force myself to swallow, an when my stomach heaves – turns out I still have my guts after all – I take another gulp of mead to calm it. It seems to work.

I open the twist of cloth an look at what my cousin gave me.

The cart jerks, Fetch whines, my head swims. The sun sinks towards the mountains, turnin the sky to fresh blood.

Berengar turns towards me, an his face don't fit. I can see it stretched over the bones, the edges of the mouth all wrong an splittin.

I open my mouth to scream, but a wave of sickness chokes me.

"*Eyes up*," he says, only it en't him. Next to me my Follower's wearin my friend's skin, talkin to me like this is a dream.

It en't no dream.

"Ebba? Your eyes are wrong."

I blink. It's Berengar again, his face fittin over his own skull, his eyes wide. *He's frightened*, I think, but the thought comes from far away, like some else's.

Everythin's wrong. Inside me there's only emptiness, but outside . . .

Outside a web stretches around me, an I feel the threads thrum.

Ahead lie the black woods, an I feel em thick wi my uncle's men, their blades ready.

I feel Ulf headed into the foothills, his anger an pride fillin him up. I feel Rafe's sickness, an the moon heavy beneath the horizon.

Bloodnight.

I turn to Berengar. "My brother's back there," I say, "an we're goin to be ambushed."

Berengar gapes at me. "You said he was gone."

"They lied," I say, an I know I'm right. That wrongness I bin feelin has snapped into place: Ulf's eagerness to get us gone, an Rafe's gift.

Berengar signals Erland, who rides up.

"There are men in those woods," I tell him, "an I need to speak wi the prester. Right now."

Maybe it's somethin in my eyes or voice. Erland glances at Berengar, then jerks his head. I climb up behind him an we fly ahead. Erland whistles, loud an harsh, an the soldiers draw in, changin formation.

"What is it?" the prester asks, lookin at Erland, not me.

"My uncle's sent men ahead of us," I say, "an I have to go back for my brother."

The prester looks ahead to the woods. I can feel his thoughts slippin away, forgettin me.

"They're goin to kill him!" I say. "Look!"

An I pass him Rafe's gift.

A silver pendant in the shape of a horse.

"It's Bloodnight," I say. "You know what that means."

"Yes," says the prester, lookin from the pendant to me. "I was there. I saw Arn hung from the Harm Tree, I saw his queen murdered in her chamber, and I swore an oath."

He straightens, an pulls from his belt a heavy war axe, one side a curved an gleamin blade, the other a long, sharp spike.

"There was a time no man could stand before me without pissing himself," he says, an grins. The sudden coarseness of his words shakes me. His massive shoulders roll back, an I see a spark in his eyes I en't seen before, somethin different from his slow, steady willpower. It looks like pleasure.

"When I wear the armour of the Lord, no blade may hurt me," he says, an it's almost a chant. "His Word is my blade, his Covenant my helm." His voice wraps around me like smoke. "I it was who cut down Arn's defiled corpse, and I who led Prince Kolrand to his mother's death chamber. It was I who hunted down and brought him the hags who spawned the crime, and I who held them down while the axe was dulled, so that they should die the death they deserved. Then I swore a new oath to God, who is the King of Kings, that as I dealt with those vipers so shall I deal with all of his foes."

He reins in, an raises his axe the way he raises the cross at the ceremony.

"The Lord is my strength. He teaches my hands to war!" His great mule dances an screams its horrible noise. "Tonight we teach them the fear of God, and you, Erland of Hellingap, shall guard my back once more!"

As the first of the men hidden in the woods break cover, sendin arrows towards the on-comin soldiers, Erland's whistle pierces me again. In a flash, Medard is beside him. "Take the girl," Erland orders. Medard swings me up behind him like I'm nothin. "Go where she tells you and bring her back safe. God be with you."

As Medard turns I see Erland and Grimulf charge, Adelhard an the other men around em, an I see Fetch fightin free of the cart, lopin after Medard's horse, his mouth open an his fangs flashin yellow. I look for Berengar but we're too far away, an then Medard is shoutin for me to tell him where to go.

The sacred grove is up in the foothills. The horse wheels into the sunset an its mane seems like fire, our bodies like ash.

My arms wrapped around Medard's waist, I pray for real for the first time. All those other times, like when I was hopin for a good harvest or missin Ma, or because people were watchin me, that weren't prayin.

As we fly across the white fields into the bloody sun, I pray the White God will teach my hands what they need to learn.

Fifteen
SLAUGHTER

GALEN'S TALE

Camp of the Slipskins

I 've spent the last three days wondering how they'd greet me, these men I lived and killed with – whether they'd be as lonely for the past as me, and open their arms to the piece of it I carried, or whether they'd turn from it. Somehow I never believed they'd kill me.

I did run, though never so thief-like as Thorkel makes out. But then he always was one for putting pictures in your head. Pictures of heroes in the Great Hall, and there with them your brothers, who ate and laughed with you last night, and who died beside you this morning. That was a favourite, and he was good at it. Others he used sparingly: a knife in the dark, maybe, its spark quenched in your sleeping blood, if you didn't up and leave before dawn.

Thorkel's blow knocked me sideways in the mud, and my ears

are ringing, but I get the gist of his brag. *Kill em all*. That knife, the one he whispered about to me the night I ran, must of become a favourite picture too. Maybe it even usurped the other. If back then I was golden, Thorkel was a jug of honey, his words dripping sweetness into the barley-slush of the world. It stuck to everything, and we were happy to return to it, to sup from it, *brotherhood, glory, loyalty* . . . The words replaced spoils, replaced family and land, telling us this war, these men, this death, were all better than the things we'd given up.

They were, for me. All of it was. The one time in my life it was so. My happiness began with the day the old king cut off my hand. It wasn't unmixed, but from my mutilation to my banishing, I lived in bliss. As I left that night I crept into the still-open barrow and kissed my prince's brow, there where the arrow had not stove it in, and I knew there was nothin left for me, so I ran.

Often since I've thought I should have stayed, and taken Thorkel's knife gladly, if only I'd known what living would be like.

As the ringing fades and I spit mud from my tongue, I notice the quiet. I shove myself up on my bad hand, leaving strands of bloody drool in the mud, and see her coming down the track from the barrows.

This is the one who sheared Roaki. Of Lambtail, the girl who named her horse and turned handstands, there's no trace. When I left her yesterday her pleading followed me, her fear. I didn't know whether to believe her breathlessness. I thought some of that fever I'd seen in her had come back. I thought if it was so, and she was lying, she'd follow me.

Her face is painted with blood and earth. Her pale hair and her grey eyes glimmer through the grime, and she holds the spade I gave her yesterday in both hands, dirty knuckles white as she grips the handle. What did the boy say? *She dug her way out?*

Maybe this really isn't Lambtail, then.

There's silence as she approaches. I look up at Thorkel. The white shows all around his one eye. Thorkel was good at conjuring pictures, but now I remember he wasn't so good at things he hadn't conjured up himself. I look round. Faces familiar despite the years, but they all have the same dazed look.

The pale-haired creature stops before us, and plants the spade in the dirt, holding his gaze.

"That man is mine," she says, in a voice that is deep and rasping, not hers at all. She doesn't need to point. We all know she means me.

"And who are you?" Thorkel sneers.

"Don't you remember me?" she says.

"No one will remember you," says Thorkel, "whoever you are. Take her," he orders, and men step towards her, but hesitantly.

"I'm not here for the others," she says, her strange voice rasping. "I, Roaki of Ridgemouth, am here for *you*."

She stands tall in the thin light of sunset, and behind her I think I glimpse another shape, broader, darker, like a man made of shadow.

"Don't try to trick me, girl," says Thorkel, grabbing a handful of my hair and hauling me to my knees. "Roaki died a thief's death in Frithberg. This one told me so. He's paid for his betrayal."

"We all pay," says the dead man's voice on the child's tongue. "You too have a debt owing. Your prince ordered you to follow the Staffbearers' choice, and you swore. But here you are."

Thorkel's fist tightens in my hair. Only me and Thorkel heard my prince's dying wish, and that's why Thorkel took such care to run me off. He didn't trust the Staffbearers, and he wouldn't submit to them.

The maimed remains of the Slipskins gaze between the man with poison honey on his tongue, and the filthy child with a voice that's not hers. They don't seem surprised. Their eyes flicker like they're seein things that aren't there.

"Did he tell you that as well?" spits Thorkel. "The Sungiven was a whore, and a vassal of whores. We are the last true men."

"The world has changed. Let him go, or give me a sword."

"Even if it is you," says Thorkel. "I'll kill this girl before you can blink. Then where will you be? No body, no mouth for speaking lies. You'll be worse than nothing, Roaki."

"Give me a sword."

Thorkel flicks his hand, and the thrall-boy rushes over with a single-edged sword from the smithy and a round shield. I close my eyes. With the strongest Luck in the world this girl can't face Thorkel and live.

"Hold your Luck close, girl," Thorkel tells her, kicking me aside. "Maybe I'll kill you quickly."

He takes the shield that's passed to him, and draws his sword.

I scramble backwards in the mud like the rest, my legs still hobbled. Thorkel whips his head so his braids dance and the beads clatter, and he bellows at the darkening sky. The sound echoes through the camp.

A Slipskin tosses the bullroarer up and sets it spinning. The droning buzz fills up the valley, presses on our ears like water.

Roaki, Lambtail, whoever she is, stands with her feet wide, but the sword point dips down to the mud. Her eyes are wide, the grey eaten up by black.

They begin to circle. The light is dying, but no one expects this to last long.

Thorkel charges forward, his sword swinging up and under her shield, but she leaps back like a deer, catching the blow and cutting towards his unprotected shoulder. Her blow is knocked away; she's too far away to hit him fast, and coming closer means getting in reach of a man so big he could hug her to death. He charges again, and this time she can't dodge. His first blow knocks her sideways and his second seeks her shoulder, even as she catches herself and side-steps.

The movement saves her – the cut isn't deep, and her arm still works. Her sword lunges up and under, Thorkel knocks it away, and she steps up smartly and smashes the edge of her shield up into his face. Blood pours from his nose, and she steps out again, her sword snaking up to cut into his blind shoulder, the same cut he just inflicted on her.

The bullroarer fails as the man turning it loses the steady rhythm, his mouth hanging open.

Thorkel has his face towards me now, so I can see the same shock in his eyes.

Strong hands haul me up onto my feet as she closes with him again. I look round into bright blue eyes in a familiar scarred face.

"Laugi?" I ask.

"Aye," says the blue-eyed man. His eyes don't flicker like his companions'. "An I can see it's you, Galen. Is it true?"

"That Roaki's in her?" I twist to keep my eyes on the two. Blood bubbles from Thorkel's nose as well as two more cuts. "I don't know. But he used to bloody his enemies the same, didn't he?"

"That's no proof —" says Laugi, but his eye follows the girl weaving through the dusk.

He's seeing what I've been seeing, then. Something inside us recognises her.

Thorkel's decided to use what she hasn't – brute strength. If he can lock with her she'll go down. He forces her to dance around him, leaping and dodging. She won't be able to keep that up and hold the sword, strong as she is. She's lasted longer than anyone would have guessed, but she's tiring, and Thorkel is used to the weight of his weapon.

"Laugi," I say, "when she dies —"

"I won't save you," he says, almost kindly.

"Unhobble me," I say, "give me a chance. For old times' sake."

"Was it true about the Sungiven? Did the prince say to follow her?"

I nod. Thorkel's blade crashes into the girl's shield and it splinters. She cries out, and Thorkel laughs. I know her arm must be numb from the blow, maybe even broken.

"What's the world like?" Laugi asks, bending to cut the hobble from my ankles now that the fight seems decided.

"You'll have to go see it," I say, but as I do something changes.

The girl has been dodging, but now she flings away the shield, pushing Thorkel's sword aside and diving in. Her scream rents the air, and the blade feints down, dances up, and then slams down into Thorkel's shoulder. I can hear the crunch of the blade chopping the collar bone, and then she lets go, diving away from his sword as he sweeps it round to her. She rolls, jumps to her feet and snatches up the spade from where it stands in the mud.

She brings it down on Thorkel's sword hand, a shattering blow.

Her sword is still lodged in his shoulder. It's dark enough now that the blood looks black.

The men are quiet. Thorkel is on his knees, staring through her, his breath gurgling in his throat.

I stagger towards her on numb feet, pins and needles stabbing up my legs.

"Roaki?" I ask, but the face staring back at me is hers, white and sweating under the blood and grime. "You have to kill him," I say, careful not to turn my back on Thorkel. "No one can heal of that blow."

I look into her eyes and I can see her horror.

"You've slaughtered pigs?" I ask in a low voice. She nods. "This is the same. You did well, but if you show weakness now, we're dead."

"I can't," she whispers.

"You have to."

The thrall-boy is at her side, offering her a long sharp knife. I press it into her hands.

"Every warrior learns this," I tell her. "This is what it means to be merciful."

She grips the hilt and steps towards Thorkel. He's still on his knees, each breath a horrible drawn-out retch. He's staring at her, and as she comes up to him, he lifts his broken hand in what looks like welcome.

All around us, the Slipskins drop to their knees – first Laugi, then the others – till we're the only ones standing.

Lambtail steps behind Thorkel, cradling his chin almost lovingly in her left hand. With her right, she raises the knife, but she hesitates. Her eyes find mine.

"Give him a warrior's death," I say, loud enough for the watching men to hear. "He'll lie with our prince, the last retainer of Geir Arnson."

Still she hesitates, but I keep my eyes on her, and she pulls back his head, and cuts.

I remember it being easy, that cut, but she struggles with it. Struggles to keep it clean, as her blade goes too deep and catches. Struggles with the weight of him as he twitches and bleeds out, her arm across his chest slippery with gore.

I look away. Maybe I should be glad for his suffering, but I understand at least a little why he stayed here; why he chose to ignore the passing of the world we made for ourselves into a world where we had no place. Landless men, without family, without fealty. Less than the lowest thrall.

At last the lifeless body drops.

I look round at the men.

"Is there any here who believes it was unfairly done?" I ask loudly, but I get no reply. They're gazing at the blood-covered girl, their eyes rolling. It's a horrible sight.

"Laugi," I say, "see to the body."

I don't want to stay and watch them open the barrow.

The boy is at my side. "Packs and horses ready," he says, smiling. He hands me a full ale skin, and the relief makes me sweat.

"Who are you?" I ask, gulping down a mouthful. Rot-gut, of course, but sweet as mead to my thirst.

"That's Fenn," says Lambtail, limping towards us. "He's coming with us."

"Then we'd better go," I say. "I see you're not fainting anymore, girl."

"I think that's over," she says, her voice hoarse. "Will they hunt us?"

"Not tonight, at least," I say, and Fenn shakes his head in agreement. "But we can't cross the Floodlands in the dark."

Lambtail looks at Fenn, whose smile widens.

"Come," he says, and without waiting, he turns and heads off into the night.

I look at Lambtail, who shrugs.

"It's worked so far," she says.

Sixteen

BLOODNIGHT

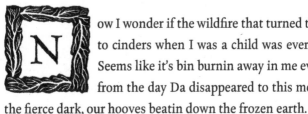ow I wonder if the wildfire that turned the world to cinders when I was a child was ever put out. Seems like it's bin burnin away in me ever since, from the day Da disappeared to this moment in the fierce dark, our hooves beatin down the frozen earth.

We come to the buryin ground just as the full moon slips out of the soil.

Medard pulls up, his horse tossin its head, an he raises his arm to cross himself, but I'm in the way.

I point across the humped ground an up the slopes. The trees grow thick, but we can see the fire glow.

"That's it," I say, hoarse from the cold. "That's them."

Medard says somethin in Southern that sounds like swearin. I suddenly feel alone, no matter I'm sat close enough to feel his body's warmth. I'm closer to the cold bones in their cold graves than I am to this outlander.

"What they do?" Medard asks in my ear.

I try to speak, but my body feels like it's strung out on a thread that passes from the hazy white of the moon right through me to the hot red of the sacred fires. I'm bein pulled apart. Behind me the prester whirlin with his axe. Ahead . . .

I know what's ahead. I bin among the worshippers for Bloodnight since I was old enough. The knobbled club, the sharp knife, the sacred oak. The firelight an the shadows. The spray of warm blood across our faces.

But that was just beasts, I think. A bull, a ram, a boar. Led each in turn to the Harm Tree, so's we might offer em up an give thanks an feast.

I know, I *know* it en't so this night.

A thin, tight thread piercin my heart. Pullin me away an towards.

I could turn, I think. *Turn an leave an never come back here again. Ulf's dug his grave. Grimulf will be back in the spring to finish him. His land will be taken, an the prester an the merchant will have their road to the East. I could leave an be free.*

An Medard whispers in my ear, in a voice that en't his, in a voice full of teeth: "*You won't ever be free, farm girl. This is family. This is blood. Eyes Up.*"

The world slips an shivers around me, pulled tight. The threads are criss-crossed, knotted up. Time to cut through em.

"I'll lead you," I say, turnin. Medard's face is close to mine. I'm glad to see it's him wearin it. "Let me down."

I guide him through the dark, around the graves an up the path to the grove. When we reach the sheep pens he tethers his horse an we go on foot. He walks beside me, his knife out. As we get nearer the glow I see a man standin across the path above us. It's one of the labourers I grew up knowin. Medard presses me back, meanin I should wait, then slips into the forest. I stand there listenin to the fire an the voices, the flute an the drum. I wish Fetch were wi me, but he fell behind as we rode. I tell myself he'll be here soon.

A figure rises up from the dark beside the man ahead of me, puts an arm around him, an dances with him. A jerky, leg-kickin, arm-flyin dance, that ends wi stillness an heaviness.

Medard walks back to me, his knife dark an drippin.

"Shhh," he says. "Secret, yes?"

I nod, my heart poundin, an he nods me on. We pass the man, sprawled to the side of the path. His head is thrown back, his throat gapes open.

I look towards the fire. I feel like a skin full of embers.

Medard steers me away from the path. We circle the red glow, echoin the worshippers in the grove as they sway an circle the fire. The flute an the drums are just warmin up, an the dance is light. Later, once all these lit-up faces are speckled red, the dance will go faster an faster, until the fire dies low enough to drive the sheep through the ashes, to keep em from ague an to protect next year's lambs from the snows.

My eyes rake through the dancers, lookin for Stig. If he's among em I'm wrong, an we can leave before they find the dead man on the path.

He en't there. I knew it already, but I wanted to be wrong.

I find Ulf easy, watchin over the rest from beside the big oak, an close to him stands the Staffbearer, her fur cap framin her painted face. She holds her iron staff, an behind her hangs the noose. My hands remember the scarred branch of the oak at Birchold, where a similar noose must of hung before the villagers turned from it.

Restin in Ulf's hands is the hard-wood club, knobbled an cruel. I don't need imagination, I *know* what it does to an ox's skull. A man's skull is probably much the same.

I turn to Medard to tell him what'll happen next. I en't ready for what I see.

Horror spoils his handsome face. His lips twist in disgust. His eyes are fixed on the oak an the two standin beneath it, an I find I daren't touch him. This is all familiar to me, even if my gut's sick from guessin how it's bin changed this year, but to him it's unnatural, evil. Heathen.

I see em the way he must. The dancers cry out with the drums an flutes, an I see their slack jaws, their wild eyes.

Then out among em I see one slacker an wilder than the rest. Dark hair tangled an loose. Dark eyes rollin. Dark hands flung high.

Ma.

I lose sight of her an sink to my knees, dizzy. But it was her. You can't mistake your own flesh like that. She's here. She en't dead.

Medard's got his arm around me, pullin me up, but my legs won't work.

She's alive. She knows what's goin to happen, an she's here.

"Brother?" asks Medard. I shake my head, tryin to stand. I want to run. I wish I'd listened to myself an run. It's far too late for that now.

One soldier an a girl, against more'n a hundred of em.

They could tear us apart.

I should of known that before, but I din't. I guess I thought if we told em to stop, they would. That if we took the boy maybe they'd be content wi the bull an the ram an the boar, like most years.

Rafe's red head catches my eye. I focus on it through the whirlin, burnin dark, an I see he leads a figure in white.

Tall an thin, hair lopped short on his neck. Dark patches under his already dark skin, where blows have coloured him up. The loose white robe, his feet bare on the winter ground.

Stig stumbles into the firelight, blinkin an shiverin, shyin away from the dancers.

I tug on Medard's sleeve, my eyes never leavin my brother. I don't even have to point. He's my shadow, after all. You can see at once he don't belong. We never did. An now they're gettin rid of him, same as they got rid of me.

The knotted threads, held tight in the dark, slip open.

Same as they got rid of Da.

Everyone's got their place, Ma used to tell me. *Everyone's got a use. You owe your life to your family. Every bite.*

The drums drown everythin out. They beat faster an faster, till the flute falls behind an the dancers are stilled, shudderin an yellin as the drums fill em.

I know what that feels like. It feels good. It feels joyful.

The drums stop. The dancers are gathered round the oak, the fire at their backs. Medard starts to move again, an I follow him round towards the oak. The fire shines through the dancers' hair, leavin their faces in shadow.

The Staffbearer moves forward, her heavy iron staff raised into the firelight. One side of her face is painted black, an her blue eye stands out in its bed of white. Tonight she works for the Wise One, the winter god, the god of the dead.

She spreads her arms, an two women come forward with

Walpurgis, who used to be the Cornmaiden. Her wooden statue has a crown an garland woven out of the last sheaf of corn left standin on Ulf's land. The women set the statue up on a chair beside the Harm Tree to watch. Later her crown an garland will be thrown on the fire, before the sheep are driven through it.

The women come forward an kneel before the tree with wide shallow bowls. I know what's comin. It will be very quick now.

The Staffbearer opens up her mouth an sings. It's the song of the Wise One's death, the story of how he learned the secret of godhead.

"I'll speak to em," I say, turnin to Medard.

"Wolves no speak," he says.

"These en't wolves," I say. "They're my people."

I can tell from his hard face what he thinks of that, but I have to try.

"How would you save him?" I ask.

I see his answer before he can form it. We en't goin to save Stig. There's too many of em. We're just goin to watch.

I move quicker than I knew I could. If I don't, he'll stop me. I slip away from him to the edges of the grove, where these people I grew up wi stand swayin to the Staffbearer's song, an I join em, they givin me no more pause than if a dog stepped back among em, or a sheep to the flock. They're all caught up, all yearnin forwards.

The Staffbearer's song stops, an her voice calls out the Wise One's words.

"I know that I hung on a windy tree nine long nights," she says, an it's a whisper, like the fire's tongue. "Sacrificed on that Harm Tree whose roots run deeper than man can dig."

The drum starts. I start pushin my way through, but everyone is pushin, everyone is fightin to be at the front.

"No bread nor mead to wet my lips, yet I died not," hisses the Staffbearer. "No mercy from the world, yet I remained whole."

I fight harder, shovin wi hands an elbows. All the times I seen it done, this is when they noose the bull. Strong, broad shoulders block my view. I scream, but it don't matter, other voices drown me out.

"Downwards I dove, the harrier at my heels, down among the dead, where I hunted the runes," says the Staffbearer, an she en't whisperin no more. I double over, an push between the legs of those in front of me. "Howling I took them, and downwards I fell."

I burst out of the crowd into the space before the oak. I barrel past the Staffbearer, knock Rafe aside, the noose still in his hands, an press Stig against the oak's rough bark.

I turn to face em.

This is the moment, I think. *If you're comin, God, this is the time.*

I look into their faces, best I can. I remember the faces when I walked the fire, the way they waited on my words. If only I can find the right ones now, maybe I don't need anythin more.

But no words come. The fire behind the dancers throws us all in shadow. All save Ulf, who's already steppin up to me, club raised.

Fetch leaps out of the dark, his fangs out an his tongue a wet red banner. His front paws slam into Ulf's shoulders, the long claws dig in, an the fangs snap an inch from Ulf's face.

The dancers sway, not knowin whether to rush forward or back, but the Staffbearer steps towards me, hand reachin for her knife. Quicker than words, Medard is there, wrestlin her down an pinnin her arms.

The dancers sway forward a step.

"Stand back!" I shout, an I hear my voice crack. It don't sound like a command. It sounds like a scared girl.

I'm back in the hall, all those years ago, callin Rafe a liar. All the men an women turnin their faces from me, pretendin they couldn't hear nor see. Ma's smile when Stig put it right by beatin me.

I should hate them. I think I do. I wonder if that's what kept the fire burnin, all the pain an humiliation, every blow I took, every wrong I dropped my eyes to, just like they dropped theirs. It fills me up wi black smoke, chokes out everythin else.

Everythin slows, everythin softens. The dancers set down roots. Medard holds down the Staffbearer, his knee in the small of her back. She writhes like a trapped eel. Ulf an Fetch growl at one another, the club dropped, the yellow fangs seekin flesh. Rafe watches his father, eyes wide wi fright.

I can barely feel Stig behind me. He's huddled into himself, skin an bone. The place where my back pushes against him is cold.

My heart cracks open like an egg. Somethin inside fights its way out, an somethin outside of me streams in.

My eyes fill up wi fire. My whole body is burnin, not hot nor cold, but alight, an each breath is bliss. The thick smoke has bin cleaned out, an now the wildfire has become pure flame.

My eyes clear, an I see again. Only this time there's nothin but this pure light within me. It lights up their faces stronger than day. My body's flooded an warm, the way it felt when Da held me in my dream.

"Stop," I say, an my voice is strong. "If you kill this boy, it'll be like you placed your own heads in the noose."

They falter, an they en't dancers no more, just a band of people I know. We've worked together, eaten together. I know their fear, because it's bin my own.

"Rafe," I say. He steps round Ulf, whose right hand is trapped in Fetch's jaws. My uncle's whimperin, an I can hear the crackle of bone. Rafe glances at him, but I call him again an he comes. We're all bred to obedience, after all.

"We grew up side by side," I say to him. "All three of us. So what's this?"

I look into his eyes an I see what a thin line I have him on. If Ulf escapes Fetch, or any of the others start up, he's lost to me. But he's the one who gave me the sign, who brought me here. He must of wanted me to come.

"What did he do, Rafe?" I can feel Stig shiverin behind me, a hard, bone-deep shiver that won't let up. "I want to understand. I need to know so's I can forgive you. I want to forgive you."

Rafe seems to be havin trouble with his words. There's a scuffle among the watchers an someone stumbles through the line.

"He en't right," says Ma. "None of us are. It's our fault."

After that first glimpse, I thought seein her like this would be too much. That I'd fall or cry or die. But now that she's here, I feel a muffled crunch, like Ulf's bones in Fetch's jaws, an that's all. Just a child's love bein buried, an sadness growin in its place.

"I din't ask you," I say, an though I say it gentle, she draws up like she bin slapped. "You had your chance. Twice-over, if Da was the first. I'm done wi you." I turn back to Rafe. "Is that what you think? We en't right?"

Rafe just shakes his head, dumb.

"This land is cursed," croaks the Staffbearer. Medard mashes her face into the dirt, but I stop him. She raises her painted face an spits to clear her mouth. "The seed dies in the soil."

"I saw enough wealth today to know you lie," I tell her.

"The curse can be held off," she says, "but it takes a man's blood, every nine years. You saw it yourself girl. Death entered the soil last year. A reminder."

"Like the Raiders' fire was a reminder?" I ask. "Is every bad year a reminder? Elsewhere it's just bad luck. This en't no curse."

"It's the Raiders' curse on you," says the Staffbearer, twistin her neck to stare her blue eyes at me. "It was set when your ma was took, an it ends if the blood of the land's master is spilled."

"But that would be . . ." the words dry up on my tongue. I look at Rafe, who hangs his head. I look at Ma, in her own little space cos the others don't want to be near her.

Blood's thicker'n water. You owe your family your life.

"My da died for *him*?" I ask, pointin at Ulf. "An now he wants my brother too?" My uncle's curled under Fetch's claws, his face bloodless. "When was it goin to stop? When you ran out of brothers an nephews? When you ran out of sons?" Rafe bites his lip, face as white as his father's. "Or when they'd had enough, an strung you up themselves?"

The light that seemed so strong an pure within me wavers, washed by sickness. The faces of the watchers sink back into shadow, melt into one another. I'm forgettin their names, their places in my life.

If blood's what they want, maybe that's what I should give em.

A scream like the mountain breakin open tears through the night. The earth trembles, an Grimulf on his horse-beast lunges into the clearin, flanked by the other soldiers.

The prester roars. His axe is bloody, an as his mule rears, its hooves flash red. It's like my sickness called him, to do what I can't. The people near him scatter, only to be ringed by Erland's men.

The light inside me flares.

"You want forgiveness," I say to Rafe, "this is your only chance. Get em to kneel to him, an he won't kill you." He hesitates, sweat standin out on his brow. I think of what he must of gone through, bein told it's his father or his cousin. That he had to help.

"You want this curse wiped out without havin to kill your own father?" I ask him, an I make sure my voice is loud enough to carry.

He nods, hope in his eyes.

"Then you have to fight it. The White God can do that. Will you take him to be your Lord an Master?"

The Staffbearer twists an yowls like a cat. One arm comes free, an her silver knife darts to Medard's side. He falls, trappin her legs, an she kicks herself free just as Grimulf cuts his way through the crowd. She stands, graspin her iron staff before her.

"Our time will come again!" she screams. "Even now —"

Her lips are still movin when the clotted iron spike of the axe drives into her skull, in one slick motion.

Blood sprays over me, warm flecks on my face an chest. Dimly I see Medard's mouth movin, like he's gaspin for air.

Grimulf drops easily beside me. The body of the Staffbearer with its ruined head lies at his feet.

"What will it be?" he asks, his teeth bared in a grin.

Rafe looks from the dead Staffbearer to his whimperin father, then from Grimulf to me.

He drops to his knees. "Protect us, sister," he says to me.

"I en't your sister," I tell him, "but I'll stand for you same as I stood for my own brother." I turn to the watchin crowd as Erland runs to Medard's side.

"This is the last Bloodnight," I say, loud an clear, an no one dares look away. "The White God is here among us, an the Wise

One's Staffbearer is defeated. Is there any other who'll be the old god's champion this night?"

No one moves. I reckon Grimulf's bloody face an toothy smile have somethin to do wi that.

"Then kneel!" bellows Grimulf, wieldin his axe. The spike drips gore. "Any who stays standing will be judged a challenger."

They drop so quick you'd think they'd bin felled. Grimulf looks a little disappointed, truth be told. But then they've lived under Ulf, same as me an Stig, same as Ma and Rafe. They've learnt to obey.

I'm glad not to see em cut down, but it makes my heart hurt to know em for what they are.

I call Fetch off Ulf. My uncle looks smaller curled round his ruined hand. I remember what Stig said once, about Ulf dyin a coward's death. Seems he was right.

"Rafe," I say, "get us mead an bread. I know there'll be some."

Rafe scutters between the soldiers, away from Grimulf an me.

I turn at last to Stig. I find I'm scared.

"Stig?" I say. "It's me. Ebba."

His eyes are rolled up under his lids, an he leans against the oak like it's holdin him up. His right cheek is scratched where he pressed it against the bark. His left cheek is yellow with old bruises. He's taller, same as Rafe, but his bones show through the skin.

I'm glad I din't see him properly first time. If I had I might not have given Rafe an the others a chance to kneel.

"I'm takin you wi me this time," I tell him, an it's a promise.

There's a ragged scream. Ulf is on his feet, one hand hangin useless, but with the other he swings the club at my head.

The axe flashes, an Ulf's head spins into the dark. His body falls an shudders, blood spurtin over the soil.

In the silence, I hear someone bein sick. *That should be me*, I think, but it's like I'm empty again. I look from Ulf's body to Medard's, then back to Stig's face. *This is all you can afford to think of*, I tell myself.

So I kneel as Grimulf stands before the oak an leads the ceremony, quicker than I seen it done in Birchold, and gorier. This time I en't there to heal. I'm cupbearer, like I used to be in my uncle's hall, an I offer each person the cup of mead, givin each one a sip. Even green-faced Rafe an slack-jawed Ma. This is the blood of the Lord, I tell em, an now it's in you.

Grimulf hands out the bread. My morsel has a bloody thumb print on it. I swallow it down, an it feeds the fire till I can't sleep for the light of my God fillin me.

Part Three:
NO WAY
HOME

Seventeen

FLOOD

TORNY'S TALE

Across the Floodlands to the North

I make Galen go with Fenn to help with the horses. He doesn't want to leave me, but I make him. Seems I can do that now.

The mist from the Floodlands has crept up into the camp. I tell myself that's why I'm so cold, why I can't stop shivering. I keep my hands on my belt so no one can see how they're shaking. My shield arm is clumsy from Thorkel's blows, and the gash in my shoulder should hurt more than it does, but for now the pain seems far off.

"You," I say to the blue-eyed man called Laugi. "Show me your master's goods."

He takes me into the largest of the shacks dug into the hillside. No windows, no air, just the close stink of unwashed bodies and smoke. I try not to cough. In the light of a dying fire, he opens a chest and lays out his master's wealth.

Thorkel's belongings are few enough. Armour and weapons, once good, now worn and mended in patches. Laugi seems almost protective of them as he lays them out, caressing them as he might a nervous creature. His bright blue eyes never leave me.

I stare at them, but the objects dance before my eyes, and if the price were death I could not choose among them.

"Mistress," says Laugi, "if I may ask, do you look for yourself or for comrade Roaki?"

I almost laugh. This man is speaking to me the way a craftsman on Smithgate might treat a wealthy customer, as if these are goods for sale, not the grave.

"You knew him," I say. "Choose for me."

So he picks out a warrior's choice from the battered wares, wrapping them in a cloak, while I hide my impatience.

At last he's done, and I turn to leave.

"Mistress," he says. "You've taken nothing for yourself."

"I've taken enough," I say. Thorkel's blood itches as it dries on my skin.

But Laugi reaches into the chest and pulls out a soft leather bag. He opens it, and draws out a helm. It's finer than the rest, gold-washed, and the visor is in the shape of a hawk, wings outstretched.

He holds it out to me.

"I can't take it," I say.

"It's yours," says Laugi, his blue eyes unblinking. "No one's earned it since Geir fell. The Harrier Helm is yours."

But I don't want it.

"Bring the rest," I say, and I force myself to walk, not run, from that dank hole.

My strength drains as I step outside, like water from a leaking bowl. My hands shake so hard I cannot stop them, and all the hurts of my body clamour. My legs turn weak.

At once, Fenn is at my side, propping me upright.

"Good," he says quietly. "Very good. Your butcher is leaving. Don't show it."

I straighten as Laugi comes out. Fenn darts forward to take the bundle from his arms, and I follow him towards the shore, as straight and upright as I can.

I feel Laugi's eyes on me until the mist swallows us up.

The long, flat-bottomed boat is ready, and Galen waits by its stern, a tall pole resting in the crook of his arm. Hero and Sweetpea are already aboard, penned in makeshift stalls. They don't like it. I hold Hero's head and talk to her. I try to feel nothing but her warm breath. I press my face into her neck and breathe in the homely mix of horse-sweat and dust.

Fenn settles himself in the bow and calls to Galen, who sets the pole into the shallows behind us, and pushes off.

Fenn seems to find his way by smell. He sits with his face turned up, like a hound casting for a scent. In the guttering rushlight his iron collar looks like a ring of dirty shadow about his neck. He calls instructions back to Galen, guiding us between floating tufts of marsh-grass. We slide quietly through the rippling dark, the splash and swirl of the long punting pole the only sound of our passage.

I wrap myself in blankets and settle myself among our packs, but the trembling doesn't stop. Soon my whole body's shaking so hard my teeth click. In the flickering light the mist hangs like cold sweat on a fevered body.

I can't close my eyes. Exhaustion pierces me like a needle, and images rush out of the night. Blows rain down on me, making me flinch. My throat aches as I speak words I can't hear. Thorkel's blade throbs in my flesh, and the awful crunch of my sword biting into his collar-bone jars me. I feel a weight on my chest, huge and slippery, and deep inside me something slick and eel-like slithers up my spine between my organs, full of sickening joy.

The filth has seeped inside of me. I am unclean.

A long way away, through the mist and the shaking, someone's swearing.

"We need to land. She's burning up."

"No land."

"One of these islands —"

"No islands. Just weeds."

"If we don't get her warm —"

The shaking takes me away from the voices and into the mist. It crashes through me in waves, wearing me down.

A light appears, and heat washes over my face. My chin is caught in a tight grip, holding me over the light.

"Drink," someone says, and a cup is held to my lips. The fumes make me cough, but I drink it. It's bitter, and laced with the strong spirits I've smelt on Galen's breath. It blazes a warm line from my throat to my stomach.

The warmth brings me round. A small fire burns in an earthenware pot, scorching my cheeks. I'm wrapped in cloaks and blankets, like a baby in swaddling, and Galen is holding me in his lap.

"Do it," he says. "Quick."

He's holding my left arm tightly, too tightly, and my arm is bare, free of the layers of heavy fabric.

Fenn takes a blade from the fire pot, its blade glowing like the dawn.

I scream as it touches my shoulder. It's worse than Thorkel's blade, worse than the shaking. Galen clamps his arms around me, holding my head and arm still. I try to kick, but my legs are bound.

Fenn takes the blade away, and Galen rocks me like a child. He murmurs to me while Fenn dresses the wound on my shoulder, telling me I'm safe, but the mist is rolling in again. I go to it willingly. Fenn's blade has burned the rest to ash, and I hold that pain before me like a torch, emptying the darkness of fear.

Thorkel's dead weight lies across my chest, suffocating me. I fight my way free of it, and pull a long, cool breath into my lungs. Sweat dries on my hot skin, dampening the heat in my bones, and for a moment relief runs through me. It was a dream.

But then my shoulder throbs, the chill enters my flesh, and as the shaking begins again, I remember Thorkel. Remember how the knife snagged on his voice-box, how the blood spurted hot across my hands.

There's no order this time, just someone holding me up so I can drink, but I push it away.

"Come on," coaxes Galen, "just one sip. There we go. Not so bad. And another."

The sun is shining through the mist, and the world around us is white. I turn my face into its light. I want to forget the fathoms of dark water beneath me, the cold, dead depths. I want to stay here, where the darkness can't reach me.

I float where air and water meet, light above me, darkness below. The cold enters at the base of my spine, and when it fills me I shake, but then the sun strokes its rough fingers across my cheeks, and the shakes are burned out of me for a spell. I hang between the two, burning and trembling, longing for rest.

When the sun sets, the mist thickens, and my body shakes longer, harder. The scorching warmth of the fire pot can only drive it off for a short while.

"How much longer?"

"One night and one day."

"We're nearly out of fuel for the fire, and I need to sleep. If the fever doesn't break . . ."

The dark sweeps me up for what feels like a long time, full of noises I try not to hear.

"I can break it," says Fenn through the dark.

"You?"

"Her butcher is fighting. He doesn't want to leave."

"And what can you do about it?"

The darkness spits me out into the weak light of the fire pot. Fenn is turned away from me, looking for something. Galen's face is hagged, dark circles like bruises under his eyes. He takes a pull from a half-empty ale skin, swaying.

Fenn turns back. In his hands he holds the mirror.

"What's that?" asks Galen.

"A door," Fenn says. He bends over the mirror, his dark hair hiding his face. "I need his name."

"Roaki."

I shake so violently my teeth chatter.

"Hold her."

Galen puts my head in his lap and holds me in place with his right hand and left forearm. I cry out, although he's careful not to touch my burn. Inside I can feel something bunch and coil, wrapping itself around my spine like a snake around a branch.

I panic. My muscles stiffen, bucking up off the planks, and the sudden movement rips me out of Galen's grip. The horses shy away from me, kicking at their stalls, and Galen swears, his arms locking around my neck and shoulders, forcing me down. This time he's not so careful, and I open my mouth to scream.

A voice rips from my lungs, harsh and grating, but the words make no sense to me. It might as well be the voices of the gulls that nest on the cliffs back home, mobbing us as we walk backwards over the cliffs to steal their gold-yolked eggs. It might as well be the waves on the reef. The thing inside me will not go quietly.

Fenn is crouched over the mirror, his eyes closed. He seems not to notice the rocking boat, the awful voice, the scared horses. His mouth is open in a dark O.

The eel-like thing inside me slips, loses its grip.

Fenn's eyes snap open.

"Roaki," he says. "Don't fight. You're already dead."

The thing inside me thrashes, but I can feel it being dragged out of me, through the cold spot at the base of my spine. It slithers invisibly towards the mirror, and as it stretches between metal and flesh, blackness leaks in at my eyes and nose, and swamps me.

It's a perfect blackness, and I lie in it a long time. My body is still and silent. There's no pain, and that scares me. The pain is real, even when nothing else is.

There are breaks in the blackness. White, shimmering interruptions, unspooling like thread.

I walk between shining white lines, treading a long, slow path from the inside out.

When I wake, my lips taste of salt.

Fenn is curled up against me, his thin body nestled into my side. He looks like any small child, not like someone who could hold a white-hot blade to another's flesh, or wrestle a dead man from one world to the next.

The mist has left dew on his eyelashes. I put my arm – my left arm, painful but real – around him and in his sleep he snuggles closer to me.

The boat rocks gently, sending ripples across the grey waters. The mist thins, and starts to turn pink. Gold bars shoot through the upper veils like spears. The sun is coming up in glory, and the water and the air soften for it. I feel like I'm adrift on a sea without end, alone except for the small body at my side. I'm not afraid. I feel free.

My heart soars up into the gold and pink mist and floats there, while the wheel of the sun rises over the mountains.

At noon, we send the remains of Roaki down into the depths of the Floodlands. I say we should bury him on one of the islands, but Fenn shows me that the islands are just mats of floating weeds, with nothing solid beneath them. So into the dark water he goes, his spoils weighting down the fistful of hair. I wait to feel something, but under the flat light of the midday sun it all seems unreal.

When Galen takes up the pole again, Fenn tugs on my sleeve and holds out the mirror.

"Yours," he says, when I don't take it.

"You're the one who can use it," I say. I don't want to touch it. "You keep it."

He looks like he's going to argue, but then he shrugs and puts it away. He gives me a strange look. If he weren't wearing a collar, I'd say it was pity.

"For now," he says. "But it is yours. You must carry it soon." He takes his place in the bows.

I'm too weak to help them guide the boat, so I stay with the horses. After two days penned with nowhere to lie down, they're both fighting to stay upright. I brush them down and murmur to them, trying to soothe them. If we don't get ashore soon, they'll collapse.

The mist thickens as the sun starts to go down. I don't say anything, but my heart thuds. I don't want another night on the Floodlands.

But then Fenn calls out excitedly, and I look up. The mist thins for a moment, and above us rise the fells, russet and gold in the dying light. We're close.

Galen bends almost double over the pole, sweat standing out on his forehead. When the flat bottom of the boat crunches on pebbles, Fenn leaps out. I follow, splashing through the shallows and heaving on the rope to help pull the boat further in.

We lay down planks to make a gangway, and Fenn shows me how to dismantle the pens. When I lead Hero ashore I can't tell who's shaking worse, her or me. As soon as she reaches solid ground, she falls to her front knees, and her rump follows. Fenn leads Sweetpea to us, and she does the same.

"I'll watch them," I say, but Fenn shakes his head.

"Sleep," he says.

So I stumble to where Galen is wearily clearing a camp under the treeline, and I get into my bedroll and I'm asleep in a heartbeat.

When I wake it's dark, but the shelter is up and there's a fire in a pit before it. Fenn is cooking. The cold is starting to bite into me, so I get up and drag my bedroll to the shelter. Galen helps me stuff it inside next to his, then hands me a blanket. It's been drying in front of the fire, and it smells of woodsmoke, not the mildew damp of the Floodlands. I wrap it around me, mindful of my shoulder, and walk to the edge of the trees.

We're only a dozen yards or so above water level, but the mist lies like a blanket over the Floodlands. I shiver, remembering its clammy touch.

"Here." Galen comes up behind me, and hands me his ale skin. It's a new one. Fenn must have laid in extra. I drink from it, and this time I'm ready for the burning liquid, though I still cough. I hand it back, and we stand looking south in silence.

"Galen?" I say.

"Hmm?"

"I'm never taking one of your shortcuts again."

He laughs, a surprised, cut-off bark, and takes a drink.

"Were you looking for them?" I ask. "Thorkel and the others? Did you know they'd be here?"

He sighs and lowers himself stiffly to the ground. I sit next to him, almost as stiff. He offers me the ale skin but I shake my head.

"Yes," he says. "And no. I'd heard rumours, but I didn't think – I thought they'd be long gone, or living quietly."

"Thorkel said you betrayed them."

"The battle of Hellingap was a bloodbath. After Geir died, I went north to join the Staffbearers."

"What happened at Hellingap?"

Galen shrugs. "Kolrand had an army, and we didn't. Geir wasn't expecting an attack so soon, and the Southern troops moved fast. Most of Geir's troops were still at Sunacre when Kolrand crossed the Vell River. They were beaten, scattered . . . Hellingap wasn't a battle. It was just mopping up the dregs."

It sounds like something he's said before, many times.

"So what made you a traitor?"

Galen hesitates, and I know I'm right. The practiced words are hiding something.

"Geir told us to follow the Staffbearers," he says. He takes a swallow from the ale skin. "The Slipskins never liked the Staffbearers much. They thought magic was for women, not warriors. Thorkel made it known which one he thought I was." Another swallow. "And there was the Staffbearer of Sunacre. When Kolrand executed the Staffbearers south of the Ridge for supporting Geir, she was the only one who escaped. She rode day and night to warn us that Kolrand had taken the court and was marching on us. Thorkel didn't like her at all."

We sit looking out over the mist. The stars show between scraps of cloud.

"I was going to ask why they gave up," I say. "I thought the real war was when the Sungiven marched on Frithberg. But it sounds like it was over long before."

"The Sungiven gave us hope," says Galen. "She reminded us what we were fighting for."

"And what were you fighting for?"

"You wouldn't understand," says Galen.

"I might," I say.

"You can't," says Galen. "It was over before you were born. We watched our way of life watered down, destroyed." He drinks. "Geir was trying to protect something already dead. The war was just the death rattle."

"That's not what Thorkel said."

"Thorkel wasn't talking about the old ways," Galen says.

"What do you mean?"

Galen shakes his head. "Do you know how the world ends?" he asks.

After my father died, and Brenna stopped caring for me, or herself, or anything much, Vigdis took me in. She used to sing the sacred songs, and I would listen.

There's one about the end of the world. It was my favourite.

"Stained from the corpse-sea comes the harrier-god to the gulls' home," I recite. "I used to think 'gulls' home' meant Gullcroft, but Vigdis said it just means cliffs. Why?"

Galen doesn't answer. The firelight from behind us catches in his red-gold beard, but his eyes are deep in shadow.

"Galen?" He turns to me, but he stares through me like he did at the barrows. "Laugi tried to give me something. A helm. He called it the Harrier Helm."

Galen stares through me some more, then slowly raises his ale skin and drinks. "That was Geir's helm," he says. "He was going to lead us home. Harrier, howe, home . . ."

The drink's making him ramble. I watch the mist rise from the Floodlands, and I wonder what I'm doing here, in the middle of nowhere, with a drunk whose golden memories of old comrades nearly got us killed.

Galen points down into the Floodlands.

"D'you know there's meant to be a temple under there?" he says.

I shake my head.

"They say that once, there was ancient forest, an in the forest was a temple. But Death lived in the forest, an the priests of the temple tried to gain power over Death."

"What happened?"

Galen waves his ale skin in a wide arc and hiccups.

"The sea invaded the earth," he says. "An now Roaki's down there with em. Poor Roaki."

When we get back to the fire, Galen spills half his soup down his front. I put him to bed before he can waste the rest. Fenn and I finish eating in silence. Fenn doesn't have a bedroll so I let him share mine. He curls up in a ball, his back against my front. Even through my layers of clothes, the cold metal of his collar burns against my breastbone.

I think about Ebba. I think about the way she was so quiet when she came to the wayhouse. She used to cower at the slightest thing: a sharp word, any sign of impatience, even the way Aud put her hands on her hips. Kelda used to snap at her deliberately to see her flinch. And I – I wished she was less of a crybaby. When she kept us up at night with her bad dreams, I wished she'd go back home, if she missed it that much.

We thought she was homesick.

She said she was homesick.

Then one night it was just us. Kelda was visiting her family and Aud was out with Jarle. It was winter, the air so cold I couldn't sleep. So I was awake when Ebba began to dream.

Up until then I'd only heard her cry. That night I found out she fought.

In her dreams, Ebba didn't cower. In her dreams she stood her ground, and she always lost.

The next time Kelda made fun of Ebba, I told her to shut up.

Later, when we were friends, Ebba told me about her uncle.

I couldn't understand – I still don't understand – how she could be two people, one clever and funny, the other tongue-tied. The timid, homesick mouse who spent her nights fighting tooth and nail.

Fenn snores gently, tucked against my chest. Fenn I understand. He took the first chance he got to escape, and he grabbed it. I couldn't protect Ebba much, but maybe I can protect Fenn.

The warmth from our bodies has deadened the chill of the iron collar.

"I'll get that thing off you," I whisper, though I know he can't hear me.

Sleep comes to me, and I dream I'm standing by a lake. In the blackness a sunken path shines under the surface like a drowned moon. I limp to the edge of the water, and send ripples sliding from shore to shore.

We spend most of the morning trying to find a way up through the trees onto the fells. Galen leads Hero and Sweetpea on the long rein, while Fenn and I scout ahead.

The tug to the North is back. Now that the ache in my arm has dulled, I can feel it under my ribs like a fishhook. Every time we have to turn back or loop round, the line goes taut, like a cramp in my side, but then we find a path the horses can manage, and it eases.

The climb winds me more than I expected, and I have to stop to catch my breath. Galen offers me his ale skin, but I shake my head. Now and then I catch Fenn staring back the way we've come, frowning.

Galen sees too, and we exchange glances. I wonder if he's thinking what I'm thinking – that the boat we took could only have held eight or so men, packed tight. There must have been others.

The fells are wilder than the pastures of the hill country. As we journey further in, the slopes below us grow desolate, some of them nothing but bare scree. The brittle shale splinters and slithers underfoot, and when I kick some off the path it starts a small landslide. The valleys are narrow and choked, so we stay as high as we can.

Up on the fell tops, silvery tarns lie in the pale gold grass. They reflect the low grey sky like blind, unblinking eyes. We stop at one to let the horses drink, and I see myself, a black, featureless shadow. I plunge my hands into the cold water, sending ripples across the surface, and focus on trying to clean the packed dirt from under my nails. There's still dried blood in the creases around my nails, and I scratch at it to get it out.

The valleys are impossible to camp in, so we spend the night on the lee of a felltop. When I'm not dreaming of sliding down an endless slope, I dream I've fallen in the tarn, and all around me is a dark, dead world of shadows.

The next day is much the same, but now when we skirt valleys or treacherous screes, the cramps in my chest are more pronounced. I catch Fenn watching me when they make me pull up short, though when he meets my eyes he grins.

Galen works his way through a third ale skin. I wonder how many Fenn thought to bring.

Still we climb.

In front of us rises a black mass, riven with white valleys – the northern spur of the mountains that march from north to south, cutting off the east from the rest of Arngard. Our path bends to the west, circling the impassable peaks and ice-fields. The bald, black rock sticks up like a great bone breaking the skin of the earth. The slopes are nothing but tumbled rocks and scree, and freezing rivulets cut across our path. The uneven ground shifts beneath our feet, and the horses sweat and stumble. We walk at their sides, hiding from the wind in their shadows.

Just after noon, we pass right under the choked mouth of a glacier. The dirty wall of ice rears dozens of feet above us, and the black rubble is slippery with its melt water. In spring this will be a torrent. Fenn dashes away from us, scrambling up to the ice face and reaching out with both hands to touch it. He almost looks like he's trying to embrace it.

"We don't have time for that," says Galen. "Go fetch him back."

So I climb after Fenn, half upright, half on my hands and knees.

"Fenn! Come on, we have to keep going!"

He turns to me, his face alight.

"Listen," he says.

He beckons me close to the ice, and I put out my hand.

"Can you hear?" he asks. He puts a hand to his chest, his eyes half-closed in pleasure. "Here," he says, tapping his breastbone.

I try. I cut out Galen's distant, impatient calls, and I let the icy wind sough through me, and I try, over the trickle of the streams, to hear what he hears.

At first there's just emptiness, a gap in the sounds of the world. But then I feel a shiver going through me in the middle of that emptiness. Like the way whalesong shivers through the cliffs back home, or the way the bullroarer thrummed in Thorkel's hands, except this is deeper, so deep it's not a sound, and it doesn't waver or change.

I open my eyes. Fenn is beaming at me.

"What is it?" I ask.

Fenn says a word I don't understand. He says it lovingly, like a beautiful name, or something he lost long ago.

Aimu.

"The world breathing," he says. "My mother taught me to hear it."

I open my mouth to ask about his mother, but he interrupts, smiling.

"Your eyes," he says. "Like ice."

I never thought that was a beautiful thing. A cold thing, a hard thing, useful maybe, but never beautiful.

I smile back at him, and then my chest cramps up harder than before, and I bend over, hands on my thighs, trying to catch my breath. The pain blots out the beauty, and I feel myself again – aching, numb, alone.

Fenn watches me, his smile gone.

"Where?" he asks, and I know he's talking about the tugging.

I touch the spot where my ribs meet over my stomach.

"Can you see anything?" I ask. "Like you could see Roaki? Can you stop it?"

But he shakes his head.

"Something has you," he says. "Calling you."

I feel the panic building in my chest, and maybe he sees it, because all at once he is the smiling boy again, darting ahead of me down the scree, looking back to urge me on, and obediently I follow.

We catch up with Galen at the edge of the glacier bed. None of us speak until we're down among the grass and heather, and the great black head of the mountains is hidden behind clouds.

The cramps in my chest die away as we turn north again, and now only the tug is left, almost gentle.

The stream we've been following grows wider, faster, then levels out. A steady roar starts at the edge of hearing, growing until it fills the air.

We stand at the top of the waterfall and stare north. At our feet the ground drops away to green lowlands. The waterfall feeds a river that meanders across the grass and down towards the long dark line of the sea. I scan the horizon, and there, in the north west, I see the familiar double hump of Whalescar, the cliff that shelters Gullcroft, and beyond it, out in the grey waters, a small, dark spot. Far Isle.

I point, but Galen has already found it, as if he knew as well as I what signs to look for.

The north wind carries the scent of guano to me across the miles, and spray dusts my cheeks like tears.

When I imagined coming home, I always pictured Gullcroft in the spring. I'd come over the cliffs from the west, and the carved boundary post would be fresh-painted under my hand, the new grass like spears.

The boundary post is flaking, its colours bleached. There's no smoke over the green turf that hides the roof of the home I grew up in, but I already knew something was wrong. The wind's been in my face all day, and I haven't smelt smoke once. There's no noise. No movement. For days now I haven't thought of the soldiers, but now my ears strain to hear hoofbeats.

Galen puts his stump on my shoulder.

"Better no smoke than too much," he says.

I know what he means, but the quiet unnerves me. What if they were caught unawares? Raiders never bother with Gullcroft, so we rarely set lookouts. There's nothing here. Just smoked fish and peat fires and —

Home.

I squint into the wind. If my eyes are watering I tell myself it's that.

"I'll just check," I say.

"Go with her," Galen says to Fenn, who slithers off Hero's back and joins me. "I'll take them the easy road," he says, meaning the horses. Sweetpea's lame in one foot, and both animals need to rest. He starts off down the path to the village.

The ground rises and falls just past the boundary post, like a gentle summer swell washed over the land and turned to earth. Just over the second swell the ground dips steeper, and I look down on the turf roof and dirt yard of the place I grew up in.

I skitter down the slope to the yard, arms out to keep my balance. The yard is empty, the trough clogged with stagnant rainwater. I use the edge of my knife to shimmy the latch on the door, and pull it open.

The house is empty. The hearth is clean, the bench pushed back along the wall. By the bed at the left end of the room there's a wooden cradle, and when I check the storeroom, there are dried pulses and a barrel of preserved fish.

"Winter camp," says Fenn. He's been telling me about his people, how they followed the *peku*-deer between the summer calving grounds and the winter pastures. In the summer his family lived in hide tents, but in winter they returned to more permanent settlements. Looking round, I know what he means. The small, everyday things are gone, but the bulkier things, the things that will keep – cradle, cauldron, a cask of beer – they've been left.

So they had time to plan before they left, and they meant to come back. But why? And where?

I shut the door carefully and Fenn follows me towards the village. He doesn't complain when I climb back up the slope, away from the path Galen took. Neither of us feel like being caught on the low ground.

"That's Whalescar," I say, pointing to the humpbacked cliff above us.

"Who lives there?" Fenn asks.

Right on the edge of the cliff there's a circular hut with steep eaves, black against the grey sky.

"Vigdis," I say. "My father's sister. She's like you. A Spirit Walker." I feel the cramp growing in my chest. "She'd know what's wrong with me."

"Let's ask," says Fenn, smiling.

I look from him to the clifftop hut and back again before I see it.

Smoke, trickling through the thatch into the sea breeze.

Before I know it, I'm running. Fenn shouts after me, but I don't stop. Images are streaming through my mind too quickly to catch.

Standing on the reef with my father, my skin slippery with scales and spray, and turning to wave up at the cliff where Vigdis stood, singing the fish into our nets . . . watching the fishing fleet come back in at sunset, running before a storm, and Vigdis chanting, her eyes fixed on the tiny boats until every one was safe behind the reef . . . waiting, one night, long past sunset, Brenna pleading over and over until her throat was raw, and Vigdis just sitting there, staring out into the dark sea, as if she couldn't hear her sister-in-law's heart breaking . . . breaking so hard that she left us and went somewhere else. No spark of recognition in her eyes, not when I said her name or put the comb in her hand for her to braid my hair, just that long stare that seemed fixed on the horizon, even indoors, watching for the boat that never came back.

I'm pounding up the slope to the cliff path, my lungs and legs aching, but still the memories come, like spurs in my flesh.

Vigdis taking me up to the hut when Brenna wouldn't care for me anymore, keeping my hands and head busy, singing me the sacred songs . . . Thorpe the pigherd calling my father a coward, until I learned to fight and broke his nose . . . Sleeping in the hut, feeling the whalesong come up through the cliffs into my bones . . . Being sent back to Brenna, older, awkward, and the way she looked right through me, like I was a nuisance, a mistake. And then Sklep, his visits, his courting, the way he held me down while he sheared me, though I fought. Brenna watching with her long, blank gaze, and a small smile, as if she couldn't hear my cries.

I've reached the path, and I bend over, hands on my knees, chest burning. Fenn is toiling up the slope below me. Up here the gulls yell into the wind, the waves break on the rocks below, and a hooded figure makes its way along the path from the hut.

The figure has a long staff, its iron rods twisted into whorls at the top, like a distaff. It lands heavily with each step, and with each step I seem to feel its thump through the ground, travelling towards me.

I push myself up, and wait. As she gets closer, my heart jumps. The blue hooded cloak, the silver pendants at her breast; everything is so familiar.

We're only a few paces apart when my chest cramps so hard I bend over again, twice-winded.

Something's wrong.

The figure lowers her blue hood and I look up into a stranger's face. Her dark grey eyes are hard, and her iron-grey hair falls over her shoulders, tangled in the wind.

Below me, on the path out of the village, Galen comes galloping. He's on Hero's back, leaning over her neck, and he shouts to me, but the wind steals his voice. I watch him pass as if in a dream.

"We've been expecting you," the woman says to me. "I'm Ranvig, Staffbearer of the North."

She holds out both hands to greet me.

Her white forearms are covered with twining blue tattoos.

I try to run, but a fish on a line can't outswim the hook. The vicious cramping stops my breath, drags me to my knees, gasping. I let the darkness take me.

In it, I'm underwater, where the sun can't reach. Then I step off the sunken path and haul myself dripping up onto the land.

Snow falls my first night back in Gullcroft, and by the time I wake, all escape is cut off.

Eighteen
INHERITANCE

lf's blood is still wet around the Harm Tree's roots when the prester comes to cut it down. The wide black scar of the burned-out fire is still warm. A score of labourers are penned in by Adelhard's men on their horses. Two yoked oxen churn the ash wi their hooves.

I'm not there to help, but I watch. I make sure I watch. Fetch sits quiet beside me, an though I don't touch him, I can feel his warmth. He is a kind of holy horror for the people of Eldinghope, an they keep their eyes from us both.

Grimulf calls Rafe out from among the farm men an puts an axe in his hands. I en't had a chance to talk to Rafe since last night. He was kept among the soldiers, in case any of Ulf's people thought to have revenge. Maybe I'm a bit surprised they din't try it anyhow. But without Rafe they'd lose the land entire, for who would own it then? Stig? The boy they was goin to see hanged an slaughtered a few short hours ago? The boy they've seen beaten an shamed since he first learned to walk?

Of course not. That's why Erland had Stig an Ma sleep with us, under guard. They'll never be safe here again.

So when I feel pity needlin me as Rafe stands helpless, the big axe weighin him down, I stamp it out.

"Don't you know how to cut down a tree, boy?" Prester Grimulf roars, his hand at his belt on his own axe hilt. There's not much of the prester in him today. His eyes are still smoulderin wi the pleasure of battle. Next to him, Berengar sits with his writin frame across his knees, his stylus ready.

Rafe steps up to the oak. There's a spray of dark droplets across the bark an Rafe puts his hand over them, the axe restin at his side. He bows his head.

The men start to shift. Funny how it takes less'n a moment for em to get restless. The prester feels it too, but he lets it happen. I'm watchin him, I see it.

"Well, boy?" he says.

Rafe turns, his face pale. He shakes his head.

"I won't," he says.

I get a strange feelin, like I'm seein somethin that's already happened. Like I've watched this exact same moment before.

I look from Rafe to the prester, an I see those hooded eyes all lit up an smilin. I know what he's goin to do.

"If you want to see your sire well buried, cut down the tree," Grimulf says. "Or you can treat your slaughtering post with respect, and feed your father's body to the pigs yourself. It's him or the tree."

The labourers cry out, but Adelhard circles them, whip in hand.

Rafe takes up the axe. I see the weight of it in every line of his body. He raises it an swings blindly, his eyes turned from his work.

I feel it like I felt the lash from my brother's hands.

They make you destroy what you hold dear. It's how they come to own you. At first they give you a choice, but if you accept their bargain, you'll have to choose again, over an over, until you realise all your choices were false.

When Rafe's hands are too blistered to continue, Ulf's foreman is forced to pick up the axe.

Berengar's scratchin away at the barkpaper. I wonder what it says. If the words were mine, it would start like this:

'On the tenth day of winter, in the year of Ulf Berrson's death, the Harm Tree at Eldinghope fell.'

The tree falls at dusk, but I'm not there to see it. I'm back at the farm carin for Stig. He's bin laid in one of the small rooms that open off the main hall. He's grey under his tan, soaked in cold sweat, an his large eyes roll under his lids. The bruises on his arms an body are old, brown an yellow, but his back is crossed with long lash strokes, half-closed. They must of whipped him before they led him to the tree. I wonder if that Staffbearer din't drug him too. I seen folk rave wi fever, but Stig is unconscious, lollin like a sick babe off the edge of his bed.

More'n once I wish I had Mistress Una's help, but all I got is one girl who's too kind or too stupid to know that helpin me will win her no praise with her fellows. She's a bit older'n me, but she jus stares at Stig wi wet blue eyes an is barely no use at all save for buildin the fire an fetchin water.

Ma keeps tryin to get in, but I close the door in her face an stop my ears to her words.

It's dark when the wagon rolls back into the yard, an I hear Erland shoutin orders. I go out into the hall to see what's what, Fetch at my side. The labourers are bein coralled in the main barn, an from the hall I can sense the ugly mood on em. That's when Berengar comes in, supportin Rafe.

"The prester says you're to tend him," he says, his breath short from holdin up the boy.

I nod him through to the back room. The fire is high an the small space is like a furnace. Rafe stumbles to the bed, puts out a hand an cries out. No one's removed the splinters from his bloody palms.

I send the girl for cold water.

"What can I do?" Berengar asks me.

"Get me a needle, staunchweed an sunwort," I tell him, already at Rafe's side. Rafe's holdin himself up, his face turned from me. I take his wrists, wonderin if he'll pull away from me, but he don't. "Let me see those hands," I say, the same way I talked to the sick at Birchold. The blood comes mainly from burst blisters. I click my tongue. "A pretty mess, but no worse'n that. I'll make em sting, but I promise they'll be better for it. Show me your back."

When I've got him turned round, I stare at the fresh lash strokes, the blood all seeped through his shirt an clotted, an I don't know whether to rage or cry. Underneath the sheets an blankets, Stig's got the same long lines on his back.

"What did you do to get this?" I ask, tryin to make a joke of it.

"Yer vexed," Rafe says, muffled, as I start to cut the shirt from his back.

"I don't think vexed is enough," I tell him. "Let me guess. You swore to avenge Ulf's death."

He don't answer, but I know him. He's not just Ulf's son, he could be my brother, if my brother had received preference instead of scorn. I grew by his side, though he walked in the light an I in the dark. The scorch of my uncle's spite sometimes touched him, but he never could bring himself to stand with us when it was turned our way. Rafe loved him, however cruel he was.

"There's no point," I say, tryin to make him see it. "The East en't closed to the world no more. Grimulf is the rooster on the hayrick. King Kolrand is not a boy any longer, an others have their eyes on Eldinghope than those who live here. If you rise up it will not be against ten men, but an army."

"They'll say I lost the land of my fathers," Rafe says, turnin to me for the first time. The firelight dances in his bright red hair.

"Ulf lost it, by playin the strong man," I say. "You don't have to make his mistakes." But even as I say it I think of the labourers under guard, watchin as the prester made Rafe take up the axe, an I wonder what it would be like, every day of your life, bein urged not to drop your eyes, but to raise your fists.

"It's my land," Rafe says, "an he's a monster."

"If it's monsters you're lookin for," I start, but the servin girl is back, an maybe it's just as well. I tell her to bathe his hands, an she bows her head over her work, but I think I catch her weepin into the basin as the water turns rosy.

Berengar comes back, lookin harrassed. "Here," he says. "I found them. Ebba, will you see your mother? She —"

"No," I say, turnin from him an closin the door.

I sit over Rafe's hands, cursin the firelight an the seepin

blisters, an one by painful one I needle the splinters from his stubborn flesh.

We eat soon after, an the soldiers are given their watches. Rafe, Ma an Stig are to sleep in the hall again, but everyone else is sent to the outbuildings. The girl who helped me asks to stay, but I remember how she wept over Rafe's hands an tell her to come back in the mornin. Whether she's brave or stupid I don't want her tempted to try anythin that might get her killed. I've seen enough of that.

I sit in the small hot room wi Stig an keep him warm an watered. Fetch dislikes the heat, but he lies across the door outside, an I feel safe in the closeness of the room, alone wi my witless brother.

It suits me well to have a task that keeps me awake, because when I close my eyes I see Ulf, or poor handsome Medard, or the painted face of the Staffbearer crushed beneath the prester's axe. I wonder if there was any way I could have kept them all three alive somehow, whether there was a moment I missed, words that would of bound em. Now that it's quiet I let myself take out the memory of how I felt before the killin, when all the smoke was burned away an there was just pure light. It's like a story cut off before the end. What would of happened?

Maybe Stig would of hung an I beside him. Maybe the blood was owed an someone was always goin to have to pay it.

As the night wears on I worry more for Stig. The fever en't high enough to be the cause of his senselessness, but still he don't wake.

Fetch's growls outside the door rouse me. I jump up an open the door a crack.

"Who's there?"

A line of light falls on Ma's face. She bites her lip in fear, her eyes on Fetch, an I feel a sickness sweep through me at the sight of her. "Go away," I say.

"Abda, wait!" She calls me usin the name only she has ever used, an only when I was very little. "Please."

"Don't call me that," I say, horrified to find I'm cryin. "Don't speak to me."

"Let me see him," she begs.

Here is somethin I can grasp an turn on her.

"Don't pretend you care," I say. "If it was up to you he'd be dead. Leave us alone."

"He's drugged," she says. "Please, Abda. I can help."

So I was right, for all the good it does. I let her in. What else can I do? I do not have half her lore, an I need help. She's brought herbs with her, an soon the small room is thick wi sweet smoke. The smoke makes my eyes stream, so I close em.

It's only when I wake that I know I've slept. I start up, missin Fetch beside me. The hall beyond the room is lit wi the mornin sun. The room is still warm, but the fire en't so built up, an Ma is strainin somethin through a cloth into a bowl. The girl who helped me yesterday fusses wi Stig's blankets.

I slip out into the hall, rubbin the sleep from my eyes. Berengar sits by the fire, writin as usual, Fetch stretched out at his feet.

"Your mother is good at her work," he says, not waitin to greet me. "I think we should take her with us to the hospital at Birchold."

I grunt. "Why? What's a hospital?"

"A place of healing," he says, bent over what looks like a list.

"Last time I was there, it was just a barn full of sick people," I say.

"Yes, with barely any stores," he says. "This is the list you had me make with Mistress Una. Everything Birchold lacks, your mother has. The barn full of sick people will be very grateful."

"What if I don't want her with us?" I say.

"Then she will probably die," says Berengar. "Your uncle's people are not forgiving."

I watch him carefully draw up a new list from his notes. Ink stains his fingers, an his brows meet over his straight nose. There's a smutch of ink on the end of that too. I see why the soldiers don't accept him. Here he is, in his enemy's hall, worryin over people he don't even know. They're not his responsibility, but still he worries, an he writes up a list, an he thinks on how to save em.

My muscles unlock a little, an my heart warms.

"You're right," I say, settin myself on the floor beside him. Fetch raises his mighty head an licks my hands in welcome. "Ten men on horses can't hold Eldinghope. The men who paid tithe to Ulf are only holdin off till they know Rafe's mind, an he will stand against Grimulf."

Berengar scowls down at his birch bark, an he looks very young. "You should not tell me this, Ebba," he says. "I should tell Erland, and he Grimulf, and your cousin will be put to death."

"But you won't," I say, "not yet. Rafe is still in our care, an I'll see if I can talk him out of it, at least until we go. Grimulf may have a fight on his hands come spring, but not till then if Rafe has sense."

Berengar looks down into my eyes, an all that warmth rushes into my face. He nods. "Try," he says. "Grimulf says we need only hold the farm a day or two more, then we can leave."

"Thank you," I say. "I'll talk with him."

Erland strides through the door, one hand is on his sword hilt.

He snaps his fingers at Berengar. "Up, up," he says, an we both scramble to our feet. "We're going to the grove. Bring the boy." He means Rafe. "Ebba, you stay here. Grimulf's got a job for you. Two of the men will stay with you, same as yesterday. If there's any trouble do as they say."

The prester strides in, all heavy-lidded dignity. The fiery warrior has passed. Behind him come several labourers, carryin a makeshift stretcher. They lay it on the table. The foreman's wife follows.

"My child," the prester says to me, "Here is a heavy duty. Your uncle must be prepared for his last journey with all honour. This good woman will help you."

He signals to Erland, an they leave, Berengar an Rafe behind em.

I go to the stretcher, knowin what I will see won't be pleasant.

The foreman's wife eyes me. Her face is unfriendly, but I see the need for her, someone the people of Eldinghope will trust. Neither Ma nor me can fill that role. The prester might have given this task to me, but I don't have the knowledge of how to put together a body torn apart, so that those who bury it see peace, not horror.

Ma an the girl come from tendin Stig, an when the foreman's wife gives em their orders, I'm happy to fall in. At first we don't speak, but then the girl starts up a mournin song, an though four voices en't quite enough, we take it up. There are no words we could say to each other that would overcome the mistrust between us, but the task fills the emptiness. We strip an wash an sew up the body of the man who ruled us.

When the noise of the men returnin fills the yard, Ulf is dressed, coins on his eyes an mouth, a heavy torque hidin the stiches round his neck. When Rafe is escorted in we kneel, but we don't wail. Normally all the women should be here makin a cry, but it would be a lie if I were to throw myself down an weep for my uncle. The others are quiet too. I wonder if Rafe guesses my thoughts. He looks over his father's corpse an turns to the foreman's wife.

"All was done well?" he asks, an his voice is cold. "My father was not mistreated?"

The bluntness of his suspicion is an insult, but I say nothin. I know his grief is held hostage just as he is, an he cannot show it.

"He was treated with respect, my master," she says.

"Then wait with him until the bearers come," he says, not lookin once at Ma or me.

I stand wi Fetch at the hall's door an watch the preparations. The hewn wood of the Harm Tree is carried up to a flat-topped grassy knoll east of the farm, lookin out towards the sea. That's where the farm beacon was lit, to tell the outlyin homesteads when Raiders were sighted, an also where Stig, Rafe an I used to play at the battle that was fought before we were born. Rafe would play Uncle Ulf, of course, an he battled the Raider King, who was Stig with his teeth an chest bared, an I was Ma, the captive crouched timid an alone in the boat, waitin for Ulf to rescue me. It always ended in Rafe stabbin Stig through the heart, an leadin me from the boat, while Stig tottered an leered an yelled, "Curse you, Ulf Berrson! Cursssse youuuuuu!"

Now I wonder what we were playin at, this make-believe story where my Da was nowhere to be seen, an Ulf led Rathna the Outlander kindly by the hand, when in all our days an nights we'd never seen him treat her with anythin but scorn. An how did Rafe feel, when he was tole this play-curse was a real an livin truth, one that'd make a murderer of him?

When the pyre is raised, an the dusk come down so I can just make it out against the dark east sky, the foreman comes with five others to carry the body. I recognise em. They are the headmen of the five dales north of Eldinghope. They visit yearly to bring their tithe to Ulf. I see their hands are bandaged, same as Rafe. The prester must of made them take up the axe after him. They nod at the foreman's wife, but they ignore me an Ma.

Fetch appears at my side like smoke, grey an warm. I put my hand in his rough mane, an I feel him growlin too low to be heard. His muscles are tense.

Somethin's goin to happen.

I lead Fetch to Stig's room. Ma follows me, her back hunched against the men's stares.

I close the door an kneel down to look into Fetch's eyes. He looks back at me, waitin. I wonder if the closeness of the room reminds him of how we met, hard by the fire in the lord's hall.

"Fetch, stay an protect em," I say, showin him Ma an Stig. "If anyone tries to hurt em, kill. You understand? Kill."

Ma cowers back from me as I rise. "Try to get Stig roused," I say. "You won't be able to move him like this, an if they attack the hall you'll need to. My guess is they'll torch it. If I come back an find you've saved your own worthless skin an left him to die, I will not hold em back. I'll leave you to em. You understand?"

Ma covers her face an nods through her sobs.

I look at my terrified mother, an I hate myself. I feel sick, but the words are out now, an nothin I can say will undo em.

"Bolt the door," I say, an I leave.

Ulf's body has bin laid on boards to be carried up to the pyre. The six men lift him onto their shoulders, an I get in line behind em.

It's a pitiful showin. First goes the body, then Rafe, then the foreman's wife an me, an finally the servin girl, who I don't seem able to shake.

The yard is empty, an Adelhard an his men guard the barn where Ulf's household is bein kept. The rest, the tenants from the homesteads an the dales, have bin sent back to their homes across the snow-patched fields.

At the top of the knoll the prester waits. His face is bland, but I see his fingers twirlin somethin in his left hand an catch a glimpse of gold. He must be impatient to be away from this corner of the kingdom, now it's bin brought into line. Erland an Berengar flank him. A light guard, I'm thinkin, an others must be too. What's the prester playin at?

The bearers lay Ulf's body in the middle of the pyre, an Erland an Berengar each thrust a torch deep into the pyre's bed. The bearers stand back an watch the fire take.

Rafe's mouth opens in the flutterin light, but suddenly all I can hear is a swarm of noise like a strong wind. I turn an next to me stands the servin girl, her face all wrong. When she opens her too-wide mouth her teeth are sharp like arrowheads.

"*Eyes up, girl,*" says my Follower, her voice a hiss.

"My father paid for this land in blood!" I hear Rafe shout, an everythin slows. The bearers turn, knives held in their hands. The foreman an three others close on Erland an Berengar, an my gaze is caught like wool on thorn.

Berengar's sword is out, already swingin, his face hidden by a helm I've never seen him wear before, an I see now that he is a soldier, as well as a word-writer. The sword bites deep into the side of one of the dalesmen, draws back, then slams back into the man's exposed neck.

It's so brutal. There en't no style, no grace, just metal edges gougin men from life to death.

Next to me, the servin girl screams, but it comes out choked wi terror.

I swing round an clamp my arm over her mouth.

"Shut up," I say in her ear, "or they'll kill you too."

I tear my eyes from Berengar in time to see Grimulf, a dalesman already dead at his feet, catch Rafe's hand an crush it, forcin him to drop his knife. The four survivin bearers, three dalesmen an the foreman, fall back from the fray, their eyes on Rafe an the prester.

The prester's face has come alive. *He was just waitin*, I realise. *He wanted Rafe to give him a reason to kill. An now he's got it.* Rafe's frightened, but he just stands there, waitin for the blow. Maybe that's what he wanted too.

Grimulf's teeth flash an he opens his mouth to yell.

If Grimulf yells, Adelhard will set his men on the servants corralled in the barn. If the killin starts, it won't stop. It'll be unarmed men an women, children caught in the crush, flesh wrenched apart beyond all stitchin.

For a moment I see two boys, their wooden practice swords raised, playin out the doom of their fathers. I remember the light that filled me on Bloodnight, an then I'm not just rememberin, I feel it, like it was waitin for me to let it in again. Pure an sweet.

My body moves between em before I can think, Grimulf's blade raised against me, Rafe at my back.

"Let him live," I say. "He en't his father. I'll be his surety."

The prester's eyes glitter, but he stays his hand.

"No!" Rafe howls behind me. "Move!"

He grabs me, but I twist like Torny an Jarle taught me, an drive the heel of my palm into his eye. He staggers back, hands over his face, an trips.

"Ulf din't love us," I tell him, "an I en't goin to watch you get our people killed for his sake. Dogs can be forgiven for lovin a bad master, but not men. Now what are you? Man or dog?"

Rafe don't answer, just turns his head away. I turn back to the others.

"You're a man," I say to the foreman. "You know I'm right. Ulf beat us when he was angry, an when he was pleased he let us watch while he beat someone else. Now you can choose. If you miss his leash, his heel on your neck, then kill us. There'll come a beatin like you've never known. But if you want to go home, an weather the winter, an maybe see spring come again, go now."

I see the foreman's eyes dart to his wife, who has stood unflinchingly by. She must of come up here ready to share her husband's fate, an now he's lookin to her to seal it, one way or another.

She nods.

He looks back to me. "We'll go," he says, "an we'll see in the spring. But if we don't like what we sees then —"

"Then it'll be spring," I say, "an not tomorrow, nor the day after. In fact, tomorrow you an your families will be out of the barn an back in the hall, en't that so my lord?"

The prester has not said a word till now, an still his silence stretches. At once our noses are filled with a stench. The fire has reached Ulf's body, an burnin flesh an hair poison the good woodsmoke.

"It shall be so, Salvebearer," the prester says at last, an though his face is closed again, the bloodlust tamped down, his eyes are lit up like warnin fires. The foreman an his wife bow an turn to leave, but he calls em back. "Wait," he says, "for we are not done with judgements."

"No!" I say, but with a look he tells me my part is done.

"You were loyal to your master," he tells the foreman, "an so I pardon you, for it is not for the hound to judge how the master acts."

Anger flashes across the foreman's face, but he has the sense to hold his tongue.

"But these men," Grimulf says, turnin to the dalesmen, "these men are guilty not only of misplaced loyalty, but of treason, and that I cannot pardon."

He holds up his palm to them, an whatever they see there turns their faces pale. Out of the corner of my eye, I see Erland's face. Full of sorrow.

The execution is swift. The dalesmen maybe think it's their idea to charge, but up out of the shadows come the three soldiers Medard used to command. They trap the dalesmen an slay em before they can cry out.

Very neat. No ends. Like it was planned.

Like me an my speeches were part of that plan.

Grimulf turns smilin to us. The servin girl has fallen to her knees an retches onto the grass. The foreman an his wife hold one another, eyes on the corpses.

"Tell me," he says to the foreman, "have you ever seen this?"

He holds out his hand. In the great calloused palm lies the golden horse, the sun-shield on its back.

The foreman shakes his head. "My master din't trust any of us to handle his treasures," he says, "not even his own kin. I swear we never saw it."

"Then you may thank him for this at least," says Grimulf. "Your ignorance, and the supplications of your mistress, shall lengthen your lives to the spring. But if I do not like what I see then . . ." He smiles. "You understand."

They bow an leave, takin the servin girl with em. They keep their eyes down.

I stand in the acrid smoke, the pure sweet light inside me eaten up by bitterness.

"It seems to me you've won inheritance of this land," the prester says to me, though he's watchin Rafe where he sits on the ground, his hand over his eye. "In single combat, no less." Rafe's one good eye glares at him.

"You're mistaken," I say. "A thrall can't inherit, even one who's bin freed."

"But maybe a believer, unjustly enslaved, can," says Grimulf. "There are several examples in the annals of the South of the White God's believers enslaved and sold by heathen kings. In such cases where they lived, the Lord saw fit to restore to them their freedom and their estates."

In such cases where they lived. Don't think I en't noticed that.

But at that moment the servin girl flies back up the slope.

"He's awake!" she pants. "Stig Arfson's awake!"

Stig's sittin up in bed. His upper lip is still beaded wi sweat, but the brown of his skin is warm again, the greyish tinge chased from his cheeks.

I sit an take his hand in mine. His fingers are long an slender, an his palm narrow. I'd forgotten how beautiful his hands are. A little clammy, maybe, but I stroke em an they're dear to me, as

298

dear as his gaunt face with its black stubble an his large dark eyes.

"How are you?" I ask, an my voice wobbles.

"Ebba," he says, with effort. "When did you get back? Did Rafe bring you with him from Frithberg?"

I shake my head an tears spill over my cheeks. "No," I manage thickly, "I came by myself. How d'you feel?"

"Tired," he says, blinkin his long black lashes. "Where's Ma?"

"In the hall," I say. "Stig, do you remember?"

"R'member what?" he asks sleepily.

"Bloodnight," I say. "D'you —"

"Silly," he says. "Bloodnight en't come yet. Don't worry, you en't missed it. I'm goin to sleep some more now."

I sit by him till his fingers loosen an fall from mine.

Berengar coughs from the door.

"How is he?" he asks. "Will he be able to travel?"

"In the cart, maybe," I say, "but it's gettin colder, an sleepin on the road at night won't do him any good. He's weak, an it's two nights an a day back to Birchold."

Berengar sits on the stool beside me an looks at Stig's face, then at mine. I wait for him to say we look alike, like everyone does. Same dark hair, same dark skin. Outlanders.

"He looks like your mother," he says instead. "He has her eyes, her hair. You take after your father?" I shrug. "You have the red hair of your cousin, at least," he says. "I see it in the sun. Red under brown. Like fire under wood." I look away, but he takes my hands in his. "Tell me what is the matter, Ebba."

It sounds stupid, but I feel like my heart lies poundin in my hands, an his ink-stained, sword-callused fingers are my ribs. His hands tighten on mine, an I feel my heart trip.

"He don't remember," I say, pullin my hands away an my thoughts back to Stig. "He thinks it's half a moon ago, an I'm come back wi Rafe from Frithberg. I can understand the Staffbearer would drug him. No one wants the sacrifice screamin an spoilin things, do they? But why can't he remember the days before that?"

Berengar's still leanin towards me. He says nothin, but his eyes flicker to the door, an just like that, I know.

"No," I say, shakin my head. "No. She wouldn't."

"I think," he says gently, "it was the only mercy she could give."

I gaze blankly at my brother's limp hand, wonderin what would make a woman drug her only son for his death.

"Maybe that is a blessing," says Berengar. "Would you have him remember what was done to him?"

"Yes!" My voice is so forceful, I surprise myself. "We were told! You protect your family, and your family protects you! Without family what are you? What keeps you from harm? But look at him. Look at me."

Berengar puts his arm around my shoulders an hugs me close. This time I don't pull back. I screw up my eyes against the tears, against the thin bruised face of my brother, the cowerin shape of my mother, against Ulf lyin headless an Rafe with his death-wish. I am so full of pain I can't breathe.

"You were lied to," Berengar says. "It was a fine lie, made of noble thoughts, but it was told by a man with no nobility or goodness in him. It is not your fault you believed him. You had no one to teach you better. And look! Even though you were taught a lie, you tried to make it true. Because of you, your brother lives, and your cousin, and not just them."

But others have died, so many of em, an I watched.

The bitterness, the pain, the sickness . . . it all comes to a point. A certain, unmovin point. Berengar thinks he's talkin about my uncle, but all I can see are the burnin eyes an axe of Prester Grimulf.

Nineteen
SECOND SKIN

o you know how whales hunt? she asked.

The piebald whales, with their sharp teeth, they catch a seal and toss it, like a cat plays with a mouse.

The tusked whales spear their prey on their long horn, like the shrike spears the frog.

But the great grey whales, they dive up singing from the deep, and all the little fishes dance on their tongues, not even knowing they're caught.

That's how the whales hunt, she said.

I'm in a warm, soft embrace. I feel light, contented.

Then my body catches up, the dull pain in my shoulder, the ache in my legs, and a subtle weight descends on my heart. The sheepskin bedroll feels too warm, and I squirm out of it.

I know at once where I am. The low walls are covered with

animal skins, and behind my bed hangs a heavy curtain of horse hide, cutting the round room in two. On the other side of the curtain I can hear voices, and the chink of a ladle against a cauldron's rim. I turn to look at the slit in the hide curtain, and jump.

The tall Staffbearer stands there, watching me. Her skin is winter-white over her angular cheeks, and her face is completely still. Her blank expression reminds me of Aud, the way she could keep her thoughts out of her face. The Staffbearer's arms are folded across her chest. Everything about her says *I'm not afraid of you.*

Whereas I just jumped out of my skin at the sight of her.

Her forearms are bare, and the blue tattoos stand out dark against her skin. This time I'm sure. The dream I had every night when Roaki was in me, with the boat and the island, and the cloaked figure leading me . . . that figure had the same tattoos.

"I'm Ranvig," she says.

"I'm Torny," I say. "Torny Vafrisdota."

A small smile of satisfaction appears on her otherwise still face.

"Vafrisdota?" she says. "Is that what she told you?" She nods to where my clothes lie folded at the foot of the bed. "Get dressed. You need to eat."

She slips back through the flap in the curtain, and I pull on my clothes. My knife, cloak and boots are missing, but where would I go? Galen took Hero, and anyway, I don't even know if I could leave.

I stick my head through the flap in the curtain, and the voices fall silent.

Around the hearth are a group of women. Ranvig sits in Vigdis's chair with its thick bearskin cover. The others also wear blue, and they range from Ranvig's fifty years to a blonde woman about ten years older than me. The youngest is the first to move, offering me a bowl of broth and boiled meat. They all move aside, making space at the hearth for me.

No one says a word. They watch me eat, and when I ask for a drink, the youngest Staffbearer passes me a cup of water. Then they watch me drink.

"What are you doing here?" I ask, wiping my mouth on the back of my hand. "Where is everyone?"

The women glance at Ranvig.

"We were waiting," she says.

"We've been looking for you," says another of the women, and there's an eagerness in her voice that makes my skin creep.

I look around the circle of fire-lit eyes.

"Vigdis told us you were dead," says Ranvig. "But Drifa here saw you."

A woman sitting next to Ranvig turns her head. Her blind eyes are milky blue.

"Where's Vigdis?" I ask. My muscles are tensed, as if expecting an attack.

"She's preparing," says Ranvig.

"What for?"

Ranvig smiles.

"Bloodnight," she says.

I'd forgotten. I'd lost count of the days. But now here I am, home again.

"Where is everyone?" I ask again. Bloodnight is important. We build a big fire before the Harm Tree at the foot of Whalescar, where the path down from the cliff reaches level ground, and we choose the best beasts for slaughter. Everyone takes part.

"They're safe," says Ranvig. "The people of Bern's Kettil have taken them in." She names a village half a day's travel from Gullcroft. "But the child who came with you is still out there. It ran away from us last night."

"He," I say. "Not it."

"Come and help me find him then," says Ranvig. When I hesitate she raises her eyebrows. "He's had one night in the snow, without food. He won't last another."

I find that hard to believe. Fenn's sensible enough to be hiding in one of the empty houses, and we saw enough food and fuel left by that he's unlikely to freeze or starve. But on the other hand . . .

Staffbearers have converged on Gullcroft, and I've never known more than two visit, not in my whole life. I don't trust Ranvig. Why would Vigdis tell them I was dead? Why would they be waiting for me? Why did Galen flee?

Why have I been brought here, reeled in on an invisible line, to an empty village and the tattooed woman from my dream?

Fenn understands these things. He's born to it, like Vigdis hoped I'd be when she took me in after my father perished. Fenn recognised the mirror for what it was, and he wrestled Roaki from me when he wouldn't go.

Fenn can help me.

"If you hurt him, I'll kill you," I say.

"He's just a child," says Ranvig. "We're not going to hurt him."

"I'll need my boots," I say.

The snow is thick on the steep path down from the hut. I end up sliding some of the way on my bottom, and it isn't until I get down to the level ground that I see what made Galen abandon me.

Someone's raised a curse-pole before the Harm Tree, looking

over the village. I've never seen one before, but I recognise it from the stories I've heard. The sharpened pole is topped with a horse's severed head; the drooping lips bare yellowed teeth at the distant mountains. The headless body has been opened up, the meat removed, and the pole driven between its gaping ribs. The head and pole are rimed in frost. There'll be runes on the pole, laying out the curse, but I make no move to read them.

"Is this your work?" I ask Ranvig, but she just smiles.

There are two headless bodies strung from the Harm Tree. Big, male, wearing the bloody remains of dark red cloth, trimmed with fur.

I remember my fear of soldiers reaching Gullcroft before me.

Seems I shouldn't have worried.

"You'd better stay here," I tell her. "He won't come if you're with me."

"You know what will happen if you run," she says, and she holds up something.

It's a braid of pale hair, bound up in coloured yarn. My hand rises to touch my nape, but of course she didn't just make it. That's from when Sklep sheared me, before I left Gullcroft. Vigdis must have kept it.

And Ranvig used it to bring me here.

The cold numbs me. I walk down into the deserted village. In the bay, the boats have been dragged high up from the shingle beach, up-ended, and pegged under sailcloth. The stream that runs through the village spills into the sea, and the waves crash on the reef, sending spray up into the dull grey sky.

The houses are silent. I wander between them, calling Fenn's name. Finally, at the eastern edge of the village, where the east headland rises too steep to climb, I turn to see Fenn's dark head watching me from a doorway.

He has his finger to his lips.

Quietly, I walk over to him and put my arms around him. At first he stiffens, but then he returns the hug. The heavy iron collar burns cold against my neck.

"She wants you to come back with us," I tell him.

He pulls back and looks at me solemnly.

"It's her," he says. "Calling you."

"I know," I say. "Fenn, I've seen her before. When Roaki was in me, I had these dreams. She was in them."

"Not safe," he says. "Don't trust her."

I can't meet his eyes. I know what I should say. I should tell him to hide, to only come out when it's safe. But I'm alone, and I'm scared.

"Please," I whisper. "Come with me."

For a moment he seems to hover, unsure whether to run or stay.

Then he reaches out and puts his hand in mine.

He leads me back to where Ranvig waits under the curse-pole, her face unreadable.

Ebba taught me that when you're worried, the best thing you can do is keep your hands busy. I'll have to tell her that, when I see her. I was paying attention, even when it didn't seem like it.

I fill a cauldron with snow, and lay a fire in the small pit behind the horse-hide curtain, away from the watching Staffbearers. I tell Ranvig I need clean clothes for us both, and the youngest Staffbearer is sent out to find some. Then I give Fenn a bowl of warm water, a thick slab of ash-soap, and tell him to clean himself.

I sit with my back to the fire, a sheepskin across my lap, and I try not think.

When he's done I hand him the sheepskin to wrap around himself, and it's his turn to sit with his back to me as I wash.

The water from the cauldron scalds my skin, but the winter wolf has sunk its teeth into my bones, and nothing will chase it out. The blistered skin on my left shoulder itches.

Vigdis is preparing for Bloodnight, but there are no boars, no rams, no bulls left in this forsaken place. When she stands by the Harm Tree, when she recites the song of the Wise One, and how he gained the secrets of life and death, what kind of offering will be strung up beside her?

The water splashes on my face, and I remember the hot spray of blood on my face as the offerings are slaughtered, as my sword bites into Thorkel —

I dunk my head in the bowl and scrub my skin until it's red, telling myself not to be stupid. I could have died on Thorkel's blade or from fever out on the Floodlands. But I'm still here, aren't I? And this is Vigdis we're talking about. My aunt, who took me in, when even my own mother didn't want me.

Vigdis is not going to harm me. Ranvig I don't trust, but Vigdis will help me.

I'm just pulling on a pair of new wool leggings, my wet hair still slicked back, when there's a commotion outside the hut. I stop to listen, but before I can catch anything, the curtain is pushed aside and Galen is thrust into the room.

He staggers, and I move to steady him. He looks up at me and flinches. There are heavy pouches under his eyes.

"Galen?"

A laugh from the slit in the curtain makes us turn. Ranvig is watching us, and for the first time her face is animated.

"See it now, Golden Boy?" she sneers.

Galen glances at me and looks away.

"I've been drinking," he says. "Can't trust my eyes."

"How long have you been telling yourself that?"

Galen looks at me, and there's something so helpless, so tired in his face, that I step back. Ranvig laughs again.

"I remember when every girl between here and Sunacre would have fought for the chance to share your bed," she says. Her voice is soft as fur. "You used to have this glow about you. But the only person you loved was that prince of yours. You played at war together and then he died, and there were no more games, and no more gold. There's just the drink, and whatever reminds you of him."

Galen faces her. He's shivering with cold and exhaustion, but he's not flinching anymore.

"I know Geir's dead," he says. "I've been carrying him for nine years. You can't hurt me like that."

"I think you've been chasing him," says Ranvig. "That's why you agreed to carry the pendant, isn't it? That's why you travelled with Roaki to Frithberg, and why you went crawling back to Thorkel. I think you hoped one of them would kill you. That they'd send you on your way to Geir Arnson, wherever he is."

She smiles.

"And now they're dead," she says, "and you're still here. Why do you think that is?"

Galen closes his eyes.

"Because I have his Luck," he says.

An icy thrill runs through me.

"That's not all you have," says Ranvig. "You've become his daughter's nursemaid."

And they both turn to look at me, their heads moving in unison. The idea is so ridiculous, I laugh.

"When would my mother have met Prince Geir?" I demand. Brenna has never slept a night away from Gullcroft before now, from what I know.

"When she was training at the sacred grove at Sunacre," says Ranvig. "She was very young, but already very powerful. We all knew she would be chosen to succeed the old Staffbearer."

For a long moment I don't understand, but Ranvig keeps talking, and slowly it creeps up on me.

The Staffbearer of Sunacre, who helped Prince Geir hang his father Arn on the Harm Tree. Vigdis. My mother.

As it sinks in, I feel warm blood on my face.

"Why do you think Geir chose Vigdis to help him?" Ranvig says to Galen. "When Kolrand took Sunacre and marched on Hellingap, Vigdis rode three horses to their deaths, just so she could reach Geir and tell him. Why do you think she did that?"

"I don't believe you," I say, but they ignore me.

"And just think," Ranvig says, "while Arn was cutting off your hand for undue loyalty to his son, that same son was bedding the girl who would kill his father."

Galen groans, his mouth twisted in agony.

"I have always admired," Ranvig says, "how the threads are laid, one after another, and how a single knot can form a noose."

She leaves us.

For a moment, I don't trust myself to speak. Galen stumbles to one of the beds and sits heavily, a deep, hacking cough shaking his whole body. Fenn nips up onto a stool to reach some of the dried plants hanging from the beams above us, but I stay standing, frozen to the spot.

"What's your name?" he asks me.

"Torny," I say. "Why didn't you tell me?"

Galen's bent over, still coughing. Fenn jumps down and busies himself over the fire.

"Tell you what?" Galen says. "That I knew Gullcroft? That I saw something in you that reminded me of Geir?"

I don't really care about that. I'm thinking of Vidgis, of the thin thread of blood Ranvig has spun between us.

"Why did you run?" I ask, but what I really mean is, why did you stop? If he'd kept going, maybe Ranvig wouldn't have told me.

"I'm good at running," says Galen, and I know there's something he's not telling me.

Fenn thrusts hot cups into our hands. The steam smells sweet and a little rotten, like hay under the sun after a summer storm.

"What did you mean about having Geir's Luck?"

Galen sips from his cup, bright droplets shining in his beard.

"He gave it to me," he says quietly. "When Vidgis came to him, right before Hellingap. He made her bind his Luck to me. The others never forgave me."

The anger inside me drains away. To give up your Luck is to give up your life. I want to ask why anyone would do that, but then I think of Ebba, and I know.

"He loved you," I say. "He wanted to protect you."

"He cursed me," Galen says bitterly. "I had to watch him die, but he never thought I might not want to be the one left behind."

"Were you there?" I ask. "When he was killed?"

"I was so close, I felt the breeze of the arrow on my face."

His coughing has eased, and we sit in silence.

"If Geir loved you, why would he sleep with Vigdis?" I ask. The hurt in Galen's face makes me sorry as soon as I've said it, but it nags at me.

"I don't know," he says. "There are people who love both men and women, and love doesn't guard against desire. Or maybe he just did what was needed. So that there would be an heir."

And both he and Fenn look at me.

"Oh no," I say, "don't even think it."

"An heir could challenge Kolrand," says Galen.

"If they could survive that long," I say.

"That's why Vigdis kept you hidden."

"She kept me hidden from everyone. Ranvig said Vigdis told the other Staffbearers I was dead."

Galen frowns. "Maybe she was keeping you secret until she knew you could be useful."

"A princess isn't the same as a prince," I say shortly. "The only thing I'd be useful for is marrying."

"This is not a wedding," says Fenn, but neither of us laugh.

"He's right," I say. "But you know what this is, don't you Galen?"

He looks away.

"Just say it," I order.

"The last time they emptied the village," he says, "was when they made the Sungiven."

I'm on the cliffs. The wind buffets me, but I lean into it, testing the rope around my waist. The gulls scream in my ears.

I'm on the reef. The fish are leaping out of the water and into my arms. I wrestle them like unwilling treasure, my skin sparkling with scales.

A girl with hair like the lowland corn stands over me. I've never seen cornfields like they have on the plains, acres of soft rich gold, but I've heard it in the songs and I know. Hair like corn, eyes like summer, and armour made of bright scales. She looks at me and smiles.

"Do you know how whales hunt?" she asks me.

I shake my head.

"Watch," she says.

The cliffs shake with whalesong. Out beyond the reef, where the seafloor drops away, a patch of black water boils with silver herring. They're turning, turning, caught in a cage of white bubbles. All at once the great hidden things burst upwards, mouths gaping, and the herring jump and twist between the lipless jaws, before the lined throats close on them, and the huge black heads bow beneath the waves.

"There's not much difference," says Vigdis, her spindle bobbing on the end of a new thread, "between driving men and driving fish. But if you were a fish, who would you want rid of? The children on the reef? Or the monsters from the deep?"

The knot at my waist is tight. The golden-haired girl holds Vigdis's spindle in her hands, the thread stretches between us. The gulls scream.

I walk backwards over the cliff.

When Ranvig comes for us at the end of the day, I don't ask where we're going. My brief sleep has deadened me, made me mute and clumsy. We follow her down the path to the village, slipping on the packed snow. On the beach waits a boat made ready for us. Ranvig sits in the bows, Galen lifts me in and Fenn jumps in beside me. Galen sets a long-handled oar in its notch, and sculls us past the shadowed reef, between the cliffs, and onto the open sea.

There's only one place we can be going.

The end of the world, I think, in my sleep-muddled head, and the song I began reciting for Galen comes back to me.

Stained from the corpse-sea comes
the harrier-god to the gulls' home,
fish-like, out of the fear-flow leaping
to the far isle, and the fair-faced keeper.

Vigdis is on Far Isle.

The setting sun dips out from under the heavy clouds, sending its beams across the sea. I watch the cliffs fall away from us, and feel the island growing at my back like a shadow.

This has all happened before, I think.

At last Galen brings us alongside the island's bare shore. He straddles the gap between the boat and the rocks, and hands me across the gap. Fenn jumps out beside me.

"We'll be back at dawn," says Ranvig.

I stand on the hard rocks and I watch as Galen sculls back across the black and gold swell. I can't speak, I can't think, I can't feel. I'm weary, and my injured arm aches.

Fenn pulls me up.

"We need shelter," he says.

"There'll be shelter," I say, starting to climb.

When I reach the top of the tumbled rocks, the west is a bloody line. In its red light I look across the island. At the northern end the rock juts up in black pillars, a forest of sharp edges and flat, six-sided faces. From here to there the flat ground is strewn with small boulders. In the middle stands a single black pillar.

I cross to it and run my hand over the hard stone. Fenn follows me, weaving between the small boulders, casting around, but I've already seen what I'm looking for.

On the north edge of the island, where the black pillars of rock pile up against the north wind, there's a flutter of blue cloth. Against the black rock it's as shocking as a glimpse of blue sky in a thunder storm.

I run towards it, jumping boulders, and there she is.

Her blue cloak flows around her, and her silver pendants shine on her breast. Her long pale hair streams out of her hood, but instead of blonde, it's white. I hesitate, half-wanting to run, but she pulls back her hood.

Eyes so grey they're almost colourless, long hair tangling across her face and the stones around her. Her face is thinner, older, but she holds out her arms, and I run into them.

She strokes my short springy hair, my cold nape, and her other arm wraps around my waist like mooring rope. I bury my face in her shoulder and feel hot tears spilling into her salt-rimed cloak.

"Torny," she says, "I'm so sorry."

"I know," I say. "She told me."

She stiffens in my arms.

"What did she tell you?"

I pull away, cuffing tears from my eyes.

"That you're my mother, and about my father. And Galen said —"

"Galen!"

"He came with me. He said they're doing the same thing they did for the Sungiven."

She holds my shoulders, searching my face for something.

"Come on," she says, turning on her heel. "You'll freeze."

She's limping badly. I don't say anything, just turn to call Fenn.

He's standing on a boulder at the edge of the stone forest, looking back across the island. I step up beside him. The last light of the setting sun sends shadows sprawling east, where the full moon is lifting out of the waters.

The boulders aren't strewn randomly. They're laid out in loops and swirls. The lonely pillar marks the centre of the labyrinth.

Under the forest of black stone there's a cave. Fenn doesn't want to go in, but the wind makes him shiver, and finally he gives up and lets me lead him down into the cramped, smokey space. He wraps himself in one of the sheepskins from Vigdis's bed, and tucks himself beside me like a shadow. Fish stew bubbles over a small fire, and when Vigdis fills a bowl for me, I pass it to Fenn first.

Vigdis has settled herself with her right leg stuck straight out, as if she can't bend it. There are new lines on her face, and her mouth is thin with pain.

"Did Ranvig do this to you?"

Vigdis barks with laughter.

"Age did this to me," she says. "And pride. Ranvig was just the tool."

"What does she want?"

"She's trying to raise the dead," Vigdis says. "She wants to go back. She wants to win this time."

Fenn wolfs down the stew. Vigdis fills the bowl again and hands it back to me. Fenn curls up at my side while I eat.

"You never told me —" I begin, but I stop when I think how stupid it sounds. She never told me anything.

Vigdis leans back against the black stone wall. In the smoke and the firelight, her face stands out like bone.

"This is your chance," she says. "Ask."

I could ask her a hundred things. I could ask her about the man I believed was my father, or the man who really was, or why Ranvig wants to change things now. But there's a story in my head, and if it turns out I'm part of it, I need to know.

"You killed King Arn," I say.

Vigdis tries to keeps her face expressionless, but she can't snuff out a flicker of pride.

"Yes," she says. "At least, I put the noose around his neck. Geir did the honours."

She might as well be talking about slaughtering livestock.

"Why?"

She frowns.

"Arn was vile," she says. "He sold out his own people to the Southern Emperor in return for gold and men. He turned his back on the gods of his fathers. He had no respect. Staffbearers used to be part of the king's counsel, but my teacher was treated like a senile old granny, though she was the wisest person at his table. The only reason we were allowed to train was Arn liked having young girls around. Of course I helped Geir kill him."

I don't say anything. I wonder if the Vigdis of Arn's court saw the power she should have had slipping away, even as she came into it. I wonder if that's what she killed for.

Beside me, Fenn sleeps like a dog, his eyes closed and his chest rising and falling with his breath.

"Did you think I would be like you?"

She prods the fire, though it doesn't need it.

"What do you mean?"

"You know. A Staffbearer." I can't stop the bitterness entering my voice. "You must have been disappointed."

She keeps her eyes down.

"Why do you say that?"

So I tell her about Roaki, how in my hunger for a second Luck I went to him on the Harm Tree and haggled with a dead man. Vigdis listens all the way through to Thorkel's death, hissing through her teeth when I tell her about how Roaki closed my throat, and the fight. But I don't mention Sleeper's Howe, or what happened inside it, and I skip over Fenn's part in the story.

"And then Roaki wouldn't leave," I tell her, unable to meet her eyes. "He tried to stay in me. I thought I was going to die."

"And how did you get him to leave?" asks Vigdis.

What can I say? I can't tell her about Fenn and the mirror, because I've left them both out of the story. Partly it's instinct – if Vigdis or Ranvig know about Fenn, they might not let him stay with me. But partly I'm jealous; Fenn has something I should have had. If I'd been able to do what he can, maybe . . . maybe Vigdis would have told me she was my mother.

"I told him he was already dead," I say.

Her head snaps up, her eyes sharp.

"What?"

"I told him he was dead, and he left," I say, uncomfortable. "He shouted a bit, but he went."

Vigdis is trying to control her excitement, but she can't. She tugs at her silver pendants, staring at me.

"I never guessed . . ." she says to herself.

"Never guessed what?"

She looks at me, distracted. "Did he show you things? The dead man?"

"He showed me Ranvig. We were here, on the island, and so was he, and he kept asking my name."

"But you didn't tell him?"

I shake my head.

She laughs. It's such a strange, victorious sound, it excites me and scares me all at once.

"You idiot," she says. "You lucky, lucky idiot. Whatever made you think of taking a dead man's Luck?"

"I wanted to be a warrior," I mutter, the heat back in my cheeks. "I was training with Jarle. I wasn't bad, but he kept telling me how much weaker I was because I'm a girl. I thought a second Luck sounded useful."

She laughs again. "How old is Jarle now?"

"Eighteen," I say. "But how do you —"

"I knew his mother, Suniva," Vigdis says, and the smile is for herself now, not me. "When I sent you off, I wondered if you'd like him any better than the boy Thorpe." She looks me over. "But you don't, do you?"

"He's all right," I say, sidetracked. "He taught me how to spar."

"Oh well," she says, "that's not important anymore. You invited him in! That was so stupid. I'm proud."

I look at her in surprise.

"It takes a strong mind and a strong body to carry a spirit rider," she says. "Do you think just anyone would have done? Most people would have died. But you . . . you didn't just carry him, you threw him off." She shakes her head. "Ranvig was right. I was so short-sighted; I should have taught you properly."

❧ 319 ❧

"What was she right about?"

"That with you, we could win." Her face is alight with excitement. "She wants you to be the next Sungiven, and lead the North to victory. That's why I sent you to Frithberg, so you'd be out of her reach, and that's why she made me call you back."

"You kept my hair," I whisper.

"Yes, I did." She reaches out and strokes my short curls off my face. "I missed you, Torny."

I feel the tears pricking my eyes again.

"Did you name me?"

"Yes." She smiles. "When I had you, I gave you to Vafri to take with him to his wife in the North. But I named you for the thunder, because I knew a storm was coming, and I wanted you to ride it."

"Did you love my father?"

She flinches, as if she wasn't expecting the question.

"Of course not."

"Then why —"

"We don't always do things for love."

I sit back, her words ringing like a slap. She touches the place where her ribs meet over her stomach, an echo of the way a new mother rests her hands over her pregnant belly, and something about it seems false.

"I'm sorry," she says. "I didn't want Ranvig to call you. But it's turned out all right."

For the first time, I feel as if I'm seeing into her the way she sees into others.

She's lying.

She tries to disguise it, but it's there in her voice, her face. This new warmth, this mother-talk, it's all because I told her about

Roaki. She was excited and . . . relieved. As if something she'd felt guilty about had been resolved.

There's no struggle – her ambition won long ago, when Geir asked her to hold the noose. Maybe even before that, when she was a newcomer to Arn's court, when a man she didn't love put a baby in her belly. She wanted the power.

Even if Vigdis is my mother, she'll still let Ranvig have me. She'll be pleased that the Sungiven is her flesh and blood.

"You have a chance to be a hero," Vigdis says. "Won't you take it?"

I think of my practice fights with Jarle, and my first sight of a warrior in Smithgate, the shining new-made weapons hanging up in the forge, and the smith spitting on the name of the Sungiven. I think about all the heroes in all the stories I've ever heard, and about the golden-haired woman in my memory, standing on the cliffs and smiling at me. I think about Galen and his dead prince, and one-eyed Thorkel, guarding his men like a jealous husband. I think about Fenn, curled warm by my side, and the Sleeper in its howe, cold and alone.

Finally, I think about Ebba, her smile, her strength.

"Yes," I say. "Yes."

I don't sleep. I watch the flames dance blue and violet on the driftwood until they die. I feel empty, adrift on the night. I stare into the blackness, and for a moment I think I'm back on the stony beach at Gullcroft, the waves lapping at my feet. I walk out into the cold black sea, and feel the waves close over me.

Before dawn, Vigdis calls me. I put on the undyed shift she leaves for me, wincing as I expose my bare skin to the cold air.

I shake Fenn. He mutters and curls up tighter, and I wonder if I should let him sleep, but when I think of walking out there alone, fear twists my guts. I shake him harder.

"Fenn," I whisper, "it's time. Fenn!"

Still half-asleep, he follows me out into the freezing cold.

In the grey light, Vigdis and Ranvig wait for us at the far end of the island, the other Staffbearers behind them. Seeing them side by side is a shock. Ranvig must be twenty years older than Vigdis, but she stands tall and strong, while Vigdis leans heavily on her staff, her face drawn.

I take off my cloak and wrap it around Fenn. I look around for Galen, but there's no sign of him. Maybe he wasn't allowed to be here. Instead I lead Fenn to blind Drifa, who stands apart from the rest.

"This is Fenn," I say. "Look after him."

Drifa puts a hand on his shoulder, and Fenn leans against her, bundled up in the comically large cloak. His chin nods down to his chest.

Vigdis hands me the drink she was brewing all night. It's like the one Fenn fed me, under the thorns near Sleeper's Howe. I screw up my face, but I don't vomit.

Ranvig is fidgeting with excitement.

"Quickly," she says, pulling me to the entrance of the labyrinth and taking hold of my wrists. The blue tattoos spool across her white skin like threads. She holds my eyes with hers, and steps back between the stones that mark the labyrinth's entrance.

A straight path has been opened, leading to the black pillar. Ranvig leads me to the centre and binds me to the pillar. Vigdis explained this bit but I still hate it. I feel so helpless. Ranvig draws her long knife, and though I know what's coming, the pain of the blade being drawn across my chest makes me bite my lips until they bleed. The shallow cut stains the plain shift a bright, perfect red.

Drifa takes a bullroarer from her belt and tosses it into the air with a practised flick of her wrist. The buzz starts in my body and rushes out to fill the grey world, blending with the wind and the waves. Ranvig hurries back to Vigdis, and the other Staffbearers ring the labyrinth.

The sun isn't over the horizon, but the world is lighter.

When it rises, Vigdis said, she'll enter you.

Who? I asked.

These days they call her the Cornmaiden, Vigdis said, but long ago she was the Queen of Horses, the Mother of Peace, and she ruled this land and many others. Then the Wise One took her crown and made her the goddess of farmers, but still she sows, and still she reaps.

It'll be like molten gold, she said.

Vigdis and Ranvig stand on either side of the entrance stones, so that the labyrinth's path is unhindered. It looks out over the rocks I climbed last night, over the sea and south to the gap in the cliffs where Gullcroft lies.

I gasp.

With a sickening lurch, the distant cliffs seem to rush closer. I see a boat on the waves, the beach, men gathered by the curse-pole, and then over the turf to the glacier-plains, the fells, the glittering expanse of the Floodlands. Under their silver skin I seem to see a sunken path that leads from shore to shore, through the Slipskins' abandoned camp, and between the windswept thorns to Sleeper's Howe.

With another lurch I'm back in my body, looking across the white-topped waves to the far-off cliffs.

Something is climbing out of the sea onto the rocks, just out of sight. I can't see it, but I can feel it: waterlogged, dead, black as bog oak.

I scream. The sky is getting lighter, but the sun won't come in time. All I need is to feel the sun, and I know its gold will fill me, will make me what I'm meant to be, and send this crawling thing back down the long road to its grave forever.

But the sun is swaddled in clouds, and as the bullroarer thrums through the rock, the thing pulls itself over the ledge.

It's like a hole in the world. Everything bends around it, and it keeps coming, limping towards me. I scream and try to rip myself away from the pole. Vigdis is moving her lips, but I can't hear anything over the buzz in my bones, and then, horribly, I feel the flesh at the base of my spine opening.

Tell me your name.

"Stop it!" I scream. "Stop!"

But Drifa spins the bullroarer, and Ranvig opens her arms in glory, as if she can't see the horror moving towards me.

"Vigdis!" I scream, as the thing limps between the boulders that mark the entrance. "It's wrong! Stop!"

But Vigdis ignores me, her lips moving, her gaze far away, nursing some past hope like a future promise. Ranvig pushes the stones back into place, closing off the straight path to the heart of the maze.

I feel the walls of power blaze around me as the labyrinth closes. I could no more cross the boulders than I could run through stone. The thing halts and sways. It knows it's trapped now, but it doesn't care. I'm trapped with it, and all it wants is me.

"Fenn!" I scream, as it takes another step towards me. It's only a few feet away. I close my eyes and remember Fenn leading me across the lines of white pebbles in the burial chamber. The way he pulled me over them. He's the only one who can help me.

"*Fenn!*"

The thing is right in front of me. I can feel its cold breath, if such a thing can breathe. Mist wraps around me like a shroud.

The bullroarer dies. I look at Drifa in time to see her snatch her hand away from Fenn, bright beads of blood in toothmarks on the skin. The cloak lies crumpled at her feet. Fenn dodges Vigdis and runs to me, his dark eyes determined.

Ranvig steps in front of him, her fist out, and he shudders.

The light goes out of his eyes, and he slides off her knife.

I scream as he falls, scream as the thing reaches round and finds the hole in my back. Mist curls up my spine like an eel.

I'm here, it says. *Everything that was mine is yours. Tell me your name.*

So I tell it, and as I do the sun rises. But the mist is with me now, I move through it and breathe it, and the sun seems sickly and far off to me. At my heart where I once felt that hungry red joy there's nothing, just a chasm.

I step outside myself.

My body hangs spent from its bonds, like a rag on the wind and the waves. I watch as Ranvig treads the labyrinth, circling towards the pole with impatient steps. Her eyes and lips are wide, and her hands shake. Her knife is still bloody. She cuts through my body's bonds, and leads it by the hand along the circling path, like a groom might lead his bride. I watch from outside, wrapped in mist.

As Ranvig steps across the threshold she turns, and holds out her arms in welcome.

My hand slides her own blade into her breast like the prow cuts the wave. The mist around me muffles me, dampens any shock, any horror.

The knife drops.

I am the butcher. I am the Harrower.

Vigdis and the others stumble back, their mouths slack.

Behind them, on the rocks, stands a man.

Laugi, one eye freshly plucked, holds the golden helm in his hands.

"Mistress," he says, bowing to me.

My body stoops and gathers Fenn into its arms, and the mist wraps around us both. I can see where the hard metal of his collar digs into his thin neck, imagine the chill of his cold body against my own, but I can't feel it. He lolls in my arms like a sleepy child.

I am the gates of the land of the dead, and you are all prey to me.

Twenty
WINTER

EBBA'S TALE

Eldinghope, the East

he ships arrive the next day. I'm makin sure Stig's comfy in the wagon when Adelhard rides into the yard. He calls to Erland in the Southern tongue an the two of em ride out again. I leave Berengar helpin Ma into the wagon. Seein her leanin on his arm makes me angry, so I climb up to where Ulf's pyre still smokes in the cold mornin air, Fetch by my side.

Longships lie offshore. I watch the soldiers march up the beach, along the track through the dunes an into the yard. I pluck the last of the long grass an tear the blades to shreds. I try to count the marchin soldiers, but I can't keep my mind on it. Fetch sits on his haunches beside me, a low growl rumblin in his chest. I reach up to scratch behind his ears.

"I know, boy," I say.

There must be close to a hundred men. They en't Southerners, I can see that, but they en't like warriors neither. They all wear the same deep red tunic over dark breeches, though some of em have cloaks trimmed wi heavy fur, an gold an silver rings on their forearms. The ships fly a flag with a great black bear on red.

I hear footsteps an turn. Erland comes to stand beside me, shadin his eyes against the mornin sun. Fetch's rumblin dies away, an he lays down, his head on his paws.

"I thought the King's token was an eagle," I say.

"It is," says Erland. "But these are the Bearskins." His voice is warm. "They're what the Slipskins should have been. Well-trained men with good blades and good purpose."

One of the fur-cloaked soldiers sees Erland an salutes, his armrings glintin. Erland raises his arm in reply.

"You're proud of em," I say.

"They have the strength of good men, not barren gods," he says.

I look up at him. His face is calm an peaceful, like a farmer lookin over a healthy crop.

"They're yours, en't they?"

Erland smiles. "This is my company," he says. "You didn't think I had just nine men under my command?"

I din't think on it at all, an he sees it, which makes me a little sharper than I mean to be.

"If they're so perfect, why bring outlanders on this dance?"

"The evil of the Staffbearers is rooted deep," he says. "Grimulf needed men he knew would serve him, no matter what."

"Like you," I say. He don't answer. I've remembered somethin else: two riders in dark red an fur bein sent north from Frithberg.

I wonder if they found what – who – they were lookin for, an my heart is heavy. "D'you really believe they're evil?"

"How can you ask me that, after what you've seen?"

I look down at my lapful of shredded grass. "Is that why you took to the White God? Because the Staffbearers hurt someone you loved?"

"They hurt this whole country with their meddling," says Erland. "I saw brother killing brother because those hags wouldn't accept that their time was ending."

He's lookin away, over the heads of the soldiers beneath us, over the ships to the horizon. "It was terrible," people say. "Brother killing brother." But mostly they don't *mean* brothers, not really. Kin killin kin should be unthinkable, so if they say that, they don't have to say what they really saw or what they really did.

But Erland don't mean it like that. In his mouth, a brother means a brother.

"You're from Hellingap," I say, "an Hellingap supported Geir."

"They disowned me long before that," Erland says. "I was sent to Sunacre to join the Slipskins, but instead I joined Kolrand's household."

"Why?"

"For love," he says. "But she died. The Slipskins killed her. By the time I faced my brother at the battle of Hellingap, we had not called ourselves brothers for years. When we're rid of the Staffbearers we can start over," he says, like he's repeatin somethin he's bin told. "Our wounds will finally heal."

I scratch Fetch's ears, an think of Ulf an Arf, swallowed up in flames an blood, an me an Rafe an Stig an Ma, all of us burned an bloodied. Rafe cryin when I wouldn't let him die. Ma watchin over the son she'd drugged, not knowin if her mercy might turn to murder. When will those wounds heal?

I watch the last of the soldiers crest the dunes.

"I thought that if Ulf had bin polite an did as Grimulf asked, he might of bin spared," I say. "An I thought Grimulf was reckless to threaten Ulf when all he had was a handful of men. But he knew he wouldn't be waitin till spring, din't he?"

Erland has the decency to look away.

"If your uncle had welcomed us with open arms, Grimulf would still have found a reason to remove him."

So there it is. If things had bin different, like maybe the curse had never bin said, an my da had lived, an all had bin well in Eldinghope, an none of us ever suffered . . . even then, Grimulf would have come just the same, an it could of bin Arf's pyre smokin behind me, an me weepin cause I couldn't die repayin that debt.

I stand up and brush grass from my dress. My mind returns to all the Prester's talk of sheep an shepherds that seemed so strange when I first heard it. Now I understand it.

"Back in Frithberg, Grimulf an the merchant were talkin about black sheep that came to the East in ships," I say. "They meant people like Ma, din't they? People like me. Now that your Bearskins are here, the Raiders will have a fight on their hands . . ."

"And the slave route from the East will be open," says Erland. "Yes. King Kolrand and the Emperor will be pleased."

The sun sends light dancin over the wavelets. Fetch stretches an yawns hugely beside me.

"Is that all I am?" I ask. "Livestock?"

Erland turns me to face him, his hands on my shoulders. "You are going to be free, Ebba Rathnasdota. You are going to be so much more than a slave, or a farmgirl, or even a saint with a magic salve. You're going to heal not just the people, but the kingdom. You're going to change the world."

"I couldn't even save my home," I say.

The last of the soldiers pass the knoll.

"I'll look after your people," Erland says. "If they don't take arms against us, they won't be hurt. Birchold needs you, and so does your family." He follows my gaze to where Berengar is passin the reins up to Rafe on the wagon's seat. "I need my armsman for now," he says, half-smilin, "but I've promised him he can take the rest of your mother's supplies to Birchold at the new moon. I believe he has a list."

I sniff. "Only one? Last time I checked he had at least five."

"Four," says Erland. "One was a request to spend midwinter in Birchold. He says he wants to record local customs and dress." I snort, and he smiles properly. "If we aren't snowed in, who knows? Maybe I'll grant it." He nods towards the farm. "Go on, Ebba. They're waiting."

Fetch at my heels, I run down the knoll. Some of the newcomers stare at me openly, a small dark girl with a hound so big it comes up to her shoulder, talkin to their captain like an equal. Others try to look from the corners of their eyes. I ignore em, go straight to Berengar. *I en't like you*, I think, an there's somethin in me, somethin powerful. *You think you know who's important an who en't, but you don't know me.*

"Are you sure about this?" Berengar asks, holding Medard's horse by the reins.

I'm not, but I'm damned if I'm going to ride on the wagon like a servant anymore.

"How hard can it be?" I ask.

"Well," says Berengar, his straight dark brows pullin together, "the first time, I broke —"

"Just help me up, will you?"

I don't fall off till a mile later, when there's no one to see me. At least, no one who matters. Rafe forgets himself an laughs like a goat, but he don't count.

✿

TORNY'S TALE
Gullcroft, the North

When I surface, I'm in a boat with Laugi and two of his men. Fenn lies across my lap, and my feet rest on a pile of iron staffs. Far Isle is just a low dark smudge in the mist.

"Harrier," says Laugi. "Your warriors have come to welcome you."

I twist round. The beach is visible between the cliffs, thronged with men in armour, their spears upright in the mist like a dead forest.

The Slipskins.

The cold wind cuts across my face. I search back in my memory. I remember Fenn falling from Ranvig's knife, the thing entering me, and Laugi stepping up onto the rocks . . . but everything else is blackness.

Far Isle has vanished, and Vigdis isn't with us.

The mist swirls around me, thicker, until everything is muffled and quiet. My thoughts disperse, drawing back, the way any living thing flinches from pain. We pass the reef, the cliffs close about us, and shingle crunches under the bow. The two oarsmen leap out, holding the boat fast.

Laugi kneels before me, and puts the Harrier Helm on my head.

I'm back in the dark, airless grave. White bones, white skin. I reach out and touch – loneliness. A loss that would not fade. And then the man with an eye like a mirror, who made such insidious promises and would not die, who tricked us, trapped us, tore us apart. Long, unbearable captivity. And then a terrible warmth, of flesh, of blood, and an inescapable heartbeat, drumming out the moments of life, so awful it had to be torn out of me. Torn over and over, until I understood there was no path back, and they put a sword in my hands and said, "Now use this." And the cloak of flesh grew familiar, and the task demanded of me became habit, and I learned to love the measure of my cage, its golden bars and deep red nights. And then the key, come to me in a small, quick form, in a pair of dark, laughing eyes.

No matter how rich the cage, all captives dream of a key.

The cold wind scours my body, but the helm narrows my view, deadens noise.

I gather Fenn into my arms as I rise, and I turn to face the shore.

A shout goes up from the warriors, a solid wall of sound, blasting through the deadening mist. I feel it like a weight on my chest.

Row by row, the warriors kneel.

"Harrier," says Laugi, "We have honoured you and made sacrifice to you these last nine years. We felt you rise and we followed. Now, will you lead us to the end of all things?"

Yes, I say. At least, my lips move, but the voice is not mine.

The men's cheers engulf me, but the helm makes it seem far away.

Two warriors drag forward Galen. His face is bloodied, and he looks at me in horror. He sees my burden, and lets out a strangled cry, but that too is distant, flat, and my eyes slide off him.

At Galen's shoulder stands the form of a man with bright blue eyes under straight brows, his sharp cheekbones narrowing to a strong chin. His beard is trimmed short, and his mouth is hard and sensual at once. There is a glow about him, and where it falls on Galen, Galen seems doubled, as if there is a younger, softer self inside him, whole and freckled and red-gold. And I know that these golden creatures are Galen's two Lucks, one his own, one his prince's, clothed in the form and beauty of his love.

I stare into the radiant face of Geir Arnson, trying to remember why he should be important to me. But it's no good. Galen's memory of him is too golden; it chases out all other thoughts. I look away, and Galen stands before me as he is: bloodied, alone, broken.

This man is mine, says the Sleeper. *He lives until his debt is paid.*

The warriors part before me like water round a stone, and dimly I see each one has a golden shadow. The men themselves darken, their features hard to tell apart, but their Lucks stand out between the dull flesh. Some are steady and some waver, but the mist is thicker now, and the world feels insubstantial.

The only solid thing is the dead weight in my arms.

Bring me a smith, we say.

And then I bury Fenn.

I choose a place on the cliff where he can see the rising and the setting sun, and I dig the hole and lay him in it. I wrap him in a warm cloak, and put a meal at his left hand, so he won't be hungry. Under his right I lay the broken thrall collar I had the smith cut off him. I told the smith if he so much as scratched the skin, I'd kill him. The smith looked from me to Galen, and worked as gently as if he had a newborn under his chisel.

Galen said looking into my eyes just then was like looking into two white holes.

"You're not like Suniva," he says. "She was mostly human."

But I don't know or care who he means. He's scared of me, and sometimes he prattles to cover it, but still he follows me everywhere.

"The Slipskins call me your dog," he says.

The Slipskins want him dead. That's why he follows me even when every muscle in his body would rather run. I know, I can tell. Sometimes he even quivers like a dog.

Laugi tries to tell me I can't trust Galen. He says he worries that someday Galen will slide a knife between my ribs.

I just laugh at him.

The Sleeper won't let anyone hurt me.

The world is dull and choked with fog. The days are so short they slur together, brief flickers of light in a long darkness. As the world fades away I discover new senses. I can feel minds.

Laugi's mind is coiled tight, like a serpent around treasure, feeding on itself. Before I was free, there were only minds like this. I lay in the dark, in my prison of twisting paths, and felt them growing on the other side, pressing against the walls that held me. But they were no good to me. They would worship, but they wouldn't come to me.

And finally, he came back. I hadn't felt him for so long. My long lost boy, with a mind like a key. And he could feel me too, and that made him careful. He didn't want to be used, and I have no power over the living but fear.

The dead are my domain, but they seldom walk.

Until she came. Until he followed.

My lock and key.

My freedom.

❧

EBBA'S TALE
Birchold, the East

Mistress Una seems pleased to have me back. She makes up beds for us in her own home, an when she sees the supplies we've brought from Ma's store, she takes Ma's hand an squeezes it. I look away an call up Fetch. I see Mistress Una hold her back when Ma tries to follow me.

I want to say goodbye to Adelhard an his men, but they're already gone. I guess they need to make the pass before next snowfall, but all the same I wish they'd waited.

I see Rafe helpin stable the cart an horses alongside some village boys. They're laughin an talkin, but as I pass the stables one of em sees me, an bows. The others follow, an Rafe looks up to see who they're greetin. When he sees me he gets a complicated look on his face, an I turn away before it turns bitter.

Who am I?

It's like Erland cut me loose when he said I was goin to be free, an now I can't find a foothold.

I avoid the barn where the sick lie. I loop round the hall an down the path to the clearin, where the black scar of the coals I trod is hidden under fresh snow. It reminds me of the other scars, up in the Eldinghope grove an down on the knoll by the dunes.

There's no runnin from this. I guess I knew that.

I go back past the cottage where I stayed wi the prester. I'm glad to be free of him for now. The owners have moved back in. Fetch trots up to sniff noses wi the family mutt, an the wife an her husband see me an offer me warm cider. I sit on the bench outside their door where Berengar used to sit, an ask to hold their babe, an with him in my lap they speak that much freer, tellin me the winter stores are good, an the prester has made sure they had grain enough to protect against last year's want.

"He's been a blessin to this village," says the wife, takin back her son to nurse him. "The headman says change is comin, thanks to him, an Birchold shall have wealth from it."

"Did he say what kind of wealth?" I ask, but they don't know. I scratch Fetch behind the ears an think of Dagomar's black sheep. It makes my heart heavy. I grew up in fear, but I could of bin in chains. I could never of known Ma an Stig, could of bin sold outright, my family a blank.

Is that what happened to Ma?

This new thought makes me stumble. How come I en't never asked myself that before?

Because you blamed her, I tell myself. *You were angry that she couldn't protect you, that she taught you to look away an be thankful when Ulf's anger fell elsewhere. That she looked away when it fell on you. You din't wonder if she'd ever known her own Ma. You din't want to know.*

I take my leave of the family an head back the way I came. When I walk into Mistress Una's kitchen I find her an Ma workin at the big table, arguin over the best way to set a broken foot.

"Ma," I say, an she almost cuts herself. "I need to ask you somethin."

"Oh Abda," she says, her eyes fillin. "I'm sorry. I drugged him. I just couldn't stand him knowin what was —"

I feel that same sickness I felt before lookin at her, but this time I push it aside. I find I'm scared.

"Not that," I say, rougher than I mean to. "I know *that*. I want to know how you came here. How the Raiders came to have you."

Mistress Una wipes her hands on her apron. "You two sit," she says, guidin Ma to the hearth. "I got barley needs toastin."

So we sit by the hearthstone, our hands workin by themselves, an Ma tells me what she's never told me before. She tells me how her name was Roshna, before she came to Eldinghope an Arf named her Rathna, so's she'd have a name fit for Arngard. She can't remember her family much, an thinks she must of bin sold young, because before the Raiders took her she remembers a big house, all made of stone, in a land where the summer lasted most of the year an she never wore furs. The family had a daughter just older'n her, an Ma cared for her rooms. It was a beautiful place, a rich place, but if she upset her young mistress, the girl would beat Ma on the soles of her feet. Ma was sold when she started to bleed, an the merchants took her down a long wide river to the sea, where the Raiders attacked an carried her off, an that's how she came to be there when Ulf an Arf captured the ship.

"Ulf was for sellin me," she said, "but your da liked me. I remember em arguin. Ulf said we could sell me after, but Arf put his foot down an said he'd take me instead of his share of the spoils."

"Dad *bought* you from Ulf?" I ask.

Ma shrugs. "He saved me," she says. "If I'd of bin sold I wouldn't of lasted. He wanted to marry me, an I wanted to live."

"So . . . din't you love da?"

She looks into the fire, her eyes far away. "He saved me," she says again. "I was grateful. An he was a kind man. While he lived he sheltered us, an when he died, Ulf kept us."

"Would of bin kinder to let us go," I say, but Ma shakes her head.

"You don't know what the world is like, Abda."

"I know what Ulf was like," I say, tryin to keep my voice even. "An I've seen a bit of the world. It en't all bad."

"But there are always men like Ulf," says Ma. "If you don't have someone to shelter you, sooner or later you'll come under their hands."

I breathe in the warm barley-scent, tryin to bite down my anger.

"Ulf din't need to chain you," I say, "did he? He put chains in your head, an he knew they'd hold."

"Abda —"

"Why d'you call me that?"

Ma draws back. "Arf let me choose your name. He chose Stig, an I chose Abda, only they all called you Ebba cause that's one of their names."

"Why Abda? Does it mean somethin?"

Ma looks at me slant-ways an says, "It was the name of the girl I served, back in the summer land."

I don't say anythin. It breaks my heart to think Ma gave me

the name of her child-mistress, of the person who beat her, like a name might be a spell that could better the babe it was given to. Turns out all it meant was I scorned her too.

"Are you finished?" asks Mistress Una, wipin her hands on her apron. "Only your boy is awake, an he's askin for you."

Ma jumps up an goes without a backward glance. Mistress Una is watchin me, so I keep my face empty an gather up her toasted grain.

"I've bin meanin to talk wi you, Salvebearer," she says. "Now you're here for a spell, we should think about the hospital. Roshna says she can make up the salves an tinctures we'll need most often, an you an I will have work enough. I've found a couple of good strong girls who en't squeamish, an I can show you all the bits you don't know yet. But your Ma's got more knowledge'n me, so what I want to know is, will you be workin with her? Cause she tells me that savin just now, you en't spoken to her since you two met."

I think about it. I think about how Ma's told Una her own name, her proper name. Roshna. Those who took it from her are dead, after all. It's beyond time she took it back.

"I'll work with her," I say after a moment. "I en't sayin everythin's fixed, but I'll learn from her, an I'll help her."

"No one asks a broken bone to mend in a day," says Mistress Una, "but it's got to mend straight as it can, or you'll never get the use of it."

The next day I go wi Mistress Una to the barn, an meet the two girls who'll be learnin alongside me. Rafe is there too, sulkin cause Mistress Una tole him she needed a strong boy, though seein the arms on Nanna an Hella I en't sure why. Anyway, he's there all day, an the next mornin he comes again, so in the end there's four of us learnin from Una.

It en't nothin like bein the Salvebearer. It's a lot more messy an a lot less grand, but I don't dread it the way I used to dread the ceremonies in the shrine, because I en't lyin. I fall dead to sleep every evenin an that's all I ask. To be busy or sleepin, an free from thoughts of Grimulf or Ma or Ulf, or the memory of that light I felt an tried to touch, before death blotted it out.

❧

TORNY'S TALE
Gullcroft, the North

I stop sleeping. I only know because Galen hates it, hates the way I sit with my eyes open for hours at a time, the way I can't feel cold or heat. One day he finds me sitting in the snow on Fenn's grave, watching my own fingers turn red and then white as I hold the mirror in my bare hands. I took it from Fenn before we buried him. It's always shining these days, but without Fenn nothing passes through.

"She won't let me die," I tell him dreamily as he leads me back to the hut.

"I don't think she understands bodies," says Galen, holding my hands in a bowl of warm water. The hut is dim and smoky. "She's never had one of her own, only someone else's."

I hazily remember something about tearing, tearing off flesh the way you'd tear off a heavy blanket on a summer's night . . .

"She won't let me die," I say. "She needs me."

"Let's hope she remembers that," he says. "Here, eat this."

I screw up my face as he feeds me, my hands still held under water. My mouth feels tender and numb, as if it's been burnt.

"I don't want to," I say, turning my face away.

"Torny," Galen says, and he's not angry, he's begging. "This is the first time you've come back to me in days. I don't know where you go when she takes over, but I need you to eat, and I need you to sleep."

"Don't worry," I murmur. "She's taught me how to do it. How to cross over. I'm all right now."

"You're not all right, Torny. You disappear for days. Your body —"

I look down at it and laugh.

"I'm stronger than ever," I say. "Don't be silly, Galen. I could snap you in two."

He looks at me helplessly.

"I know," he says.

"All right," I say, "I'll eat." He looks so much like a kicked puppy, I want to pat him, but my hands are tingling and aching as the warmth creeps back into them. "But I'll be going soon, so do it quickly."

I can feel her tugging me back, into her kingdom. It's hard to resist, so I don't bother. Everything is so delicious there, so soft. There are no edges. Things flow into one another like light. The whole valley is golden-green, streams criss-cross beneath the ancient trees, and the air is full of sweetness and music. Fenn's there too. He's well fed, richly dressed, and he keeps the Sleeper's horses. The Sleeper loves him like a son. She tousles his hair, and jokes with him, and when one of the hunting dogs bites him, she has all its teeth pulled out.

Every hurt you feel will be paid in blood, she tells Fenn. I promise.

Who wouldn't want to live there?

The Sleeper's horses are light-footed and fast. They break like a wave across the land, across the valley's enemies. Fenn is decked in gold, the Sleeper in red. The valley is peaceful, the deer cries under the hunter's arrows. The valley is safe, the enemy cries under the Sleeper's hooves. All her movements are slow and graceful, as if she moves through water. The horses gallop across the land like waves, the green grass breathes like flesh, and the Sleeper gives Fenn gold anklets and bracelets. Even in the dim green shadows under the oaks, he gleams.

You have given me joy, says the Sleeper, when I thought my cup could hold nothing but sorrow. I lay in starless night, but you have brought me the sun in your palms.

She rarely wears the same face twice.

Sometimes I wonder who she is, this queen who inhabits the bodies of others. I wonder why she loves the merry dark-haired boy so intensely. But between the trees lie dark shadows, and the streams are far deeper than they seem. Thinking is dangerous in the gold-green valley. If I try to ask questions, she sends me back, and then I find myself in the deep winter, where the frost-wolf gnaws my skin, and Galen worries at me like a terrier, and there is no Fenn.

So instead I roll through the warm sweet air, and I try as hard as I can to stay here, on the other side, where I am safe.

"Come back," Galen's saying. He daren't touch me, but his voice is urgent. "Torny?"

I open my eyes.

343

"Oh," he says. "It's you."

They've come. Give me the helm.

Below the cliffs, under the rotting shambles of the curse-pole, minds are gathering. I can feel them. Some are familiar, those curled, obedient serpents who have felt me in their dreams for many years now, so that they can't remember what it's like not to feel me there. But there are new minds too, unregimented, unruly, different and divided in their thoughts, their ways. Some are fearful and some are doubting, but still they have come.

I walk out of the hut. The bay is thick with the smoke from their fires. Mist curls around me like cold thread and the smith's hammer rings out from the forge, a steady, singing rhythm. I breathe in, and the smells of smoke and metal fill me up like food.

I am their goddess, and these are their offerings. I don't need anything else.

The level ground by the Harm Tree is too small to hold them all. They trail down the slopes to the village, grizzled veterans, young men in their strength, and mingled among them the ghostly glow of their Lucks. They turn the hillside luminous.

Laugi stands above the crowd, halfway down the path. His empty socket, the mark of his self-ordained priesthood, has healed.

A heavy man with a shaved, tattooed head stands just below Laugi. His shaggy fur cape covers one shoulder, and a wide studded belt glints under his brown cloak.

"We were convened by the Staffbearers," he says, his voice raised. "Where are they?"

I can feel the snake-minds uncurling, waking up. The Slipskins fan out around the upper edges of the level ground, their hard faces scanning the crowd for signs of trouble.

"The Staffbearers will no longer intervene in the business of men," says Laugi.

The crowd quiets instantly.

"They have given up their staffs and gone into seclusion," he says. "Look."

He points to the curse-pole. The skull is almost bare now, the skin in ribbons, and the ribs stick up through the snow. Around the pole stand six iron staffs. One in particular —

I feel a sharp, squeezing pain under my ribs and I falter. It passes, and I right myself before Galen can steady me, but still, I try not to look at the staffs.

"What have you done to them?"

"Nothing." Laugi meets the man's glare. "They called you here because the time has come to finish what was started with Arn's death."

"It's too late," says the man, and I can feel the minds below drawing back from him. The crowd don't know what to think of Laugi, but the Slipskins are the largest faction there, and the tattooed man is making them angry. "The Cub is protected by a beast bigger than any of us. No army of ours can face them."

"And who are you?" asks Laugi.

"Carr of Hellingap," says the man, squaring up to him, "and plenty here will tell you. Who are you? No one here knows you. You and your men are nameless among us, and the nameless have no honour."

"I am Laugi One-Eye, follower of Thorkel One-Eye, leader of the Slipskins. Any man who was at Hellingap should know me."

I watch fascinated as, by his side, Carr's Luck flickers.

"I will tell you where the Staffbearers are," says Laugi. "They went open-eyed before us, to tread the path that we must follow. But they sent someone back to us, to lead us."

And I let myself into their heads.

There is a space for me in each and every one. Because everyone knows death. All I need is a crack, a hair's breadth.

I walk down the path towards the crowd, and I feel the fear rising from them. Even the Slipskins.

Carr is sweating, but he holds his ground.

"I fought with the Sungiven," he says. "It didn't work the first time, why should it work now?"

The Sleeper surges inside my skin like a tide at the flood. She fills my eyes with white. She speaks through my mouth, in a voice like hounds.

Your Sungiven was a symbol, a promise. She was your hope, and she lied. I am the Harrower and I will not lie.

Through the mist I feel the space before me growing as the crowd steps back.

The old ways are already dead. I am not your lost leader and this is not the war of your youth. This is the last war. If you are here for your homes, your families, go back. We have none. Whoever stands with me stands alone.

"Those are pitiless words," says Carr, his voice shaking. "But what do they mean? Hellingap sent me to answer the Staffbearers' call, even though there are those who say peace has been kind to us. There are those who pay their tithes gladly, even visit the White God's kirk in Frithberg. And so I come, knowing that by coming I tear apart the peace of our lives, and you tell me that this is war without meaning, without purpose. I fought the Cub and his imperial handlers, but I fought because I believed in life. In peace."

There is a change, a turn, as the crowd hears his words, and Carr feels it.

"We who fought at Frithberg were defeated, and yet we survived. We lost so much, but we rebuilt our homes, we cared for those we had left, we found new loves, we raised children. Are we going to watch them die all over again? When the Sungiven led us, it was with the promise of a life to come. And even though we lost, we were given that. She didn't lie to us. Our hope was real, and it was rewarded."

And do others feel as you do?

Slowly, men step forward to stand with Carr.

The Sleeper smiles.

All hope is fatal, she says. *Let me show you.*

As their Lucks wink out, Laugi and his men step forward, blades drawn. In the distance I hear Galen crying out, feel him pushing past me, but I'm already gone, fleeing back to the green-and-gold, to Fenn.

The next day the curse-pole is ringed by nine heads on spikes, but my heart hurts when I see them, so I turn away.

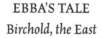

EBBA'S TALE
Birchold, the East

In the end it snows too heavily over midwinter for anyone to come or go. Branches crack under the weight, an durin the worst of it everyone moves into the hall. We sleep together like we did back at

Eldinghope. Fetch warms my back, an though my dreams are not always quiet, I do not see my Follower again. After each snowfall we dig tunnels to the barn. The barn has bin built up, but it's still not as warm as the hall, an we lose more of the sick than we hoped. The headman says words over em that the prester taught him, words that'll take em to the White God. I'm only needed for the look of the thing.

The White God likes his dead buried, but the ground is frozen hard. We lay em out in the cold under a cairn of rocks an wait for the thaw.

One day, when the air has lost its sharpness, an the thaw en't far off, Stig comes to find me in the sick-barn. I sit up from my work an watch him weave between the beds – we have proper beds now, not just pallets – an as I watch I see all the changes he's bin through. For the first time since I came back I'm really seein him, not the ghost of the boy he was. His skin en't as dark as mine, an his large eyes jump out below his black brows. He's got a beard while Rafe still has only reddish stubble. He's still skinny from the fever, but I can see that it's passin. His limbs are still long, but the gawkiness is gone.

"Ma wants you," he says, an his voice tugs on me like it always does. He sounds like Da. He can't hear it, but I know Ma does cause I've seen her listenin to him, smilin.

I cross the village to Mistress Una's, wipin my hands on my apron.

"And do you remember what you wore?" I hear.

Ma's workin at the table, her pestle mulchin in a big stone mortar. "I wore what I stood up in," she says. "Arf gave me a necklace of coins from the Raider's hoard an said that could be my price, but everythin I had was a gift."

"And how were you married?"

Berengar is leanin over his writin frame, an all I can see of him is his coal black hair. It's bin cut short, an the nape of his neck is white an delicate. Fetch lies across his feet, peaceful. He opens an eye as we come in, but he don't move.

"We weren't," says Ma. "This was before the war; we din't know anythin of the Blessed Walpurgis nor your White God. If I'd of bin the daughter of a dalesman, which is what Ulf wanted for Arf, we'd of bin married by the new-sown crops, where the Cornmaiden's stone used to stand, before they toppled her an put Walpurgis in her place."

"So you were not married?" Berengar asks, puzzled.

"In Ulf's eyes I should of bin a thrall," says Ma. "I had no family, an no wealth. So Arf had to take me as a concubine. Ulf wanted his brother free to marry. Or maybe not," she says, after a moment. "He knew by then what he intended. Maybe he din't want nephews an nieces that looked like his brother, after he'd killed him. Lookin at you two he could always say you were mine."

An she looks up at me as Stig comes in behind me.

Berengar turns an goggles.

"Alright," I say, an I feel heat risin in my cheeks, though I en't blushed all winter. "Far as I know I en't grown a second head." But I have grown in other places, cos Kelda's blue smock fits me properly now, an for the last moon I've bin lettin Ma braid my hair. It's pinned up at the nape of my neck, an Hella'n Nanna tell me it's fetchin.

Berengar's as red as I am, which en't helpin, cause now I know what this is, an I en't ready.

"Ebba. You are looking —" he starts, an as I raise my eyebrows I see panic set in. "Strong."

I can feel Ma an Stig watchin with interest.

"Strong?" I en't exactly spoutin poetry, but bein called strong by an outlander in front of my family is . . . not how I thought this might go, whenever I thought about how it might go, which was, if I'm bein fair, not since last year what with everythin else, but when I did think on it, right, firstly, it was with Jarle, maybe in the stables, an second, there was just *us*, an *third* . . . he din't say I was strong. But since that is what Berengar said, actually, it en't that bad. There's worse things to be.

"Well . . . you're lookin . . . clean," I say, not doin much better.

"I have been directed in the use of the steam bath," says Berengar, his cheeks flamin.

Ma turns away abruptly, her shoulders shakin. "I forgot somethin," she says, an leaves.

Stig looks between us an sits down, scowlin. "Who's this?"

"This is Berengar of Vellsberg, a border town of the Empire. Berengar, my brother, Stig Ra — Stig Arfson," I correct myself. Stig's taken our da's name for good.

"It is a pleasure to meet you," says Berengar, bowin over the writin frame on his lap.

Stig glares at him. "This is my sister," he says, "an if you put your Southern paws on her I'll kill you."

"Stig Arfson! I think I can look after myself!"

"I'm seventeen! I'm your guardian!"

"When I want you to be my guardian I'll tell you, thank you very much."

We glare at each other until Berengar says, "You will be coming with her?"

"What?" We both look round.

Berengar en't blushin no more. "The captain sent me to ready you," he says. He meets my eyes seriously now. "The prester says a horde will march on Frithberg as soon as the roads are passable. He has ordered your presence."

"A horde?" Berengar nods. "What are you talkin about?"

"An what's Ebba's place in this?" asks Stig, still tryin.

"She is the Salvebearer," says Berengar. "She will lead prayers against the heathens."

Stig tenses, but I lay my hand on his shoulder. I knew my service weren't ended yet.

Berengar looks at me. "The horses," he says. "They were symbols, worn by the generals of the rebellion, in the time of the Sungiven. We prevented the uprising here in the East, but the North has risen. There are rumours they are led by a devil."

"That's just talk," I say. "Who needs devils when we have people?"

From what I can see, it's men an women who are at the root of evil, not gods.

Berengar shrugs, but his mouth is tight. "Erland will be here tomorrow."

"Then I'd better go tell Una," I say.

Twenty One
COLLAR

he saddle of the pass is bordered with grimy snow, packed in layers where it's fallen, frozen, fallen again. We soon see where the grime's comin from.

The ash stings our eyes, whippin tears across our cheeks. Banners of dirty smoke stream towards us, and Frithberg itself is ringed in shadow an fire. Between the town an the Ridge are blackened ruins where outlyin farms used to stand. A dark sea of tents rings Frithberg's walls like a stain, an the dead fields between the two are scattered wi lines of fire.

Berengar shudders, an at my side Fetch whines, itchin to go down into the trees below.

Erland comes up to us, leadin his horse. He scans the plain, an I see his mouth tighten. He glances north west, up past the Ridge, but he sees me lookin an forces a smile. "I didn't think they'd move so quickly," he says. "Tell me what you see, Berengar."

"Town ringed north west to north east," Berengar says, standin straighter in his captain's presence. "They have burned all the dwellings outside the walls, as well as the bridge. They use the river as a natural defence, and they have dug trenches against cavalry. They know they are weak against mounted enemies. Our cavalry will be hampered, and our infantry will pay the price."

Fetch sneezes. The smoke has a foul, cloyin smell. "They're burnin somethin," I say.

"Bodies," says Erland grimly.

"There's somethin else."

"Can you tell what it is?" Erland asks, but I shake my head.

Ma could, I think. *There's so much I en't learnt from her yet.* The leather saddle bag at my back reminds me of the supplies Ma an Una packed for me, a new box of salve among other, less famous balms, an small bone bottles of ingredients so strong you need only a few drops. It en't much, but they spared what they could. I think of Ma layin them in, meager stores against a long winter. I miss her suddenly, an it surprises me. I en't felt somethin so simple as missin her for a long time. But I know she's safe at Birchold wi Stig an Una to care for her, so I push it away.

Somewhere down there are my friends. I know it's no use hopin they're safe.

I don't let myself think of Torny. I try to tell myself she's far from here, but I en't stupid. I know the silver horse Rafe passed me was the same as the one-handed man's, an this horde is come down from the far North. I hope she had the sense to keep out of it, but Torny weren't much one for sense when it came to fights.

I take one look south, but the cloyin smoke turns my stomach. I cover my nose wi my cloak an lead my mount down from the pass an between the pines where the snow lies thinner. The guides, young men from Birchold, have bin through ahead of us, trampin down a path through the forest to the king's camp on the southern bank of the river, keepin us hidden.

I try not to think of our leavin, but it sits heavy on my heart. It was nearly noon before we left, which meant hours of waitin, hours of snipin between me an Stig. Hours of Ma cryin, tryin not to show it. I din't want to leave it like that, but I had no choice. I said things I oughtn't of to Stig.

Things like:

It's a bit late to act like my guardian.

You en't earned the right to tell me what to do.

You din't protect Ma when you should of done.

Even though I know she din't do all that well either.

But what's done is done, an she needs him now. I told em I'd be back by Walpurgis Day, but I en't sure even I believed me. They saw how the prester called an I came.

To them this war en't their business. Anythin over the mountains or beyond the sea don't concern em. Even seein soldiers land at Eldinghope, even hearin the stories of the garrison they built there, they don't really believe it'll last. But I know, don't I? Berengar's tole me, Erland's tole me, even Grimulf, in his own way – the world is big, an Arngard is small. The Empire crosses mountains an rivers an seas. Our little kingdom is nothin but a thorn.

So when Grimulf came for me, I kissed Ma an hugged Stig, an then I bowed my head to the prester an called him 'Father' like he likes me to. Without a whisper, though my whole body recoils from him. I think he knows. I think it pleases him.

Rafe din't show his face, which shows he's grown some sense, but I missed him. Then the prester had me come out an bless the soldiers for the ride to war.

That's what this is, then. War.

I hoped it weren't, but I seen it now, an I can't pretend. Those fire-filled trenches, that sea of shadows where the rebels camp. Erland took it well, but I could see it threw him, just for a second. He weren't expectin what he saw. More of em than he thought, an quicker, already in position. Warned against the Southern cavalry, the mounted soldiers sent by the Emperor to help King Kolrand.

But still not enough, part of me thinks, the part of me that's proud, that don't like the thought of Grimulf spreadin his hand over this earth of ours.

I remember what else I saw from the pass. Lined up across the open plains to the south of Frithberg, with the War Road runnin like a broad arrow through its centre all the way to the burnin bridge outside Frithberg's gate. The king's army. Tents of white sailcloth, all rosy in the sunset, open spaces where the horses are corralled, an a train of wagons comin down the open road from the palace at Sunacre, loaded with all they need.

There are two sides, that view said. I never saw it drawn up so clear. The side of order an the side of ash. Which are you on?

I have a tent to myself, pitched alongside the prester. I don't like it, but I en't got a choice. I'm his Salvebearer, an everyone must see it. Erland an Berengar are pitched on his other side, but now when I see Berengar, my stomach swoops an dips like it used to with Jarle. All the soldiers treat me like the Salvebearer, bowin an crossin themselves when I pass, even Adelhard who knows me from before. It makes me uncomfortable, an I try to stay out of their way.

I've got another reason to avoid em. These soldiers are from the garrison at Eldinghope. I want to ask em how the winter went, but what if I don't like the answer?

Whatever's happened, it's beyond my power to change. When Rafe was short with us this winter, I'd tell myself he must be havin those thoughts too, but worse, harder. What's beyond my power should of bin within his. I was driven out, but he was dragged.

I sit in my tent an think of how things change. How last time we stopped here I was a curiosity, an this time I'm a saint. I en't expected to do the cookin no more, but I think I preferred it when I was. At least I had somethin to do then. I remember complainin to Berengar, askin whether I was mistress or servant. Now I know it's not whether you serve, but who.

Like he heard me, Berengar sticks his head through the tent flap.

"I have brought you food," he says. "Will you join me?"

"What are you doin?" I ask. "Countin beans?"

He smiles, but it's lopsided. "Not today," he says.

Turns out he's sharpenin Erland's blades. We sit outside the tent, as we can only be together outside, an we sit three paces apart, so the prester can't scold us. I eat the watery stew, tryin not to breathe the foul smokey air too deep, an he works his way through two swords, three daggers, an then picks up the prester's long-handled axe. I can't suppress the shudder that goes through me.

"Last time we were here, that had not yet bin used," I say.

"Lots of things were different," he says, not raisin his eyes.

"Yes," I say. "I was just a farm girl, an you weren't very impressed."

He don't answer.

"Medard was still alive," I say.

"So was your uncle," he says. "It may seem unfair, but it was a good price."

I look at him, shocked. "How can you say that?"

"Nothing is given freely," he says, his eyes still on the curved axe-head. "Your uncle and his allies were a stone in the path. Medard would have understood."

I think of the laughin young man lyin with a knife in his guts. "I think he'd of rather lived," I say.

Berengar looks up, his cheeks flushed. "Medard was a good soldier, but not respectful of you," he says. "Remember that. Soldiers die because that is the price that has been agreed. I know you wish to save your people, but sometimes the price is too high."

"Horseshit," I say.

He reddens. "Your cousin, for instance. You required that he live. How many of his people will die because they believe that while he lives, they should not allow his land to be taken?"

"I don't know," I say coldly. I know I'm pushin this somewhere we shouldn't go, for both our sakes, but I can't help it. I want to know. "Tell me. How many died for him this winter?"

Berengar sets down the axe, face red. "Five," he says. "Five men executed. Was that a good price for the boy who would have seen your brother murdered?"

"Like you would of chosen any different," I say. There are tears blockin my throat, but I don't care.

"*I* understand these things," says Berengar. "I might die

tomorrow, or the day after, and it will be a good price if this poison is drained, if it does not spread."

I know he's thinkin of his family, of Vellsburg, last outpost of the Empire, his home. I've only ever imagined the borderlands, but I know from stories that they have not bin quiet lands, an peace came only wi Kolrand's reign. To lose that peace must scare him, would scare me.

"Berengar of Vellsburg," I say. "I'm a healer, not a soldier. I can't count up lives like coins an say the price was good. But I promise, I will do everythin I can to keep your people safe, same as I would my own."

He don't say I en't done em much good so far.

Night falls, an the cold is bitter. I'm glad to have Fetch to warm my back. It takes me a long time to get to sleep, the weight of those five lives heavy on my heart. When I do, I dream of a white light, burnin through my eyelids like the dawn.

The smoke gets thicker all the next day. The thin snow is streaked with it, an our horses toss their heads, spooked by the smell. Between the bare beeches we can see it hangin heavy over the plains, an from under it comes the thunder of hooves.

"Skirmishers," says Erland. "The king's testing their lines."

We're down on the lower slopes by now, leadin the horses over the uneven forest floor.

"Does that mean they're preparin to attack?" I ask.

Erland hacks away a bramble, his movements impatient.

"It means he's waiting," he says. "For us."

It en't our numbers that interest him, I know that much. I look ahead to where the prester leads his mule, his long-handled axe shinin at his back. The king must want his holy man by his side.

"Why does he want me here?" I ask. "The prester can bless the king's warriors better'n me. What use am I?"

"Didn't you tell Berengar that you learned healing because of the Raiders? What did you do for those you knew wouldn't live?"

I'm not sure I like where this is goin. "We'd make em comfortable, give em mead, or —" I trail off.

"Or?" He don't look at me.

"Help em sleep," I say. Ma, Una, both of em tole me not to talk about this. I seen Ma do it before, once or twice, an I know I got at least one bone bottle in my pack with a black wax seal, to let me know its use should I need it.

"Well," says Erland, an it seems like he knows the rule that says these things stay unspoken. "Most soldiers don't want to meet their god sleeping. But they might want to meet him with courage, not pain." He glances at me. "And the White God might be a bit closer, if the healer is the Salvebearer."

"Will I be on the battlefield?" I ask, my body suddenly gone weak. I know it's cowardly, but I din't expect it, an it scares me.

"No," he says. "You're too valuable for that. You'll stay at the king's camp. Your prayers will be needed."

I avoid his eyes. I wonder if he guesses that since Grimulf took Eldinghope, my prayers en't bin quite what they should be.

An Berengar will be on the battlefield even if I en't.

The ground evens out, an ahead of us I hear the rush of the river.

"Did Berengar tell you what the messenger said?" Erland asks.

"He said that the rebels are led by a devil."

"Berengar thinks like a believer. To him there is only the White

God, and the devils who hinder God's work." Erland rubs the scar on his jaw. "I was at Frithberg ten years ago, and I saw the Sungiven. I know there can be gods in mortal bodies."

The river is closer, its noise makin it hard to hear.

"What —" I look round to check the prester is still far ahead of us. "What was she like?"

"Impressive," says Erland shortly, "but just a puppet. Gods are full of glory and power, but they're selfish. They don't care who follows them, or who falls for them. They make bad leaders. That girl would have done better to refuse the honour the Staffbearers offered her."

We reach the river. Erland puts my mount on a lead rein for the crossin.

"Did you know her?" I ask as we wait our turn.

"No," he says. "If the Staffbearers have tricked someone new into bearing an unnatural weight, it's sad, but not important. One hero is nothing, however gods-touched, against well-trained men. But if the Staffbearers have joined with the Slipskins, they're worse fools than I thought."

"I thought the Slipskins were dead?"

"They should be," says Erland, leadin us to the river's edge. "We hunted them hard enough. But who knows what the Staffbearers have been hiding north of the Floodlands?"

His horse fords the river, the water up to its ribs. I hold tight to my saddlehorn, my legs tucked up, an keep my thoughts to myself. If the Staffbearers have called down a second Sungiven, who might they have convinced to bear a god's weight?

I push the thought away like flotsam, an I watch Fetch swim beside me, his teeth bared above the swirlin foam.

By the time we reach the edge of the forest it's sunset, an we're worn out. In the last light, our band rides towards the long line of gutterin torches that marks the edge of the king's camp. Berengar raises the standard, an the black bear's token flutters over us.

A mounted guard meets us an guides us to the perimeter. Beside the soldiers rides a man in a long robe like the prester's, only black, an the crown of his head shaved bare. He rides close to Grimulf an speaks with him in a language like the oath I learned so long ago. Kirk-speak. It makes me uneasy, not knowin what's bin said. Now an then the man looks at me, an I don't like it.

The leader of the soldiers rides with Erland, talkin quietly at his elbow. Erland's face is hard as he listens.

"Ebba," says Berengar, joinin me as I fall back. "My place is with my lord. If you need me, send word to the Bear of Hellingap." He passes me a small wooden token. It's marked with a black bear under the blue three-pointed knot of Hellingap. I turn it over, my heart tight.

"I thought you'd be near me," I say, tryin to sound like it don't matter.

"Your quarters will be close to the prester, in the royal quadrant," he says. "If I can come to you before battle, I will."

The torchlight falls slantways across his black hair. All the air has left my lungs. I thought he'd be close to me until he had to go. I thought we'd have more time.

I reach out an touch his hand. "Don't go," I say, but just then a roar bursts from Erland. My horse dances under me, an Berengar lunges forward to pull my reins tight. Our eyes meet, an then he spurs his mount forward to his master's side.

"Salvebearer," says an unfamiliar voice behind me. The man in the black robes comes up beside me an bows. "Prester Grimulf has asked me to show you to your quarters."

"Captain Erland —"

The man looks grave. "Hellingap did not survive the infernal horde's assault. Its warriors were strung from the walls for the crows. And today the gates of Frithberg opened for the fiends."

My stomach feels sick.

My guide leads me down a wide grassy lane between tents. Looking round I see the others have disappeared. My only comfort is Fetch, trottin loyally beside us. We ride deeper into the camp, an I grow dizzier an dizzier as I realise how big it is. There must be thousands of men quartered here, not just soldiers, but armourers, smiths, cooks, farriers, grooms, servants . . . even children dart between tents, chasin dogs, cats, each other . . .

"Survivors," says my guide, followin my gaze. "Fleeing the Ridge towns and Frithberg."

"How many escaped?"

"Only those with foresight," says my guide. "Here. This is the royal quadrant." He shows a wooden token to two guards. Beyond em the lanes are wider, the tents bigger. My guide leads me to one among many, marked by a black eagle an a red cross.

"Prester Grimulf's quarters," he says. "Yours lie alongside it." He hands me a wooden token like the one Berengar gave me. It shows the same black eagle, wings spread, against the yellow sun of Sunacre. Kolrand Arnson's device. "There are servants waiting to prepare you."

"Prepare me? For what?"

"Your introduction to the king, of course." He puts up a hand to help me dismount, an I slide awkwardly from the saddle. A servant appears to take our horses, but I stop him an ask for my pack. I take it despite his protests an carry it inside the tent myself.

You can't really call it a tent. First there's a small space where a girl takes my dirtied shoes and cloak, then she ushers me through into a second room, where braziers warm two chairs an a table, an behind that hangs a pavilion of embroidered material, glowin like the harvest moon. Fetch sticks his head through the openin an I follow, an gasp when I see a bed of furs, sheets an blankets, warmed by a small brazier. Somethin sweet smokes on the coals, fillin my head with softness, an I yawn. Fetch flops down on the bed, but the girl collects me an bows me beyond the pavilion to another partition. Behind it steams a metal tub full of warm water an another chair covered with towels.

Before I can protest, the girl has me out of my travellin clothes an into the tub. She makes me hold up my hair an starts washin me. I en't bin treated like this since I was a babe. She has me soaped, sluiced an towelled so fast I've barely warmed up from the water. I sit in the chair while she combs out my hair. She gets rid of the tangles, but the smell of the horde's smoke still lingers. Then she dresses me in new clothes.

Like everythin else here, they're richer than anythin I've seen or felt before. The undershift is soft-woven wool, so fine it lies against my skin like a caress, an the dress is white, hems an bodice stiff wi gold thread. The girl braids my hair back from my face, but leaves most of it hangin loose down my back. For my feet there are soft tan leather shoes stamped wi gold emblems on the heels an toes.

Before the girl can hurry me out the front entrance, I dash back into the pavilion. Fetch is curled on the bed, his back legs twitchin as he hunts in his sleep. I open my pack an take out the box of salve, fightin off a yawn. I notice two slim bone bottles, both sealed wi black wax, an take them too. I don't want anyone openin them without knowin their danger. I put all three in my soft leather purse, an settle it safely at my belt.

I scratch Fetch's ears an hurry back to the entrance, where my black-robed guide bows an leads me past the prester's tent, which must be twice the size of mine, an down a wide grassy road lit by torches. They give out a steady light, an they smell sweet too.

Suddenly, out of the corner of my eye I see a dark shape lope between two tents. I follow it, expectin the children I saw earlier, but it's too big. It disappears behind the next tent, but at the next alley it's there again.

I turn to say somethin to my guide, but a long red tent rises up ahead of us, an he quickens his pace. No need to ask whose it is. On the entrance flap, a black eagle spreads its wings against a sun embroidered in gold thread.

Two guards in red livery bar the way, but they catch sight of us an step aside. They bow lower to me than they do to my guide.

A servant in red takes our names an bows us through into the main chamber.

Drapes of fabric hide the far end of the tent from view. The air is hazy. Braziers burn with a sweet-scented heat, an drapes of a finer material veil the figures movin behind em. The ground is covered wi rugs an furs, an sounds are muffled.

I recognise one voice easy enough though. The prester is already here.

His bulk moves towards me between the draperies. This is Grimulf the commander. Arm guards gleam at his wrists, an two gold cloak pins fashioned like wolf heads frame his chest. He holds out a fist, like a lord callin his hawk to him, but it's for me. I rest my hand palm down on his knuckles, loath to touch him.

He smiles at me as if he knows it, an draws me forward.

"Try not to speak too much," he murmurs. "You look like the Salvebearer, but you still sound like a bumpkin."

The air shimmers gold an my head swims. Behind the drapes, dark figures fall silent an watch as we walk past. I en't in my rightful place. I never bin so far from it. I feel like I'm drownin in riches, surrounded by more wealth than I ever knew existed. Under the stiff bodice of my white dress my heart batters against my ribs, till I feel anyone who looks must see it.

Somethin soft grazes my cheek, an I look up into my king's eyes.

I drop to one knee, but not before a shock goes through me.

King Kolrand must be ten years older'n me, an his curly hair is dark blonde instead of pale, but somethin in the grey eyes, the tall slim body, the wide cheekbones is . . . not familiar. Too crazy to be familiar.

You're imaginin it, I tell myself, my mind racin. *You're dazed.*

But I en't, I *en't.*

The young king is dressed all in black, seated on a raised dais. Gold at his neck, knuckles an belt, but delicate like I never seen, all set wi dark red gems. A thin golden veil ripples like hot air between the king an his subjects, gildin his blank face, his cold grey eyes. That's what I felt on my face.

"Ebba Rathnasdota, sire," the prester says. "The Salvebearer."

The muffled talk stops.

"The lamb among wolves," says the king. His voice is soft, an

I remember Kelda's pipe, how she used to charm us with it. "The girl who walks barefoot through fire. Grimulf tells me you called on the White God to strike down the devil-worshippers as they held you captive – and he did."

I look up.

I could deny it. But the dark figures have come forward – men in the colours of the kingdom, yellow for the South, green for the plains, blue for the Ridgelands. Men with armrings, torques, swords an axes at their belts. Lords an warriors, an some in robes like the prester's.

I could tell him what really happened, or try to, but I would make myself weak. I would make myself worthless. An once I am worthless in this court of gold, I will not last.

The stories are more important than I am now.

"Yes, sire," I say.

"Come here."

I rise, nearly trippin on my long hem. I drop my gaze, but it's no good. The cold grey eyes burn me like ice.

They are exactly like Torny's.

No wonder they tried to hide her. No wonder they wanted her back.

"Please excuse this poor reception," King Kolrand says. "I look forward to welcoming you properly, when we return to Sunacre."

I think my heart stops, but a crimson-clad servant is at his side, and the king is liftin somethin golden from his hands.

"You have served your lord well," he says, "and you will be rewarded as any other warrior would be."

The gold veil parts an I'm handed up onto the dais. A murmur runs through the watchin lords.

For a second the king an I stand face to face, only air between us. He puts his arms round me, an for a dizzyin moment I think he's goin to embrace me. But instead I feel my hair lifted off my back by unseen hands, an then a weight settles around my neck.

I reach up, still dazed, an touch metal.

The king has put a collar on me, in front of all his lords.

An now he's waitin for me to thank him.

Say somethin! I think, but the words won't come. The weight presses against my collarbones, an I struggle to breathe. Erland said I'd be free, but Kolrand might as well of branded me.

I look into the eyes of this slender, black-clad young man, then at Grimulf. His white curls shine in the brazier's light like sun through the clouds. I can almost see the strings leadin from his fist to the king, like a spider with a bundled up fly. Am I the same? Are there strings tuggin on my limbs, my tongue, ready to make me jump when the prester pulls?

I could cut em. I could end this.

I open my mouth.

"Sire!" A guard appears. "We've caught a spy!"

The king glances at Grimulf, who beckons sharply. Two guards drag forward a third person, scruffy, mud-caked, and throw him down at the foot of the dais, close to my hem.

Oh *no*.

I cover my mouth wi my hands, feelin sick. Grimulf smiles.

"Where did you find him?" the king demands.

"Trying to sneak into the prester's quarters, sire."

On his knees, his hands bound, Rafe lifts his head an glares. I see him take in my dress, my gold collar. Disgust fills his eyes an he looks away. He ignores the king an looks right at Grimulf.

I know Rafe. I *know* him. He's goin to get himself killed.

"Sire!"

King Kolrand turns to me, surprised.

"This man is my kinsman, sire. He must of followed me across the mountains."

There's no followed about it. Rafe din't see me off from Birchold not because he was avoidin the prester, but because he'd already left wi the guides. An to do what? Hide in Grimulf's tent an murder him?

"Your kinsman?" The king looks between us, angry. "What was he doing hiding in shadows like a thief?"

Rafe opens his mouth but I'm quicker.

"I told him to stay away from the war."

Rafe tries to speak but the guard gives him a kick to the ribs, windin him.

"I can vouch for the boy, sire," says Grimulf. It's my turn to be surprised. "A fine young man, quick to defend his family's honour." Rafe's eyes burn, but Grimulf just smiles. "Our Salvebearer has the heart of a woman, full of softness for those she loves."

I don't say anythin. Right now if you let me alone wi Rafe, I can tell you it wouldn't be softness he'd hear from me.

The king looks between us, hesitant.

"If he has come all this way to fight for you, sire," says Grimulf, his eyes locked on Rafe, "let him fight. Put him among my men. I always have need of young men of spirit."

The king nods, but the guards are already pullin Rafe to his feet. I turn, but they're draggin him away, an Grimulf is at my side. He presses me down into a chair, smilin.

Well, let him smile. At least Rafe's alive for now. Though for how long, I don't care to guess. In battle, wi the prester at his back . . .

"It is always hard," says Grimulf gently. "In battle, anything may happen. But the White God will not be deaf to your prayers. Now, the king has paid you a great honour, and you owe him your thanks."

I try to calm myself. I've got to play the prester's game. He's got Rafe now.

But we're interrupted again. Erland strides towards the dais, shovin drapes out of his way. He's dressed in fine Ridgeland blue, the triple knot of Hellingap on his chest, but his face is white.

Behind him comes Berengar. He's dressed like what he is, a young noble, an when our eyes meet somethin travels between us – a shock, a recognition.

Erland don't wait, barely bows.

"These animals need slaughtering," he says. He bows briefly to King Kolrand, but it's Grimulf he looks at.

"You've spoken to the survivors," says the prester.

"This *bitch*. I'll kill her myself."

"Not in front of the Salvebearer, captain," says Grimulf.

"She should hear this," growls Erland. "Hellingap wasn't a battle. It was a massacre. They killed everyone and used their corpses as *decoration*. How did a ragtag band of seditious farmers do *this*?"

"The survivors say they saw things. They say . . ." Kolrand hesitates. It's only a moment, but his mask cracks. "They say Geir Arnson was there." Kolrand looks from Erland to Grimulf. "My brother is *dead*, isn't he?"

"Of course he's dead," says the prester. "Do you think if Geir Arnson were alive he would have waited ten years to challenge you?"

"But some of his men survived," says Erland. "The Slipskins.

We heard rumours, but . . . it was just stories. Warriors waiting for their master to rise from the dead, for the gods to walk again . . ."

Kolrand's face is cold, but sat close to him I hear the hitch in his breath.

"Sire," says the prester, "this is no revelation. The Slipskins were beaten at the Battle of Hellingap, but some of them lived, and now they have joined this rebellion. There is no mystery. In battle, men are close to death. Is it any wonder if they think they see the dead?"

Erland's face is hard. "With your permission, sire, I'll prepare an attack at dawn. The sooner we wipe them out, the better."

The king nods. "Do what you need," he says shortly. He catches me lookin at him, an for a moment he frowns. I wonder what was showin in my face, while I was watchin his. "Your armsman had better take the Salvebearer to her quarters," he says. "She will have work to do."

Twenty Two
LABYRINTH

THE HARROWER'S TALE

The Drovers Road by Hellingap to Frithberg

I keep them close by me, the Serpent and the Dog. The Dog is useful. His worry tells me when I need to feed the body – my body – or clothe it, to keep it working. If I forget he does it for me. The Dog is always gently lit by his two Lucks, his own and his prince's. Sometimes, when he's been drinking, the Dog speaks to his prince.

I fit comfortably in the minds around me now. I find the best welcome in those already touched by death. The more loss, the more pain, the quicker the entry. The more they accept me, the more I give.

For instance, the Serpent Laugi rarely eats now. His strength comes through me, reward for his submission, his sacrifice.

When you bleed, when you suffer, you open yourself to death. You invite me in. And I come.

All of the Serpent's men are criss-crossed with the scars of their faith.

The first few villages we came to, no one died. I ordered the men from each village who had answered the Staffbearers' call to return ahead of us, to tell them our terms. When we arrived, everyone who could fight was there waiting for us, knife in hand.

If you don't join us, everything you love will die.

To join us, all you need to do is make a cut.

They have to do it themselves. No one can do it for them. But once I'm in the blood, I'm in.

As I seep into those other minds, my strength flowing like water, I find some small relief. This body holds me like a close, heavy prison, but a prison is better than the grave, and despite its demands, a body is better than none. Still it troubles me. I have encircled its mind, given it what it longs for, yet the smallest things break through. A glimpse of long dark hair can make its heart kick like a stallion. That heart! Like a fistful of thorns, bloody, senseless, so alive. It took me all winter to tame it.

But I have the secret, and they are always hunting for it.

How do you stop this pain, this fear?

At every village, every town. They taste it and they flock to me, leaving hearths untended, babes unfed. They pick up anything that might serve as a weapon and they come. They bring their wavering Lucks, their aching memories, everything they have lost. They leave the living and drink from my cup, and they whet an appetite for death that will never leave them. I know this. I know.

When you are dying the world burns. Every touch is a caress. Your petty loves count for nothing when you reach the end of the world. There is a love so strong, so irresistible, that it has not let a single one of you free from the moment of your birth. All of life is only this.

Sometimes when I look at them, I can't tell the living from the dead.

The road runs like a river, the villages pass like islands. I leave them all empty.

At nights I sit in a tent surrounded by the Serpent's men, and no one but the Dog is allowed near me. Their minds are restful, self-consumed. After so many years of living so close to my grave, they sleep very little. Why sleep, when the dreams come while you are awake?

I don't sleep. The body wants to, I can feel it, but as the darkness rises up I feel muscles and sinews trying to bind me. Its mind grows slippery, starts to escape my grip, so I haul it back into wakefulness. I let the body go limp and corral its mind in memories of my kingdom. I accompany it, show it everything I had. I get lost with it, rolling in the warm air and the softness of the sun.

But it's getting harder.

The body's mind should be weakening, but instead it's fitful. Its heart is starting to kick, even deep in the valley.

By day it is better. I ride, the beast beneath me cowed, fearful. It knows what it carries. The wind blows in my face, and it speaks to me. The mist shrouds us, travelling with us. We must cross the mouth of the Floodlands before the thaw comes, before the road is breached by the fury of spring, and the North is cut off. The mind of the body tells me this, and the wind whispers its secrets.

"They won't expect us before the thaw," the Serpent says. "If we reach Hellingap before the cold breaks . . ."

Hellingap.

That is the name of their shared wound. The Serpent's men all turn to it, feed on it, like maggots on a corpse. It peoples their waking dreams and they carry it with them.

The Dog drinks and talks to his prince.

"I'm sorry," he says, and sometimes: "Let me die."

He hopes we will be defeated.

We won't be. We can't be.

No army I lead can be stopped, I tell him. *That's why they did this to me.*

"Who?" he asks, slurring. "What did they do to you?"

But I fall back into the green-and-gold, and no more heed him than the whining of a mutt.

One night the Serpent calls me from my reveries.

"We are nearly come to Hellingap, Harrier," says the Serpent. He persists in calling me by that bastardised name. "Shall we send them their traitor's head as a warning?"

Behind him stands the man Carr, flanked by two of the Serpent's men. His face is mottled with bruises, and his hair is growing in, but under the grey bristles the blue tattoos stand out darkly. His Luck flickers.

No.

The Serpent looks surprised.

Let him go.

"He'll rally the town."

He knows our terms as well as the others. Let him tell them to his people.

The Serpent's men unbind him.

You have until noon.

The man says nothing, just glares at me.

Give him a horse, I tell the Dog, and the Dog takes him by the arm and drags him away.

"The lord of Hellingap is loyal to the Cub," the Serpent says as his men follow. "It would have been better to send him Carr's head."

When you woke me, what did you know?

His cheeks go pale.

"Thorkel said you were a god," he says hoarsely, "older than the ones we worship. We all saw you in our dreams."

And what did your dreams tell you?

"That once there was a kingdom under the waters, and that the priestesses there summoned you into human bodies, to do their bidding. But you grew too strong for them. You destroyed them."

I smell his fear.

Don't doubt me again.

"No, Harrier."

The Dog returns.

"Why'd you let him go?" he asks. "It can't be mercy."

Your prince died at Hellingap, I say. *Tell me, was he avenged?*

"Never," says the Serpent, while the Dog says, "He wasn't that kind of man."

They glare at each other.

You mean his death was required of him, I say to the Dog. *I know. I too was sacrificed, many times. But I had my revenge.*

I feel the Serpent's mind uncurling, readying itself. He has been waiting for this.

Follow him, I order. *See where he enters. Enter after him. Open the gates for me.*

"What are you going to do?" demands the Dog as the Serpent leaves.

What your prince never wanted, and you never intended.

❧ 375 ❧

"Maybe Carr can give us the town," he says.

He will fight us with everything he has.

"Then why let him live?"

Because my followers are hungry for death. Can't you feel it?

"Hellingap is well-protected."

Everything falls in the end.

"Don't do this," he begs.

This is what I am.

The Dog readies my horse. The Serpent's men have their own mounts, and they will drive the army after us.

"Quiet, Hero," says the Dog, holding my mount's head. "It's your mistress. You know her. Shhh."

The horse stamps and bucks as I come towards it, but I grasp the thick hair of its withers and pull myself onto its back. I hold the reins in my fist, short enough to force it to keep its head up. It tosses its head against the bit, and I kick its sides, hard. Its whole body shudders, but it stops trying to rear.

The Dog looks away and mounts his own animal.

The wide grassy road treads the margin of the dunes. The seagrass rustles, sand whips across the long beaches in stinging veils, but still the white mist clings to us, blotting out the sky.

The sky brightens, the tide turns. The sea crinkles on the dark horizon.

The town appears suddenly. The dunes heap above us, hiding the sea, and then the road crests and drops away into a wide estuary of silver mudflats, winding channels and three broad bridges spanning the deepest streams.

"Hellingap," says the Dog.

On the far side of the estuary, a huge tongue of grey stone lifts out of the mire. Hellingap sits on its highest point, its back protected by the sheer drop into the sea, its front heavily stockaded. The carved cross-beams of the lord's hall stand out against the lightening sky. The morning sun turns them gold.

The Dog gazes upon the town, his Lucks overlapping his flesh. For a moment there are two young men, both golden, both proud, their hands interlinked.

I look behind us. I can see glints between the dunes, where the army follows us. One of the Serpent's men rides up to me for orders.

We cross now, I say to the Serpent's man. He gallops off. I turn to the Dog. *Do you have it?*

"You gave Carr till noon," says the Dog, reaching for the bag strung across his back.

I lied, I say.

I kick my mount into motion. It leaps forward, down the dune, and across the first bridge. The sun is weak, but where it falls on my skin it stings. A prickling runs over my body like lightning through storm clouds.

The Serpent's men drive the army at a trot. They stream across the bridges and gather on the field before the town, the Serpent's men bullying them into rough formation, while here and there across the frozen ground, small groups build bonfires. When the fires are burning, I take the bag the Dog carried for me, and I scatter them with a powder. The west wind blows the smoke across the army, and their eyes start to flicker.

"What are you doing?" the Dog asks. He looks ill, and when he raises the ale skin to his lips, his hand is shaking.

I'm teaching them to see.

There are guards on the walls of Hellingap now, scurrying like rats. The wind carries the clink of armour, barked orders.

I sit on my terrified horse, and raise my face to the wind. My strength rushes through my borrowed body like a flood.

The wind swings from west to east, and the fragrant smoke covers the town.

Reins in one hand, I pull my cloak from my body. Leather straps criss-cross the torso, and against the breast, just over the kicking heart, lies the mirror. The Dog starts back, shielding his eyes. Even he can see it shining now.

The Serpent's men to either side of me take bull roarers from their belts, and toss them into the air. As the smoke catches in my body's lungs, the buzzing deepens, strengthens.

The army's Lucks are burning fiercely, gleaming through the mist and the smoke. My fighters yell, their eyes opened. They see their Lucks, solid and unwavering as the pulsing buzz of the bullroarer fills them.

A corpse-light gathers over us, streaming from the mirror. The land itself is shimmering now, the field both empty and littered with fallen bodies. The ghostly light forms a pulsing membrane between the two.

Hoarse screams break through the smoke. The corpse-light splits, a hole in the air, and the hole turns into a man looking back over his shoulder, the fletchings of an arrow sprouting from his left eye socket. On his brow is the double of the helm I wear, the gold-washed harrier with its wings outstretched. He draws his sword and at my back the screams join in awful cacophony.

By my side, the Dog whimpers.

A scouring wind howls through the slit in the world over my

breast, and the living surge after their dead prince.

As if in answer, the gates of Hellingap swing open.

I have lived so long in other's heads, in the narrow confines of borrowed flesh, that I had forgotten how sweet destruction is.

For a short while, I am free.

The Dog finds me lying glutted in the lord's hall.

"What have you done?" he asks.

I lick blood from my lips.

I've freed them.

He looks around the hall, at the bodies where they lie.

"They've killed everyone," he says. "They're hanging the bodies from the walls."

Your prince is avenged.

"Have you no mercy?"

I find I'm tired. The aura of battle is fading, the mist seeping back in. The mirror lies dull against my chest. My limbs ache.

I wasn't called here for mercy, I say.

"No," he says, "I suppose you weren't. How did you do it?"

What? Raise your prince?

"How did you make them massacre their own people?" he says.

This whole kingdom floats on a sea of blood, I say. *You think you walk on dry land, but all you need do is plough the fields, and it comes seeping up. He knew that.*

The Dog looks to where Carr's body is being dragged away by one of the Serpent's men.

"Stop," he orders, and there's iron in his voice. The man drops Carr's heels as if they burn his hands. "Don't touch him."

The man looks at me.

Leave us, I order.

He turns from the Dog with a sneer, and leaves. The Dog drops to Carr's side and closes the dead eyes.

"You did this," he says. "You sent him here to die."

Impatience breaks through my weariness.

You invited me here to kill. Don't pretend you're innocent. You helped them. You even carried the girl across the waves to be bound.

"I didn't know this would happen! I wanted —"

What? Your Sungiven? She's dead. She died, just like they knew she would.

The Dog hesitates.

The people who do this, they know the bodies they trap us in don't last long.

"No," says the Dog. "Vigdis was Torny's mother. She was the one who made the Sungiven. If she knew it would kill her, she would never —"

She knew.

He doubles over, and his one good hand fumbles for his ale skin.

I advance on him, smiling.

Bodies can't hold us, I say. *Believe me, I know. We enter, we walk, but sooner or later the bodies always die. Once a body's been a vessel, there's no cure.*

"How could she?" he says. "I thought she was keeping her safe. So that when we won —"

When you won? I laugh. *Look around you.*

I haul him up and drag him to the hall's entrance. Below us sprawls the conquered town. The houses burn, the dead are piled at every corner, and the smokey air is filled with wailing.

This isn't about winning. This is about making an ending.

He slumps beside me, his eyes closed against the sight.

I've been patient, I tell him. *But it's time you understood. There is no after.*

The Serpent climbs the steps toward us.

"Your orders," he says.

I send my strength out over the town, feeling it wash through the minds of my army.

The time for sleep is passed, I say. *They won't need it anymore. I am their strength, their purpose. Tonight we march south.*

The villages of the Ridge fall before us, our ranks swell, and the living walk in the company of the dead. One evening we stream down the sides of the Ridge, a golden wave from out of the smoke-dark North. The outlying farms have been abandoned, but in one someone waits for us.

The Serpent's men bring a wiry blond man before me. He leers in terror, and raises his hand to his chest, thumb and forefinger together to make a circle.

A tattoo of a snake runs around the circle, the gaping jaws on his thumb, the tail on his fingertip.

"I knew you'd be coming," he gabbles. He has a good voice, but his breath is shallow, and he trips over his words. "When Roaki was strung up in the autumn, and there were rumours of attacks, I knew to look for you. I was a Slipskin once, so I've been watching and waiting. I wanted to be ready."

The Serpent draws his knife, and the blond man drops to his knees.

"Don't you dare call yourself a Slipskin, Spraki," he hisses. "You fled the battlefield. You've been sitting in your lord's lap all this time —"

Hush, I tell him. *You were a Slipskin?*

Spraki nods desperately.

Would you like to be one again?

Once I've given my orders, I go back to my tent. Spraki said an army is coming against us from the South, and the Serpent is preparing for them. Spraki has fled back to the town, cut about to convince them of his escape.

The Dog follows me, cradling himself in his own arms, his face haggard. His mind is full of memories of the battle on this plain all those years ago, when he was newly heartbroken.

"Please," he says. "You're the bringer of death. Let me die soon."

I can't, I say. *Your prince protects you. Only when he releases you will you be free to die.*

He moans, and I feel something strange, something that at first I can't place.

Pity.

I reach out and stroke his face. He stiffens, but he doesn't pull away.

I know, I say. *It's unbearable.*

"What if I never die?" he whispers.

Let me tell you a story, I say.

Many years ago there was a mighty goddess. She drew the sun in her chariot, she made the earth green and the corn grow, and while she reigned there was a golden age, and no one ever went hungry. People called her the Cornmaiden, and she was beloved of all.

But still the goddess was lonely, and so she took a young boy to be her son. This son was a happy child, growing up in the glow of his mother's love, but because she was a goddess and he was mortal, he could never see her in her true form. One day when he was still young, he hid himself, and she, thinking herself alone, revealed herself, and so he died.

The goddess was distraught. In fury she cracked open the earth and descended into the underworld to try and find her son's spirit. But soon she became lost in the labyrinth of the underworld, and without her the world above grew black and withered, and people starved. Meanwhile, in the darkness beneath the earth, the goddess had undergone a terrible change. She was no longer the Cornmaiden, but a terrifying monster.

At last she found her son's spirit, who told her she must accept his death. He led her from the underworld, and once again the world grew green and the people filled their bellies. But the goddess could not forget her son, and every year on the day of her son's death, she withdrew, haunting burying grounds and the deep forests, and the earth died for a time.

She was no longer the benevolent mother of the golden age. When her fury was awoken she became monstrous, destroyed crops and made people and beasts barren, and people feared her as much as once they loved her. In the temples, priests and priestesses offered sacrifices, hoping to appease her.

After many generations of this, a man came along. He was uncommonly clever, and his heart's desire was to gain the secrets of life and death. It was said that whosoever could face the goddess in her monstrous form would gain the divine knowledge, but many had tried, and their bodies had been found hanging from oak trees deep in the forest.

The man was clever. He knew he could not defeat her, but if he could separate her two forms, the light from the dark, she would be weak.

First, he told the priestesses of the goddess that he could help them return their goddess to her old self, and they would regain the golden age long lost. With their help he fashioned a doorway between upper world and the underworld in the form of a mirror, and bound it to him. Then, on the first day of winter, he went into the woods in search of the *goddess.*

He found her deep in the forest. Like the others before him, he told her he wished to learn the secrets of life and death. The goddess hung him on an oak tree, and like the others his spirit left him and went into the underworld. But he wore the doorway, and as his spirit was dragged down, he put his arms around the goddess and pulled her through with him. She fought him, clawing out one of his eyes, but he would not let go.

For nine days, his body hung on the tree, and his Luck trod the labyrinth of the underworld, dragging the howling monster behind him. Eventually he imprisoned it at the heart of the labyrinth, and on the ninth day he returned through the doorway and sealed it. The man became the Wise One, with the power of life and death, and the monster was gone.

The goddess had been split. The Cornmaiden remained in the upper world, having lost her knowledge of who she was, and the monster was locked in the underworld. The Cornmaiden married the Wise One, who became chief of the gods, and everyone forgot what had been before.

But the Wise One gave the doorway into the keeping of the priestesses. At first they kept it secret, but as the years went by and even the oldest priestesses forgot what it was, they began to use it for divination. And that was how they discovered that the doorway led to a monster, and that the monster could be released for a short time into a child's body.

They called this monster the Harrower.

The first girl the Harrower possessed tore herself to pieces with her own hands.

The priestesses learnt. They learnt that the monster was searching for a little boy, and if they sought the one it needed, it would be quiet – for a time. Never for long. The boys always died, and the Harrower would grow so destructive that they would have to kill its human body, banishing it back to its underworld prison. But while it was quiet and contained, it could be . . . useful.

An army led by the Harrower could not be defeated. The Harrower could control the winds, and see into the hearts of mortals and read their thoughts. But it also changed people. People who spent time with the Harrower had no need for sleep or food. They saw things that others couldn't, they fell into violent frenzies. They took longer to die.

Banishing the Harrower became harder – sometimes the bodies it inhabited seemed to walk even after they had been killed. Then the Harrower started finding its way through the doorway into bodies by itself, without help from the priestesses.

At last the priestesses became frightened. They built a labyrinth in secret, and one night they tore the Harrower's most recent body to pieces, just as it had once destroyed itself. Then they killed the Harrower's companion, the boy, and they laid the two bodies in the labyrinth together with the mirror, and sealed them up.

That night the whole kingdom was swallowed up by the earth, and the sea invaded the land, and where once there was a proud palace and glorious temples, now there was nothing but treacherous marshland and impassible waters.

So the Wise One reigned, his docile wife the Cornmaiden by his side, and the Harrower was trapped in a double grave between worlds, forgotten and sleeping.

Until she came.

The Dog is silent.

I know what it is to long for release. But the only one who can release me is my son, and he always dies before he can free me. This time I felt him, long before this body came to me. He was so close. But I must be inside a body to be released.

"Fenn," says the Dog. "He died when you entered Torny."

He always dies. Since I am doomed either way, I will give these people what they want. When this body dies, I will be trapped for who knows how many ages. Why not end everything?

He reaches out tentatively, and touches my hand. I let him.

"You can't," he says. "The world is much bigger than you imagine."

I know only what I was, and what I am.

"If you were released, would Torny survive?"

I turn from him.

Why do you care so much about her?

He looks surprised.

"She's Geir's daughter," he says. "She's all that's left of him that isn't me."

Your prince? No. His Luck could not have bound itself to yours if he had a child in the world. It would have gone to her as a Follower.

He stares at me. "If she's not Geir's, then whose is she?"

But my patience is used up.

I don't know, I say. *All I know is that my son, my key, is lost, and I will never be free. All I can do is destroy. So I will do that.*

Twenty Three
CROSSING

The King's Camp and Frithberg

Berengar leads me silently from the king's tent an down a grassy lane. The cold night air clears my head, but the gold collar is still heavy at my throat.

"This en't the way to my quarters," I say after a while. "Where are we goin?"

"Wait here," is all he says.

I stand in one of the narrow alleys, jumpin at every sound.

Then Berengar is back, a bundle in his arms.

"I en't supposed to be here," I say.

"I know," he says, his face serious. "I found you these."

Inside the bundle is a blue tunic, same as his, an undershirt, britches, folded inside somethin hard.

"What's this?" I ask.

"There is something you need to see," he says.

"But —"

"We do not have much time."

"What if the servant tells the prester I never came back?"

"If you return they will keep you there," Berengar says.

I think of Fetch, curled up on the bed of furs. How he fell asleep so quickly. How I yawned in the sweet-scented heat . . .

I reach out an touch Berengar's shoulder, an feel muscle bunched under my hand. His whole body is tense.

"You're disobeying orders," I say.

He looks wretched, but still he holds out the bundle, an after a moment I take it.

"I can't change here," I say.

He takes me through the unlit alleyways until we reach a dead end, an he stands with his back to me. The cold wind moves through the sailcloth like a spirit, an all of a sudden I feel my flesh on fire.

Maybe it's this world, so unreal an powerful. Maybe it's the horror of bein a pawn in the prester's hands.

"I need help wi the ties," I say, wantin him to turn round. The dress is much more complicated than anythin I ever wore before. The kind of dress you need a servant to get you in an out of. I touch the gold collar, my heart hammerin.

He comes close, blushin. "I did not think," he mutters.

I lift my hair off my neck an turn. I feel his fingers graze my back as he feels for the knot. He finds it an tugs. I feel the laces give.

"You have to loosen em," I say, a devil on my tongue.

I want it to last, I find. In the middle of all this, I want his touch to last.

He slides his fingers under the laces, against my skin, an hooks em out.

I let my hair fall down across my back, over his hands. His breath hitches, an I realise I'm shakin, but not wi fear nor cold.

He rests one hand on my nape, an the warmth of it seems to travel in my blood.

"Ebba?" he says, an I turn. "What —"

But I don't let him finish. I reach up an kiss him.

His lips are chapped, but he opens them an I slide the tip of my tongue between them. He pulls me closer, one hand wrapped in my hair.

The tents snap an rustle in the night air. Above us the stars shine through veils of smoke. We are two livin flames in a maze of wind an shadows.

Finally we pull apart. He hugs me tightly, once, then turns his back. I strip off the white an gold dress, an pull on the britches, the undershirt, the tunic. I fasten my purse at my belt. The helmet's a bit battered, but it has nose an cheekguards. I pile my hair up under it an hope it stays put.

"How do I look?" I ask, an then kick myself for soundin like an idiot.

Berengar runs his eyes over me, an half-smiles. I feel the fire inside me blaze up.

"Like a woman," he says. "You are not made to dress as a boy."

I tug at the over-large tunic, but it's no use. If I were built like Torny, maybe I could get away with it, but I am what I am.

"Then we'd better stick to the shadows," I say, "an try not to get caught."

We hide the dress an move swiftly on. We stick to the dark alleys, only crossin lit thoroughfares when we can't avoid em. As we move out towards the edges, the camp becomes less ordered, more haphazard. We skirt campfires were men are arguin an singin, kitchens set up to feed the foot-soldiers. I try to get used to the feel of britches, after a lifetime of skirts. In lit up tents, shadows move like puppet-plays against the sailcloth.

At last the ground opens out. We skirt a corral an cut across a dark stretch of grass to two long tents. One is lit from inside, an a shadow moves slowly across the side, pacin up an down. The other is smaller, an a dim light glimmers at the far end.

We creep towards the smaller tent, an as we do I hear a low moan comin from it. Whoever's makin it sounds like they're tryin to block out the world.

I know it's a healer's tent by the smell. A brazier by the entrance is burnin sage, an I get a lungful of the warm smoke before I notice. I try not to cough.

On a bedroll near the entrance, a figure's laid on its back. Berengar kneels down an gently takes its hand in his.

"I am back," he says. "I have brought someone to see you."

I kneel beside him an take off the helmet. A grey face peers out from under the covers, the moan comin between gritted teeth.

"I'm Ebba," I say. "Can I take a look at you?"

"She is a healer," says Berengar.

I unwrap the girl, because she is a girl. Her hair an clothes are sweat-soaked, an she shivers violently as I peel the covers off her.

Her left leg has bin crushed from the foot to the knee.

I keep my face calm, an my voice soft. "What's your name?"

"Lana," she whispers, half-word, half-moan.

"How long you bin here, Lana?"

"She arrived this evening," Berengar says. "One of the scout teams brought her. They found her down by the river."

"Lana Sebsdota?" I ask, the name comin back to me. "Your brother breeds horses, don't he?"

She nods once. Jarle used to go to Sebson's farm to learn horse breakin, I remember that.

"You know Golden Jarle from Sorleyson's wayhouse?" I ask, beckonin for Berengar to give me his knife. Lana nods again, her mouth tweakin up for a moment. "I'm a friend of his. Can you tell me when this happened?"

"Lord Frithrun ordered us inside the walls," she says, gaspin as I gently cut her blood-stiff skirts away from her leg. "Two days ago. But someone – someone opened the gates. They killed – so many – I ran, but —"

I look at Berengar.

"Lana," he says. "Tell Ebba what you told me."

Tears drip down her face from the pain, but she nods.

"Their leader," she says. "I *knew* her."

My hands freeze. "Her?"

"White hair," she rasps. "White eyes. Seen her – before. With Jarle."

"A girl?" I say. "Like the Sungiven?"

"Not – a girl," says Lana, but her eyes are rollin back. "Monster —"

She says somethin that sounds like 'Harrier'.

Berengar's watchin me. I settle Lana as best I can, but she's passed out, her head lollin off the bedroll. I get up an beckon Berengar aside.

"Did she tell you anythin else?" I ask.

Berengar looks pale. "She was . . . not well," he says. "She said the rebels are led by the dead. She said the god of the dead was come against us."

A shudder goes through me. *When men are close to death, is it any wonder if they see the dead?* Lana's close to death too, but somehow I don't doubt her.

"Berengar . . ."

"I know." He's a soldier, of course he knows. "You cannot save her."

I think of the damage, of the red lines travellin from the ruined leg up the pale flesh of her thigh, an I shake my head.

"It's too late," I say. "The rot's in her."

"But you can help her," he says, an he en't askin.

Lord forgive me, I can.

Lana is moanin again, her eyes screwed shut. I sit down by her head an open the leather purse. My fingers brush the box of salve, but I reach past it.

In case you need to make more, Ma said. *The other ingredients are easy to find, but this you gotta keep on you. It en't safe lyin around.*

I take out one of the hollow bone bottles an break the black seal.

Five drops for the salve, said Ma. *An you make sure your hand's steady, cause if it en't . . .*

"Lana?" I say. "Can you hear me?" She nods, her eyes still closed. My voice catches in my throat. "Lana, I'm so sorry."

She reaches out an grips my wrist. Her broken nails dig into me.

"Help," she gasps. "Help me."

"I can't heal you," I say.

Her grip tightens, an she pulls me forward.

"Make it stop," she says.

"There's only one way I can stop it, Lana."

A tear splashes on her fist, an I realise it's mine.

"Will it hurt?"

"A bit," I say. I remember the moon pulsin under the skin of the world, the web of blood that led me to my brother's side. "You might see things."

"I already have," she says. "Do it."

"Open your mouth," I say.

Carefully, makin sure my hands don't shake, I let ten drops fall on her tongue.

Then we sit with her, me on one side, Berengar on the other. Slowly, a change comes over her. Her grip on my wrist relaxes. Under my fingers, the flutter of her pulse calms.

"Can't feel you," she mumbles. "Still there?"

"I'm here," I say.

"Says y'can speak t'the gods," she says. I glance up at Berengar, but he's lookin fiercely at the drowsy girl, not meetin my eyes. "C'n you speak to em f'r me?"

I close my eyes, my fingers linked with her slack ones. Learned oaths an mumbled blessins won't do here. She deserves better'n that. I close my eyes an reach for the red of wildfire, the white of surrender.

"The White God en't like our gods," I say. "He's always here. You en't gotta spill blood for him to take heed. If anyone ever held you an loved you, then you know. He's that, but all the time, no matter what. There en't no land of the dead, an there en't no pain. There en't no one to wish you harm. There's just light."

"But I've seen her," says the girl, twitchin. "I've seen her. She'll take me."

"No. She can't touch you." I stroke her hair back from her face. "I don't know what she is, Lana, but she en't here for you. You're safe now."

Her breathin eases.

"It's comin," she says. "I c'n feel it . . ."

Shortly after she steps outside herself, an I become a killer. I stagger to my feet, an Berengar catches me, but I push him away.

Outside a dog howls, an other distant hounds join in.

"Ebba. Ebba, we have to go."

I'm starin down at Lana, her face slack. Berengar shakes me.

"They will look for you soon."

I pull the edge of the sheet over Lana's face. "I en't goin back," I say.

"You must."

I shake my head.

"I can't," I say. "He'll make me like the king. A puppet with a golden collar. An who knows how long I'll last? I en't dyin like that. I've gotta find Torny."

"Who?"

I stopper the bone bottle an put it back at my belt.

"I need to get to Frithberg," I say, brushin past him.

"But you will die!" He runs after me.

"I'll die anyway," I say. "Someday, somewhere. Might as well be here an now."

Berengar grabs hold of my arm, hard. "You had to do it," he says. "Listen to me. You gave her a good death."

"There was nothin good about it," I say, yankin my arm away, but he holds steady.

"It was quick," he says. "You gave her comfort. You are angry, I know. But you must not die too."

I look into his face, so close we could kiss again. "You told me there's always a price," I say. "Well, this is it. I can stop her. This Harrier, or whatever she is. En't that worth it?"

"You do not know what battle is like," he says angrily.

"You don't know *her*," I say, pullin myself free. "You don't know what's waitin out there. Well I do. I know her, an she wouldn't do this. Somethin's wrong, an I can stop her."

He stares at me.

"Are you sure?" he says.

"I'm sure."

He lets out a long breath.

"We need help," he says at last. "I cannot hide you by myself. We must tell the captain."

"We can't! He'll tell Grimulf."

Berengar takes my hand, gently this time.

"Trust me," he says. "Please."

So that is how I end up standin outside Erland's tent, the sky lightening in the east, the cold gnawin my bones. Inside I hear Berengar wakin an dressin his master, his voice a murmur, an all the time I'm thinkin, *This is stupid, stupid, stupid.* But I en't no soldier, an if I'm goin into battle I need all the help I can get.

Erland himself comes out to get me, an I've half a mind to run when I see him. But there's nowhere to run, an somethin in his face tells me it's no use.

"This is stupid," he says when I'm inside. Not *Where have you been,* not *What are you wearin,* an that's when I believe he might help.

"I'm sorry for your people," I say.

"They were slaughtered," he says. "What makes you think she won't slaughter you?"

My heart clenches in my chest.

"I'm her friend," I say.

"People who do these things, they don't have friends," says Erland.

"This en't her. They've done somethin to her."

He looks me over in silence. "Another Sungiven?" he asks.

"Somethin like that."

"Listen." He sits next to me, an his face is tired. "Do you know how the Sungiven died?"

"She was defeated in battle," I say.

"She surrendered."

My jaw drops. "No she din't! She —"

"She begged for death." He reaches out an closes his hand over mine. "She knew. There's no way to dislodge a god. Once it has its hooks in you, you'll never know peace. And the Staffbearers knew that. They knew that even if she won, they would have to kill her." He squeezes my hand. "I'm sorry, Ebba. It's too late."

I think of Torny holdin me at night when I woke up dreamin of Ulf an his fists. I think what kind of dreams she must be havin now.

I pull my hand from his.

"This en't the Sungiven though, is it?" I say. "It's something else." Erland's face is troubled. "An I bet you've heard some things tonight that got you wonderin what your men will be facin when they're out there, en't you?" I continue, pushin. "The dead ridin side by side wi the livin? Heard that one, have you? Your men have, I bet."

Erland an Berengar exchange glances.

"Maybe you're right," I say. "Maybe Torny's as good as dead. But what if I can distract her? En't that worth somethin?"

Berengar shakes his head, but Erland looks from him to me.

"All right," he says.

Berengar snaps somethin at him in Southern. Erland retorts in the same tongue, an Berengar looks like he's about to argue, but he bites it down.

Erland looks at me. "I said you'd be free," he says grimly, "and I meant it. I've reminded Vellsberg that saints are sent to fight devils as well as perform miracles. Prove me right."

Things happen quickly. The camp's alive again, an Erland marches through it all, givin orders an chivvyin, a steady rock in the swirl. No one pays me any attention as I hurry in his shadow, a leather jerkin hidin the shape of my body, a round shield across my back, the helm hidin my hair. We reach the corrals on the edge of camp, an he leaves me with Adelhard, givin his orders in Southern. When he's gone, Adelhard kneels before me an his men join him, heads bowed. Lookin round I realise these men are the ones I travelled with: they know me, even in my disguise.

"Bless them," whispers Berengar by my side, "or someone will notice."

So I open my arms an say the words, an for the first time I feel somethin. Maybe it's the fear of battle workin through me, or maybe it's because of Lana, but as I say the words I feel the white light comin into me, risin close under my skin.

The men rise an move to their horses, but now an then they glance at me wi somethin like awe.

"Come," says Berengar, standin by his mount. "You ride with me."

"What did Erland say to them?"

Berengar grunts. "He said it was the prester's wish that you reach the kirk in time for our victory." He braces his hands an helps me up onto a second seat behind the saddle, then pulls himself up in front of me.

I put my arms around his waist. "An they believed it?"

His body tenses. "If you die," he says bitterly, "you will be a martyr. One of the holy dead, the witness of the true God. Your death may even win us this war."

"You're angry wi me," I say.

The back of his neck flushes, but Adelhard an his men close around us, an we reach the edge of the camp.

It's still dark beyond the camp's torches, but in the east the mountains show against the sky. Then I see the torches are movin, carried by a line of men across the dark land, a line of fire pressin north. They've already reached the river. I look over the line, searchin for the glint of torchlight on red hair, or a lopin grey shadow. But of course the torches shine only on helms an armour, an who can say if Rafe or Fetch are even alive?

The dyin night presses its cold weight on my shoulders, my heart. With a lurch we start towards the river. I press my face into Berengar's back, like once I pressed myself against poor Medard, except this time, instead of laughter, I feel his heart, beatin like a lost thing beneath the cold metal scales.

"Don't be angry," I say. "Not now."

He puts one gauntleted hand over my two at his waist, an then flames are dancin on the waters of the river to my right an I see that we've come downstream, away from the bulk of the army. Men an horses are fordin where the river runs broad an shallow, an out of the smoke that wreaths Frithberg come dark swarms of riders, cuttin down soldiers as they pull themselves out onto the north bank.

We're in the dark waters now, an the icy current shocks me awake. The smoke is thicker here, an I choke as I breathe it in. My eyes itch, but I can see the gates of Frithberg, open to let her riders through. It's only a few hundred paces, but I see bow-tips above the pallisade, an between the river an the gates, smoke rises from hidden trenches. The dim crimson glow of the embers colours the sickly fumes.

As our mount hauls us up onto the bank, a handful of riders cut towards us, small an low on their Northern ponies.

"Hold on!" shouts Berengar. Beneath us the horse seems to leap away, an I hang on for dear life. To my right one of Adelhard's men cuts away towards a rider, leanin down to drive his sword into the man, while another rider tries to slip behind him, only to end on another soldier's blade. Somethin thuds off the shield across my back, an turnin I see a rider wieldin a small curved bow. The bolt must have brushed me. A third soldier cuts behind me, runnin off the archer, but another enemy is close behind him, an cuts him across the waist from behind.

"Jump!" shouts Berengar, an I hunch close to him as our mount's hooves leave the ground.

Below us I see a pit full of flyin embers, an the heat blasts my face, fillin my lungs wi the unholy smoke. My head swims an thuds as we land heavily. The horse stumbles but Berengar kicks him on. The air is thick now, an my grip is slippin. Adelhard is still beside us, but I can't see the other soldiers through my streamin eyes. A rider comes at us through the smoke, his face twisted in a snarl, an Berengar draws his sword, slashin at the man's face. The rider swerves out of reach, an I turn to watch him circle an come after us.

"He's comin back!" I shout.

An then I see it. The rider's scarred face is suddenly doubled, tripled. The man's eyes are glazed over, but the ghost faces to either side of his – they're full of such hate, such horror, that they seem to be the livin ones.

"Go!" I scream, as a soldier cuts between us an barrels into the rider's path, hidin him from view.

We're within reach of the archers on the palisade now, because arrows are thuddin around us. Through the thick smoke come glimmers of silver. Foot soldiers have forced their way up from the river, hackin at the unhorsed riders in the shadow of the walls. A long, iron-capped batterin ram thunders against the gates, its handlers shelterin under their shields. The palisade en't made for this kind of attack, an the gates shudder an splinter in their iron bonds.

At a shout from Adelhard, the remainin soldiers tighten around us, just as the ram crushes through the wood. To my left an arrow lodges in a soldier's throat, an another strikes a horse, makin it throw its rider.

"When we get inside, *run!*" yells Berengar, his sword ready. As the first foot soldiers thrust through the ruined gates an die on its shattered wreckage, our band spurs forward into smoke an darkness.

Once more I feel the horse's muscles bunch as it launches itself over the wreck of the ram an gate, but this time as it lands it staggers.

The shock makes everythin slow. I hang in the air for a moment, but then the world moves again, an I'm thrown hard against the wall of the guardhouse. Somethin heavy an soft falls over me, an I lie winded.

In that strange emptiness between breaths, I see our horse strugglin to pull itself up with its front legs. I see a dark-haired figure in dirty blue draggin himself away from the flailin beast, fumblin for his lost sword, an a one-eyed warrior walkin towards him, his short axe raised. The air boils, thickens, an a silvery arc cuts my sight.

My breath bursts chokin back into my lungs. I shove the weight layin across me, an before the mist can lift, before my heart can break, I run.

Part of me knows the weight was a body, but I shut it out. The hell of smoke an death lies behind, cold darkness ahead. When I stumble I don't look down. Between the houses lie bodies, left where they fell. The sight of em floods through me, but I don't let myself think.

I don't stop until I come out at the far end of the market place, near the kirkrock.

At first I en't sure what I'm seein. Mist cascades down the cliff of the kirkrock, coatin my skin wi droplets. It pools around a mass of dark shapes where the hangin pole used to stand. Torches have bin set burnin by the shapes, an they burn green an sick in the greasy mist.

My skin crawls.

Where once I watched Torny talkin to a dead man, a grove of corpses hang.

Spears have bin driven in a circle, men impaled on em. I see the points risin black an wet through the open mouths. Among em I see Lord Frithrun, blond Spraki . . . an another wi long red braids an a frame so broad it's strung over three spears, not one. Big Hakon.

I press myself against the clammy rock as the mist pours over me, an I close my eyes against this sickness. Nothin Ma nor Una taught me can cure me now. It's come in at my eyes, an I will be sick with it until I die, till my flesh is burnt on the pyre.

What am I to do? Somewhere here is my friend, the person who loved an protected me before all others. An is it her who did this? Her who ordered these men killed, their bodies defiled?

How can she have done this?

Or did she do what I must? Did she too go alone, on paths no one could follow, an did she face death because there weren't no other choice?

Everythin seems simple now, yet I can't move. Gettin here, gettin inside the walls, all that was just followin a path. From here on there's no path. If I do it wrong I might end up like her.

I open my eyes. The mist swirls wi shapes, less solid than the corpses in the shudderin light, but more awful. A shadow lopes towards me, an I flinch away, still frozen against the rock, but a bark tells me it's Fetch. He butts his head into my side an whines. I fall to my knees an bury my face in his fur, to make sure he's real.

I've failed.

I've failed Ma, who married a man not for love, but so that her children would be free. I've failed every man, woman an child who knelt for my salve when I knew it weren't blessed. I've failed everyone who fought for me, died because of me; Medard, the men of Eldinghope, Rafe . . . Even Lana in her dark, lonely tent, the night filled up with her fear. An Berengar . . .

My heart drops out of me, leavin only pain.

Berengar, thrown from his horse at the gates, lost among those ghosts, among those men with empty eyes.

Fetch licks my face, his tongue warm an rough. He pushes his wet nose into my ear, licks my cheek. His pink tongue is curled at the edges like a banner. His long yellow fangs shine against his black lips.

I en't failed Fetch yet. I'm still the one who saved him. I remember how it came to me, my anger at Spraki, my courage; an I remember Stig, how I faced all of Eldinghope for him.

I reach for it, but there's nothin but fear.

I'm like Lana, laid waitin in the dark for death.

Eyes up, comes the whisper, in a voice I en't heard in months.

Fetch licks my hand. His face is all wrong, human eyes under the animal pelt.

I am the blood an the mead, the bread an the meat.

Maybe there's another way. A knife en't much use against a sword or an axe, but maybe it don't have to be. Maybe all you need is a way to get under the skin.

My hand is already closin around the slim bone bottle. I unstopper it an let two drops fall on my tongue.

Fetch whines, himself again.

"Come on, boy," I say. "It's time."

Turnin my back on the dead, I climb the path to the kirk.

Twenty Four
LAMB

EBBA'S TALE

Kirkrock, Frithberg

 p through the heavy air, through the ash that burns my lungs an the mist that numbs my body. The stone path is slippery, an half way up I trip, grazin my hands. The smartin scares me. I've seen bodies torn apart tonight, crushed an cut, an yet here I am, on my knees, a little scraped skin makin all my nerves shriek.

Fetch laps at my hands with his curled pink tongue an turns back uphill. I push myself up an follow him.

The drops are startin to work. The damp rock glistens with a thousand tiny eyes. The mist slides past me, thick wi figures, an when I stumble an look back, a wave of fire gallops an breaks against the splintered walls of Frithberg, city of peace. The horizon is black an the land writhes. A few steps from the top I drop to the ground, dizzy, while my belly twists an cramps.

I pull myself over the lip of the kirkrock, an look up. Fetch growls, settin my teeth on edge.

The world bucks around me, same way my body's tryin to buck the poison out of me. Somethin's in it that shouldn't be. Somethin wrong.

In front of the kirk there's a hole.

It's like a burn in the fabric of the world. Somethin's forced its way through, made a door where before there was none. An beyond . . .

I twitch back from its cold breath, unable to stop myself cryin out.

The void turns. Its edges scorch, silvery white. It comes towards me, an I see it has shape. Tall an long-limbed, an strong, so much stronger than her brother who sits in pomp across the river, because the drops on my tongue are workin now, an I see clearly. The grey eyes under the golden helm, the lanky body.

Arn's daughter stands before me, sword already drawn.

I pull off my helmet, an my hair spills over my shoulders. Suddenly I'm glad my disguise en't foolin anyone.

"Torny," I say. "It's me."

The sword hand falters, an the body hardens, the hole in the world shrinkin to a circle on her chest, held there by leather straps.

I hold her eyes an try not to look away.

You know me, I think. *You saw me when no one else did. C'mon Torny. I know it's you.*

"Fenn?" she says. Under the gold-washed helm her pupils are tiny dots, so small her eyes seem white. She twists her head, like she's tryin to catch somethin out of the corner of her eye. "Where?"

"It's Ebba," I say. "I'm here."

An I step forward to touch her.

The sword is at my neck so fast I almost push myself onto its edge.

No one touches me.

The voice isn't Torny's, but I know it. It used to call me in my dreams.

It's bones breakin under a beatin, an the fires that ate my land. It's Ma lookin through me with empty eyes, an the whip in my brother's hand. It's Berengar's body thrown to the ground, an the arc of the silver axe.

Fetch is crouched flat against the ground, ears back, teeth bared. His growls echo round us, but he don't leap.

What have you come for, girl?

I can't speak. The blade presses my throat, an the hole at her chest is growin again. Its silver edges blot out Torny's shape, an my eyes slide from her into the void beyond. I can feel it seepin into me, through my raw lungs, my broken skin.

You've been used, says the thing inside Torny. *Not just you. Your mother, your father, your brother . . .*

I can feel the nothin inside me now, in my thoughts, under my skin. It worms its way into all the hidden places.

And you've used others.

She's found Berengar. I din't want her to, because even to think of him is like puttin weight on a broken bone, but she reaches for my memories. Like new shoots they reach for her an blossom.

I feel him. Maybe it's the drops or maybe it's her, but I feel his breath on my nape, his lips on my lips, his heart beating through both our ribs. I'm swaddled in his presence, bound by my guilt an the last sight of him, the thing I din't let myself really see or understand.

The silver axe descendin.

The blade lifts from my throat.

What do you want?

My mouth's dry, but I answer anyway.

"I want to stop the sufferin," I whisper.

Liar, she says. *You think they haven't suffered enough.*

Up from the pit of my stomach, the base of my spine, rushes red-hot rage. It burns so hot it chokes me. The fury fills my skin, and I feel for the first time how weak I am.

I want to tear the world to pieces. I want to set fire to everythin that ever wished me harm, take vengeance for every hurt. I want to be so strong that no one will ever dare touch me again.

But I am weak. I can't protect anyone, not Rafe, not Berengar, not Torny, not myself. All I can do is drop my eyes, hold still, wait for the beatin to be over.

I can make you strong, she says. *They deserve punishment. I can give you what you want.*

I remember Ulf's hot blood on my face so vividly I can feel the spray hit me. I remember the axe.

I look her in her empty face. I open my mouth an my teeth are arrowheads.

"No," I say.

The nothingness inside me blazes, squirms like a worm in a cavity, but I grasp it, squeeze it.

"I've seen the wheel turn," I tell her. "I've seen vengeance. Seems to me there's no rest comes from it."

The nothingness tries to keep its hooks in my mind, but I force it out. The thing inside Torny screams in rage as I fling it from me.

Fetch springs up, freed from his crouch, an leaps towards her.

She moves so fast she blurs. Fetch's teeth snap on air, an I run to put my arms around him, though I don't know who I'm tryin to protect, animal or girl.

Her blade hovers close to my neck. Fetch's whole body shivers under mine, but he don't move.

"Leave her."

A man limps towards us. He's leanin on a broken spear, his red-gold beard untrimmed an tangled, dark circles under his weary eyes. He has one hand an a golden shadow.

The blade quivers.

"You can't turn everyone to your will, Harrower. Let the girl be."

For a beat the sword stays where it is. Then she steps back an lowers it.

The man rests his wrist-stump on my shoulder. I recognise him now.

"Go," he says.

"I came here for Torny," I say.

His eyes are sad.

"Torny's long gone," he says. "She's not coming back. Go, while there's still time."

"There's no time," says a deep voice.

My heart sinks.

The prester, his armour gleamin, steps out of the smoke.

"Look at this," says the prester, his blue eyes flickin between us. Beside me, the one-handed man cowers away. "Everyone thinks you're back at camp, Salvebearer, but here you are."

"How d'you find me?"

"You weren't hard to follow. I knew the Vellsberg boy would

try to help you. A pity. He was a promising student. Not much of a warrior though. I'll deal with you later."

His eyes are on the thing wearin Torny's shape. Harrower, the one-handed man called her. Harrier, Lana said, an I see now that the thing wears a helm with a harrier hawk emblazoned across the brow-piece, wings outstretched. It gleams eerily in the misty air.

The prester's axe-blade is dark wi blood, an he holds it before him, ready to strike. He steps forward.

The one-handed man stumbles back from him. The Harrower, if that's its name, just stands there, waitin.

"I wondered what you'd be like," Grimulf says softly to her. "You look just like your brother."

Things move very quickly.

Fetch bounds out of my grasp, knockin me sideways to the edge of the kirkrock. For a sick moment my head lolls over the lip, my skull jarrin against rock. As I scramble up, the prester sends Fetch flyin past me with a single blow. I cry out as Fetch plunges over the edge of the kirkrock into the mist below.

"Fetch!"

"Get out the way!" The one-handed man shouts his warnin from the kirk steps.

I roll away as the prester's axe bounces off the rock by my shoulder.

I used to watch Torny spar. She was strong an she was quick, but she was nothin like this. I en't never seen anythin close, not watchin the warriors at their practise nor the soldiers under Erland.

The Harrower's sword moves like a ribbon of light. It flows, each movement fuelin the next, a torrent of force that slides from defence to attack. It's like watchin the blade breathe. It scorches a white line in the air, a knot of bright thread gatherin round the two fighters.

The prester can't keep up. He's bigger an heavier'n her, but she moves so fast, an the great sweep of his axe takes too long. The axe strikes sparks from the rocks when it lands, an the blade shrieks.

I put the sunstone between me an them, not darin to look away.

Grimulf catches a blow and staggers back. The sword-trail hangs in the air. It seems to pulse.

"You can't do this forever!" he shouts. "It doesn't matter how much strength you give her. Bodies fail."

The Harrower closes with him again, her face hidden by the golden helm, her chest eaten up by the silvery void. The blades flash in the half-light, ring out when they touch.

I feel myself bein pulled back from the stone, away from the fight. The one-handed man has joined me.

"You can still leave," he says in my ear.

I laugh.

"There's nowhere to go," I say. I can feel the cold sweat on my brow, an my legs are weak. I turn my head to look at him, an the world follows drunkenly.

"What's wrong?"

I'm starin at his shadow.

It's a man. A beautiful man, too beautiful, and where his light falls on the one-handed man it gilds him, shows him youthful, handsome.

"Who is he?" I reach out to touch him, but my hand goes through him.

The one-handed man recoils.

"You can see him?"

I nod, but my stomach's twistin again. I double over an moan.

"Do you think you can scare me?" the prester shouts. "Like you scared fishwives and old men?" His voice echoes around us. "You're just some devil dressed in the flesh of a girl. You've got no power."

I turn my head to follow em, fightin off my dizziness.

Mist boils around the Harrower, thick with bodies, faces. It pours through the shinin tear in her chest, out from whatever lies beyond. The forms in the mist break over the prester's shoulders like spray on a stone.

"You don't scare me," says the prester, settin his feet an raisin his axe. "I've killed your kind before. You die easily."

The axe swings round in a great long-armed arc, an the flat of the blade smacks into the Harrower's side, sendin her flyin. There's a crunch I don't like.

Broken ribs, I think, feelin numb. *He's playin with her. He really en't scared.*

The Harrower catches herself an brings her sword up. The blade still flashes, but the axe blocks it every time. The prester lands another blow from with the haft, an now there's blood drippin under the golden helm an her chest is heavin with each gasp.

"Bodies break," says Grimulf, steppin back. "There's no space for you in me, see? But I can do for you what you do for them. I can give you annihilation."

The Harrower brings her sword up, but with a single blow he slams her back into the standin stone. The helm rings against the rock, an she slides down to its carved foot.

"Look at what you've done, girl," says the prester softly, almost sweetly. "You're the hag's brat, aren't you? I remember Arn boasting about your mother. One of his favourite conquests, I remember. She must have kept you secret all this time to be Arngard's hope, and for what? You've given them nothing but death. How could anyone forgive you for this?"

She seems small again. I can still see the rip on her chest, still feel the unnatural sickness of what she is. But I also see somethin lost, somethin homeless.

I remember what Erland said. *She begged for death.* But did she beg because she had no way out, or because she had no one, in this moment, to tell her otherwise?

Grimulf steps forward, an the Harrower don't move.

"Listen," says the one-handed man, shakin me. "I think there might be a way. But she's got to live."

I'm already up. I reach the stone an throw myself between the two of em.

"Stop," I say. "Don't hurt her."

An I en't sure right now which of her I mean, my friend, or the thing that wears her flesh.

I en't never felt so weak as this. I probably weigh less than the long-shafted axe the prester wields, an the drops have opened me up, unskinned me, till every breath of the world shakes me. I look up into his eyes.

They are cold an blue an they go right through me.

"You know," he says. "I've spent quite some time contemplating the means of your martyrdom. I have always favoured fire. But if beheading's good enough for the bull, it'll do for the lamb."

I catch a flicker of red out the corner of my eye, from the lip of the kirkrock.

Flame-red. Blood-red. Kin-red.

"NO!"

But Rafe has eyes only for the prester, an as he leaps his long knife snakes out to bury itself in the prester's back.

The prester twists, a knife in one hand, axe in the other, tryin to cut Rafe where he hangs from his back, an Fetch, lopin after, launches himself into the prester's face. One front paw is limp an useless, but the claws of the other dig into the prester's chainmail tunic, while the long yellow teeth sink into his cheek.

The prester bellows, tryin to fling boy an dog from him, face an back slippery wi blood. I look past him to where the one-handed man still stands, held back by fear or doubt.

"Do something!" I shout.

An then, as I watch, the golden shadow enters him, slips inside his skin, an he glows.

"Galen?"

I turn. The voice is Torny's.

She grabs me. Her freezing hand fixes on my bare wrist like a vice an I see.

I see Galen, filled up with the Luck of his long dead lover. I see Rafe, clingin on for dear life, his blood seepin from the cuts on his sides, an in his heart not his father, but three children in the dunes, playin at bein their parents, only better.

An I see me. Except it en't just me, there's two of us in the same space. A small boy wi laughin eyes an an iron collar. An me, but not so's you'd know me. Me, but beautiful. Beautiful like Galen's prince. Beautiful like the dawn, an the golden collar at my neck like the sun.

I've found you.
I've found you.

❀ 413 ❀

The two voices en't separate no more, but twined together, creeper an tree.

Galen yells, his sword bitin into the thick leather over the prester's thigh. The prester drops his knife, graspin the axe wi both hands again, but Fetch fixes his teeth into the prester's wrist-guard, draggin him back with all his weight. Rafe slides heavily from the prester's back, an Galen dodges the cut-short swing of the axe, only to lunge back in, his sword cuttin up an under at the prester's belly.

Grimulf roars. He slams the axe into Galen's side, kicks Fetch away an turns to where Rafe is crawlin away from him towards the kirk door.

"Stop him!" I yell, tryin to shake off Torny's freezin grip. "He'll kill him!"

Look.

Look.

An I look, an I see, an this time when I shake her off she lets me go, an I run between the stone and the kirk, the old an the new, to where Rafe lies scrabblin at the carven doors, paintin their intricate animals red with his bloody hands, an the prester stands over him, pantin, axe raised.

An I fall to my knees an I pray.

I open myself to the light that's bin beatin against the edges of my heart ever since that dark an bloody night in Eldinghope, and I welcome it in. It pours through me like a flame, into the empty trappins of the prester's faith.

The axe, the robes, the dead man on the tree. The gold offerins, shiverin in the candles' breath. The high carved pillars an eves, made from the wood of the sacred groves, laid like fuel for a fire that was never lit.

It is the difference between the blood an the mead, the meat an the bread.

I set the fire an I walk it.

Flames surge up the walls, engulfin the kirk. Rafe is thrown back, an Grimulf screams, but it is a broken noise. The axe drops from nerveless fingers. It lands blade down in the wooden steps, an the prester falls to his knees.

Cold hands grip my shoulders an lift me, push me to Rafe's side.

Mine, says the Harrower.

She takes her knife from her belt an puts her left hand under the prester's chin.

"Please . . ." slurs Grimulf, his eyes wide an blind.

An I, with the light still in me, say, "Give him mercy."

An she nods an makes a cut so quick an clean, that the blood spurts out hot on our faces like summer rain. An she holds him till he's gone, till the light leaves him, an lays him down gentle on the steps by his axe. The kirk still stands but its timbers are blackened. The walls shed dull heat.

She reaches up an takes off the golden helm. Just above her left ear the hair is matted wi blood. It drips down the strong line of her jaw.

"Now you do me," she says, lookin into my eyes an holdin out the knife.

I shake my head. The drops are wearin off, burnt out by the cascade of light through my flesh, an the wrongness of her is fadin. She looks more an more like Torny. The thing at her chest is a dull metal mirror, held in place by leather straps.

He was right, says the Harrower.

"You don't know what I've done," says Torny.

"I don't care," I say. "I came for you. I en't leavin alone."

She turns her head east. The mist is thinnin, an a breeze blows the smoke towards the dark outlines of the mountains. Behind em the sky is already blue. She raised her face to it an smiles.

The knife is in my hand.

"I haven't felt the sun in so long," she says.

Do it. Show me mercy.

I hesitate. I know I should throw the knife from me, tell her not to be an idiot, but . . .

She begged for it.

Does it make a difference who she asks it of?

"Lambtail."

Her head snaps round.

"Galen?"

She limps to his side. I drop the knife, unnerved. I nearly —

"Go," croaks Rafe. "I'm all right."

"You en't all right, you stupid, stupid boy," I hiss. "What were you thinkin?"

But my anger's partly for me. Fetch limps up, very sorry lookin, an flops down next to Rafe, whinin softly.

"I'll live a while yet," Rafe says, puttin his arm around Fetch. "Go see to your friend."

It only takes one look to know Galen's dyin. The livin have more blood in em. Torny hunches over him, an tears mix with her own blood, drippin off her chin in rosy droplets.

"Galen," she says. "Don't die. Please. Don't leave me."

I glance at her. Someone who wants death wouldn't say those things, surely?

�416🌿

Idiot, I think. *It's the Harrower wants to die, not her!*

"Lambtail," Galen says, an he raises his hand to her shoulder. Torny tries to take his hand in hers, but he pulls free an tugs at the mirror on her chest. "She can do it. She's your key."

Torny pulls back, confused.

"What is it?" I ask.

They made it to bind me, says the Harrower. *But my key is dead. This door only lets things into this world, not out.*

"Fenn used it to send a dead man on his way," whispers Galen. "Can you use it?"

There's an echo to his voice, like he's doubled. The gold lies faint beneath his skin, an his face don't fit right.

We'll help, says my Follower, an beside Galen I see his golden prince an his golden self, his two cursed Lucks, knelt hand in hand.

"I can try," I say. "Give me it."

Torny hesitates.

This is a kind of freedom, says the Harrower. *If I can't be free, I'd rather be like this than back in the labyrinth.*

I see em wrestlin, two wills in one body. If Torny don't win, I don't like to think what the Harrower might do to the person holdin the mirror.

"This isn't freedom," Torny whispers. "None of it. Not the memories you drugged me with, not the killing. Please let her try."

Her fingers fumble open the leather straps, an she hands the mirror to me.

I hold it in my hands, an its dull surface blazes. I see myself, red-spattered, sun-lit, lovely. I know this is me an not me all at once, the way I saw myself when Torny took my hand an the Harrower showed me the world through her eyes.

"Torny," says Galen. "Come here."

Again, she hesitates, an I realise: the Harrower is scared.

"I'm dyin," says Galen. "Don't let me die like Fenn did. Hold me."

With a jolt, Torny's eyes open wide, an I see the pupils are normal. She pulls him into her lap, an he locks his arms around her. She yelps in surprise, an I see the Harrower rise to the surface again, strugglin against his grip.

Wi the last of the drops I see how everythin fits. I see the golden lovers entwined, uncoupled from Galen's dyin flesh. My Follower, Da's dyin gift to me, lets me go, risin to join em.

I see the emptiness beyond the scorched edges of the world, an how the Harrower writhes an clings to its prison of flesh, terrified, finally, of the freedom that was taken from her.

All they need is a guide.

"This won't hurt," I say, an I hold the mirror to her face.

I open myself again. This en't the flood that travelled through me to the prester, but a thread. It twines around the golden forms of Galen an his lover's Luck, round my Follower, an they in turn reach into Torny, down to the base of her spine, and pull. The Harrower cries out, but Galen's dead arms hold her body tight, an she's dragged after the others, out of Torny, out of the world, and through the mirror like thread through the eye of a needle.

The light stitches the edges of the world together again, an the last of the mist burns away.

Galen's empty eyes stare at the sky. He lies colourless in a pool of red.

Torny is slumped on her side, her eyes closed.

I put the mirror on Galen's chest an I reach for her. I take her in my arms an hold her cold body close to mine.

"Torny," I say. "Come back to me. I'm here."

"Ebba?"

I look up.

There, on the edge of the mornin, stands Berengar.

Torny wakes wi my tears fallin on her cheeks.

EPILOGUE

TORNY'S TALE

bba lays me down gently. Her hair falls like a thick, dark veil around me. I wish I could wrap us both up in it, seal us away from the world. But I know how that ends.

She puts something soft under my head and tucks a cloak around me to keep out the chill. Then she jumps to her feet and runs to the young soldier, her hair streaming in the morning wind like a flag.

I watch him catch her up in his arms and kiss her. He reaches up and untwists the golden torque from around her neck.

The wind comes out of the dark west, pure with the smell of the sea. My body feels empty; only half of me remains.

Lying here isn't going to make it any better.

Carefully, my breath hissing between my teeth each time my broken ribs creak, I get up. I go to Ebba's cousin where he lies near the blackened kirk doors. I'm trying not to look at the body of the prester.

The grey wolfhound growls at me as I approach.

I reach out and watch in surprise as the hound lunges, its fangs closing over my wrist. I yank back, the pain in my ribs winding me. The hound's teeth have left bright red scratches on my skin. The hound stands over the young man, growling a warning.

No dog has dared come near me all winter.

I guess she really is gone.

I look past the hound to the man. Blood and freckles stand out against his white skin, and he's obviously in pain, but he's pushing himself back against the steps, away from me.

My hand drops to my side.

This is what it's going to be like, isn't it?

"Fetch! Down, boy!"

Ebba runs up beside me and crouches down face to face with the hound.

"Fetch, sit." She pushes the hound out of her way, but gently, the same gentleness she showed me. "Rafe, don't move. I need to see your wounds. Berengar?"

"Yes?" The young soldier is beside me.

"I need you to get Torny out of sight. People will be lookin for her."

The soldier and I exchange glances.

"Everyone will be looking for her," he says. "There is nowhere far enough to save her from her people, or ours."

Ebba spins on her heel, coming up to stand face to face with him. Her eyes flash.

"Berengar of Vellsberg!" she snaps. "I did *not* just save my friend to have her torn to pieces or executed, d'you understand?"

The soldier's black brows knot together.

"It is not so simple as —"

"Do I make myself clear?"

"But —"

"Do I?"

I can't stop myself. The laugh bubbles up from my stomach, and even though it hurts, I can't hold it back. They stand and stare at me as I laugh and cry all at once, the tears and the pain and the love all mixed up in me till I can't tell which is which.

"I'm sorry," I hiccup. "I'm sorry."

After a moment, the soldier turns to Ebba. "Erland is below," he says. "I will tell him."

"Are you sure?"

They both look at the prester's body.

"I think I should tell him," says Ebba. "But you get him."

I help Berengar roll the prester onto his back and close his eyes. We cross his arms over his bloody chest, and Berengar goes to find his captain. I put the golden helm and the golden torque on the ground beside the body.

Fetch still growls when I come near Ebba and Rafe, so I slip past them, through the blackened doors and into the fire-kissed kirk.

It's dark and warm, the blackened wood impossibly still standing, although it creaks around me. I wonder for a moment if it might collapse, but find I don't really care if it does. Everything inside is dead. The gold offerings are all gone, and only the pale outstretched arms of the White God's image hang in the darkness.

I walk up to it, looking at its long face, its hollow eyes.

"I'm done with gods," I say to it. "I don't know what help you gave Ebba, or even if it was you. But I know it only worked because it was her. She's the one who saved me, not you."

There's nothing. No hum, no clash of swords, no sense that anything's listening. To be honest, it's a relief.

"Torny."

I turn to Ebba's voice, her shape outlined in the open door. Gladly, I go towards my salvation.

Ebba explains to Erland why he can't kill me. It sounds thin, even to me.

She talks about prices, and how sometimes they have to be paid. That sometimes they aren't the soldier's price, death for death, but the price of the living. The price paid daily, so that there can be peace.

Which side are you on? she asks. The side of order, or the side of ash?

Erland looks at me. I wonder if he wants me to fall to my knees and beg, but my ribs warn against sudden movements, and anyway, I'd be lying.

If he decided to kill me now, I don't think I'd fight.

But instead he looks away, to the blackened kirk, and the steps where Grimulf lies.

"How did he die?" he asks.

"By fire," says Ebba. "Martyrdom by fire," and Erland meets her unblinking gaze, shaken.

And I think, Ebba argues for peace, but when she had to, she chose the soldier's price too. She fought. And she would do it again.

"There's a band of townsfolk holed up in the wayhouse," Erland says to her. "Mistress Aud wasn't exactly pleased to see me, but I think you'll get a better welcome."

They don't take me there, of course. There aren't going to be any welcomes for me no matter where I go. They hide me in a chicken coop round the back of the stables.

I sit in the hay and the mess, and the chickens fuss and scratch as they go in and out, and I begin to remember. Fragments come back to me, as if I'm being let back into my own head. Just flashes – aces, blows, voices I can't quite hear – but the feelings that come with them make me regret Erland's mercy. They fill my skin like poison. I want to vomit them out of me, to scream and spew until I'm empty. Several times I start up, determined to leave, to find someone who will run me through without hesitation. But each time I freeze, gripped by a fear so intense I think my heart will burst.

Finally, long after sunset, someone comes for me. They knock on the side of the coop, and I wriggle out of it, gasping at the now constant pain in my side.

Aud stands there, in breeches and shirt. Her mouse-coloured hair is cut short.

"You owe me a pair of trousers and a sheepskin cloak," she says.

And then she holds me while I cry.

She doesn't mind. The stables are warm. The horses in their stalls stand quietly, and that's new too. I'm used to them bucking whenever I'm near. There's a bed made up by the fire, and a steaming barrel.

Jarle's asleep in the bed, his face bandaged.

"What happened?" I ask, although the answer scares me.

"He got cut," says Aud. "One of the Slipskins. Poor boy might not be able to rely on his looks so much anymore." She puts an arm around my stiff shoulders. "Come on."

She pours water from the cauldron into the barrel. It's already quite full.

"In you get," she says.

The steam smells like hops and summer. I undress, and Aud tuts when she sees the angry red bruise across my ribs.

"Still," she says. "Could be worse."

The water turns my pale skin pink. It burns. Aud hands me a hunk of soap.

"If you drop it," she says, "you dive for it."

I crouch in the hot water, soaping every part of me I can reach. Aud does my hair, avoiding the bump above my left ear.

"Why are you being kind to me?" I ask.

Her hands, tangled in my hair, pause for a moment.

"I've done terrible things," I say, and my whole body shakes as another flash sears through me. I can't meet her eyes.

"So did Suniva," says Aud quietly. "Rinse."

She pushes down on my shoulders, and I dip my hair under the water. Behind my screwed up eyes I see a woman with hair like corn.

"She was the Sungiven," I say when I surface, "wasn't she?"

Aud nods, holding out a towel. I climb out of the barrel and scrub myself as vigorously as I can. I don't want to be cold ever again.

A smaller cauldron hangs over the fire now, and when I'm dressed again in some breeches and a shirt, Aud hands me a bowl of stew with dumplings.

"Suniva wasn't like you, Torny," Aud says. "She was a real warrior, trained and recognised, though not always respected. She helped guard the Staffbearer's sanctuary at Sunacre. She knew Vigdis and Geir. She had a son a few years before the war, and she decided to raise him away from court. It was only when Geir went north to Hellingap that she decided to join him. And I followed her."

I look at her in surprise. "But you're —"

"Too young?" Aud grins. "I was sixteen when I followed Suniva to Hellingap. We arrived the night before the battle."

"And you fought?"

"For what it was worth," says Aud. "It was a short battle. We scattered north, and the Slipskins took Geir's body into the hills. We regrouped. Vigdis was the highest ranking Staffbearer left, though not the oldest, and she had a plan. So we followed her."

"When did you find out what she was going to do?"

"She asked Suniva if she thought it would work. Whether warriors would follow a god. Suniva said she thought they would follow anyone who gave them hope." Aud smiles again, but this time it's sad. "And that person was her. The few Slipskins that joined us had relied on their prince and Thorkel, and without their brothers they were lost. Suniva was a leader. She rallied the retreat. She made sure everyone who joined had training, and she punished anyone who looted or attacked the villagers."

I feel that horrible sinking feeling in my stomach.

"But then they did the ritual."

"Were you there?"

She shakes her head. "No one was allowed to witness it. When she came back, she was glorious. She seemed to shine, even at night. She was more beautiful than I'd ever seen her." Aud closes her eyes. "But she was harder too. She could fill you with righteousness, but she couldn't remember your name. Even those of us who'd known her for years became unimportant. She was still just, but she became less and less human. She killed more and more often."

Aud looks up at me, and I'm amazed to see tears in her eyes.

"I took Jarle when she didn't recognise him anymore," she says. "I took him and I left, and then, when it was all over, I brought him back here, and wore skirts, and worked for Sorleyson, and every day I lived alongside the people whose fathers and brothers and sons had died, either for or against her. So it's not hard to be kind to you, Torny. I know what was done to you."

I look from her to the sleeping Jarle and back again, and put down my bowl.

And I say the thing that's scared me the most since my fragmented memory started coming back to me.

"I think I killed Vigdis."

Aud doesn't gasp, or pull away from me. She just says, "Why do you think that?"

So I tell her about the ritual, about Far Isle and the stone pillar and the labyrinth, and how Fenn was the only one who tried to save me, and how Ranvig killed him. I tell her how I stepped outside myself, and how the Harrower stepped in. And how there's a blankness, a gap, between the Harrower entering me and when I woke up in the boat with Laugi.

How Vigdis and the others were never mentioned again, except for when Laugi told Carr that they'd gone before us, open-eyed, and showed us their staffs around the curse pole.

Aud listens, her face calm.

"You didn't kill your mother, Torny," she says. "Laugi may have, but not you."

"But how can you know?"

Aud sighs. "Going open-eyed was a ritual the Staffbearers practised," she says. "A knowing death. If she wished, a Staffbearer could choose to take her own life. It was one of their secrets, the ingredient that allowed you passage from life to death."

Aud puts her arm around my shoulders.

"I can't take your doubt away," she says. "But it seems to me you wouldn't have killed Vigdis. Even after months of control, the Harrower couldn't make you kill Ebba, could she?"

I think of that moment, when my blade hovered at Ebba's throat an my muscles strained against each other, unsure which will to obey.

"No," I say. "She couldn't."

"Then I don't think after a few moments she could have made you kill your mother."

"But I didn't protect her."

Aud strokes my hair back from my forehead. "Vigdis didn't protect you either," she says sadly. "You could worry at this for years, Torny. For the rest of your life, if you like. But you may never know. All you can do is trust yourself."

She makes up another bed beside the fire, and lies down beside me in it, her arm around my waist. She falls asleep almost at once, but I lie there, each breath grating, listening to the horses snort and stamp, watching the rafters flicker in the firelight.

I miss Fenn. I miss him curled asleep beside me, and I wish I could have seen him in life the way I saw him in my visions, well-fed and happy. I miss Galen. I wish I could have helped him heal from the wounds of the past, from the curse of his second, unwanted Luck.

I know I'm going to miss Ebba most of all, and it seems unfair, because she's still whole and healthy, and I should have more time with her. But I know how this is going to go. She's a hero, and I can't pretend to myself that I can stay here with Aud and Jarle for long. Anyway, she can't give me what I hoped.

I get up, not as stealthily as I'd like, but Aud just rolls over and starts to snore. I take her cloak, her boots and her knife. Guess I'll just have to owe her again.

I don't know how I'm going to get away, but I can't bear to stay another day in the wreckage I caused.

I open the stable door, and look into Ebba's face.

Her hand is still outstretched to knock on the door.

"Oh good," she says. "You're ready."

I look past her. Three horses stand ready, Berengar checking their girths.

"What's this?" I say.

"You can't stay in the hen coop," she says. "Someone's goin to come lookin for their eggs sooner or later."

"You can't come with me," I say. "It'll be dangerous."

"It'll be more dangerous alone."

"I thought Berengar was Erland's armsman?"

"He's got a new one now. Rafe will help him manage Eldinghope."

I glare at her.

"Torny," she says, "I only just found you. I en't goin to lose you again." She takes my hand. "I en't sayin you gotta stick with us for always. But at least let us get you on your way."

There's only one way I can think of to make her understand why she can't do this.

"Ebba," I say, "I love you."

She puts her arms around my shoulders an squeezes.

"I know," she says. "I saw. I know I can't be your lover, an I know you might not like seein me wi Berengar. But I love you too, Torny, even if it's not the way you want. An I will always love you. So please let me come."

I hug her back. I can't think of anything else.

"You've grown," I say into her hair.

"You too," she says.

"We must leave now," says Berengar. "Can you ride?"

I let Ebba go and approach the horse whose reins he holds. I hold out my hands, and the soft white nose wrinkles and snuffs at my palms. Hero whickers softly, an I turn my face into her mane to hide my tears.

"Yes," I say.

"I can't," says Ebba cheerfully. "I'll ride wi you. You're lighter'n Berengar."

"Insolent Northerner."

"Snotty Southerner."

"Are you going to be like this all the way?" I ask, climbing into the saddle. "Ow."

"Is it your ribs?" asks Ebba. "We'd better walk instead of trot."

"You mean it'll take longer?"

"It is better to discern the path of right-thinking, than to rush onto the thoroughfare of ignorance."

"What does that mean?"

"Shut up you two, we need to leave quietly."

So we shut up, and we leave. At the broken gate a large captain and his red-headed armsman throw us salutes, and Berengar salutes back. A huge grey wolfhound by the almsman's side whuffs softly as Ebba an I pass, but doesn't follow us.

The west is still dark, but the breeze that comes out of it is the first soft breath of spring. It carries lost things in it.

I turn my face into it, Ebba's arms around my waist.

Aimu, says Fenn's voice in my ear.

The world breathes.

✳ ACKNOWLEDGEMENTS ✳

This book would not have been possible without the support and hard work of many people.

My parents have always encouraged me to write, and without them there would be no book. My brother brought me cups of tea and had to live with me while I was on deadline, and for his forbearance I am grateful.

Thank you to all of my teachers, but especially to those on the Creative Writing MSt at Oxford University. Thank you also to my fellow writers there, many of whom read this book in its early forms, and whose friendship has been a constant source of pleasure.

To my agent Sandra Sawicka at Marjacq Scripts, whose belief in my writing buoyed me when I might otherwise have faltered. To Hazel Holmes and Debbie Williams, to all the staff at UCLan Publishing and to the MA Publishing students, for the love, care and attention they gave this book. Extra special thanks to Becky Chilcott for the inspired design, to Joe McLaren for the stunning cover and to Tomislav Tovic for the beautiful map.

Thanks also to the staff and volunteers who organise the NYA LitFest, and to everyone who read and reviewed the ARC. Special thanks to Melinda Salisbury, who broke me into the world of YA panel discussions without actually breaking me.

I am lucky to have wonderful friends and family who have celebrated, shared and pre-ordered my book. Thank you so much, all of you. Particular thanks to Andy, Anita, Dechen and Ziad, who took me out for dinner, to art exhibitions and to the theatre when I was broke.

Finally, all my thanks and love to my partner, Devon, who believes in me even when I struggle to believe in myself, and in loving memory of Maggie.